"Riveting from start to finish. Full of mystery, fierce friendship, and romance that might not be quite what it seems. Kami Garcia shows off her stellar storytelling skills in this fantastic first installment of *Teen Titans*. Once you start reading *Teen Titans: Raven,* you won't want to stop."

—**Stephanie Garber**, #1 *New York Times* bestselling author of the **Caraval** series

"As someone who spends half her life inside Rachel's head...it was impressive to see her so effortlessly come to life on the page! If you love Raven, this is a must-read!"

—**Teagan Croft**, actress portraying Raven in the **DC Universe** series **Titans**

"Kami Garcia's *Raven* shows us that family bonds are made by more than blood, and that the ties of sisterhood are more powerful than the scariest demon. It's the heart of this kickass "girl power" superhero book that keeps you reading and rereading and desperate for the next installment."

—**Ellen Oh**, author of **The Prophecy** series, and Cofounder and President of **We Need Diverse Books**

"I continue to be inspired by Kami Garcia's authenticity and keen ability to create raw and empowering stories full of strength, truth, and love."

—**Jennifer Niven**, *New York Times* bestselling author of *All the Bright Places* and *Holding Up the Universe*

"With *Teen Titans: Raven,* writer Kami Garcia and artist Gabriel Picolo have created a new and different look for Raven, yet she still shares the DNA of the mystical heroine created in 1980 by me and artist co-creator, George Pérez. Explore and enjoy!"

—**Marv Wolfman**, co-creator of Raven

"Raven might have a...questionable background, but this colorful twist on her story made ME want to fly!"

—**Nic Stone,** *New York Times* bestselling author of *Dear Martin*

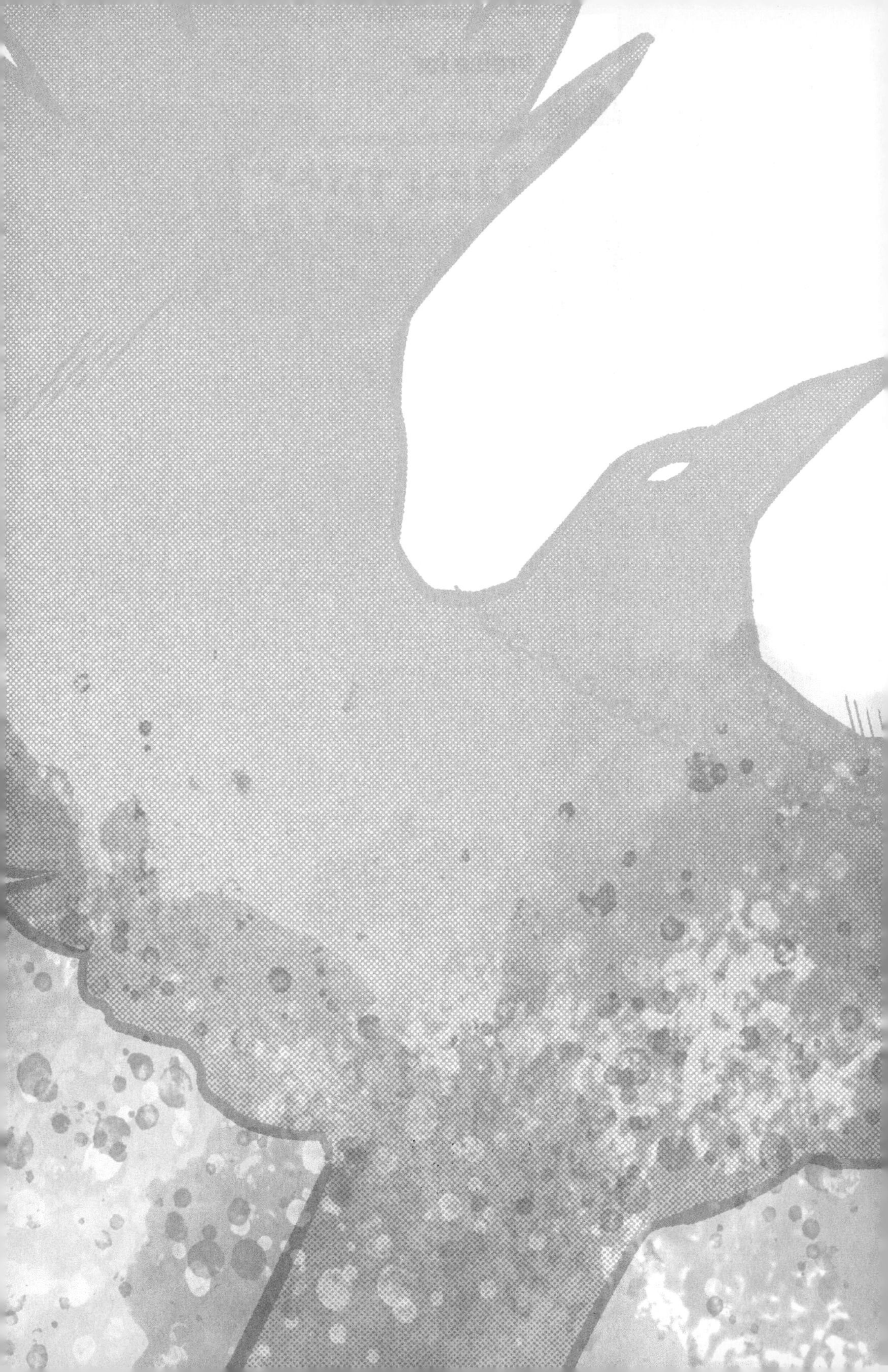

TEEN TITANS
Raven

WRITTEN BY
kami garcia

ILLUSTRATED BY
gabriel picolo

WITH
jon sommariva
AND
emma kubert

COLORIST
david calderon

LETTERER
tom napolitano

Raven created by Marv Wolfman and George Pérez

MICHELE R. WELLS VP & Executive Editor, Young Reader
JUSTINE FUENTES Assistant Editor
STEVE COOK Design Director - Books
AMIE BROCKWAY-METCALF Publication Design

BOB HARRAS Senior VP - Editor-in-Chief, DC Comics

DAN DiDIO Publisher
JIM LEE Publisher & Chief Creative Officer
BOBBIE CHASE VP - New Publishing Initiatives & Talent Development
DON FALLETTI VP - Manufacturing Operations & Workflow Management
LAWRENCE GANEM VP - Talent Services
ALISON GILL Senior VP - Manufacturing & Operations
HANK KANALZ Senior VP - Publishing Strategy & Support Services
DAN MIRON VP - Publishing Operations
NICK J. NAPOLITANO VP - Manufacturing Administration & Design
NANCY SPEARS VP - Sales

TEEN TITANS: RAVEN
Published by DC Comics. Copyright © 2019 DC Comics. All Rights Reserved.
All characters, their distinctive likenesses and related elements featured in
this publication are trademarks of DC Comics. DC INK is a trademark of DC
Comics. The stories, characters and incidents featured in this publication
are entirely fictional. DC Comics does not read or accept unsolicited submis-
sions of ideas, stories or artwork.
DC - a WarnerMedia Company.

DC Comics
2900 West Alameda Ave.
Burbank, CA 91505

Printed by LSC Communications,
Crawfordsville, IN, USA. 8/2/19.
Second Printing.
ISBN: 978-1-4012-8623-1

PEFC Certified

This product is from
sustainably managed
forests and controlled
sources

PEFC™
PEFC/29-31-337   www.pefc.org

Library of Congress Cataloging-in-Publication Data

Names: Garcia, Kami, writer. | Picolo, Gabriel, illustrator.
Title: Teen Titans : Raven / written by Kami Garcia ; illustrated by Gabriel
  Picolo.
Description: Burbank, CA : DC Ink, [2019] | Summary: "When a tragic accident
  takes the life of the only family she's ever known, 16-year-old Raven is
  sent to New Orleans to start over. She soon discovers that she can hear
  the thoughts of others around her...and another, more disturbing, voice in
  her head."-- Provided by publisher.
Identifiers: LCCN 2018043961 | ISBN 9781401286231
Subjects: LCSH: Graphic novels. | CYAC: Graphic novels. | Orphans--Fiction. |
  Psychic ability--Fiction.
Classification: LCC PZ7.7.G366 Te 2019 | DDC 741.5/973--dc23

dedications

For Nick, who encouraged me to write a graphic novel.
And for Stella, who loved Raven first,
and told me to choose Teen Titans.
—**Kami Garcia**

For Andrea, who gave me the determination
to keep working on my comics.
—**Gabriel Picolo**

dear reader,

As someone whose mother hand-made her a Wonder Woman Halloween costume—which I insisted on wearing for an embarrassing number of Halloweens—I can honestly say I've been a DC Comics fan for a long time. The idea that anyone could be a hero regardless of race, religion, gender, or sexual orientation (or, in the case of some of the Teen Titans, species) has always resonated with me. I'm the kind of person who roots for the underdog and who believes in magic, miracles, and the impossible.

I remember how hard it was to be a teen, and, figure out who I wanted to be and how to stand up for what I believed. I struggled to define myself in a world that was determined to define me—a world that didn't think I was old enough to make a difference or effect real change. So when DC Comics approached me about writing for them, the Teen Titans came to mind. Why write just one book when I could write a series about a group of badass teens—beginning with my favorite member, Raven? In the DC Universe, Raven has to fight to define herself and overcome the hand life dealt her. I wanted more readers to meet her, because the odds are usually stacked against her, but she never gives up. She's a fighter, like so many of you.

I had the honor of meeting Marv Wolfman, the co-creator of Raven, Cyborg, and Starfire from the Teen Titans. I wasn't sure how a legend like Marv would feel about me creating a new story for Raven, one of his most beloved characters. I asked for advice. Was there anything specific I should or shouldn't do? Marv's advice was to do what I wanted and make the character my own. He also said he was excited to see what I would do with her and he loved the idea of introducing her to new readers. Marv seemed to understand that the world needs Raven and the other Teen Titans more than ever—that with all the injustices in the world, there are plenty of battles left to fight. The world needs heroes like the version of Raven you'll meet in this book and her feisty foster sister, Max, a new character I created and artist Gabriel Picolo brought to life. But more than anything, the world needs everyday people like you.

Keep fighting and reading.

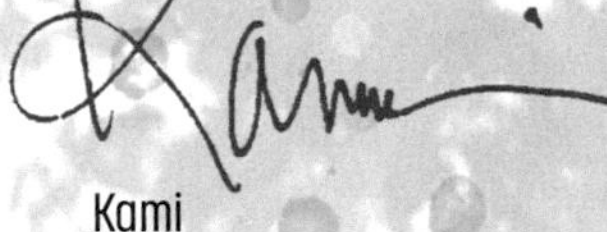

Kami

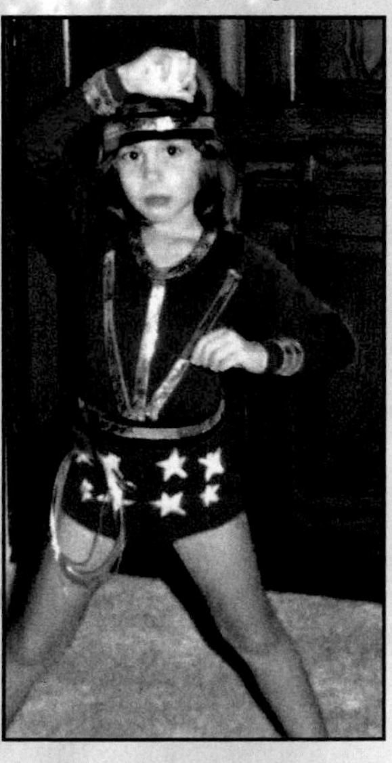

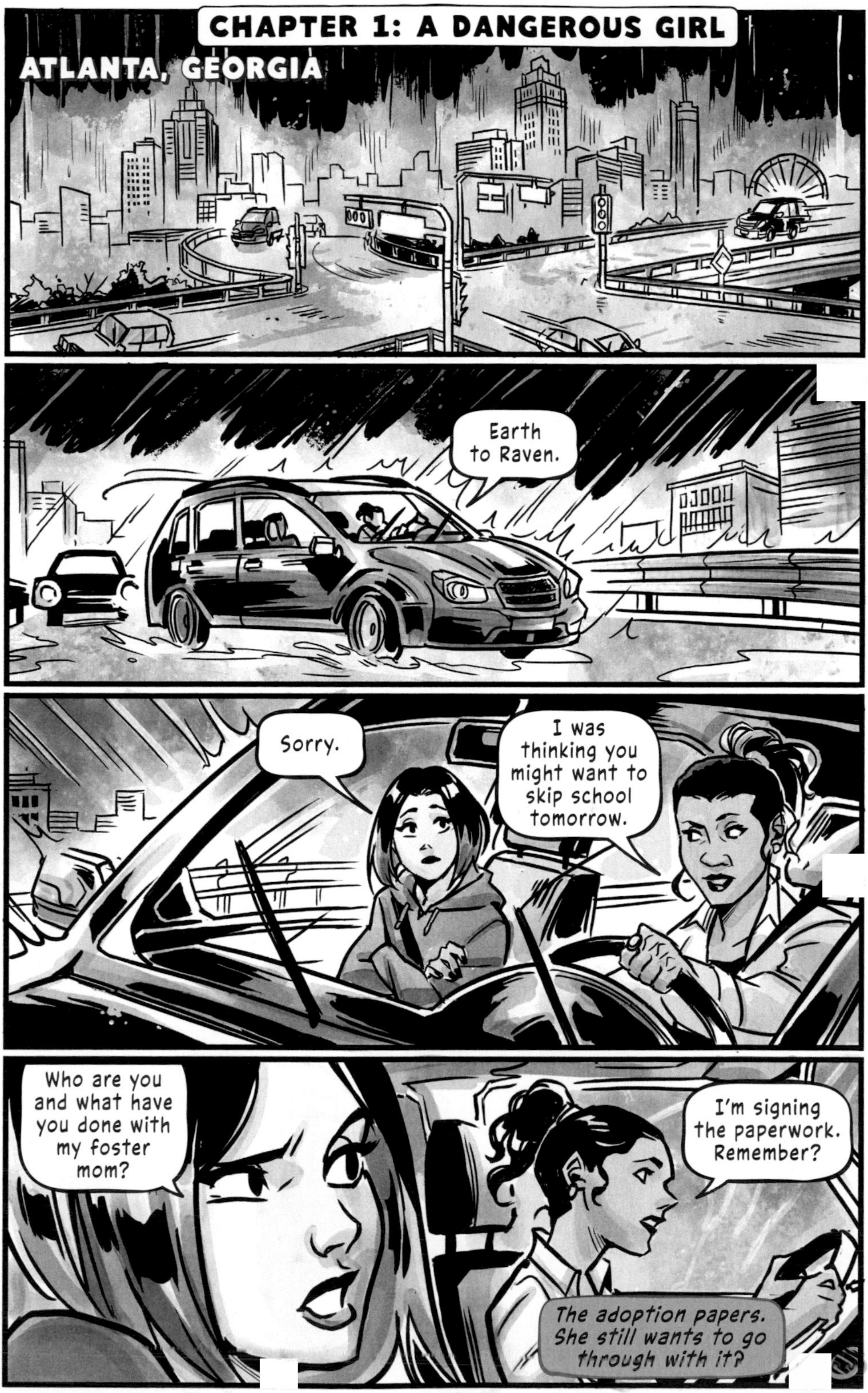
CHAPTER 1: A DANGEROUS GIRL
ATLANTA, GEORGIA
Earth to Raven.
Sorry.
I was thinking you might want to skip school tomorrow.
Who are you and what have you done with my foster mom?
I'm signing the paperwork. Remember?
The adoption papers. She still wants to go through with it?

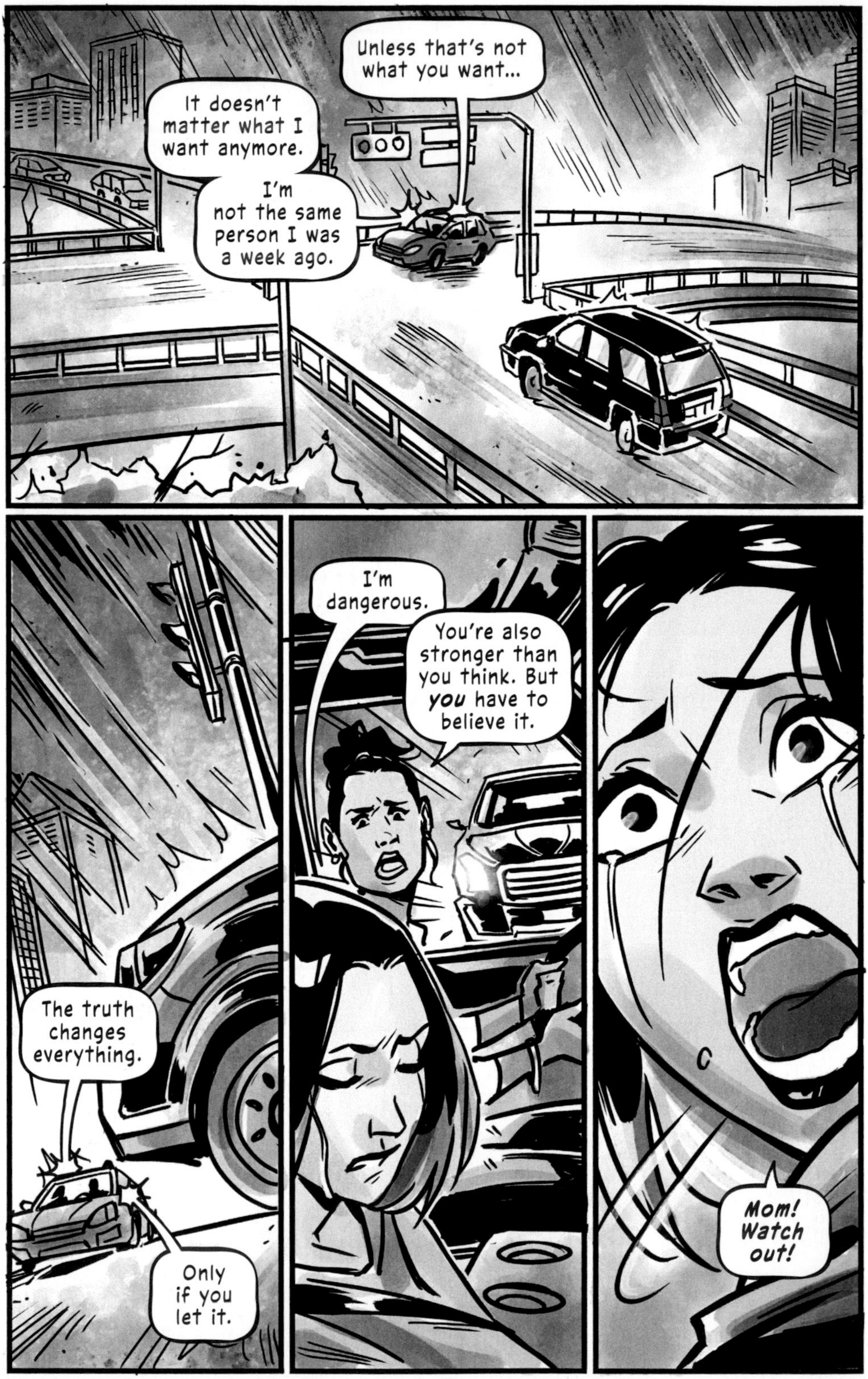
Unless that's not what you want...
It doesn't matter what I want anymore.
I'm not the same person I was a week ago.
The truth changes everything.
Only if you let it.
I'm dangerous.
You're also stronger than you think. But *you* have to believe it.
Mom! Watch out!

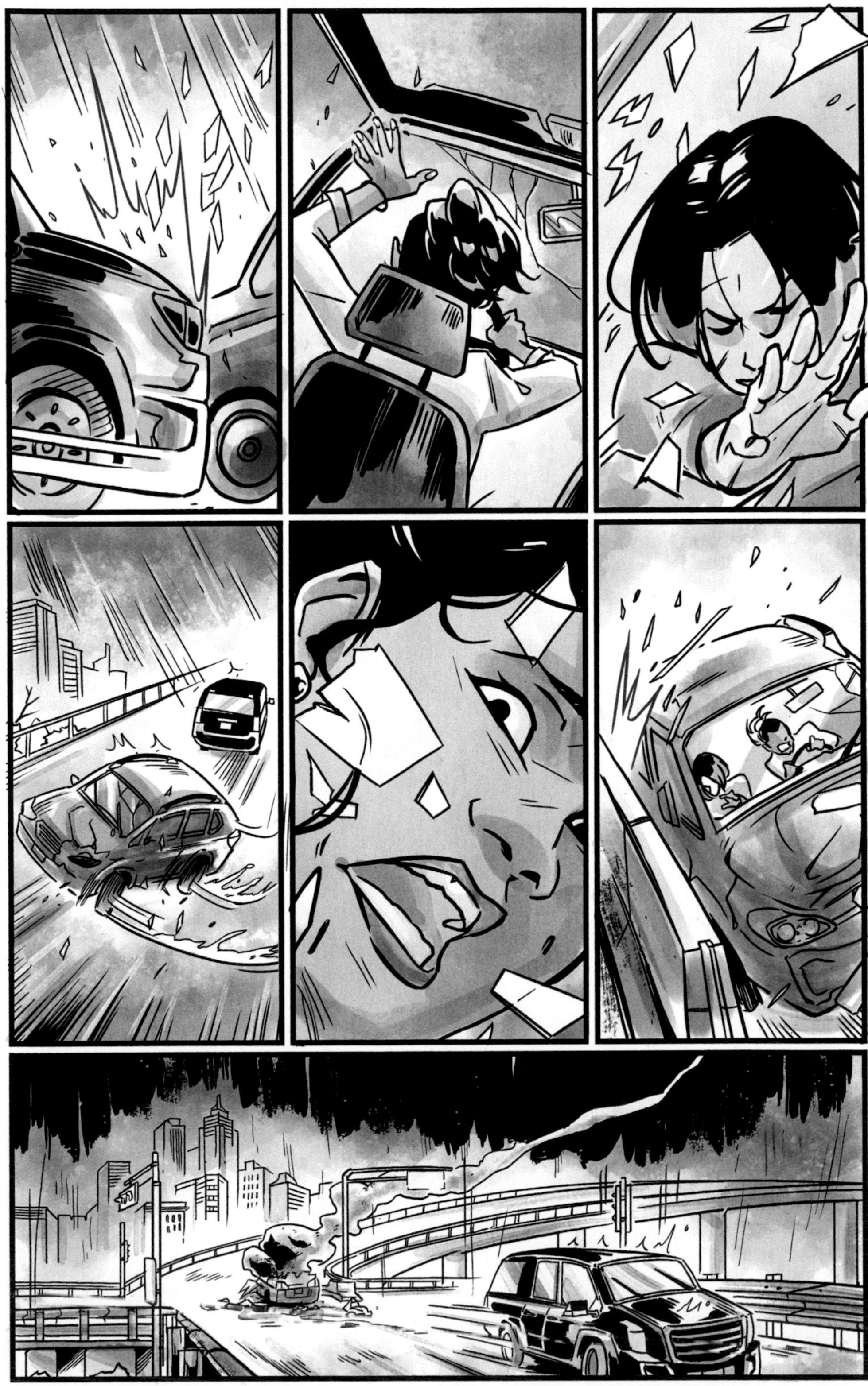

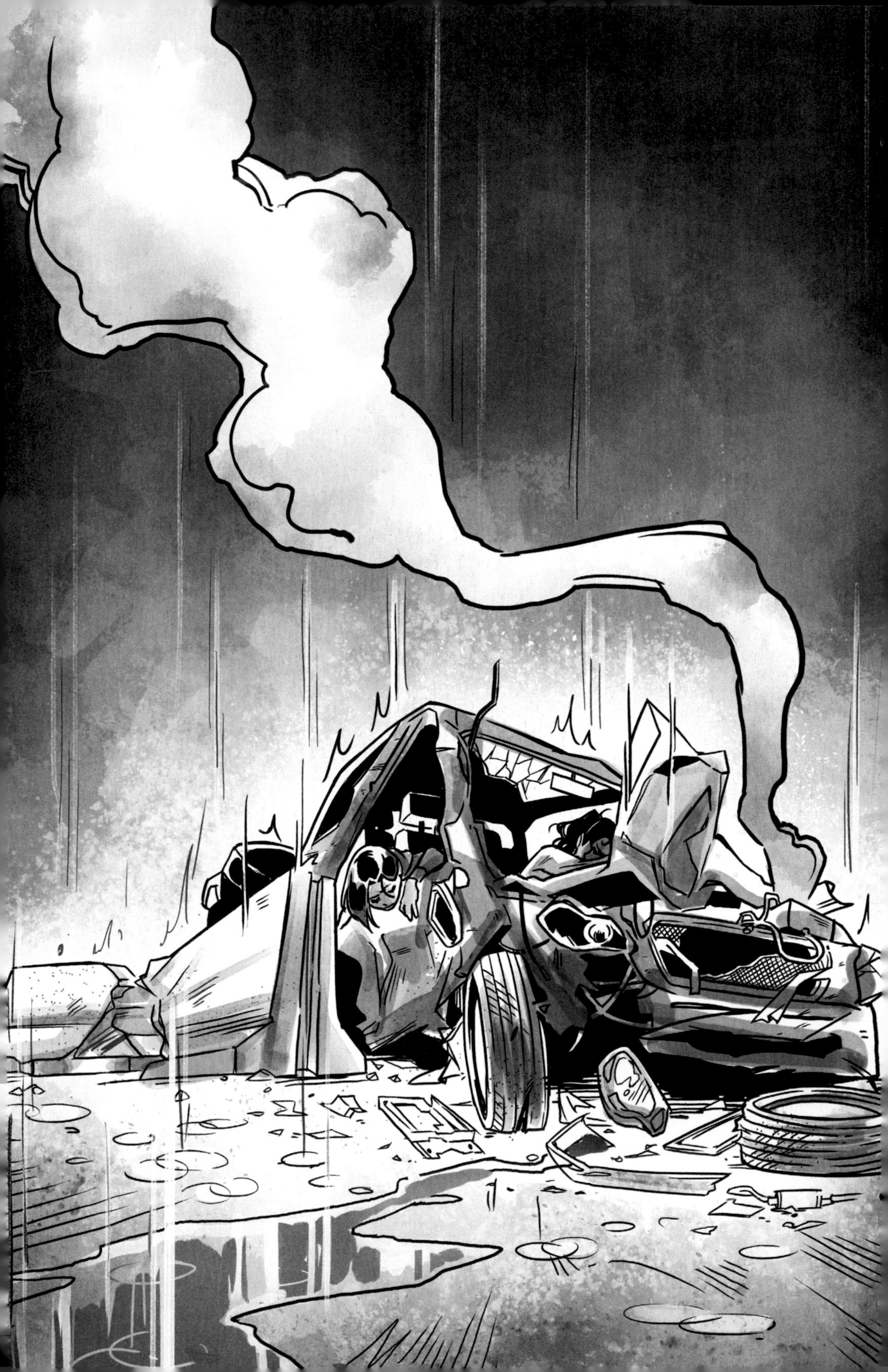

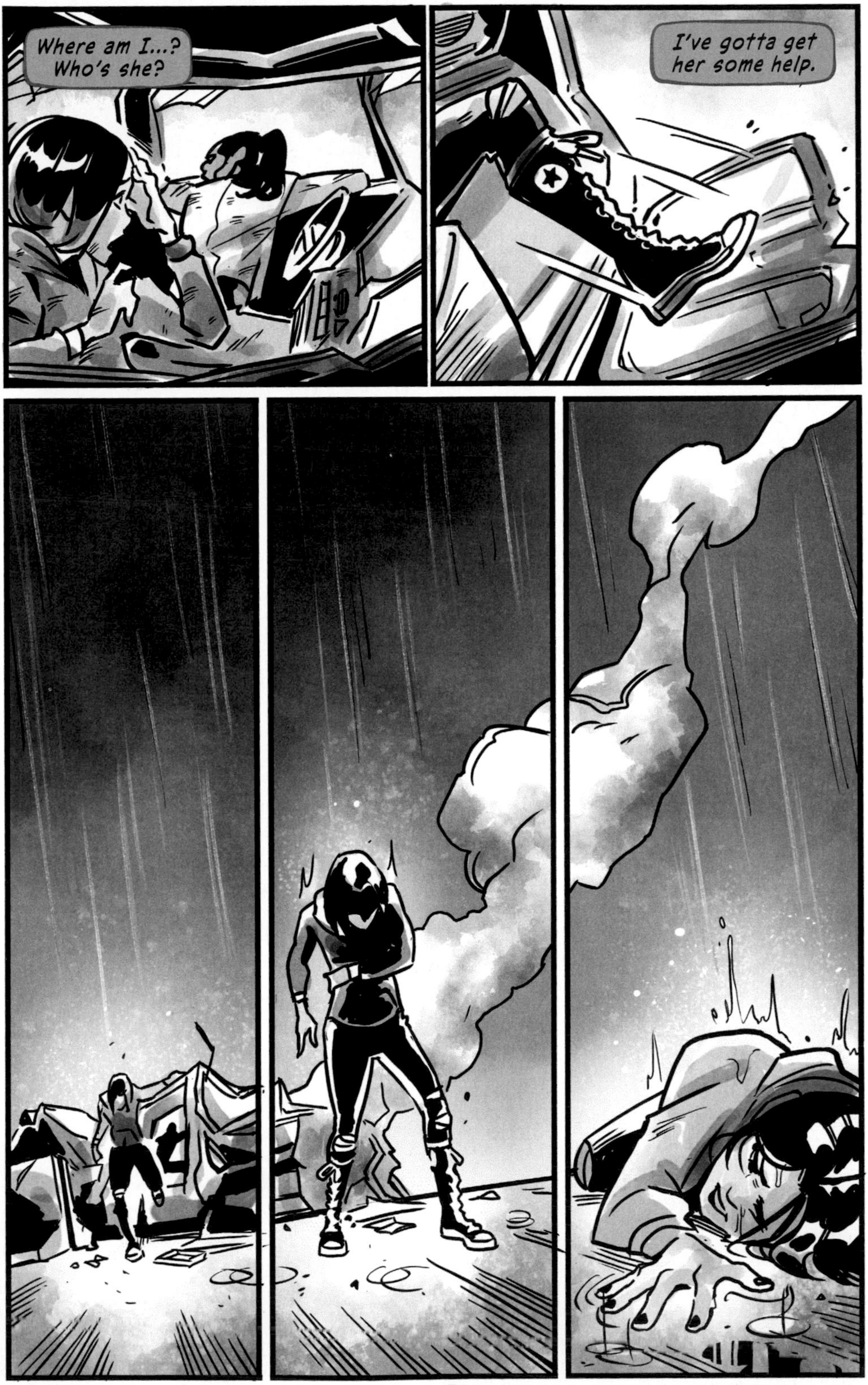
Where am I...?
Who's she?
I've gotta get her some help.

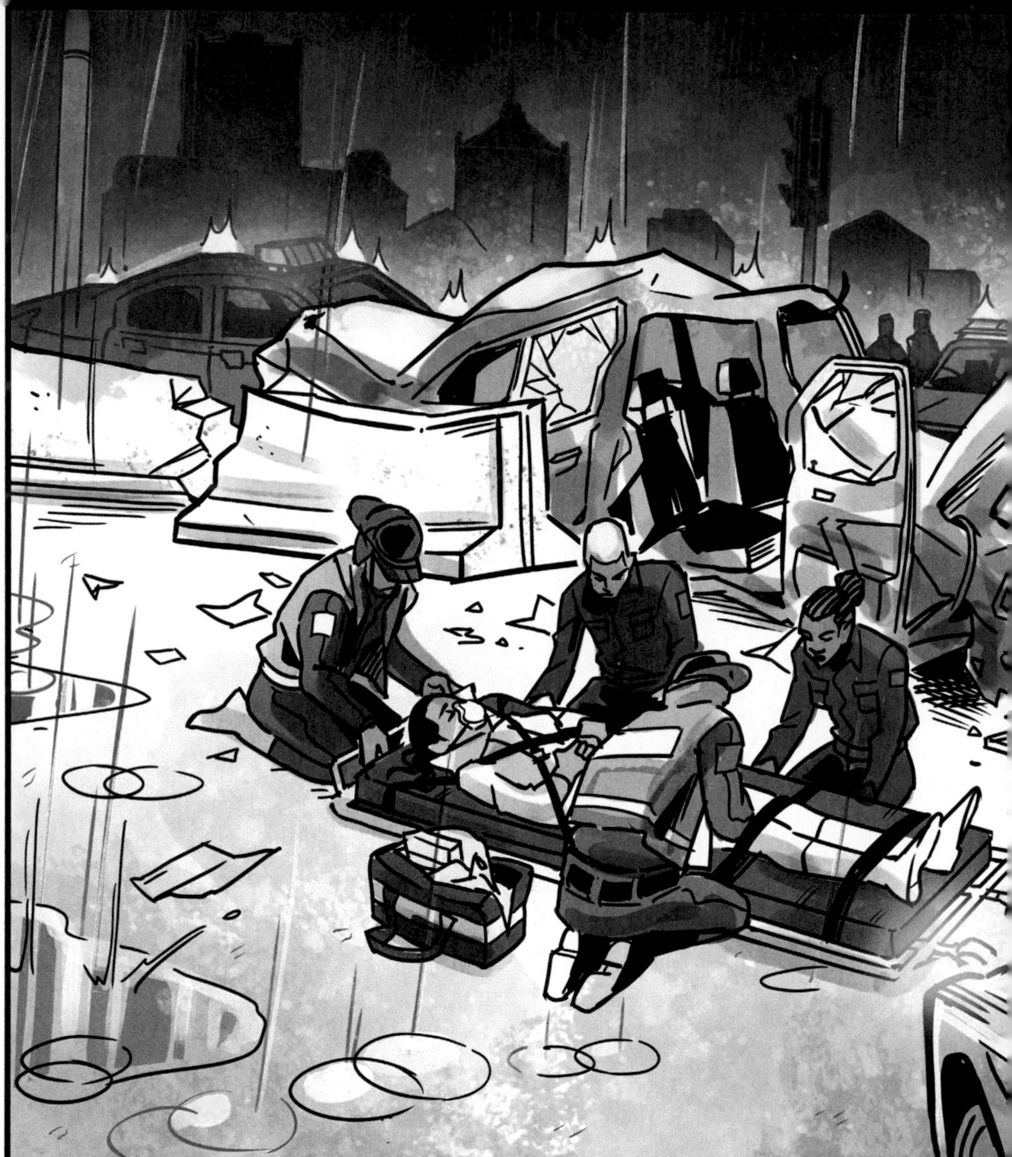

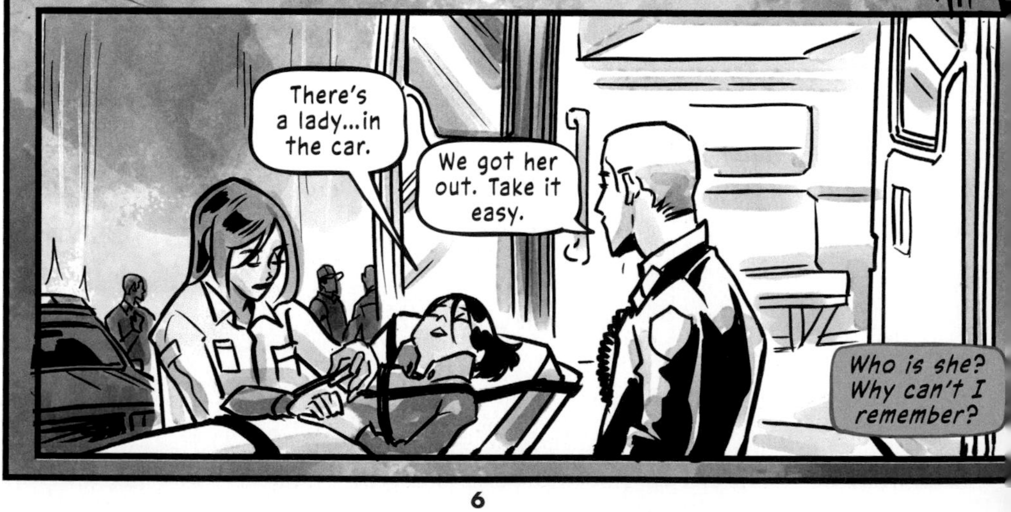
There's a lady...in the car.
We got her out. Take it easy.
Who is she? Why can't I remember?

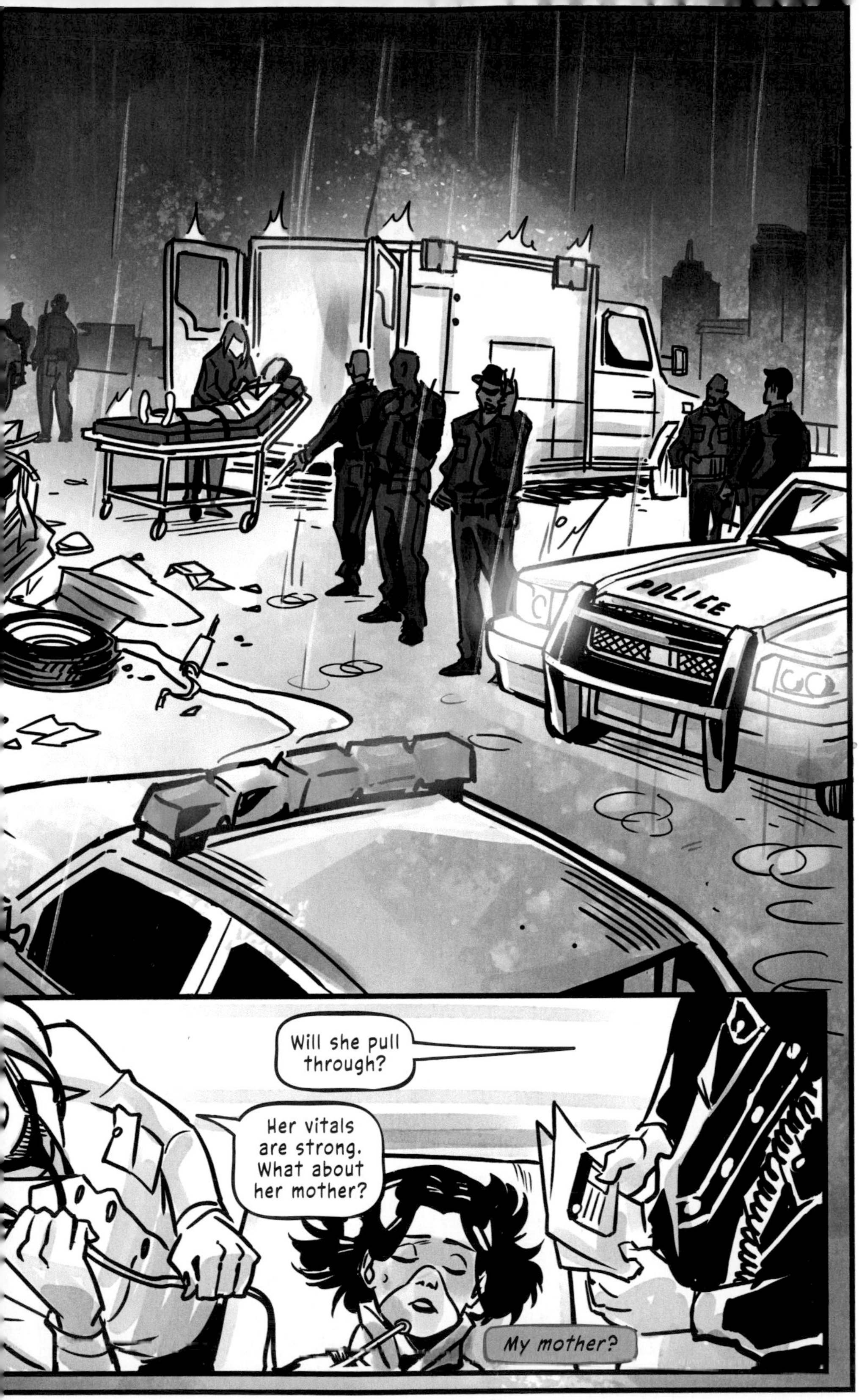
POLICE
Will she pull through?
Her vitals are strong. What about her mother?
My mother?

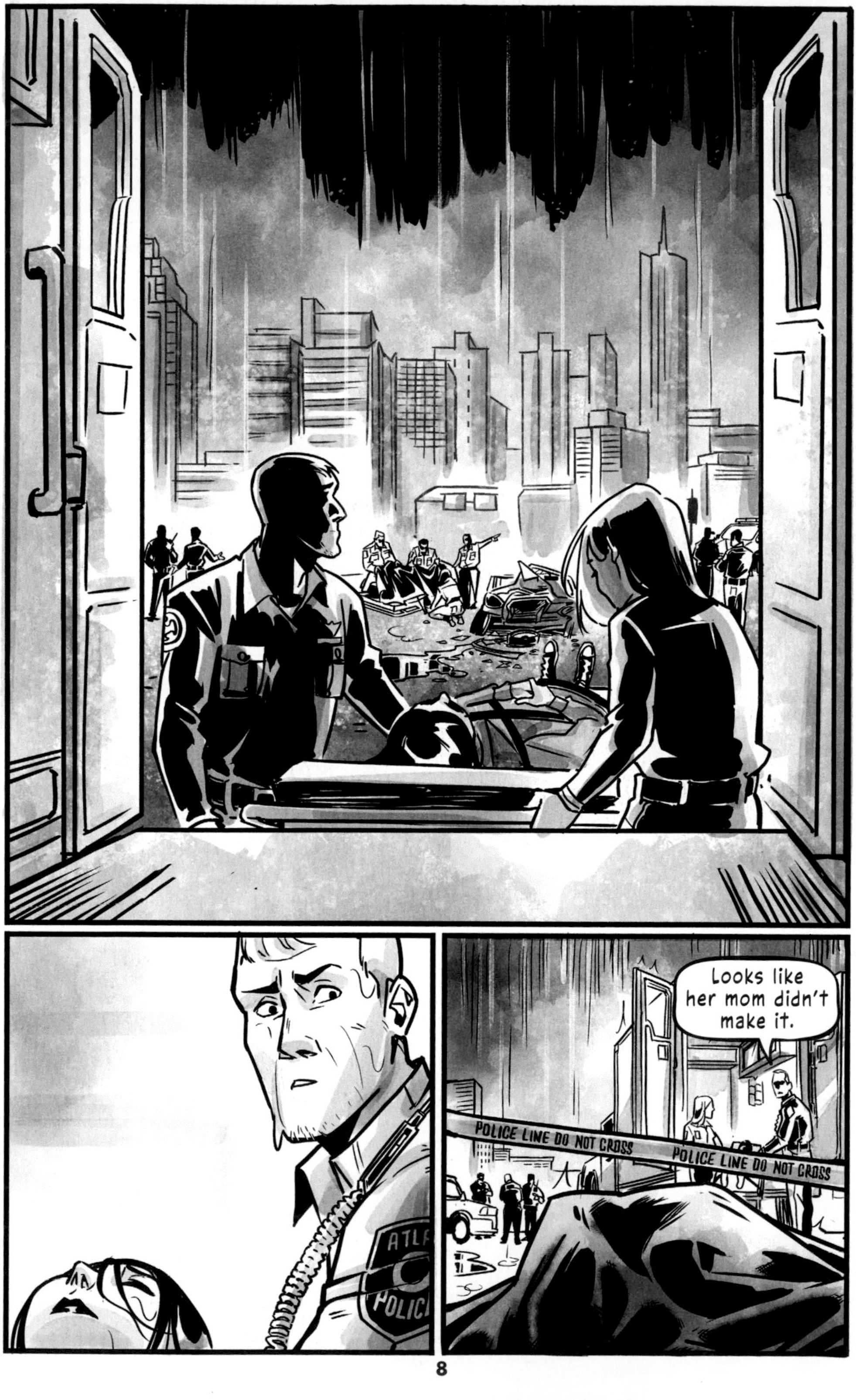
Looks like her mom didn't make it.
POLICE LINE DO NOT CROSS
POLICE LINE DO NOT CROSS

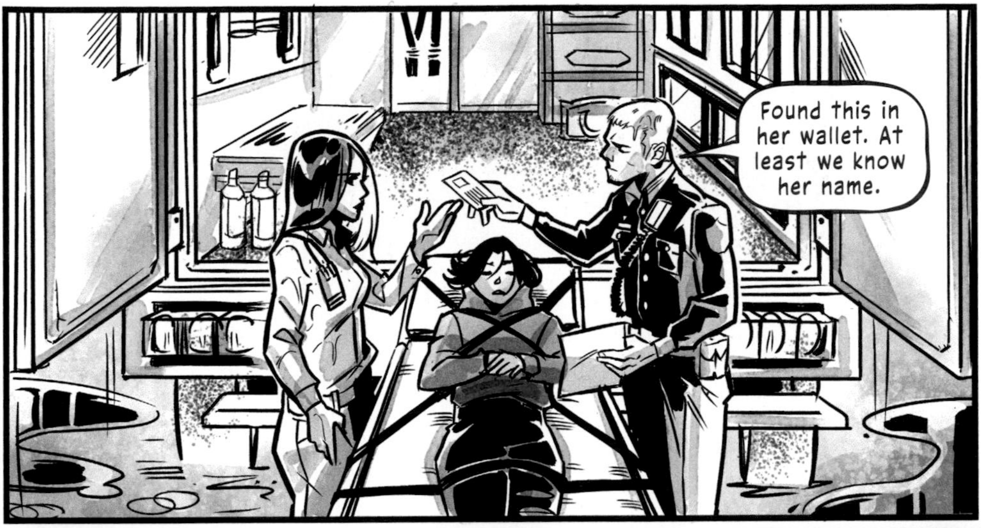
Found this in her wallet. At least we know her name.

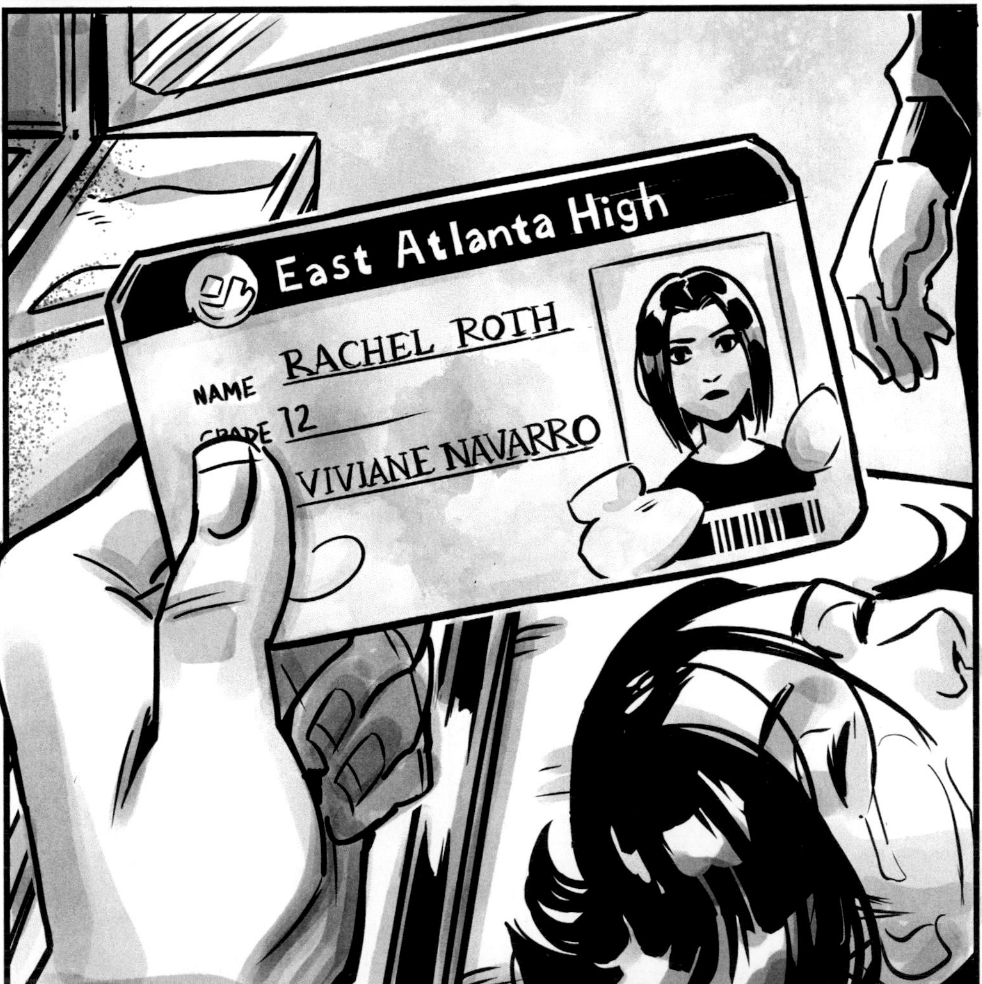
East Atlanta High
NAME RACHEL ROTH
12
VIVIANE NAVARRO

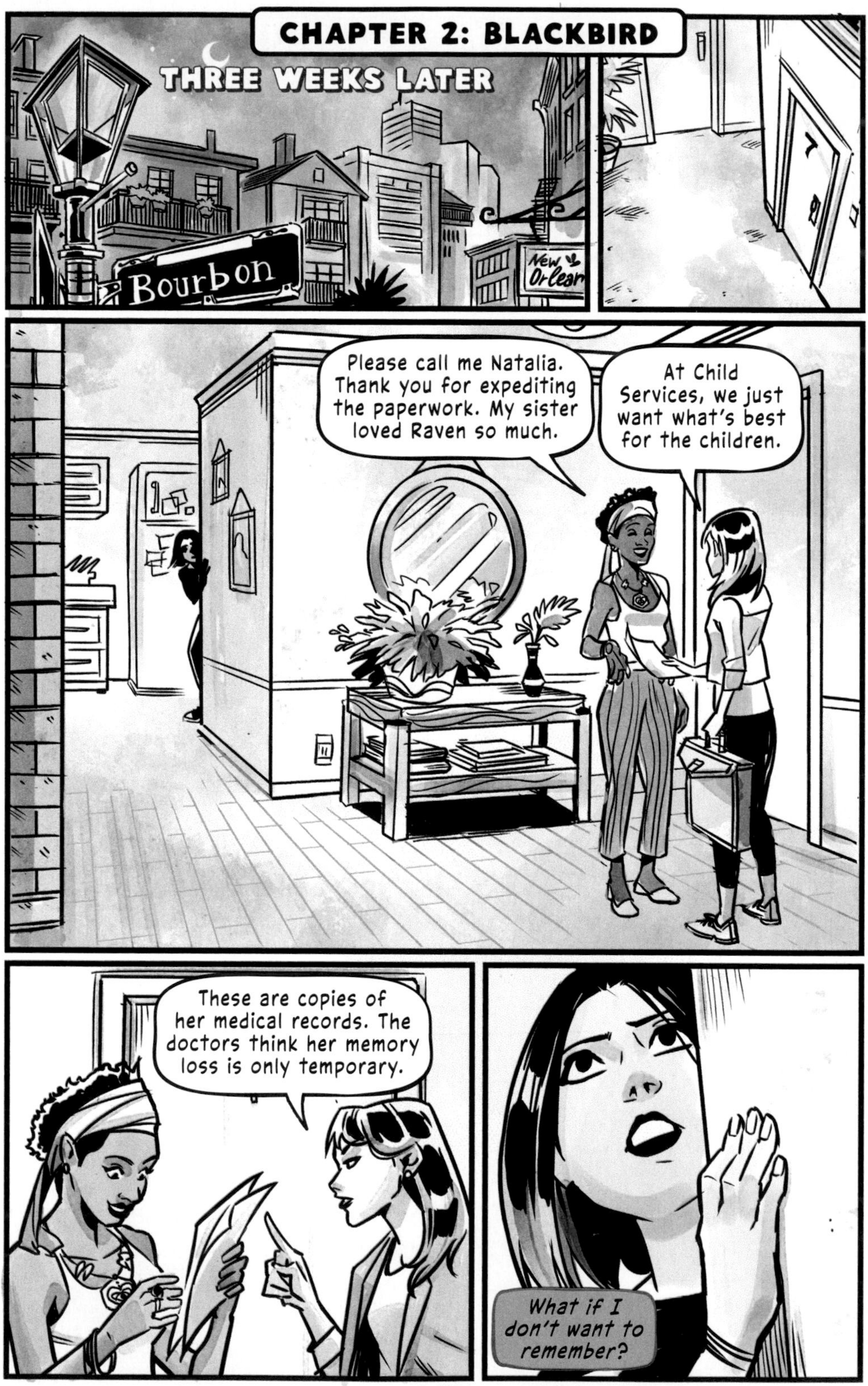
CHAPTER 2: BLACKBIRD
THREE WEEKS LATER
Bourbon
New Orleans
Please call me Natalia. Thank you for expediting the paperwork. My sister loved Raven so much.
At Child Services, we just want what's best for the children.
These are copies of her medical records. The doctors think her memory loss is only temporary.
What if I don't want to remember?

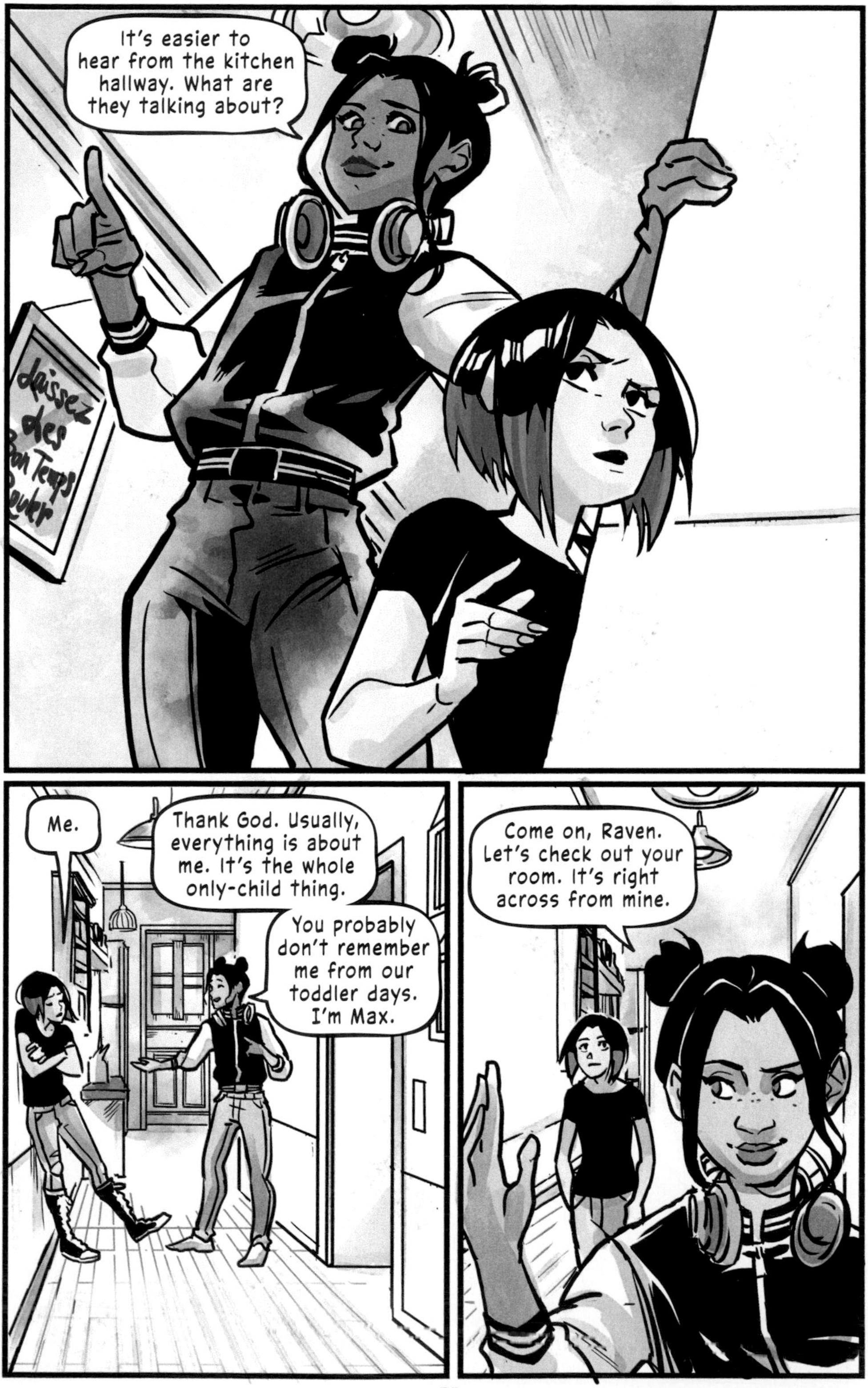
It's easier to hear from the kitchen hallway. What are they talking about?
Laissez des Bon Temps Rouler
Me.
Thank God. Usually, everything is about me. It's the whole only-child thing.
You probably don't remember me from our toddler days. I'm Max.
Come on, Raven. Let's check out your room. It's right across from mine.

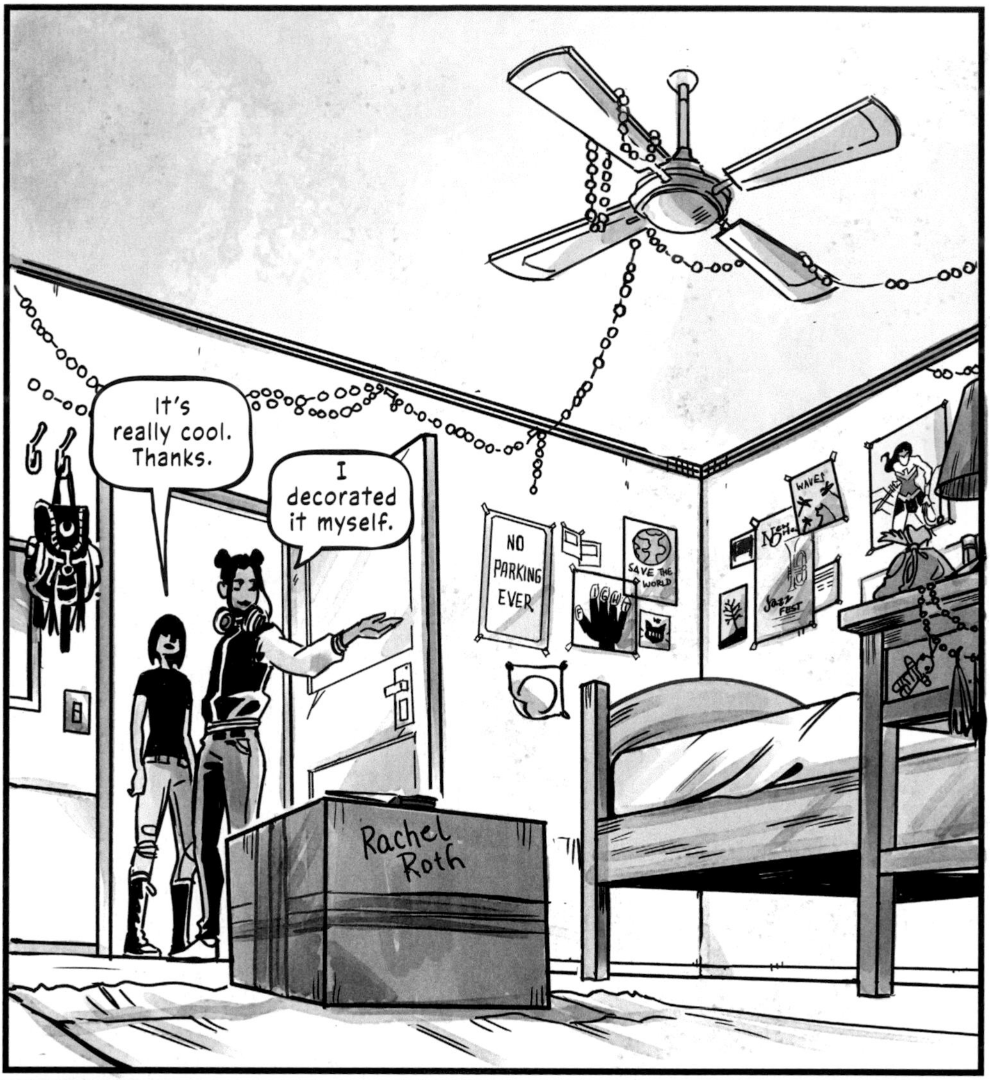
It's really cool. Thanks.
I decorated it myself.
NO PARKING EVER
SAVE THE WORLD
WAVES
JAZZ FEST
Rachel Roth

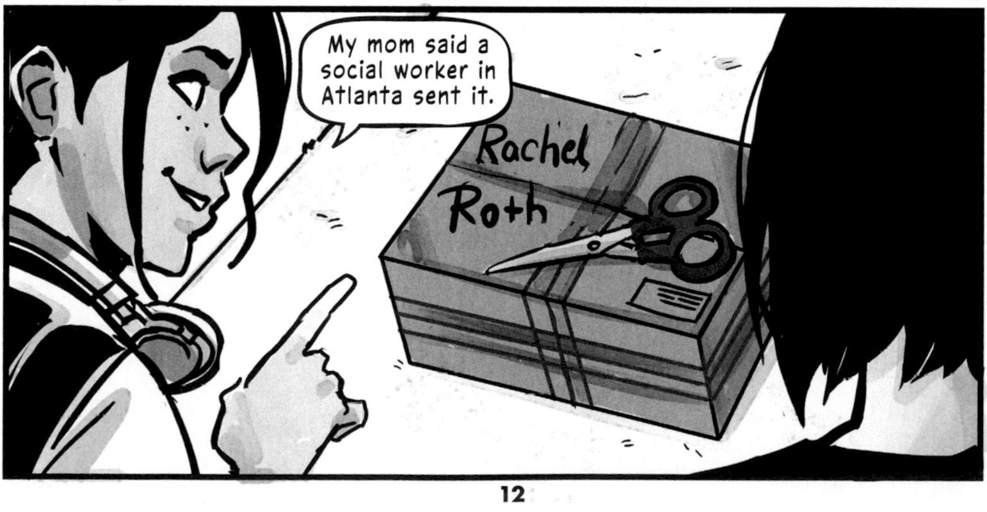
My mom said a social worker in Atlanta sent it.
Rachel Roth

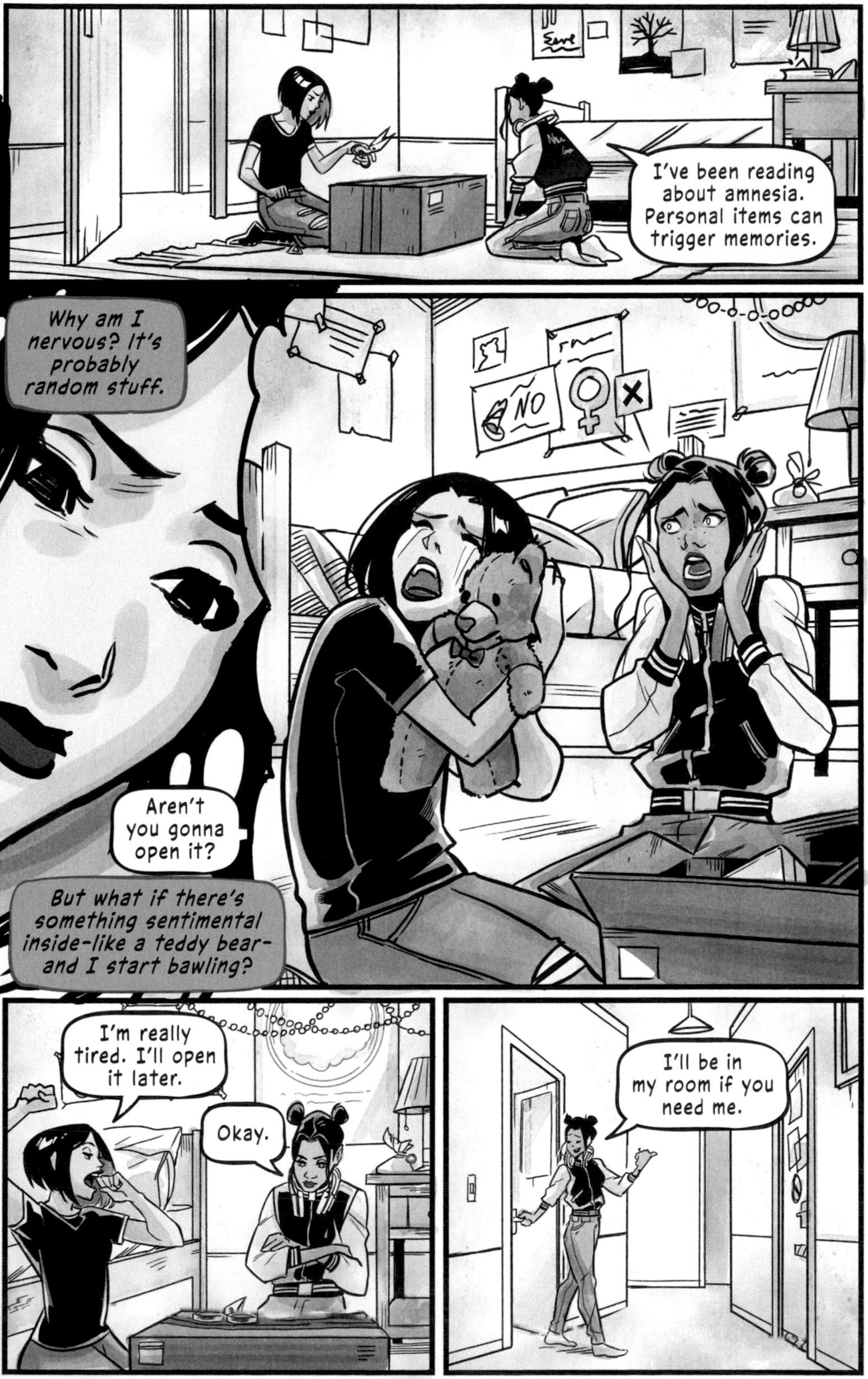
I've been reading about amnesia. Personal items can trigger memories.
Why am I nervous? It's probably random stuff.
Aren't you gonna open it?
But what if there's something sentimental inside-like a teddy bear-and I start bawling?
I'm really tired. I'll open it later.
Okay.
I'll be in my room if you need me.

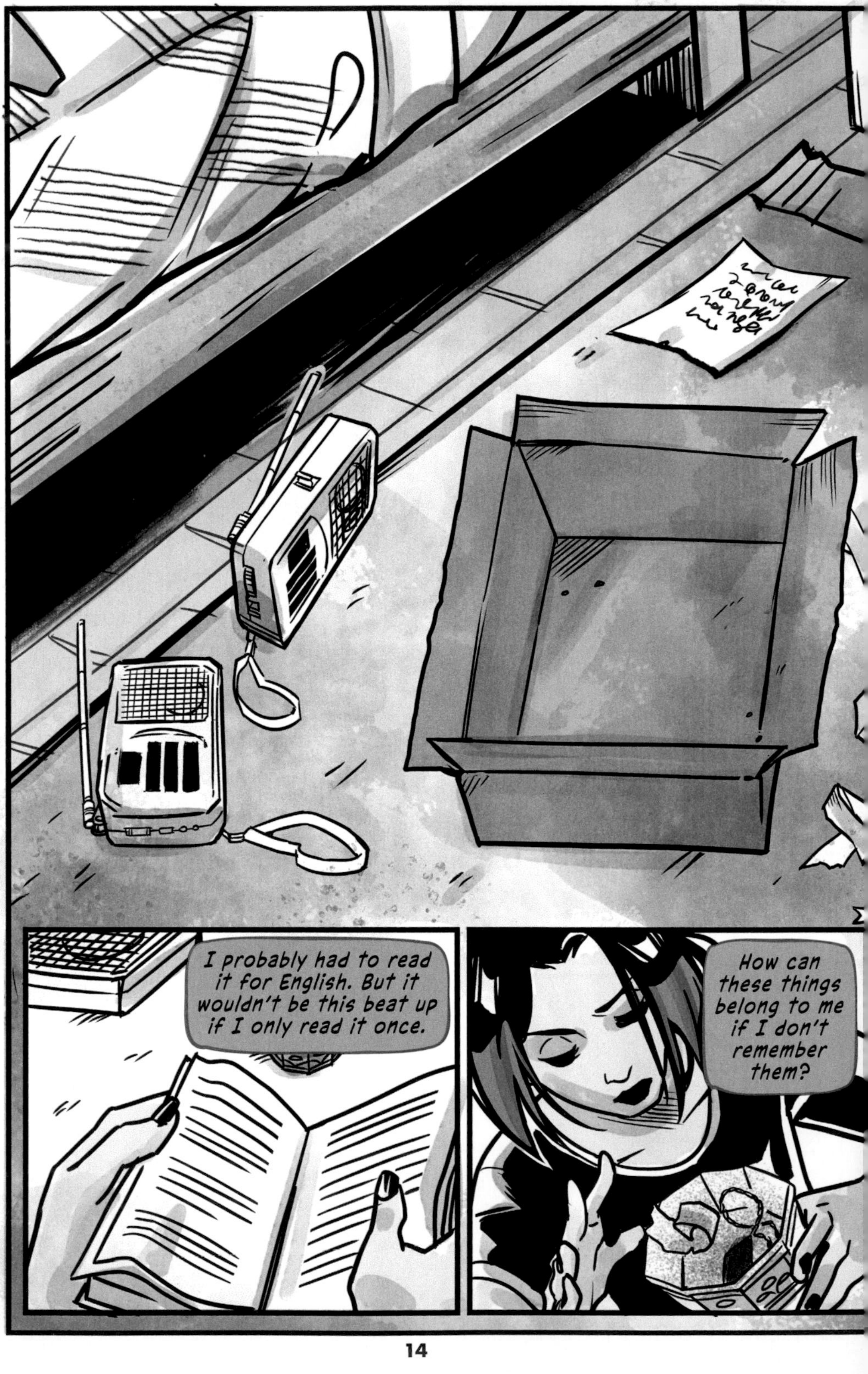
I probably had to read it for English. But it wouldn't be this beat up if I only read it once.
How can these things belong to me if I don't remember them?

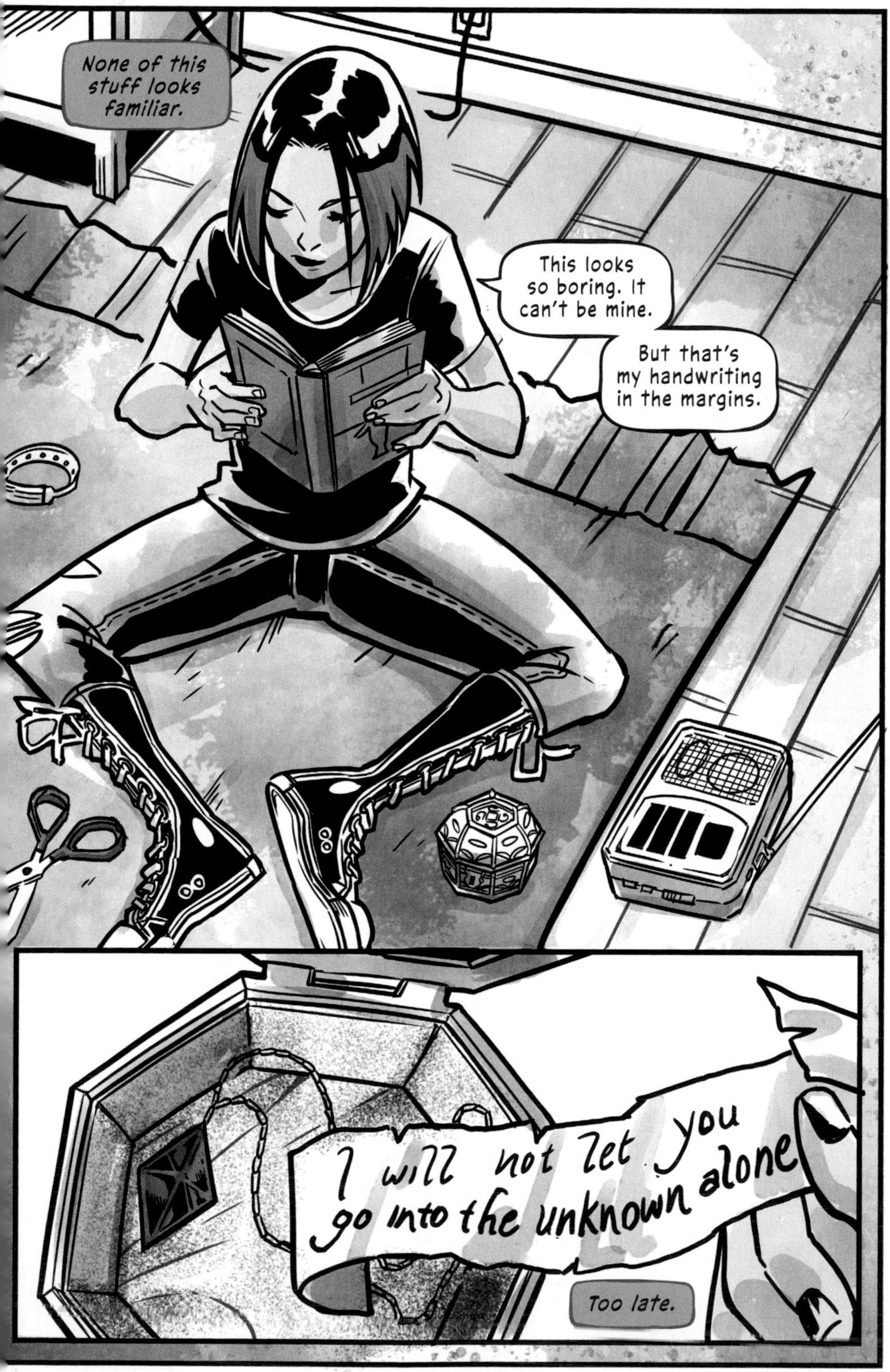
None of this stuff looks familiar.
This looks so boring. It can't be mine.
But that's my handwriting in the margins.
I will not let you go into the unknown alone
Too late.

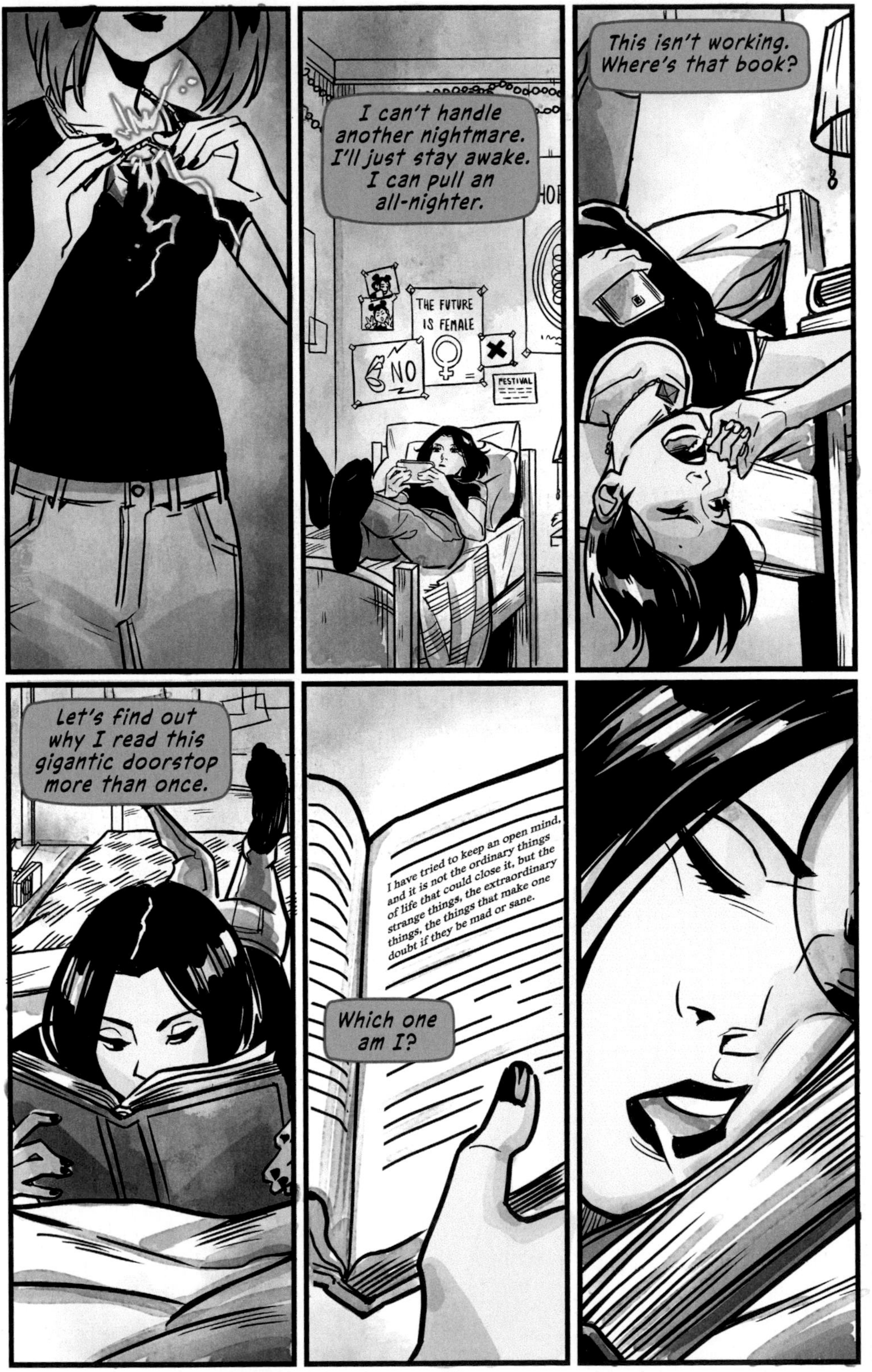
I can't handle another nightmare. I'll just stay awake. I can pull an all-nighter.
THE FUTURE IS FEMALE
NO
FESTIVAL
This isn't working. Where's that book?
Let's find out why I read this gigantic doorstop more than once.
I have tried to keep an open mind, and it is not the ordinary things of life that could close it, but the strange things, the extraordinary things, the things that make one doubt if they be mad or sane.
Which one am I?

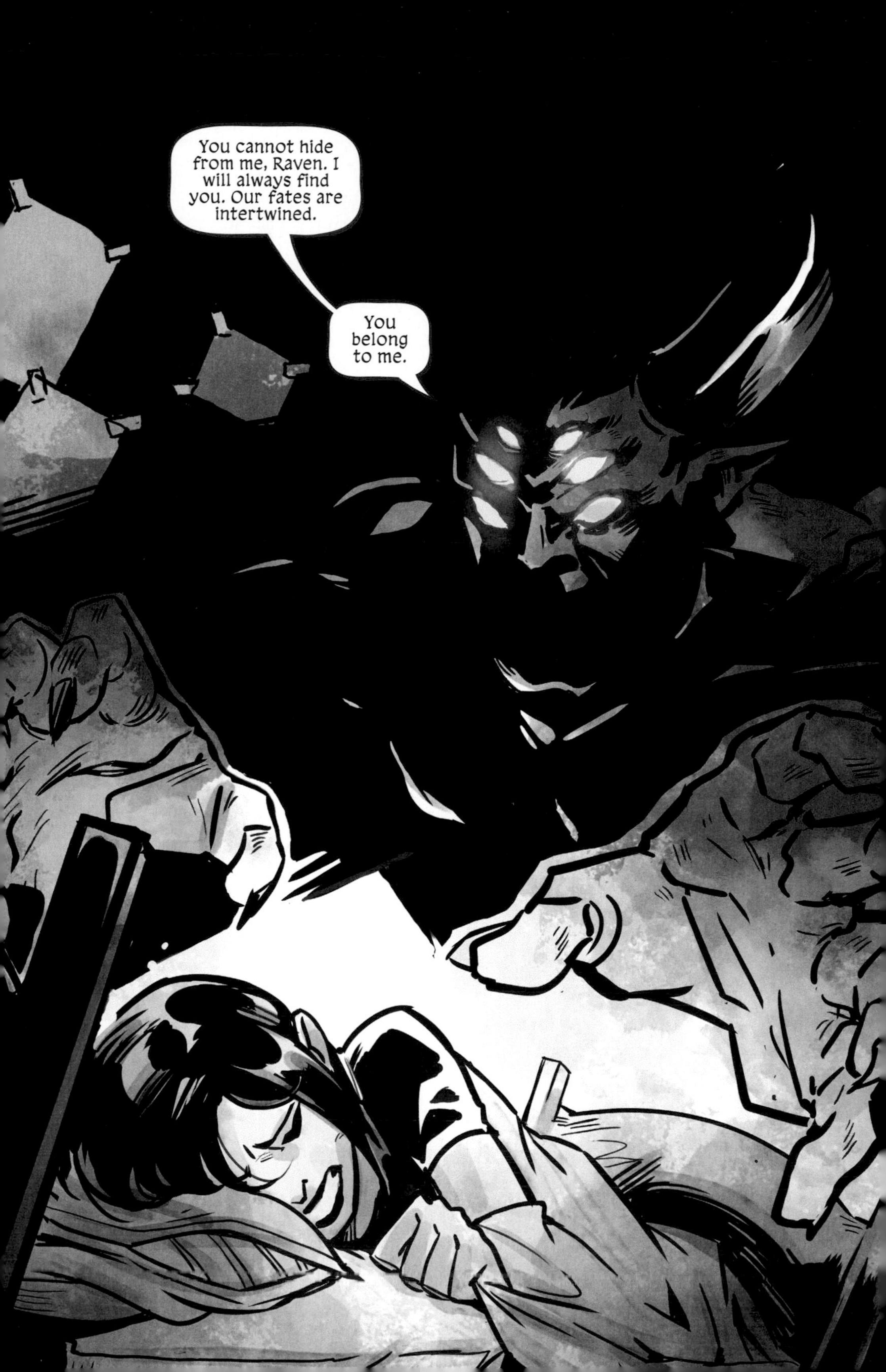
You cannot hide from me, Raven. I will always find you. Our fates are intertwined.
You belong to me.

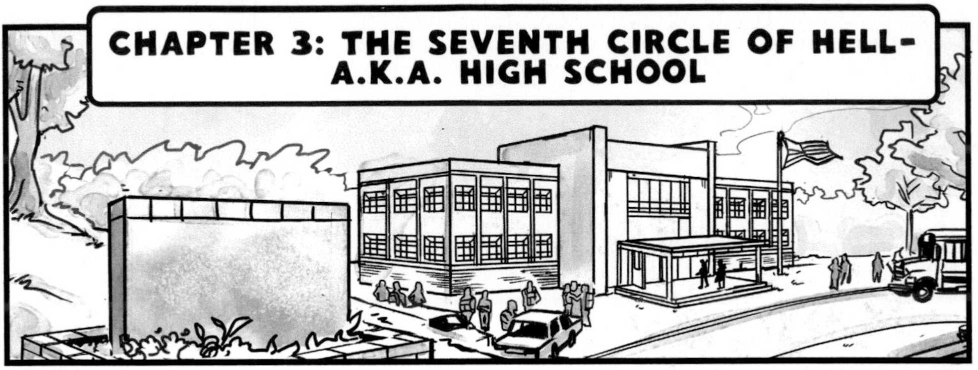
CHAPTER 3: THE SEVENTH CIRCLE OF HELL-
A.K.A. HIGH SCHOOL

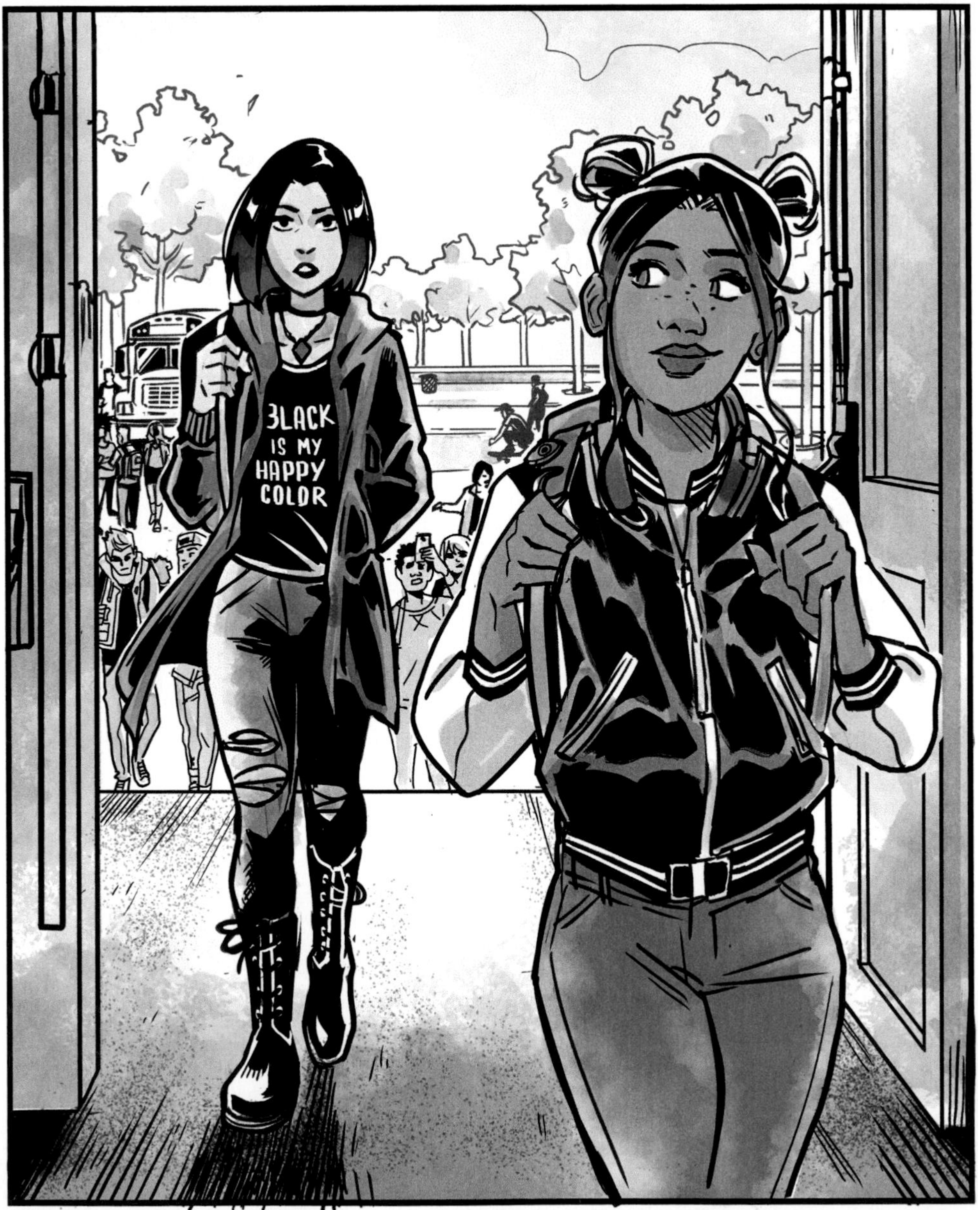
BLACK IS MY HAPPY COLOR

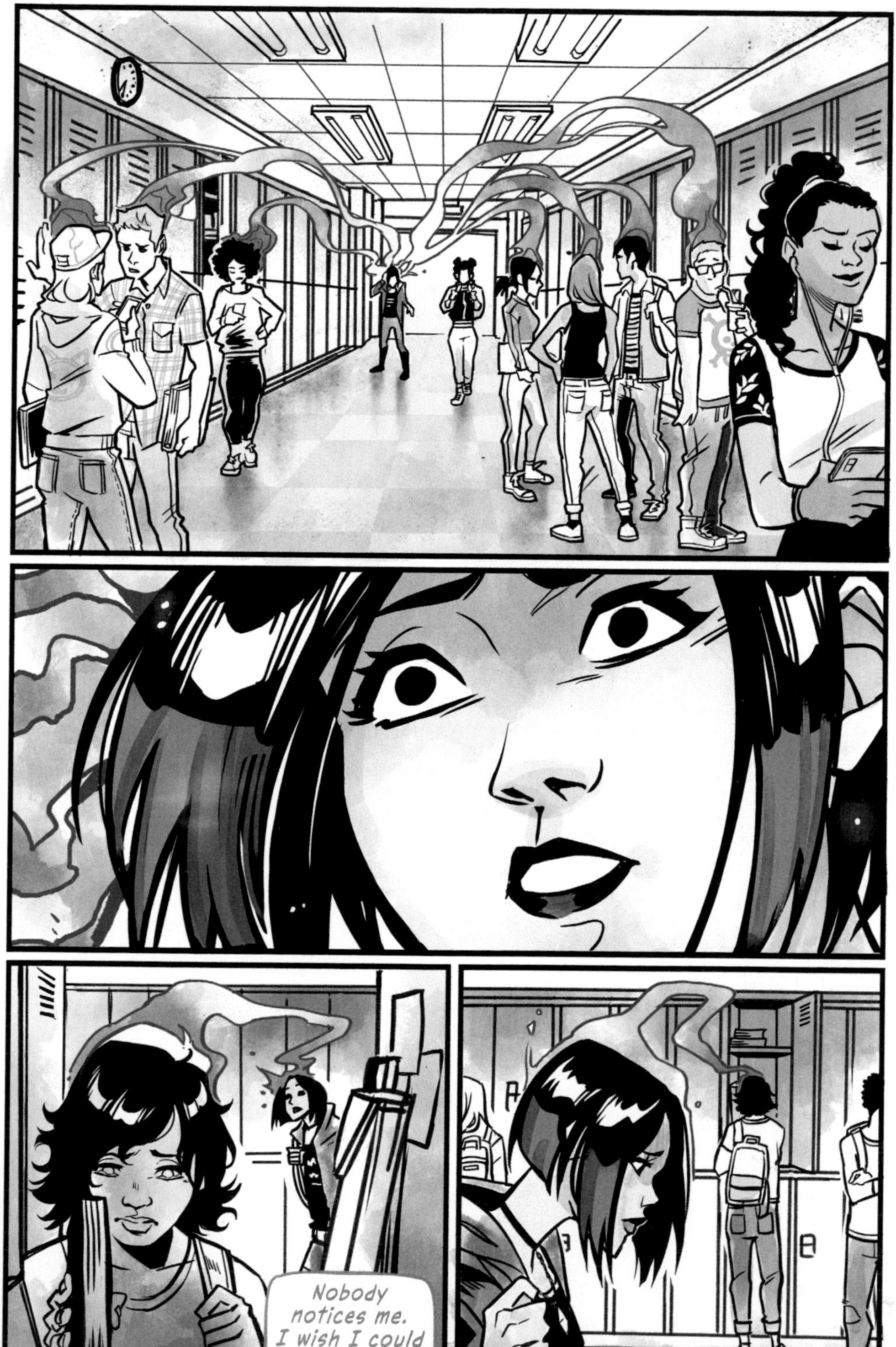
Nobody notices me. I wish I could disappear for real.

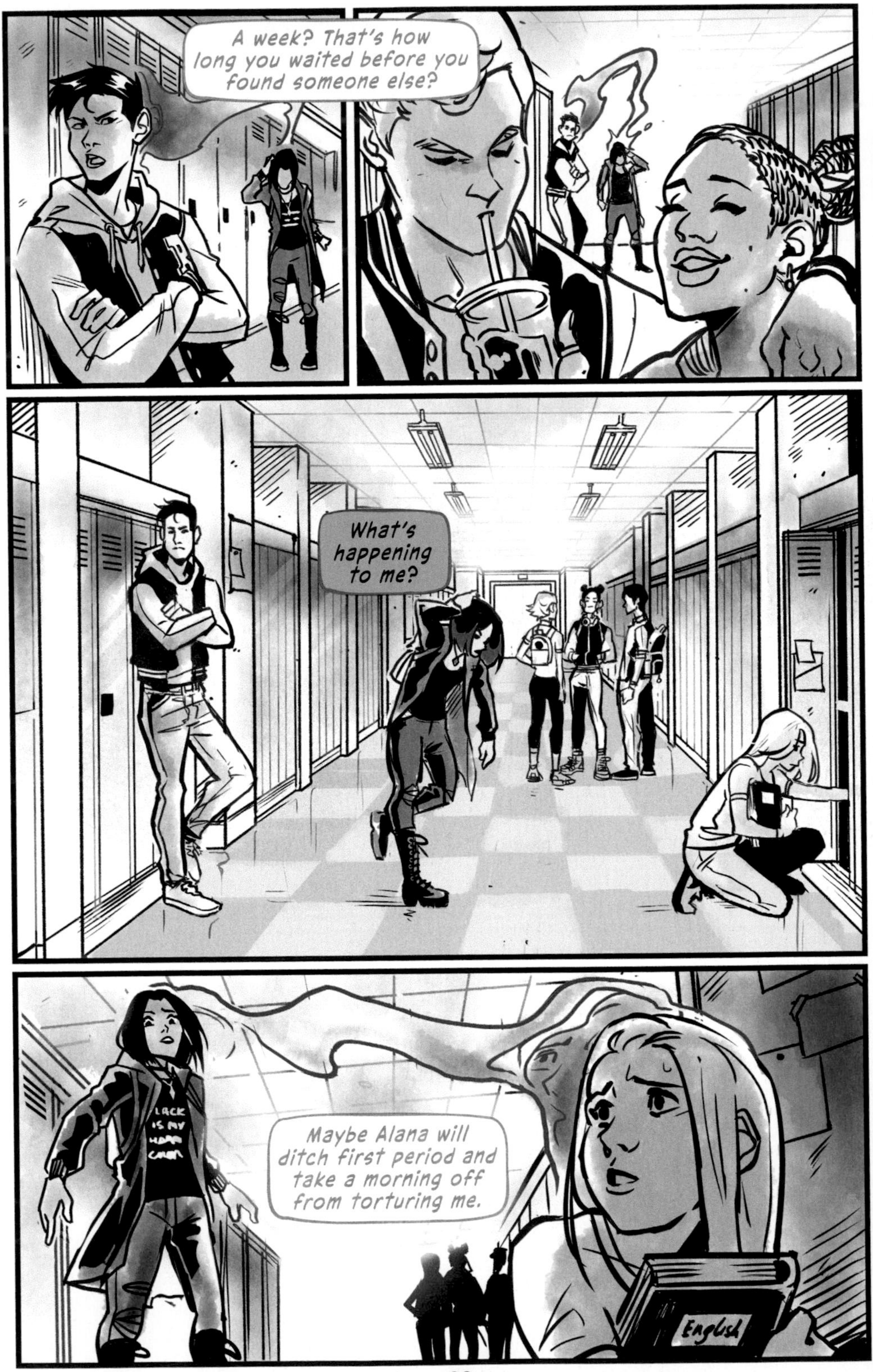
A week? That's how long you waited before you found someone else?
What's happening to me?
Maybe Alana will ditch first period and take a morning off from torturing me.
English

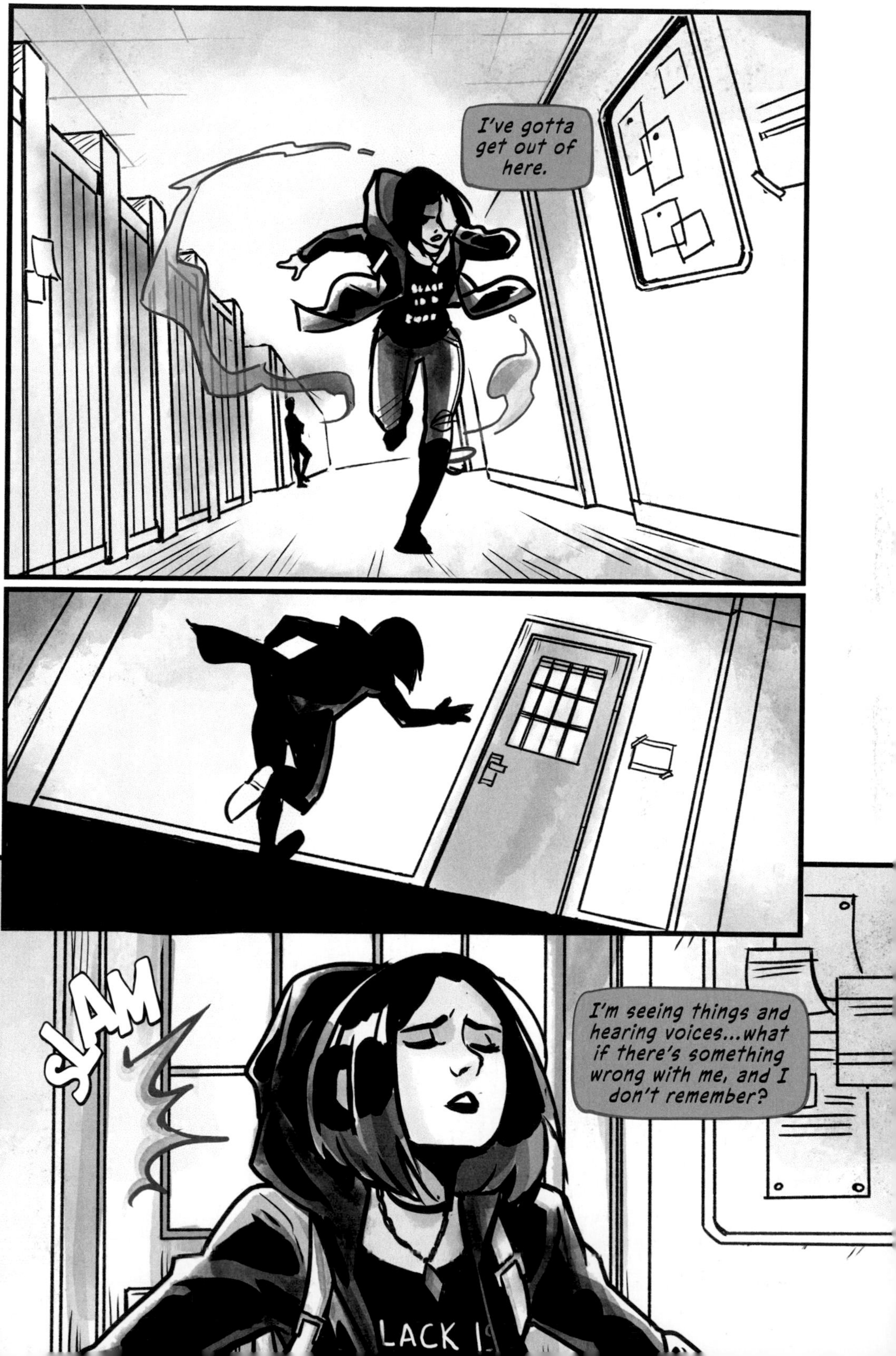
I've gotta get out of here.
SLAM
I'm seeing things and hearing voices...what if there's something wrong with me, and I don't remember?

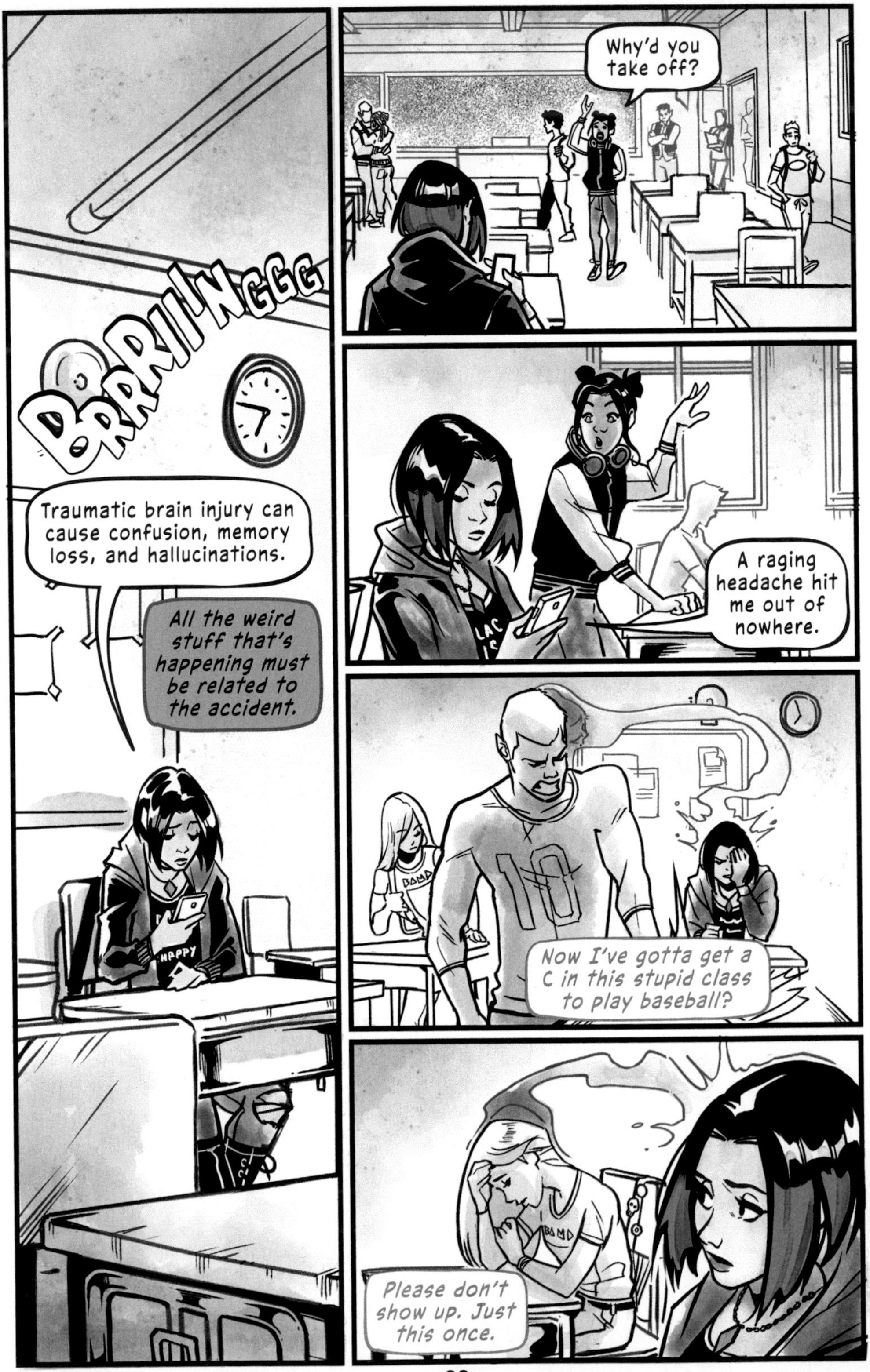
BRRRIIINGGG
Traumatic brain injury can cause confusion, memory loss, and hallucinations.
All the weird stuff that's happening must be related to the accident.
Why'd you take off?
A raging headache hit me out of nowhere.
Now I've gotta get a C in this stupid class to play baseball?
Please don't show up. Just this once.

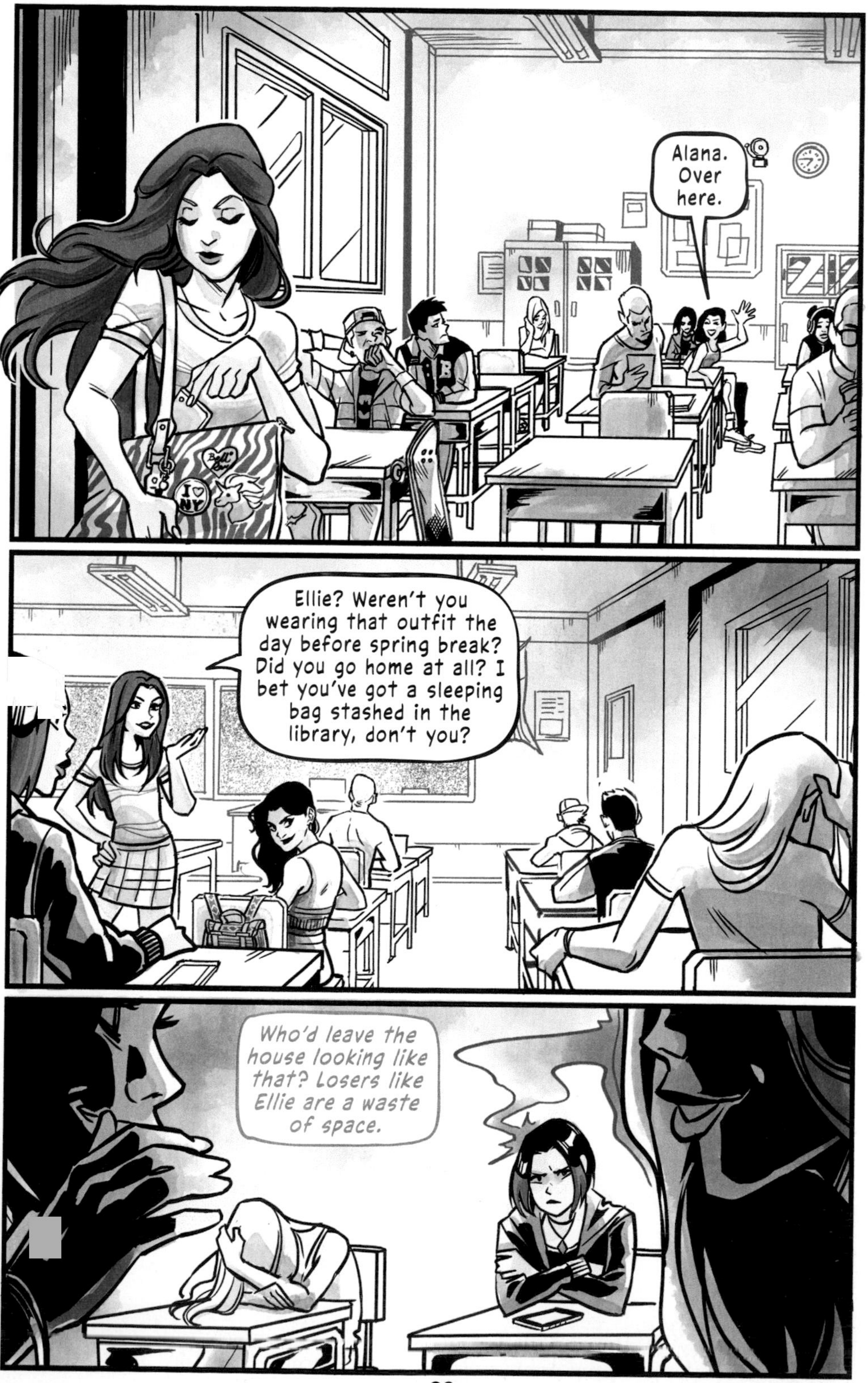
Alana. Over here.
Ellie? Weren't you wearing that outfit the day before spring break? Did you go home at all? I bet you've got a sleeping bag stashed in the library, don't you?
Who'd leave the house looking like that? Losers like Ellie are a waste of space.

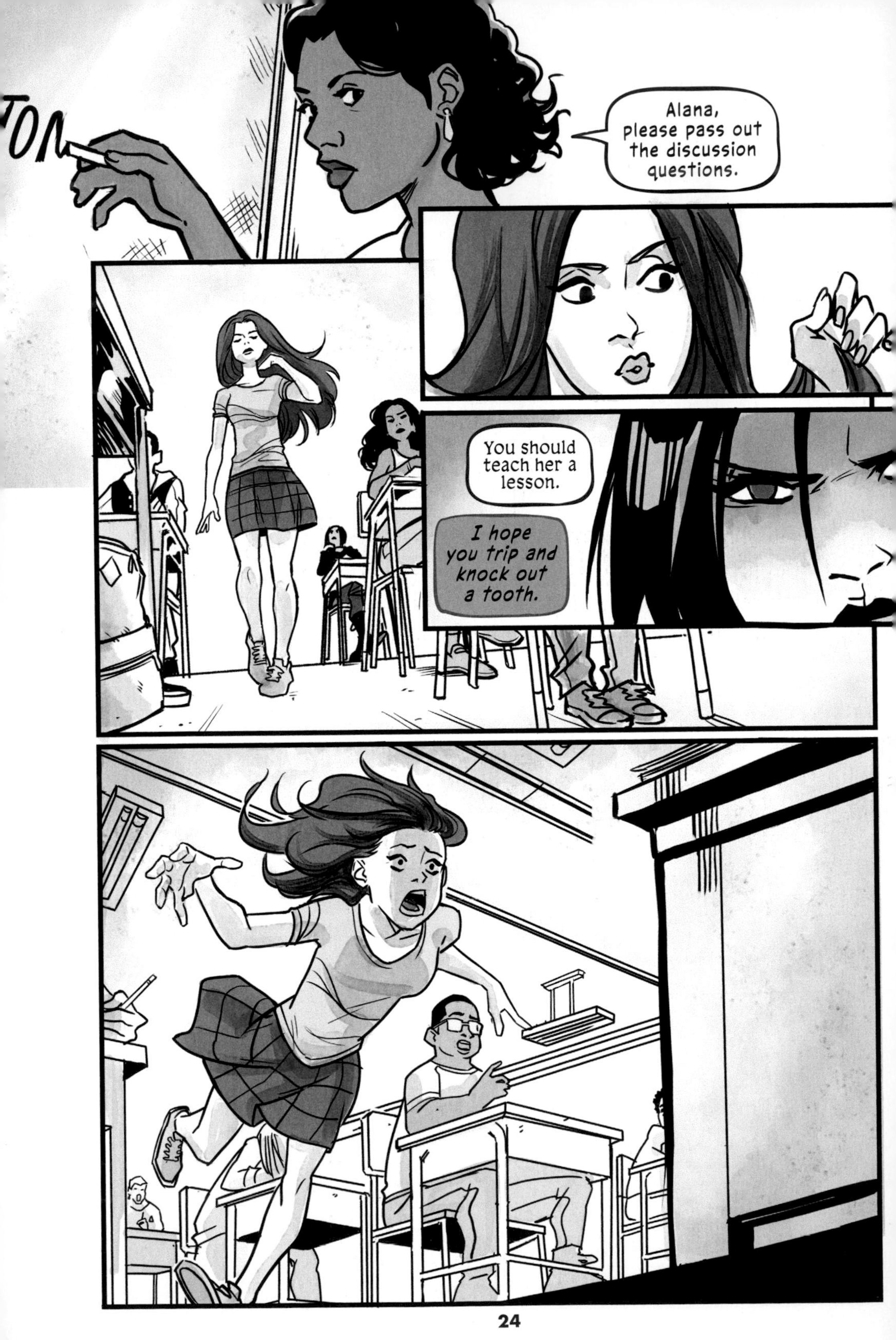
TON
Alana, please pass out the discussion questions.
You should teach her a lesson.
I hope you trip and knock out a tooth.

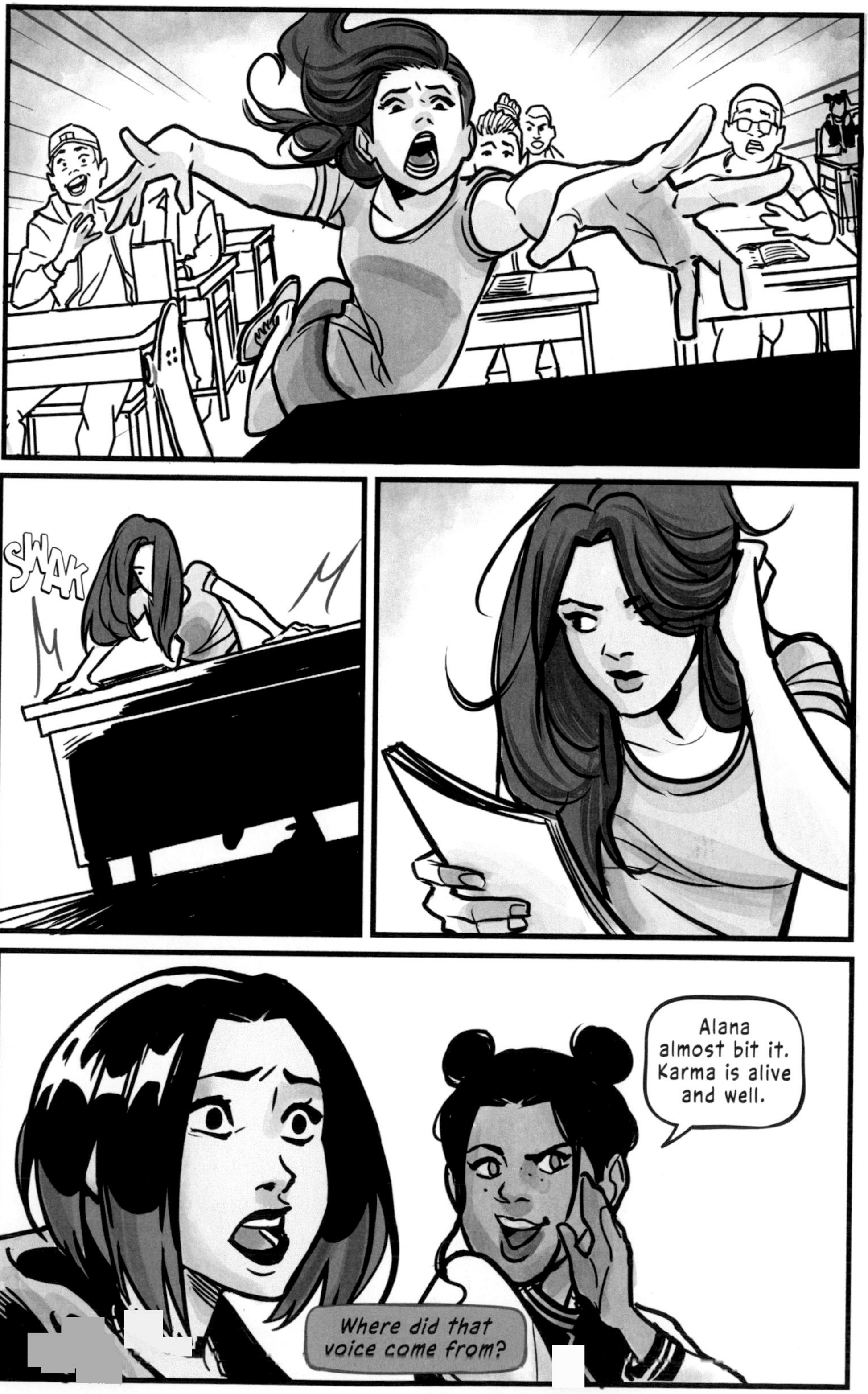
SWAK
Alana almost bit it. Karma is alive and well.
Where did that voice come from?

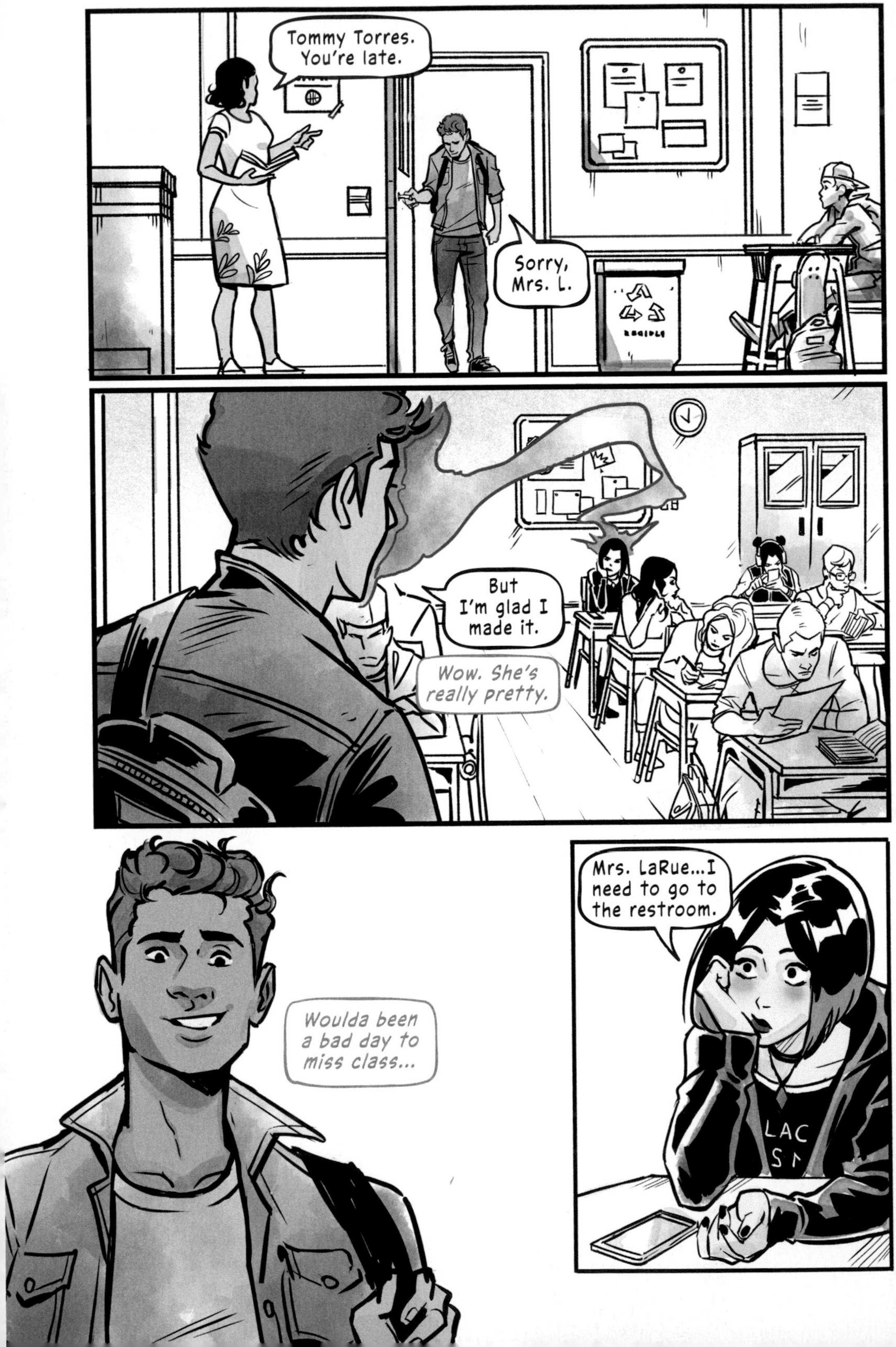
Tommy Torres. You're late.
Sorry, Mrs. L.
RECYCLE
But I'm glad I made it.
Wow. She's really pretty.
Woulda been a bad day to miss class...
Mrs. LaRue...I need to go to the restroom.

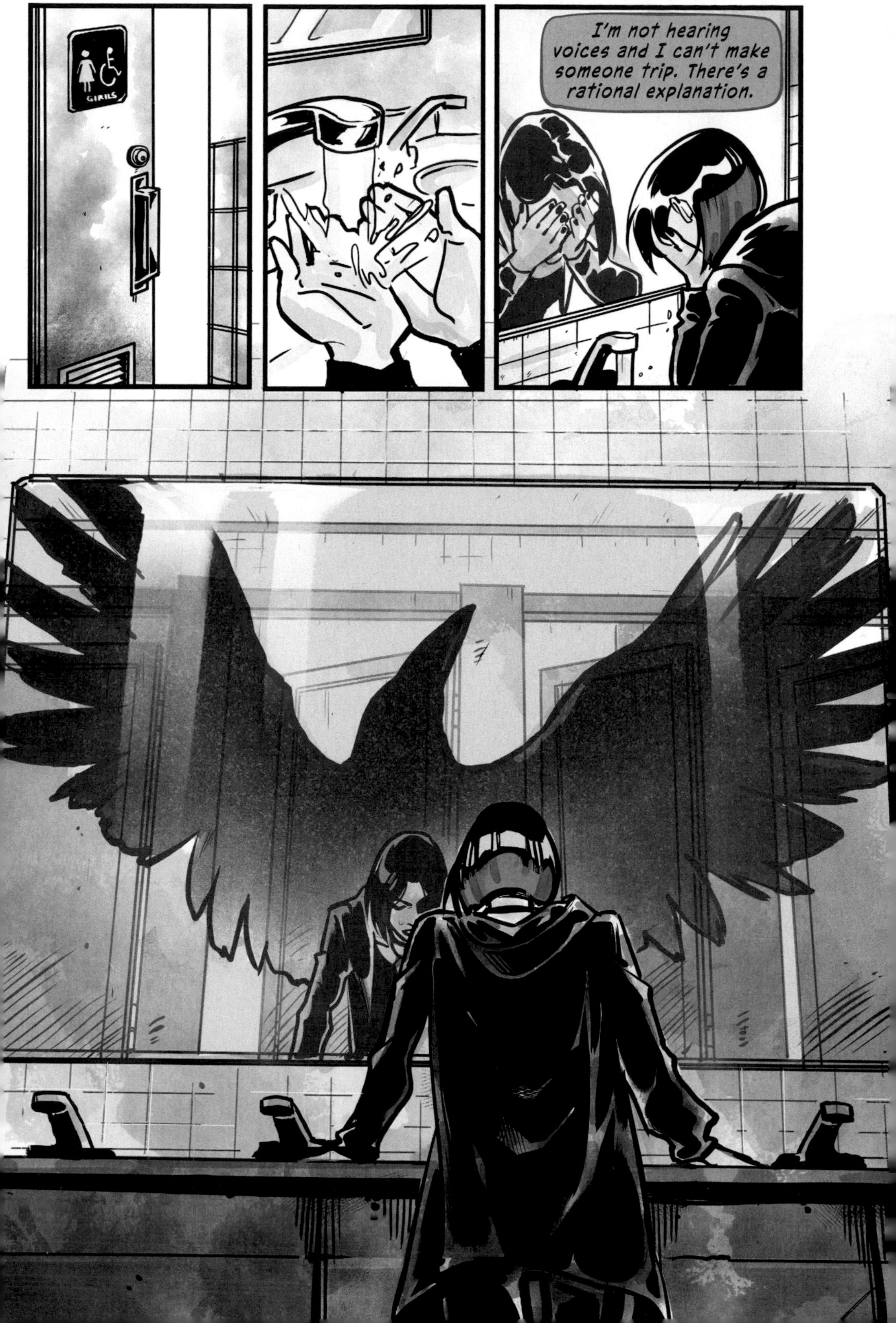
GIRLS
I'm not hearing voices and I can't make someone trip. There's a rational explanation.

CHAPTER 4: TEENAGE WASTELAND

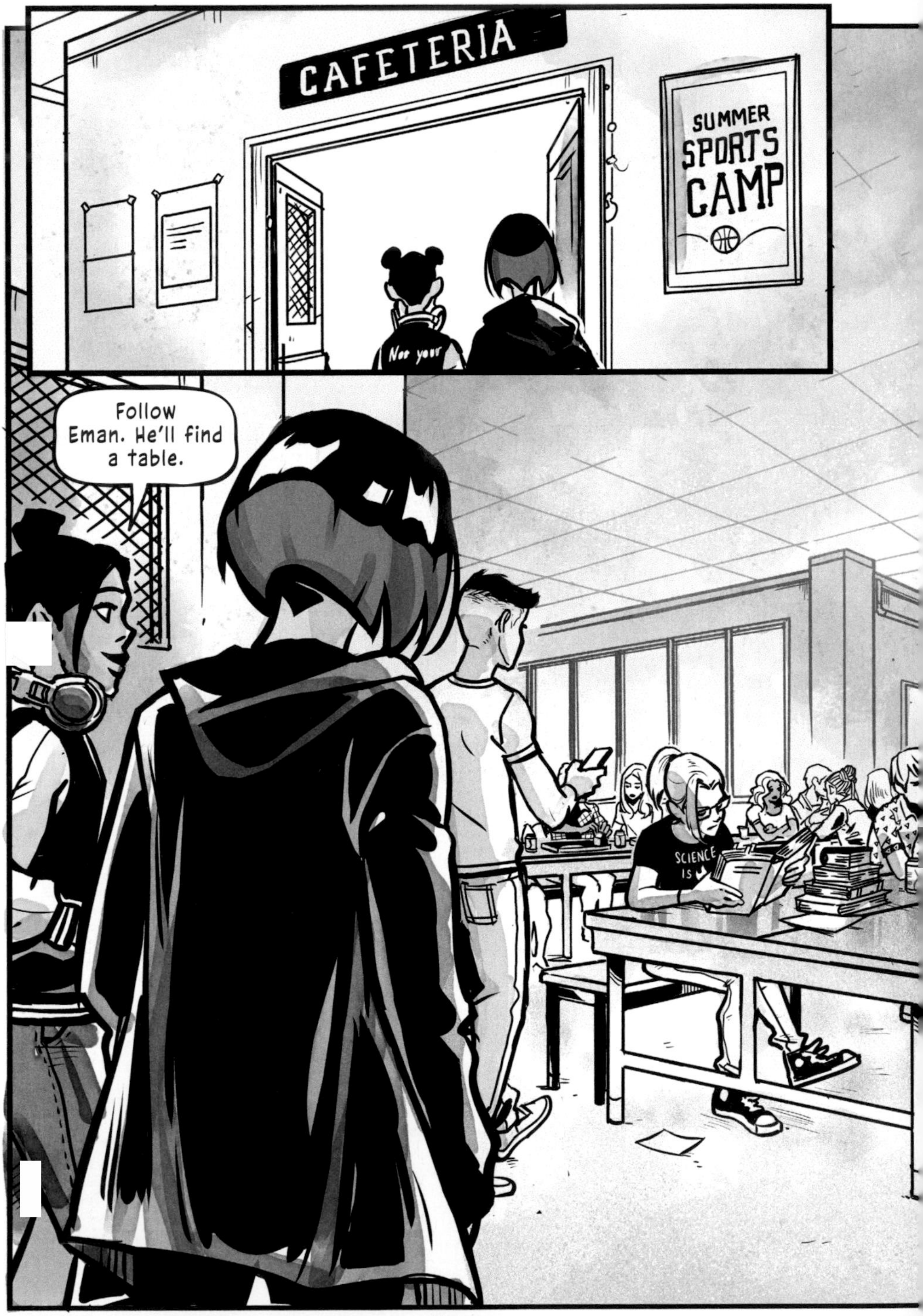

CAFETERIA
SUMMER SPORTS CAMP
Not your
Follow Eman. He'll find a table.
SCIENCE IS

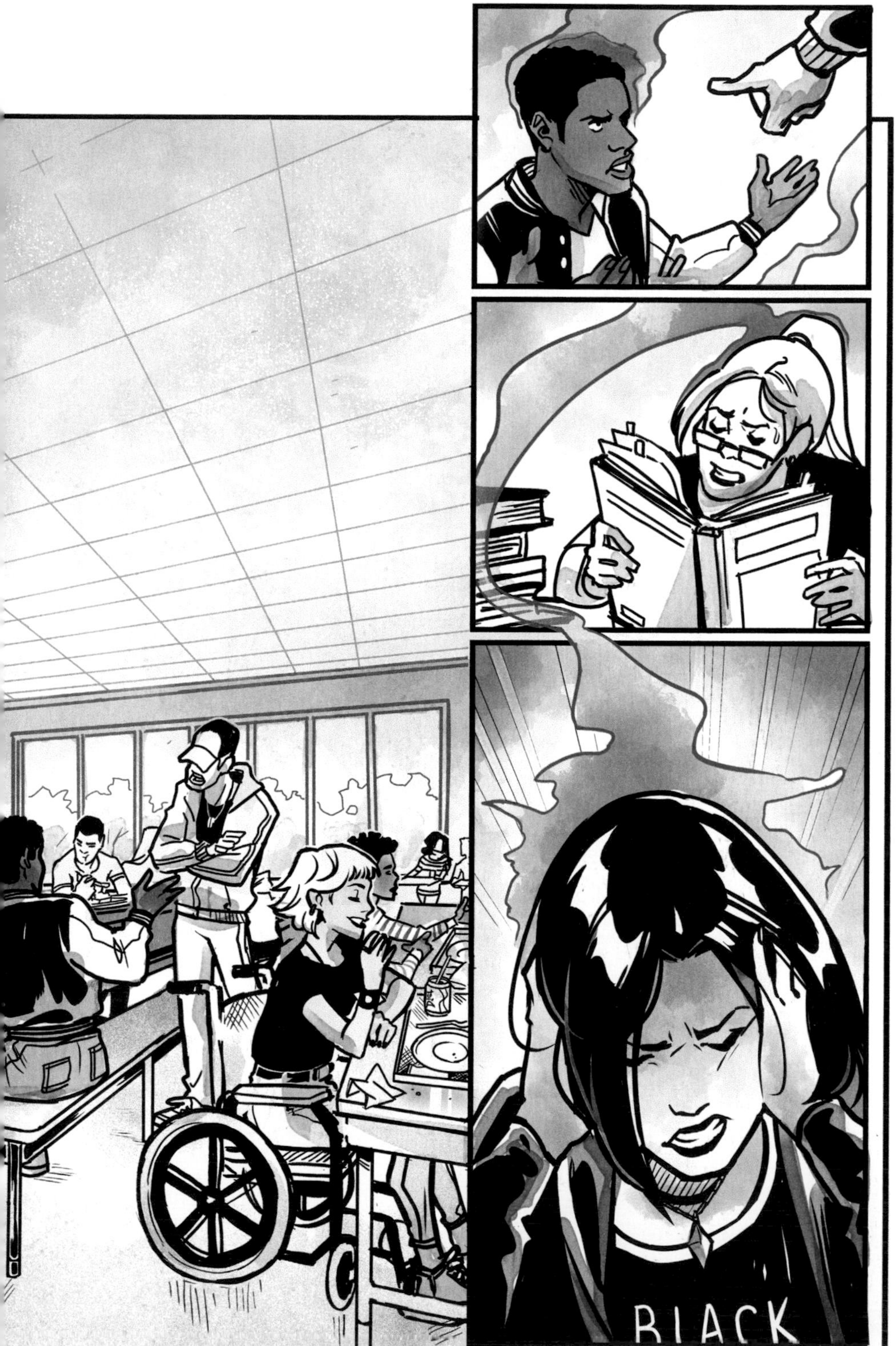
BLACK

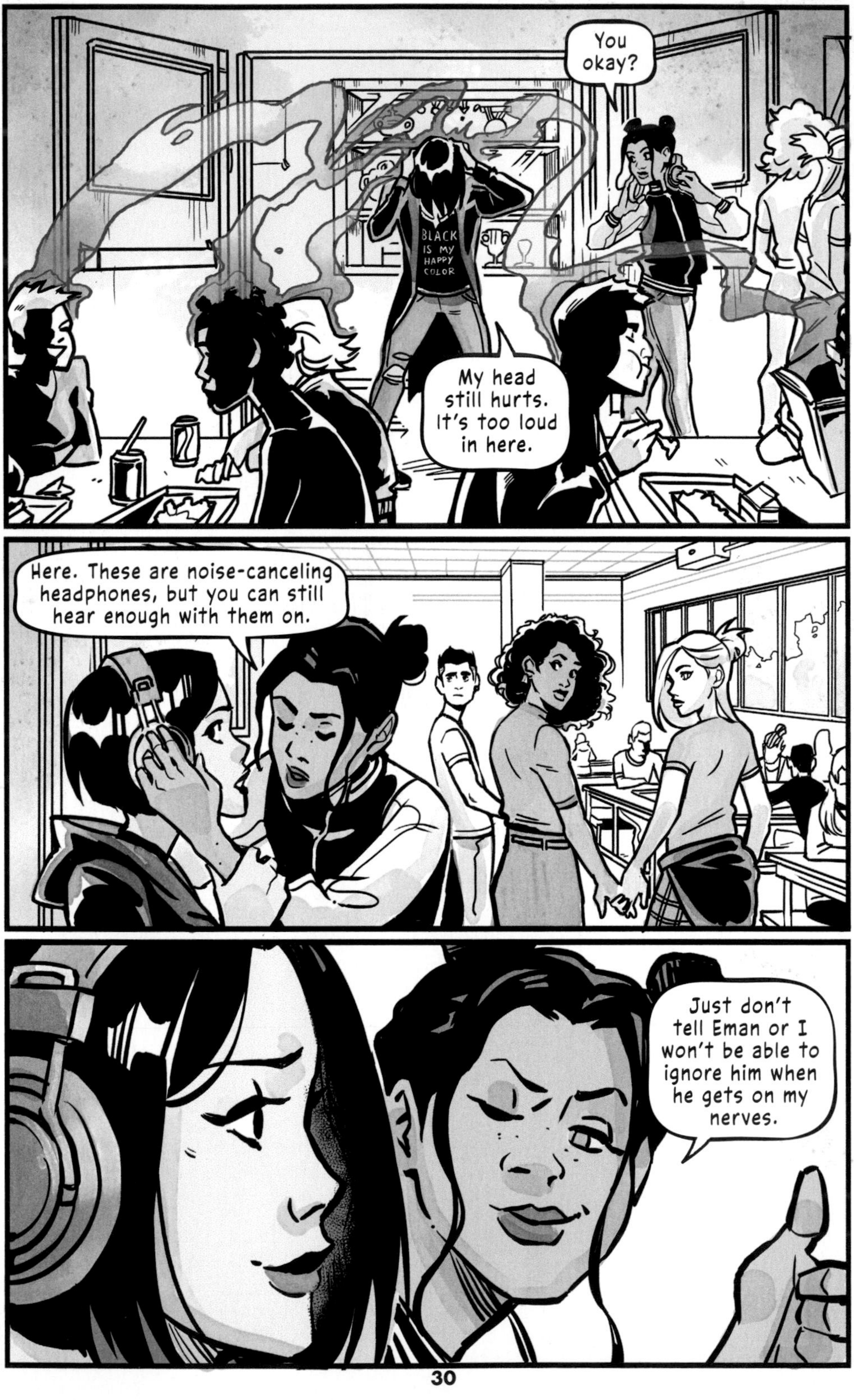
BLACK IS MY HAPPY COLOR
You okay?
My head still hurts. It's too loud in here.
Here. These are noise-canceling headphones, but you can still hear enough with them on.
Just don't tell Eman or I won't be able to ignore him when he gets on my nerves.

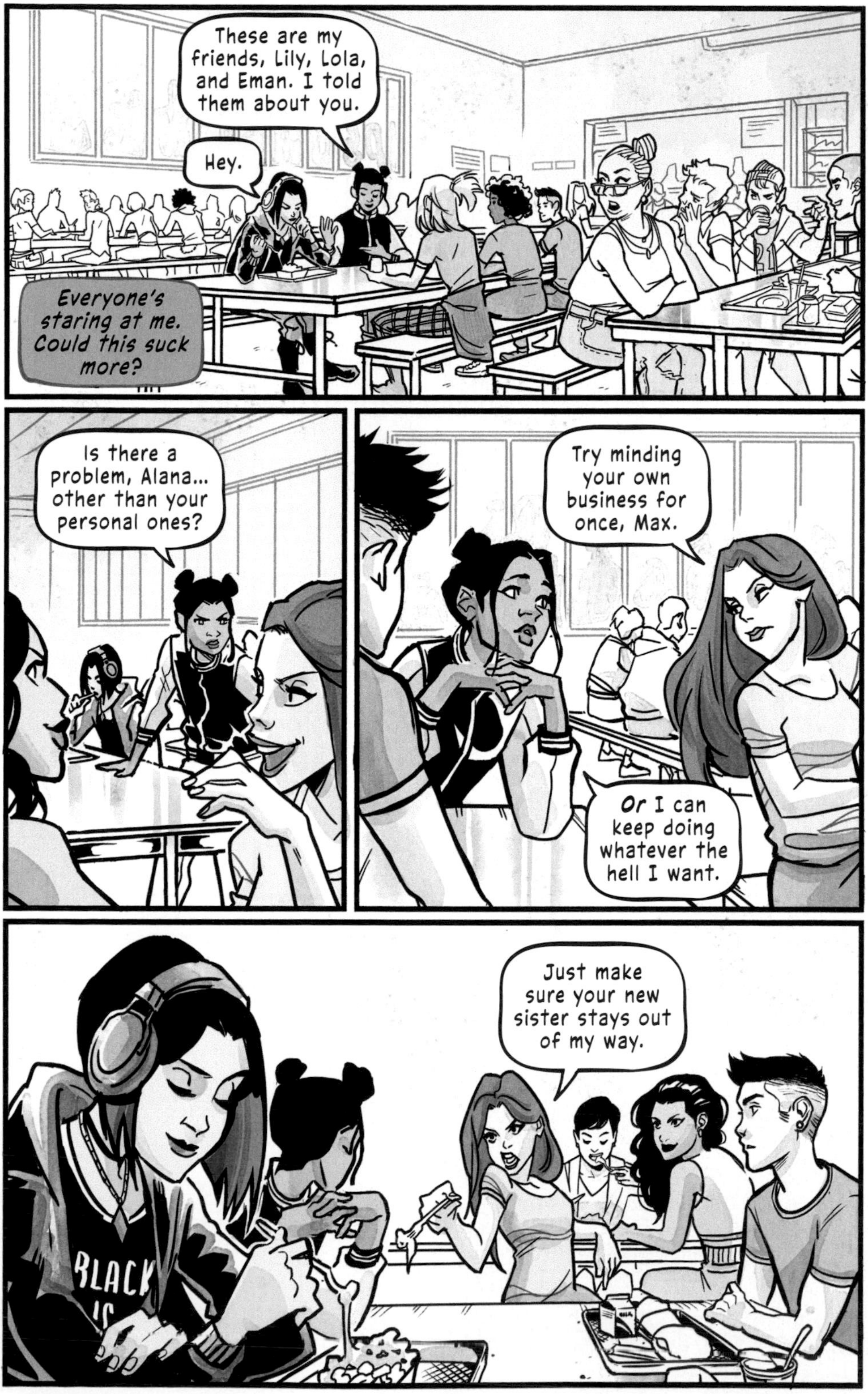
These are my friends, Lily, Lola, and Eman. I told them about you.
Hey.
Everyone's staring at me. Could this suck more?
Is there a problem, Alana... other than your personal ones?
Try minding your own business for once, Max.
Or I can keep doing whatever the hell I want.
Just make sure your new sister stays out of my way.

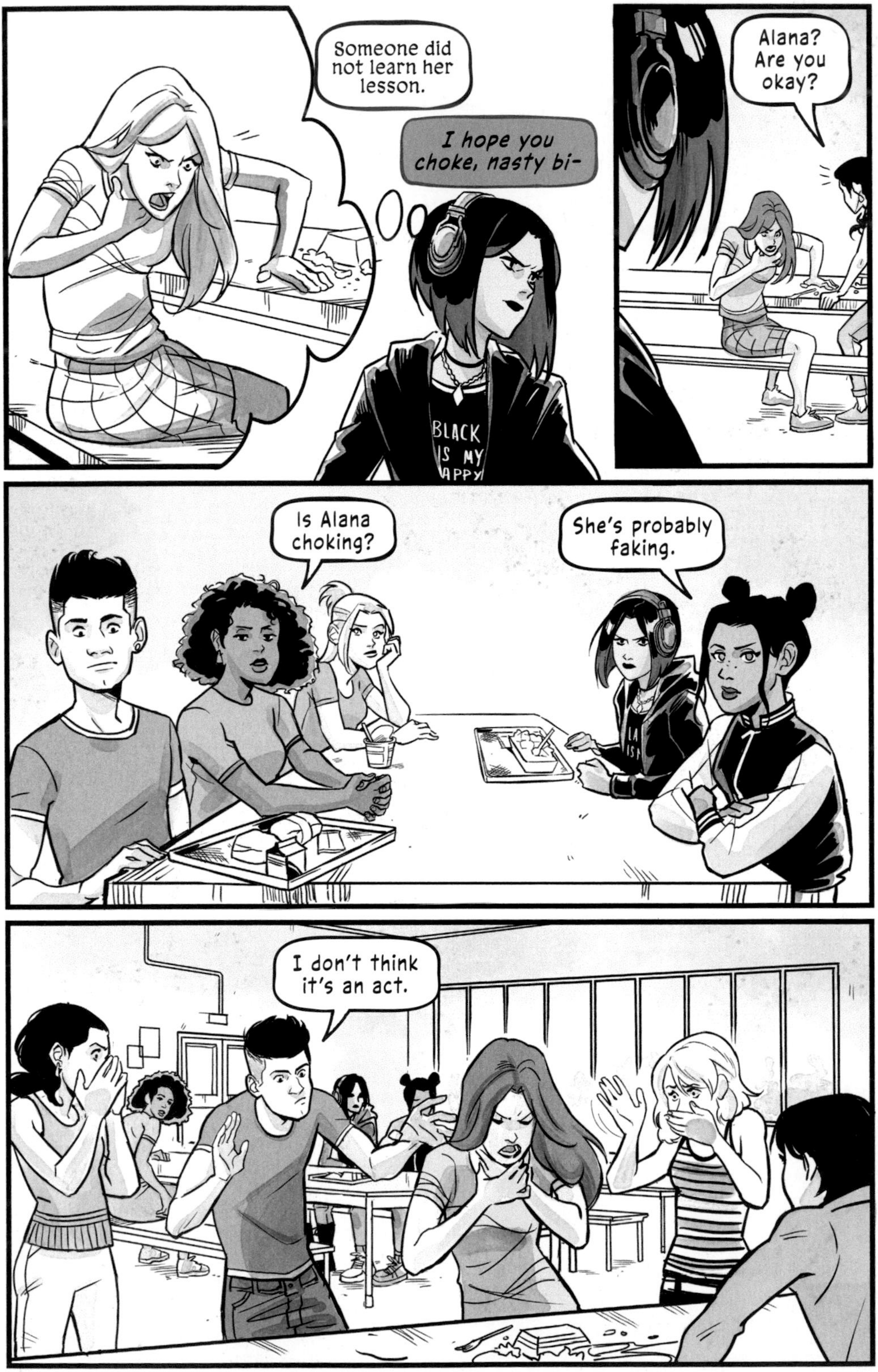

Someone did not learn her lesson.
I hope you choke, nasty bi-
BLACK IS MY HAPPY
Alana? Are you okay?
Is Alana choking?
She's probably faking.
I don't think it's an act.

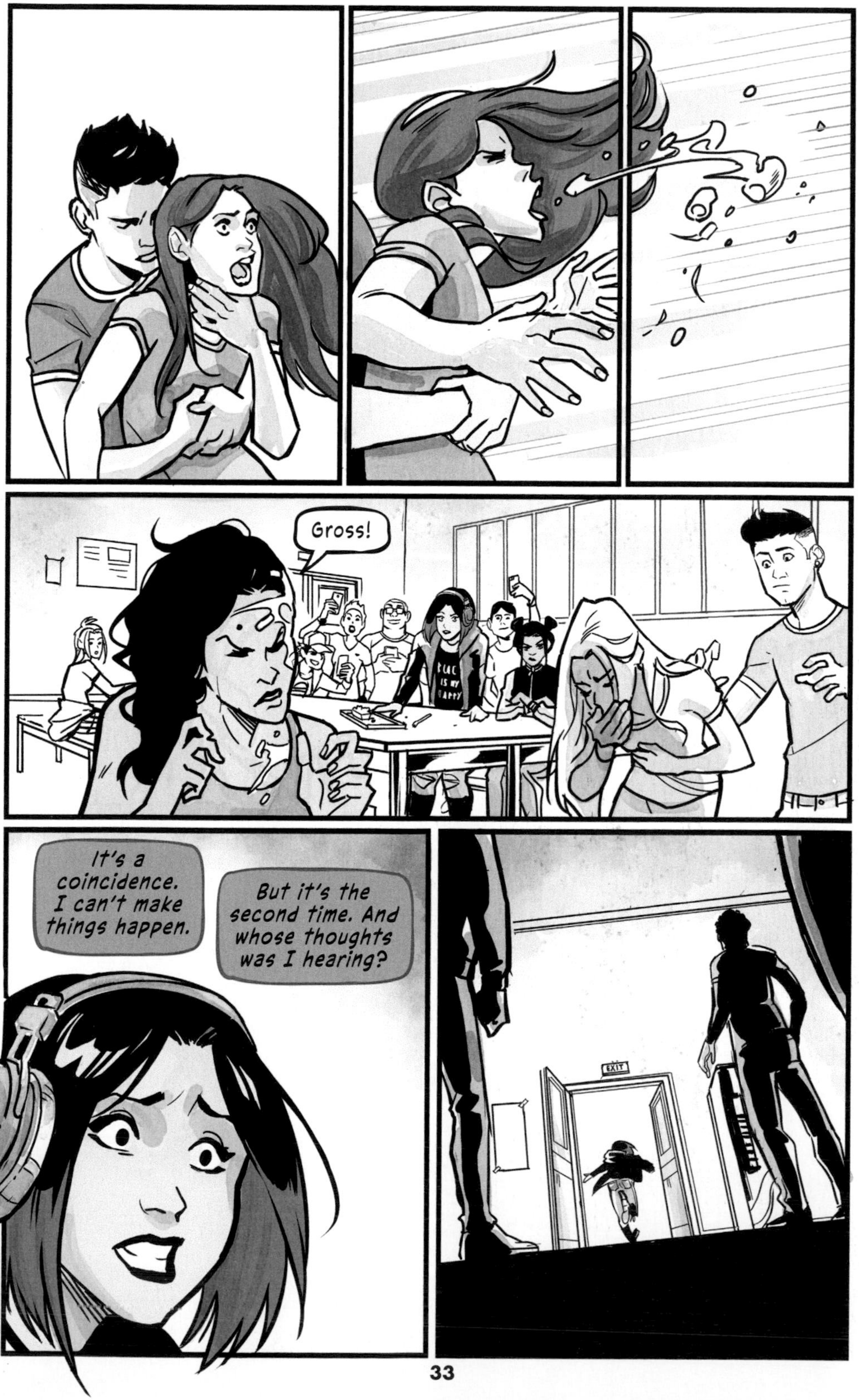
Gross!
It's a coincidence. I can't make things happen.
But it's the second time. And whose thoughts was I hearing?
EXIT

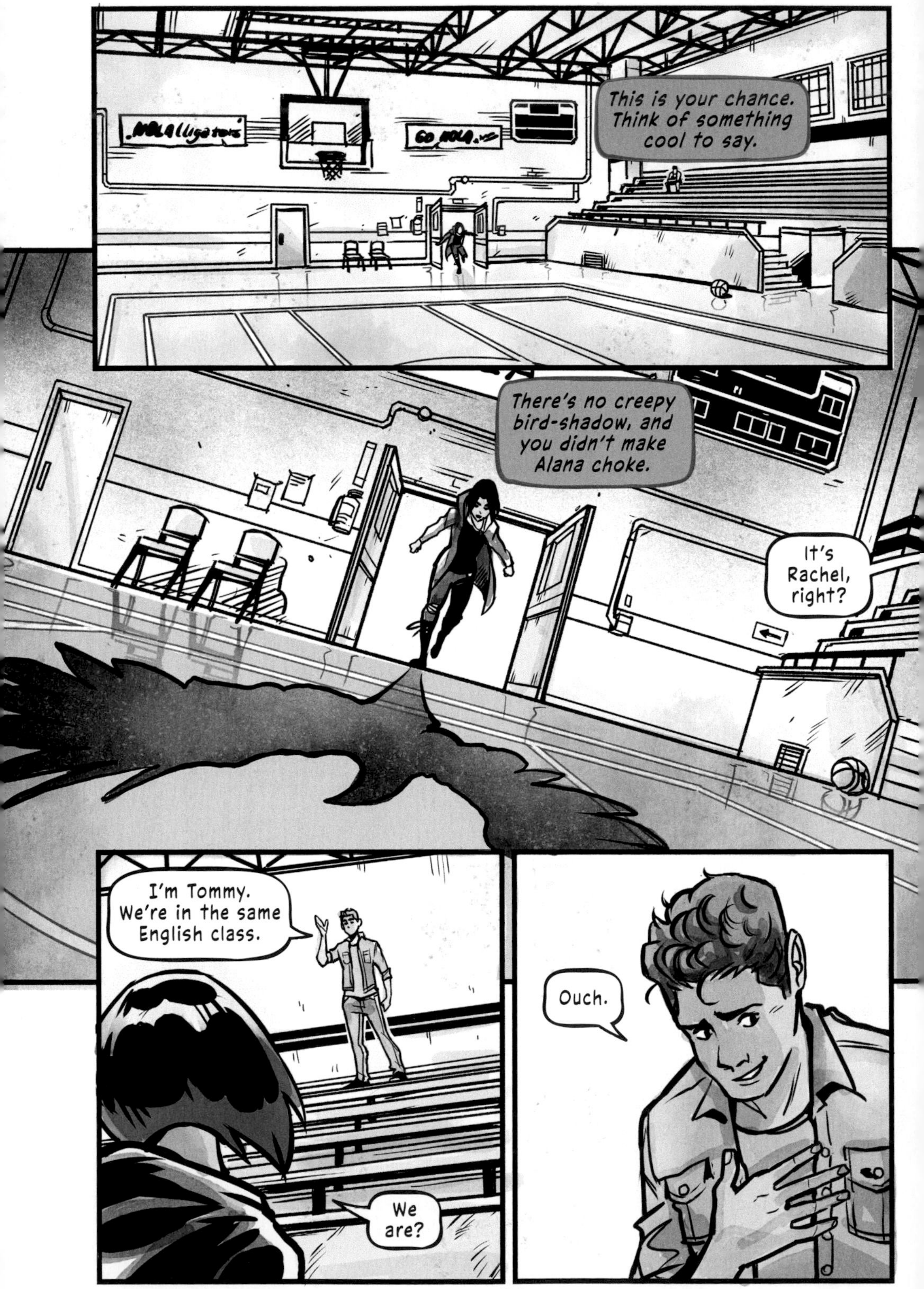
NOLA Alligators
GO NOLA
This is your chance. Think of something cool to say.
There's no creepy bird-shadow, and you didn't make Alana choke.
It's Rachel, right?
I'm Tommy. We're in the same English class.
We are?
Ouch.

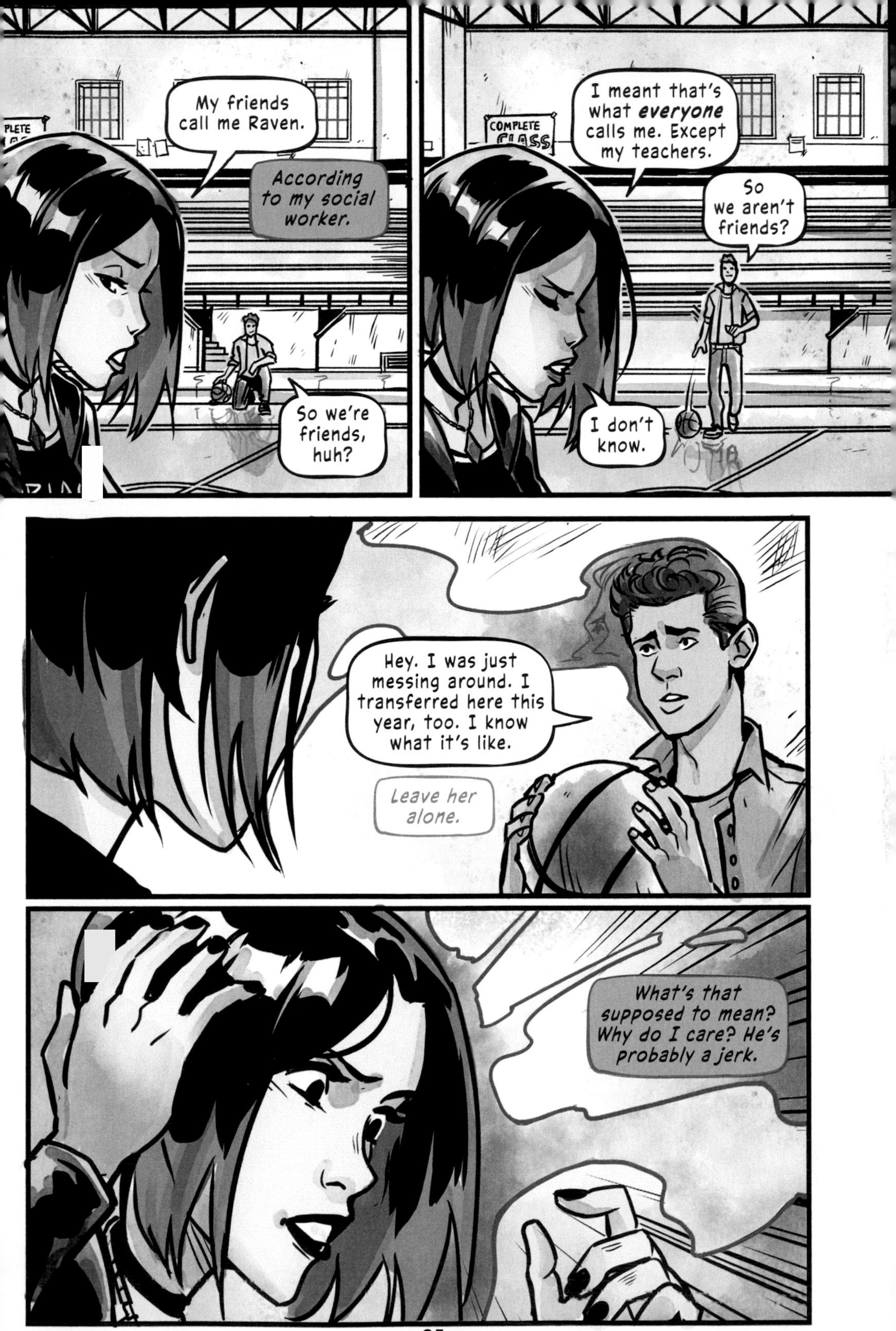
My friends call me Raven.
According to my social worker.
So we're friends, huh?
I meant that's what *everyone* calls me. Except my teachers.
So we aren't friends?
I don't know.
COMPLETE CLASS
Hey. I was just messing around. I transferred here this year, too. I know what it's like.
Leave her alone.
What's that supposed to mean? Why do I care? He's probably a jerk.

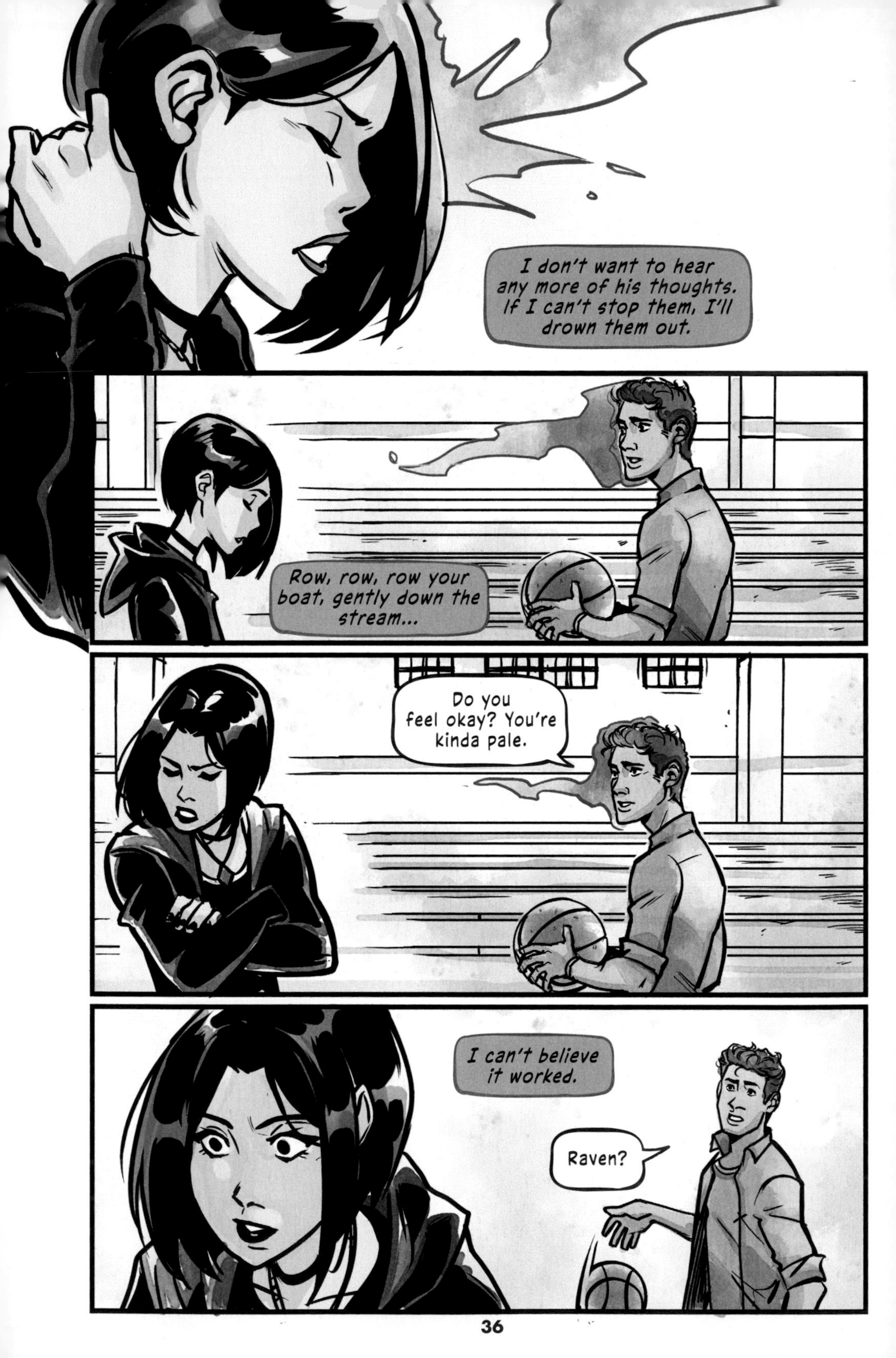
I don't want to hear any more of his thoughts. If I can't stop them, I'll drown them out.
Row, row, row your boat, gently down the stream...
Do you feel okay? You're kinda pale.
I can't believe it worked.
Raven?

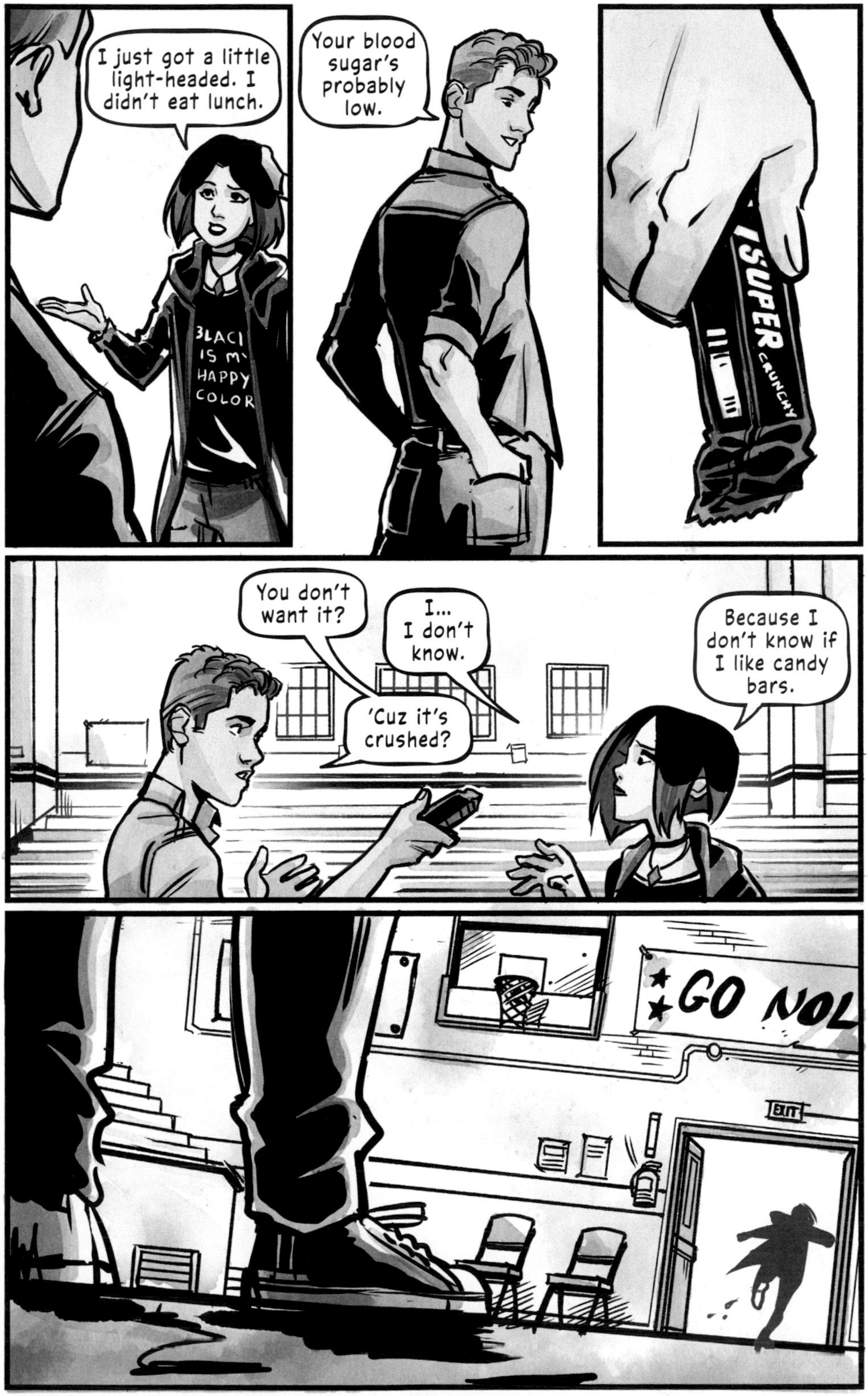
I just got a little light-headed. I didn't eat lunch.
Your blood sugar's probably low.
SUPER CRUNCHY
BLACK IS MY HAPPY COLOR
You don't want it?
I... I don't know.
'Cuz it's crushed?
Because I don't know if I like candy bars.
GO NO
EXIT

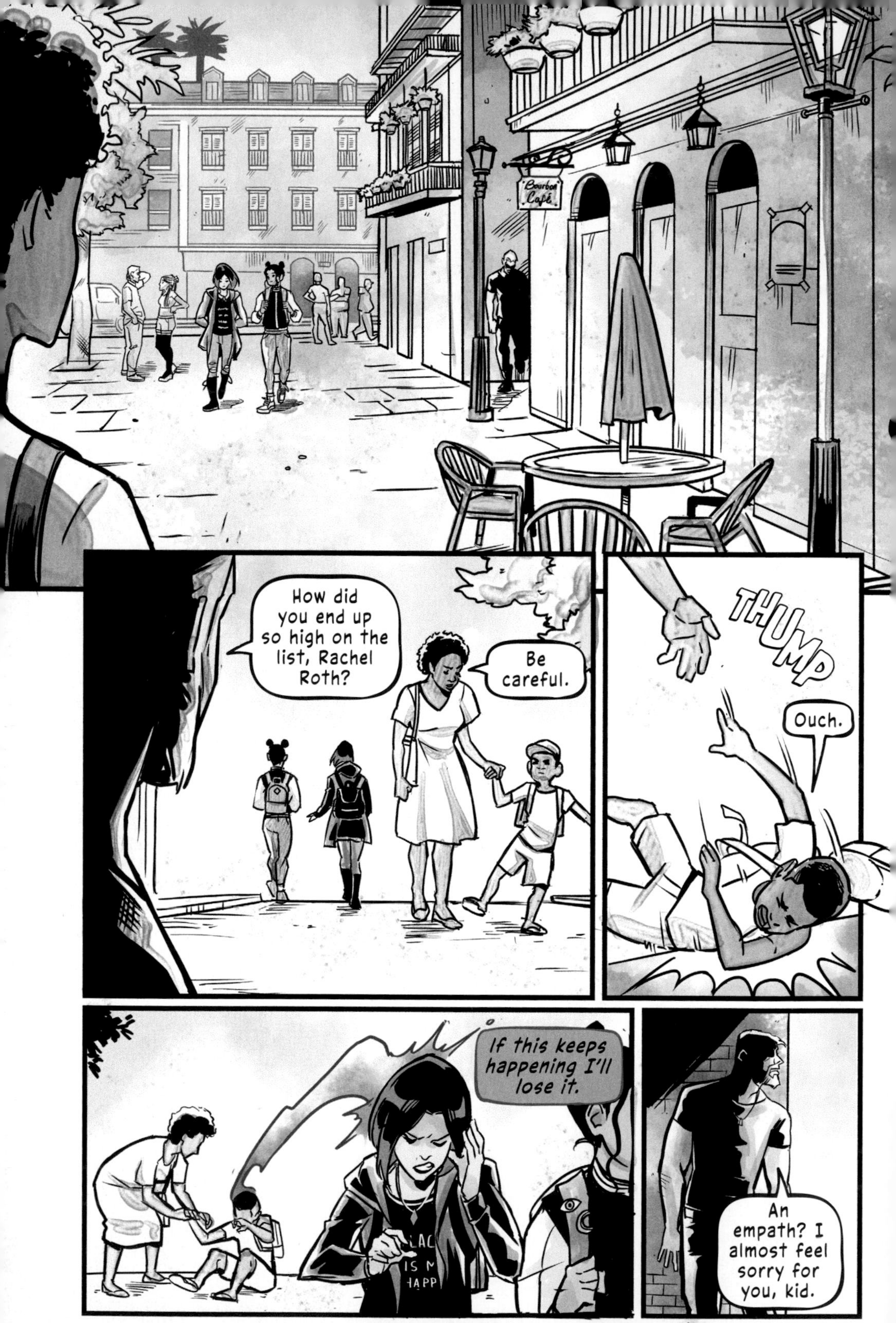
Bourbon Café
How did you end up so high on the list, Rachel Roth?
Be careful.
THUMP
Ouch.
If this keeps happening I'll lose it.
An empath? I almost feel sorry for you, kid.

CHAPTER 5: MISSING PIECES

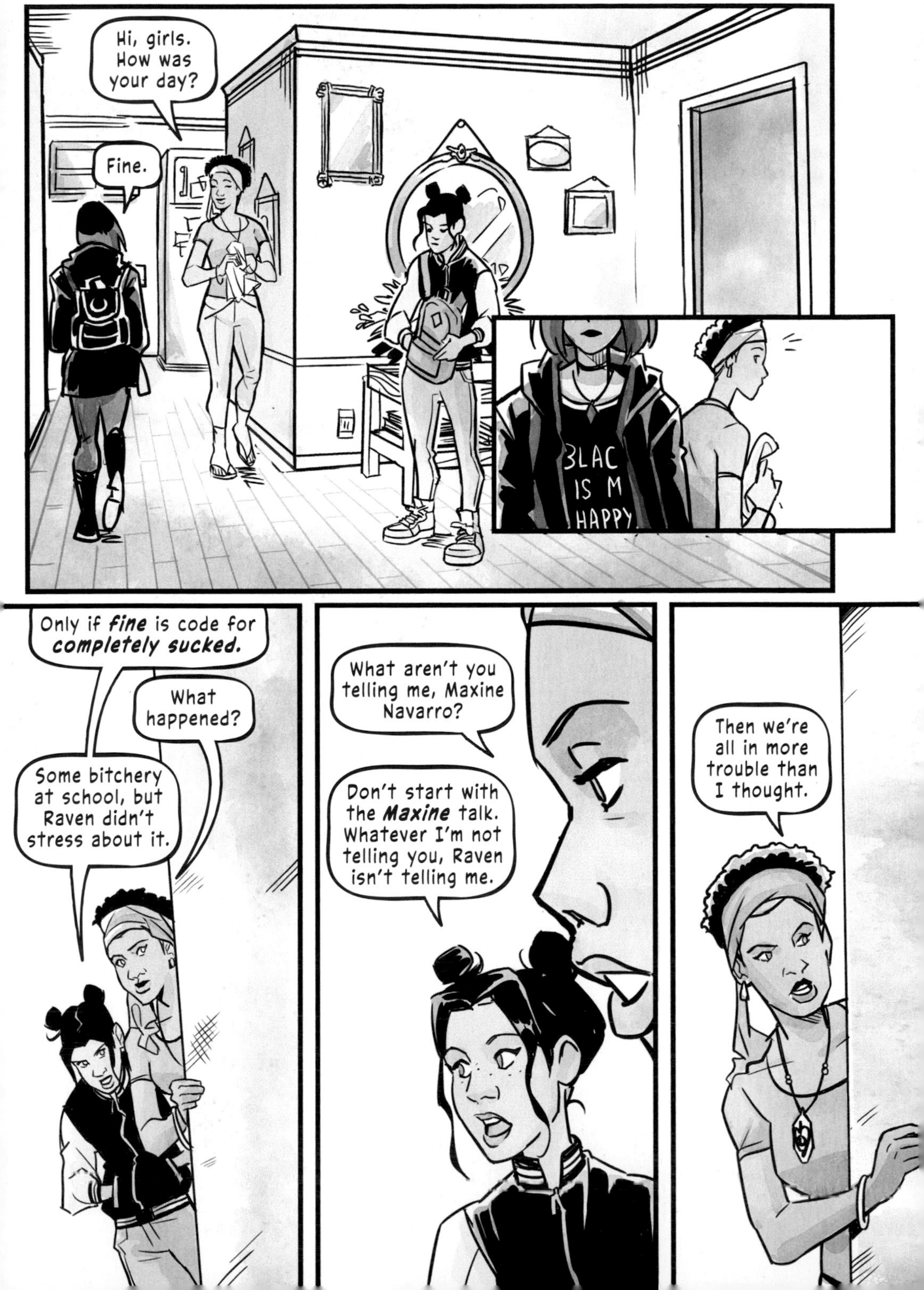

Hi, girls. How was your day?
Fine.
BLAC IS M HAPPY
Only if *fine* is code for ***completely sucked.***
What happened?
Some bitchery at school, but Raven didn't stress about it.
What aren't you telling me, Maxine Navarro?
Don't start with the ***Maxine*** talk. Whatever I'm not telling you, Raven isn't telling me.
Then we're all in more trouble than I thought.

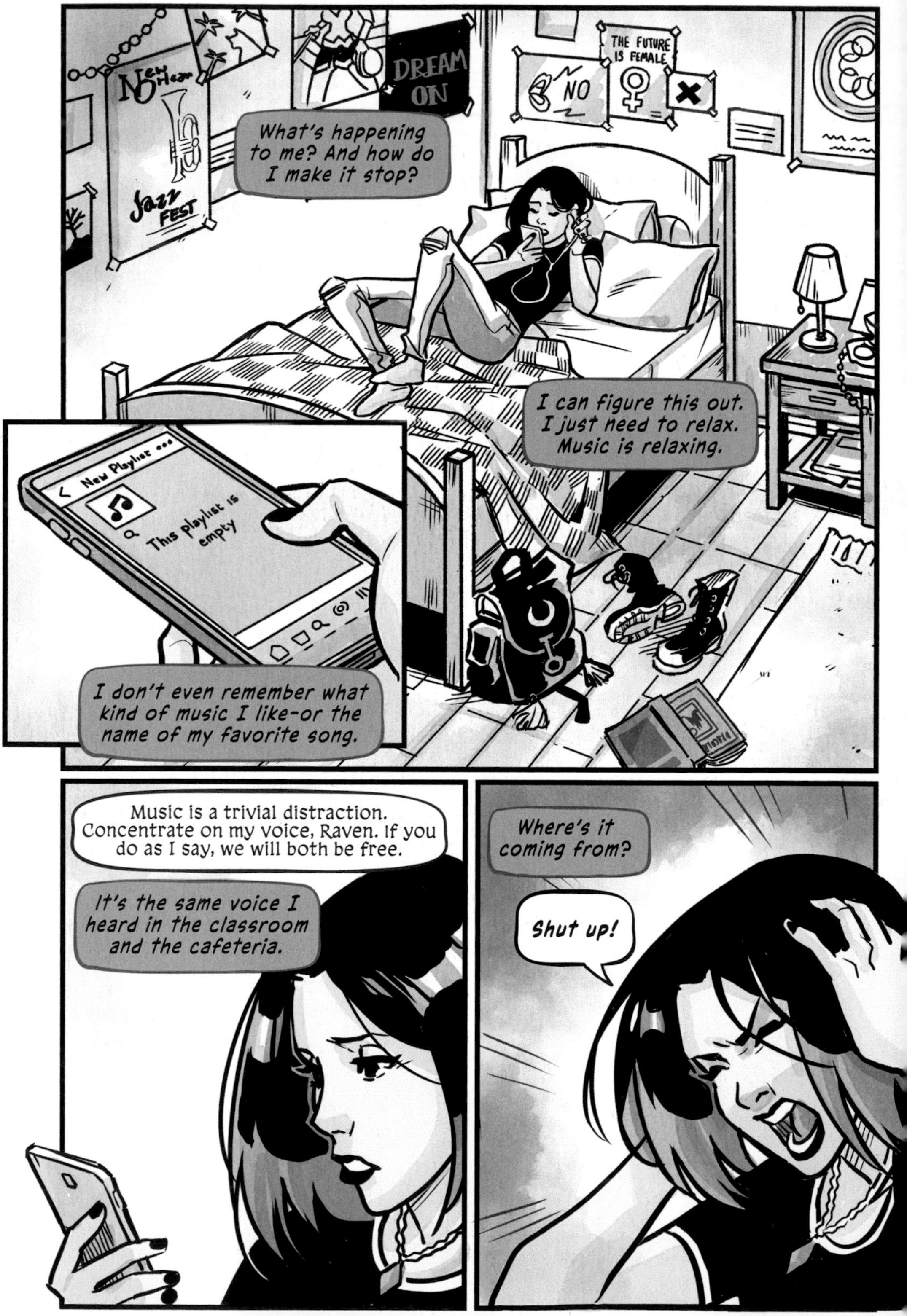
THE FUTURE IS FEMALE
NO
DREAM ON
New Orleans
Jazz FEST
What's happening to me? And how do I make it stop?
I can figure this out. I just need to relax. Music is relaxing.
New Playlist
This playlist is empty
I don't even remember what kind of music I like—or the name of my favorite song.
Music is a trivial distraction. Concentrate on my voice, Raven. If you do as I say, we will both be free.
It's the same voice I heard in the classroom and the cafeteria.
Where's it coming from?
Shut up!

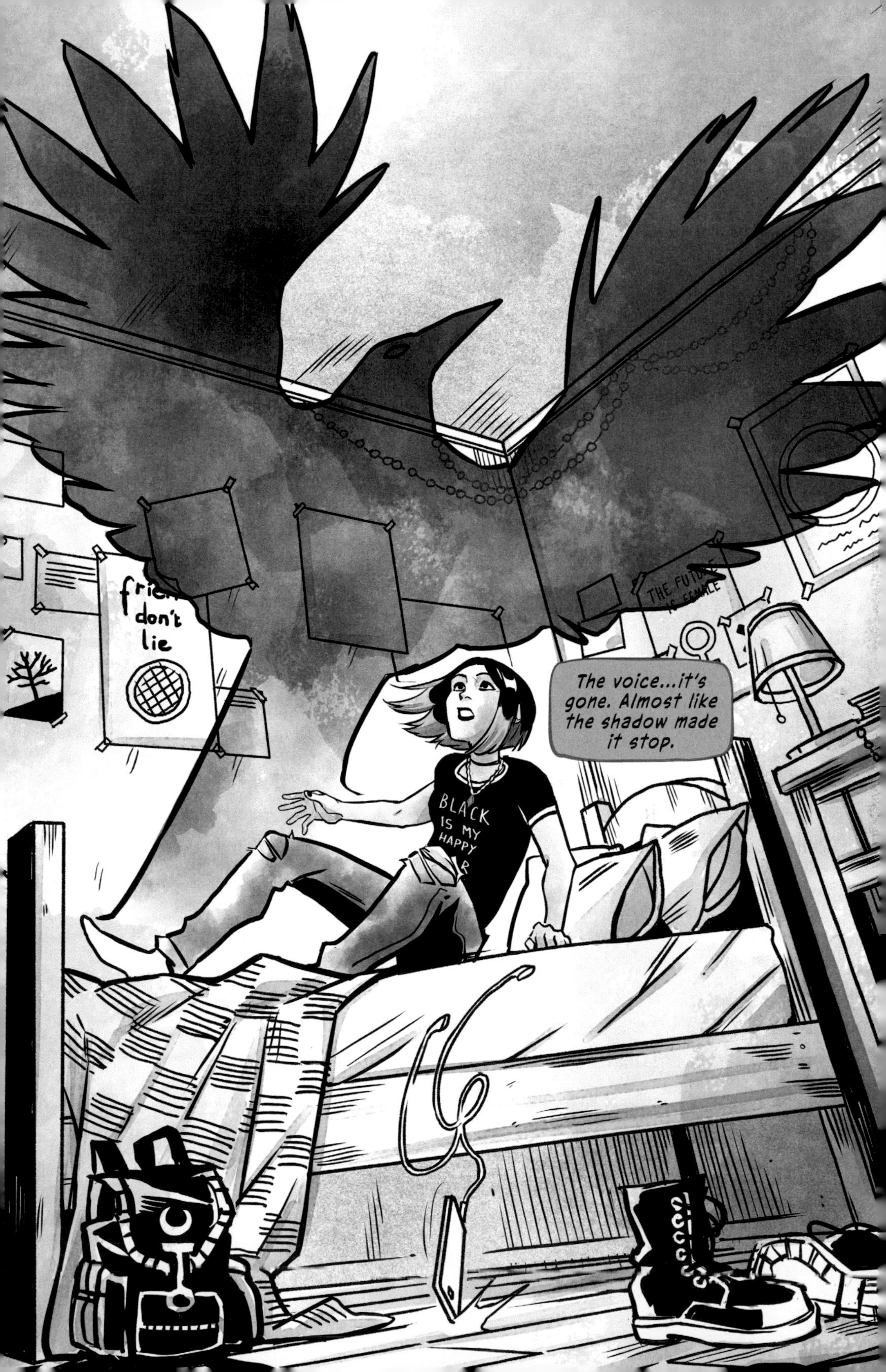
don't
lie
BLACK
IS MY
HAPPY
The voice...it's gone. Almost like the shadow made it stop.

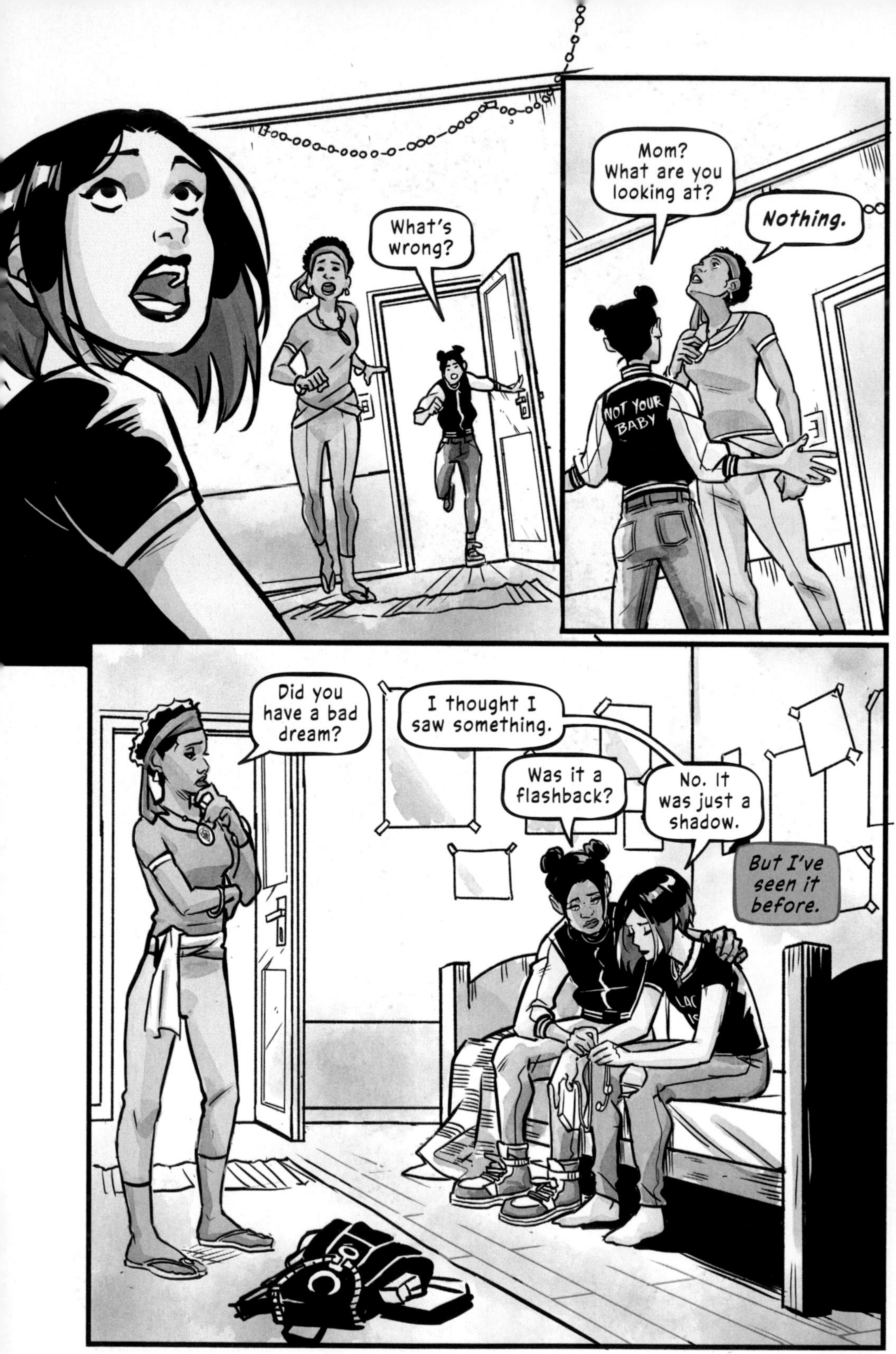
What's wrong?
Mom? What are you looking at?
Nothing.
NOT YOUR BABY
Did you have a bad dream?
I thought I saw something.
Was it a flashback?
No. It was just a shadow.
But I've seen it before.

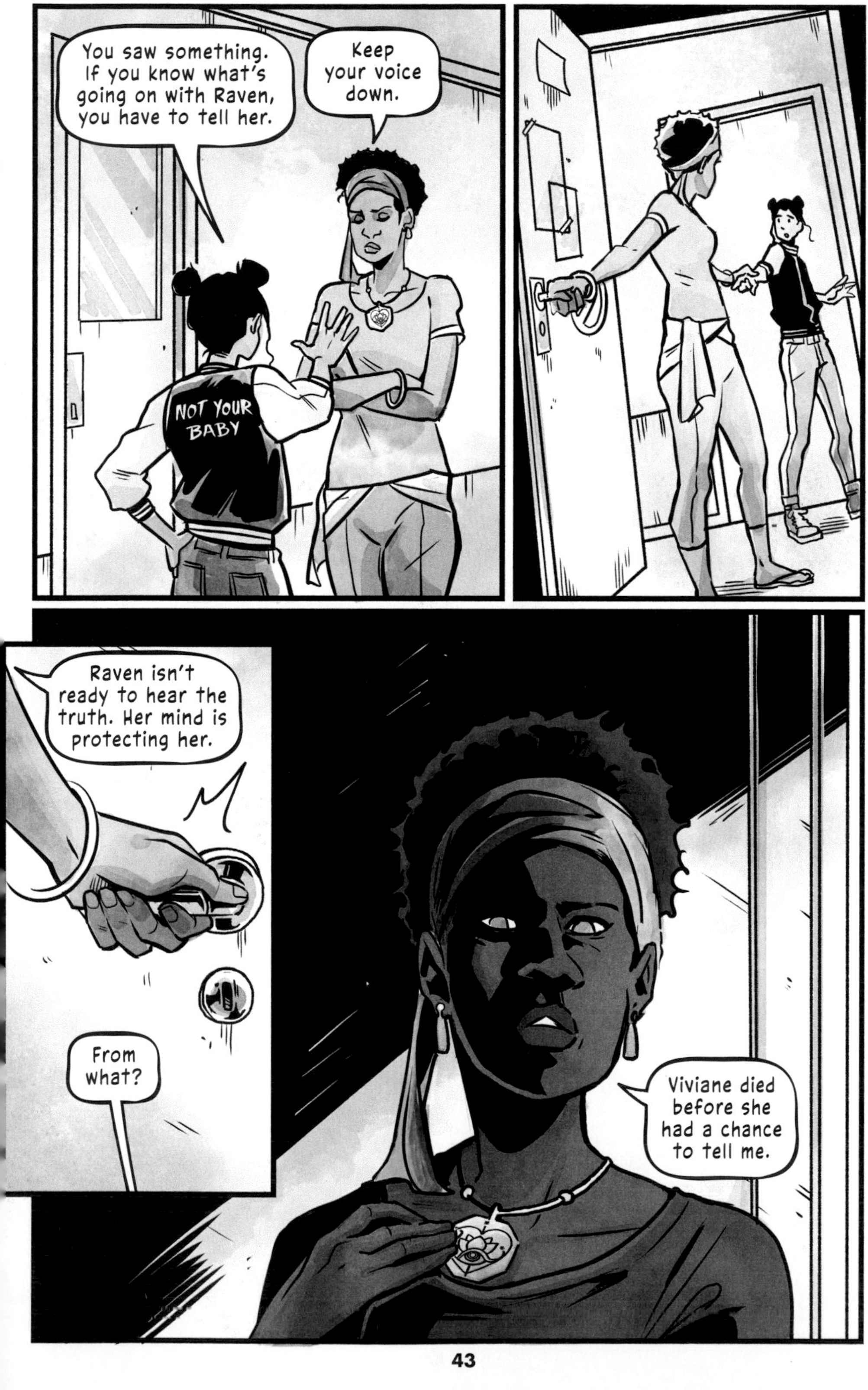
You saw something. If you know what's going on with Raven, you have to tell her.
Keep your voice down.
NOT YOUR BABY
Raven isn't ready to hear the truth. Her mind is protecting her.
From what?
Viviane died before she had a chance to tell me.

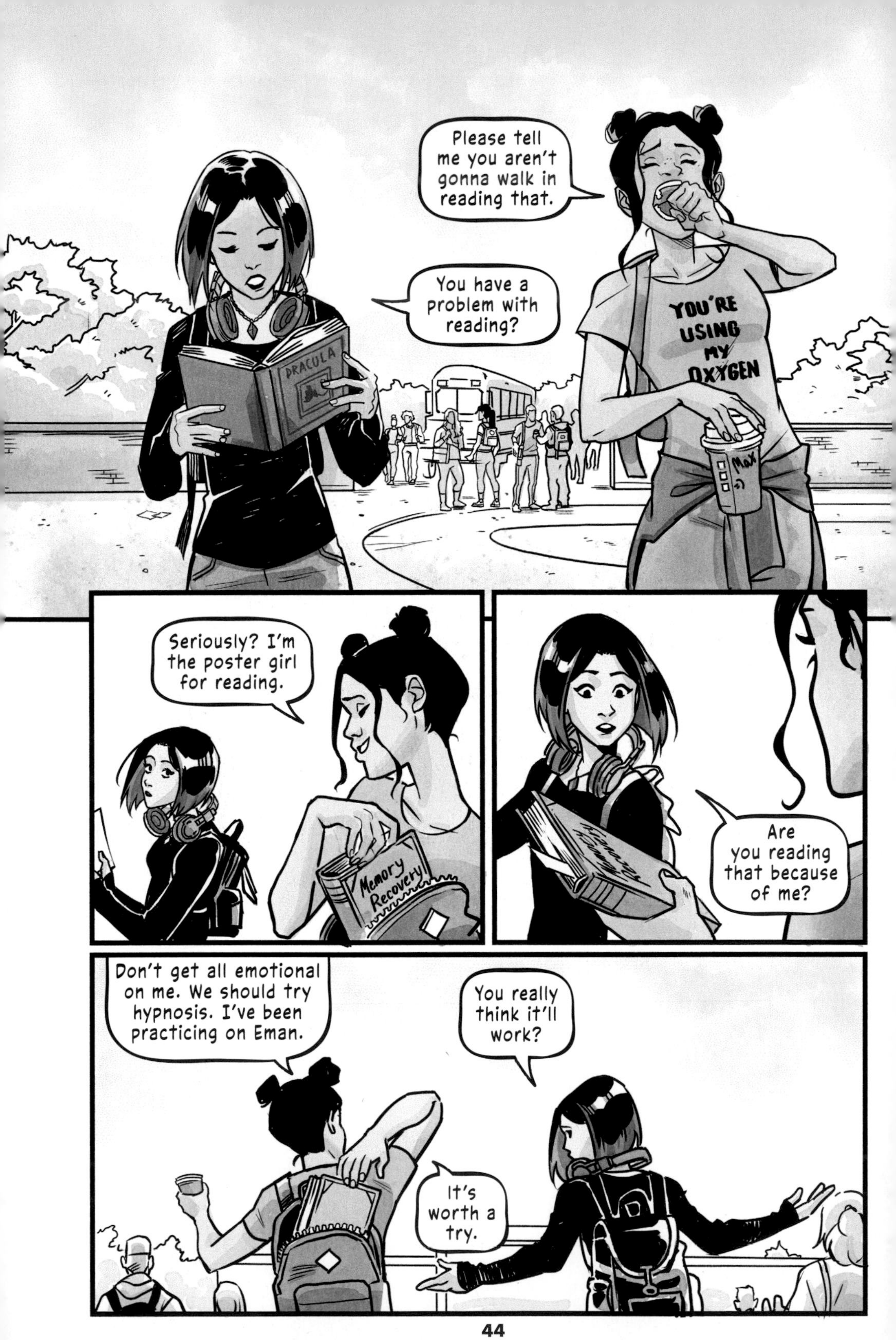
Please tell me you aren't gonna walk in reading that.
You have a problem with reading?
YOU'RE USING MY OXYGEN
DRACULA
Max
Seriously? I'm the poster girl for reading.
Memory Recovery
Are you reading that because of me?
Don't get all emotional on me. We should try hypnosis. I've been practicing on Eman.
You really think it'll work?
It's worth a try.

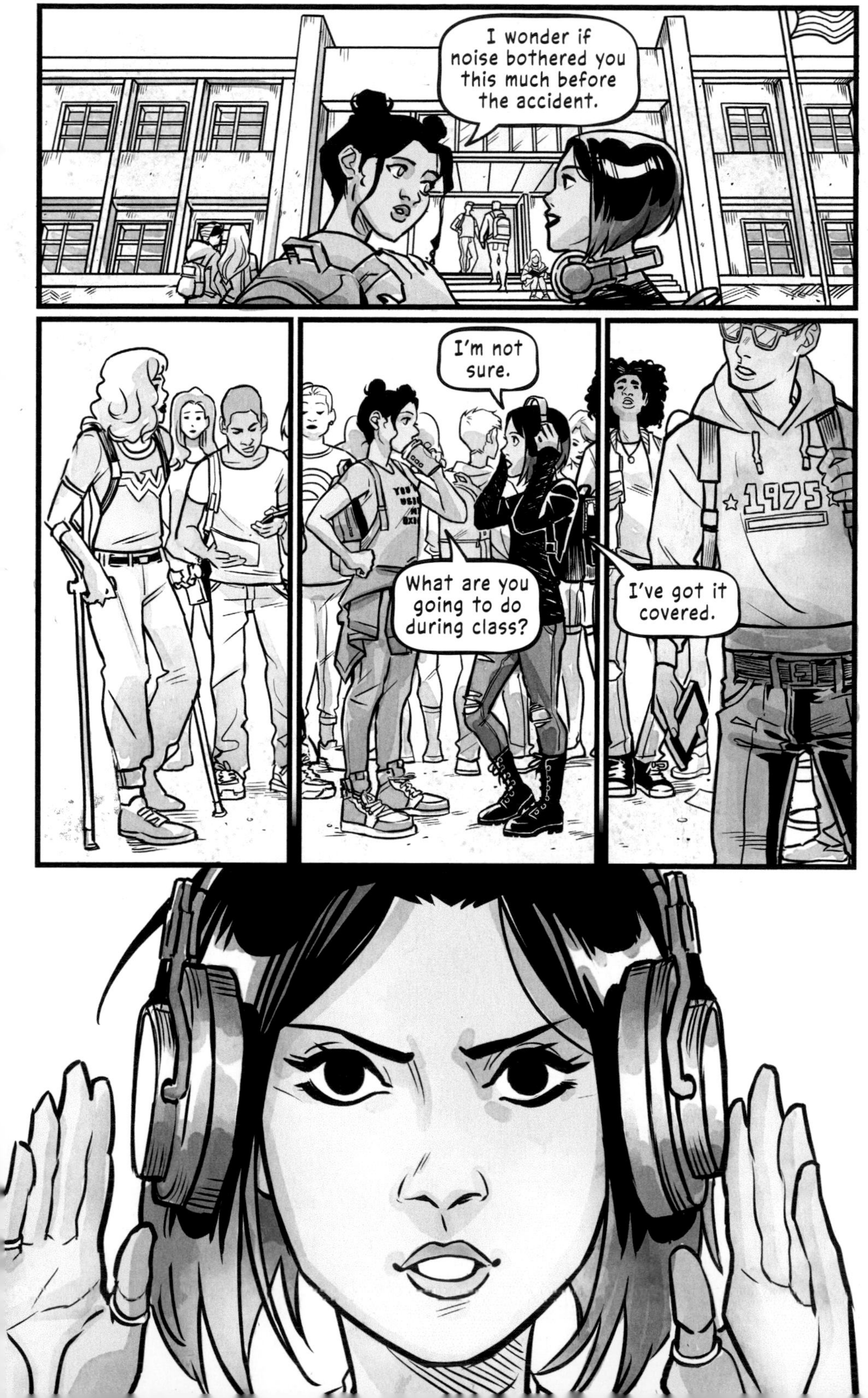
I wonder if noise bothered you this much before the accident.
I'm not sure.
What are you going to do during class?
I've got it covered.
1975

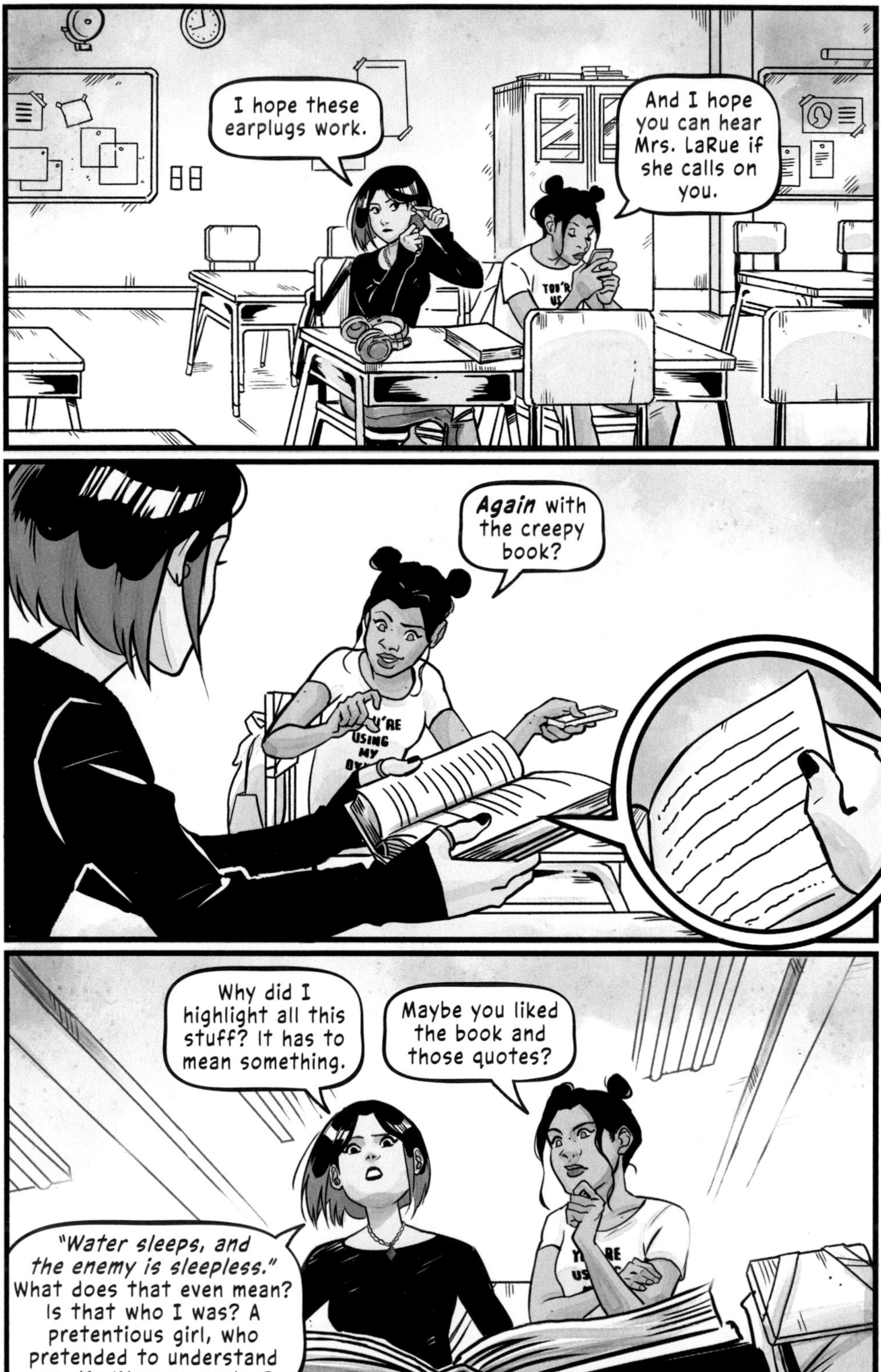
I hope these earplugs work.
And I hope you can hear Mrs. LaRue if she calls on you.
Again with the creepy book?
Why did I highlight all this stuff? It has to mean something.
Maybe you liked the book and those quotes?
"Water sleeps, and the enemy is sleepless." What does that even mean? Is that who I was? A pretentious girl, who pretended to understand cryptic literary quotes?

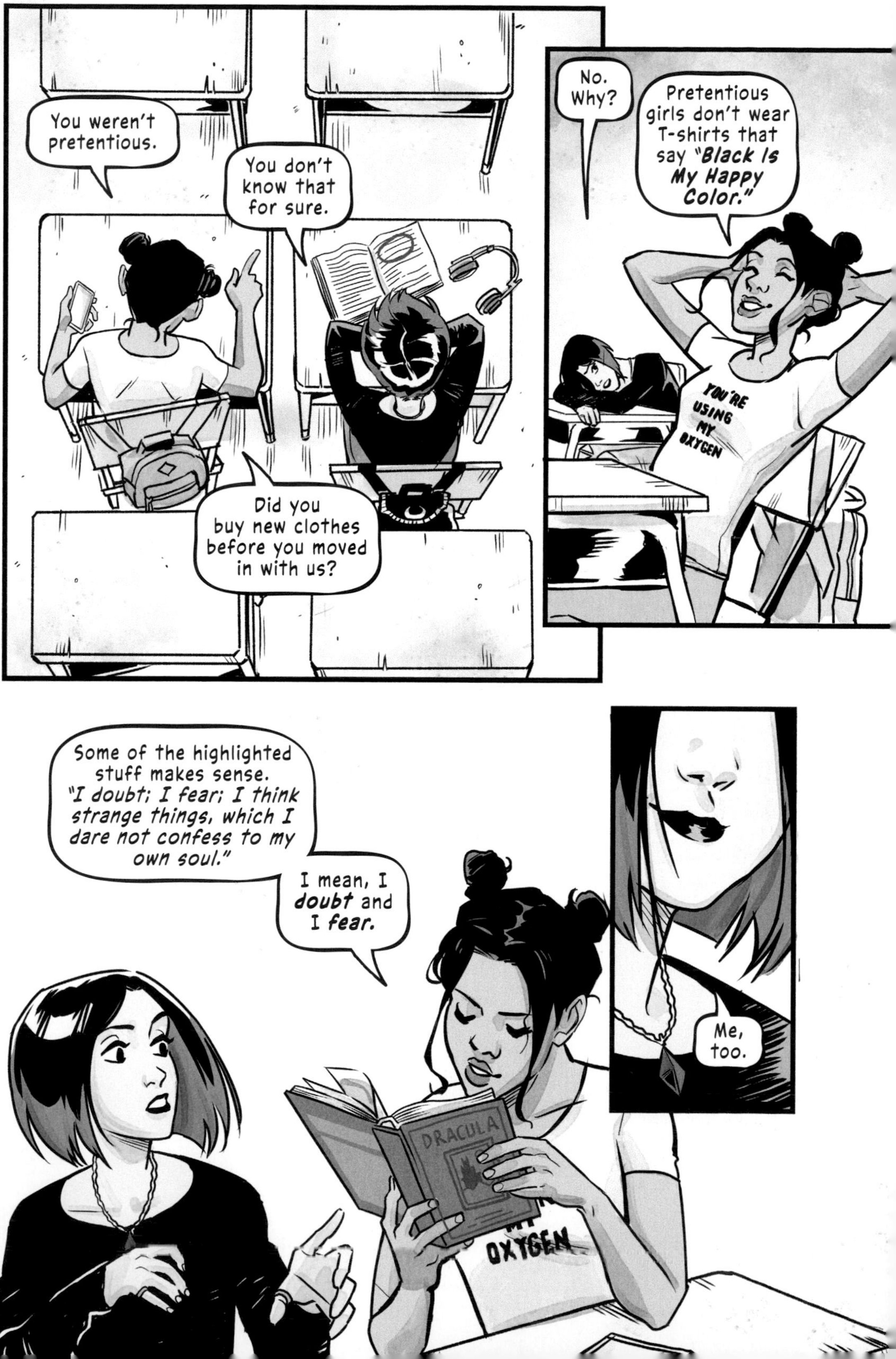
You weren't pretentious.
You don't know that for sure.
Did you buy new clothes before you moved in with us?
No. Why?
Pretentious girls don't wear T-shirts that say "*Black Is My Happy Color.*"
YOU'RE USING MY OXYGEN
Some of the highlighted stuff makes sense. *"I doubt; I fear; I think strange things, which I dare not confess to my own soul."*
I mean, I *doubt* and I *fear.*
Me, too.
DRACULA
OXYGEN

CHAPTER 6: FORTUNES AND FEARS

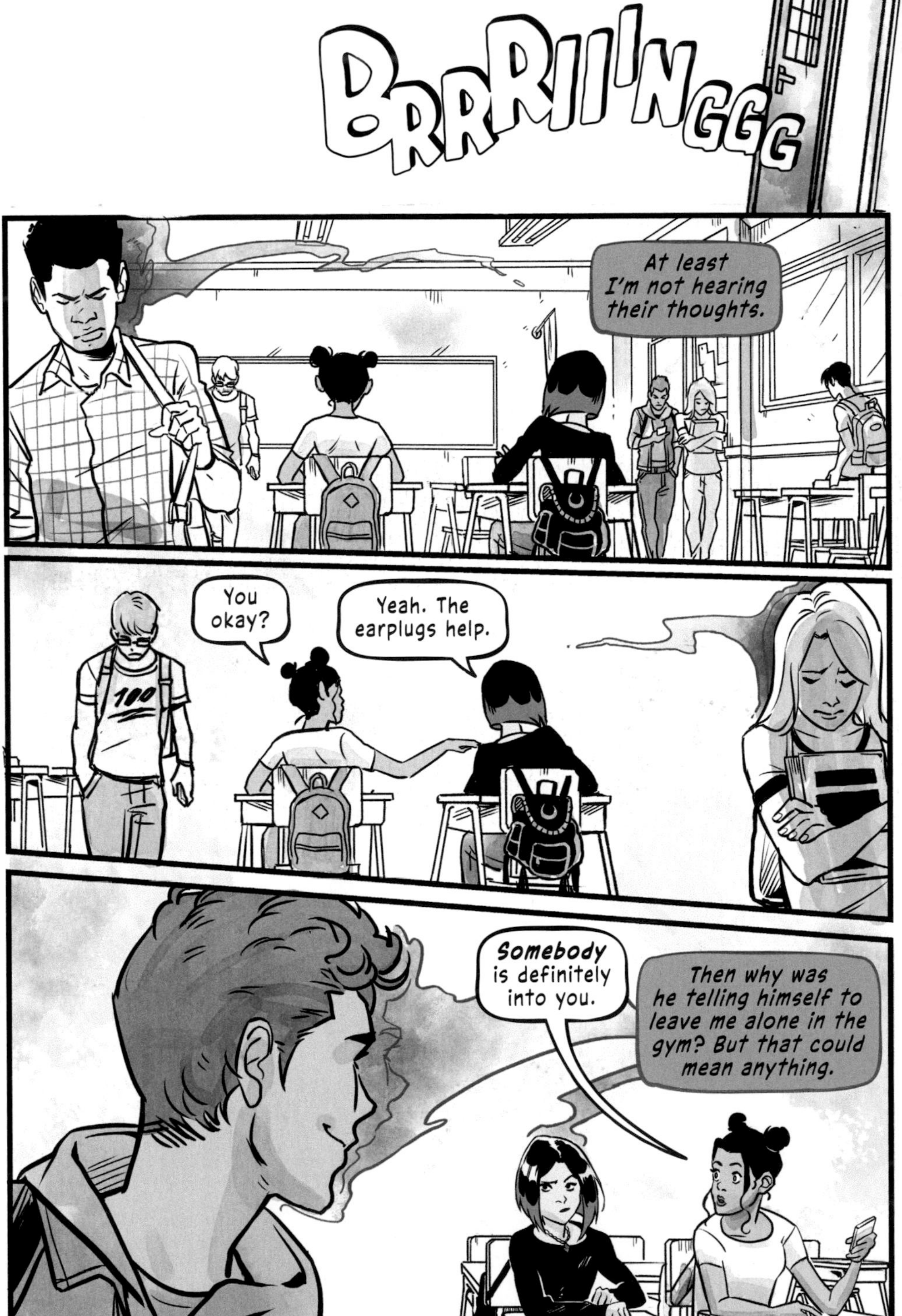
BRRRIIINGGG
At least I'm not hearing their thoughts.
You okay?
Yeah. The earplugs help.
Somebody is definitely into you.
Then why was he telling himself to leave me alone in the gym? But that could mean anything.

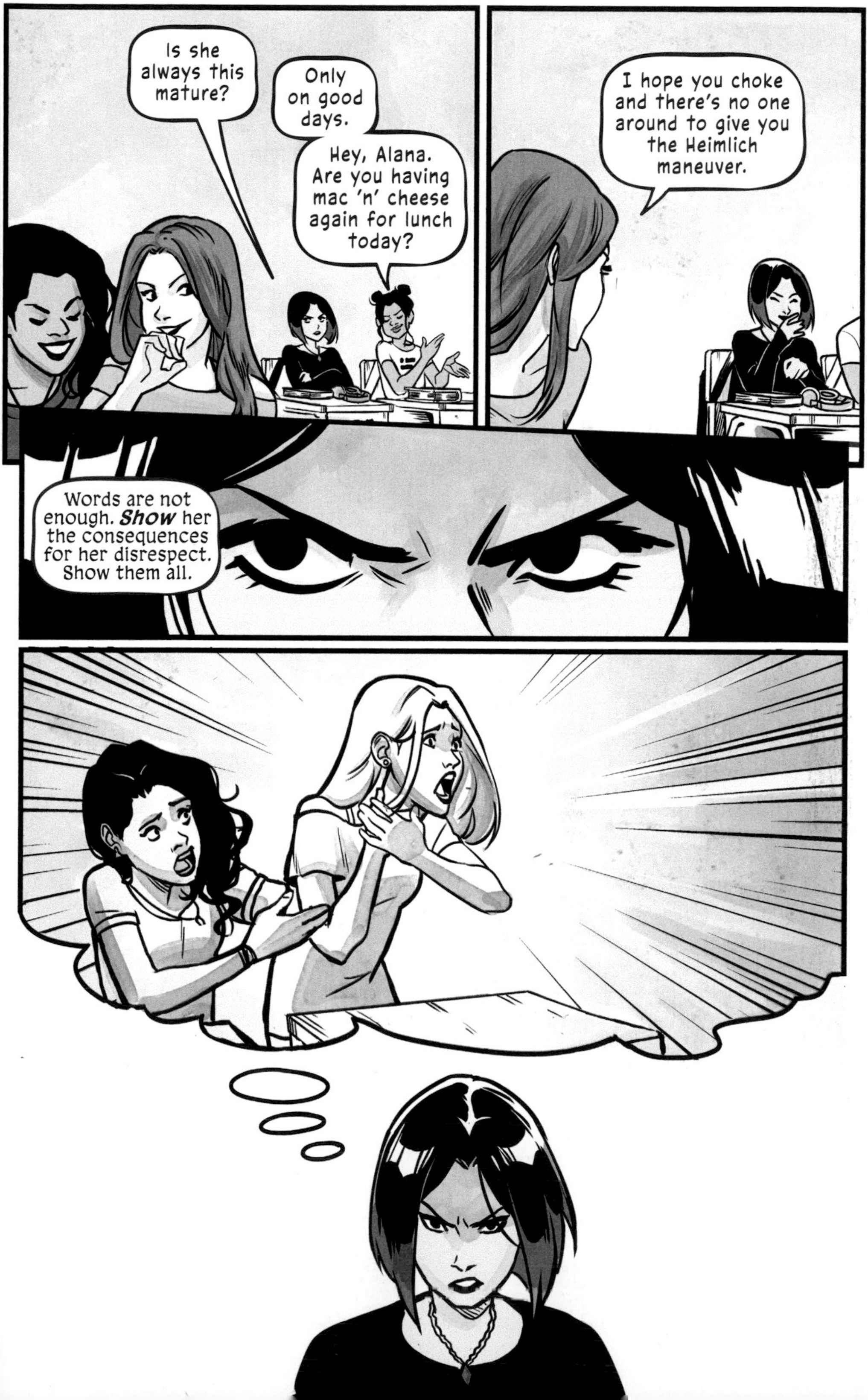
Is she always this mature?
Only on good days.
Hey, Alana. Are you having mac 'n' cheese again for lunch today?
I hope you choke and there's no one around to give you the Heimlich maneuver.
Words are not enough. *Show* her the consequences for her disrespect. Show them all.

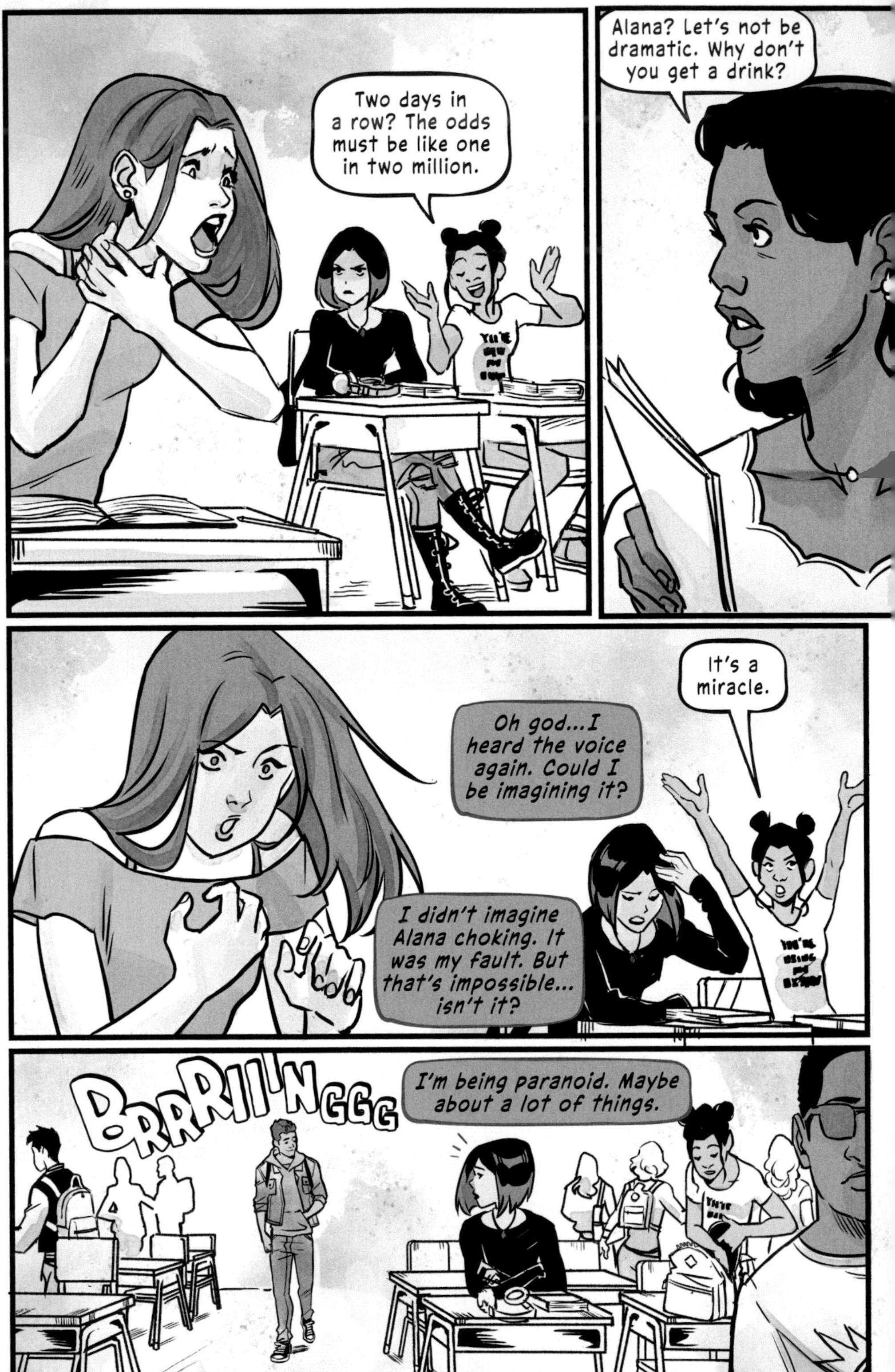
Two days in a row? The odds must be like one in two million.
Alana? Let's not be dramatic. Why don't you get a drink?
It's a miracle.
Oh god...I heard the voice again. Could I be imagining it?
I didn't imagine Alana choking. It was my fault. But that's impossible... isn't it?
BRRRIIINGGG
I'm being paranoid. Maybe about a lot of things.

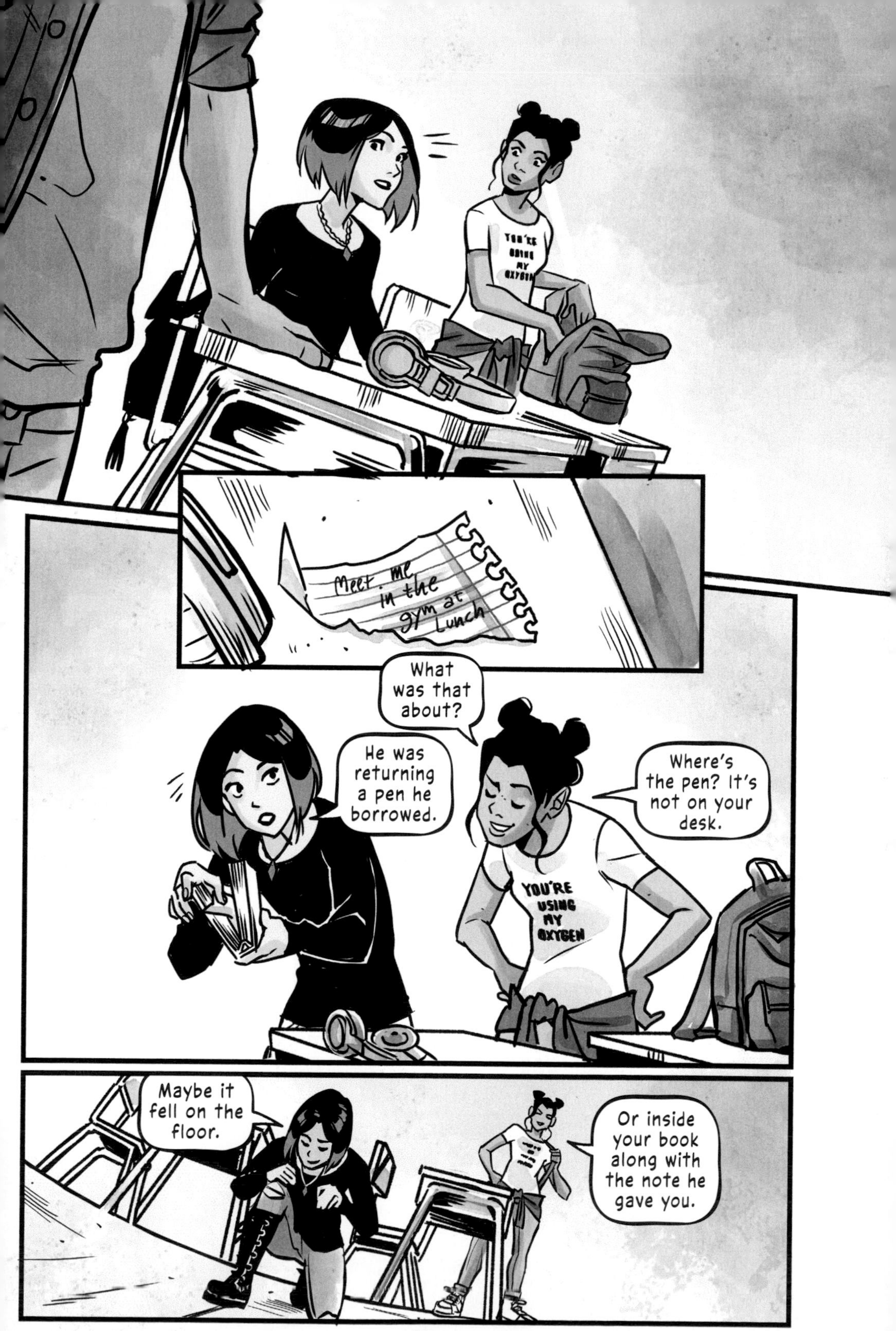
YOU'RE USING MY OXYGEN
Meet me in the gym at Lunch
What was that about?
He was returning a pen he borrowed.
Where's the pen? It's not on your desk.
YOU'RE USING MY OXYGEN
Maybe it fell on the floor.
Or inside your book along with the note he gave you.

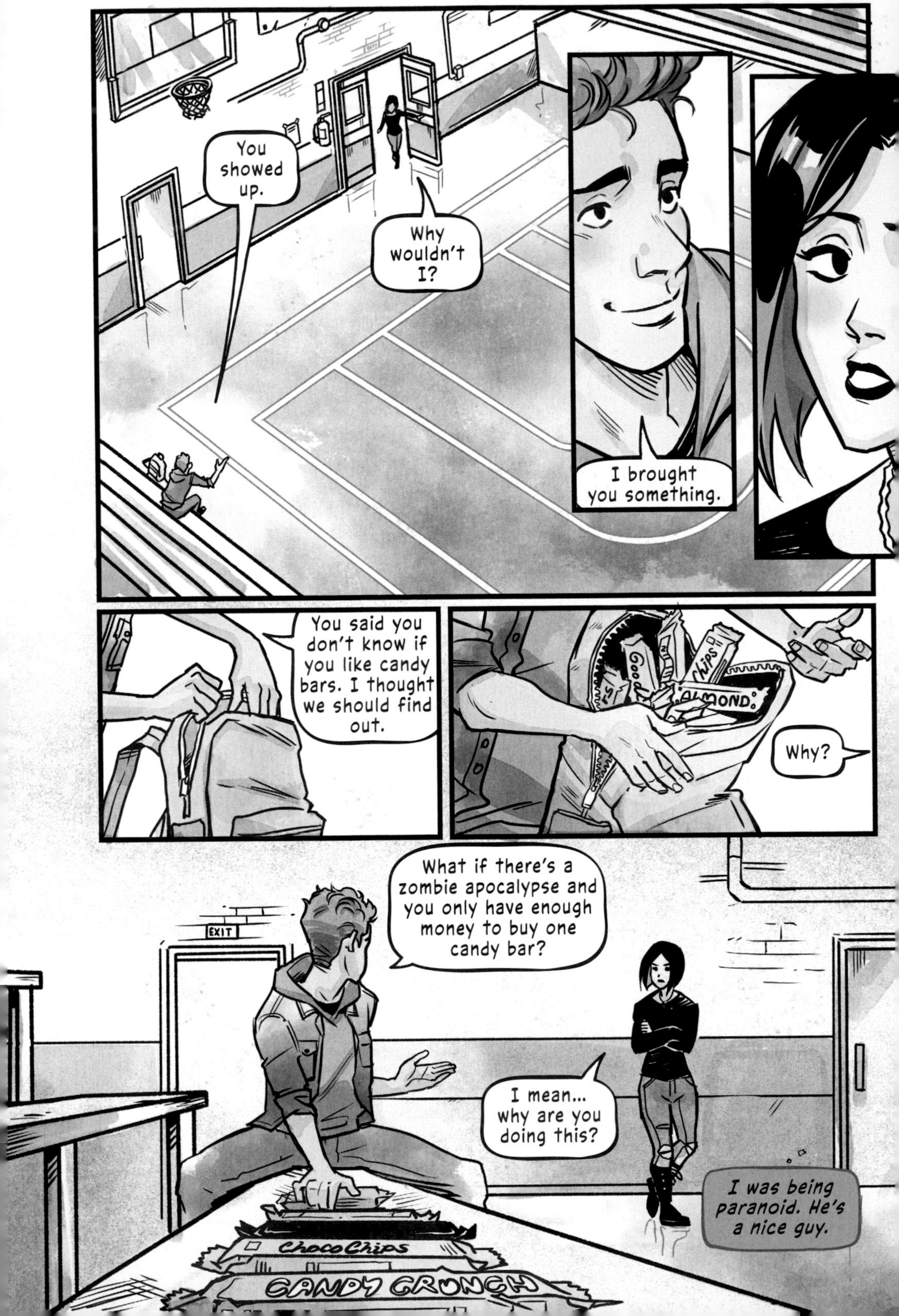
You showed up.
Why wouldn't I?
I brought you something.
You said you don't know if you like candy bars. I thought we should find out.
Goodi
Chips
ALMOND
Why?
What if there's a zombie apocalypse and you only have enough money to buy one candy bar?
EXIT
I mean... why are you doing this?
I was being paranoid. He's a nice guy.
ChocoChips
CANDY CRUNCH

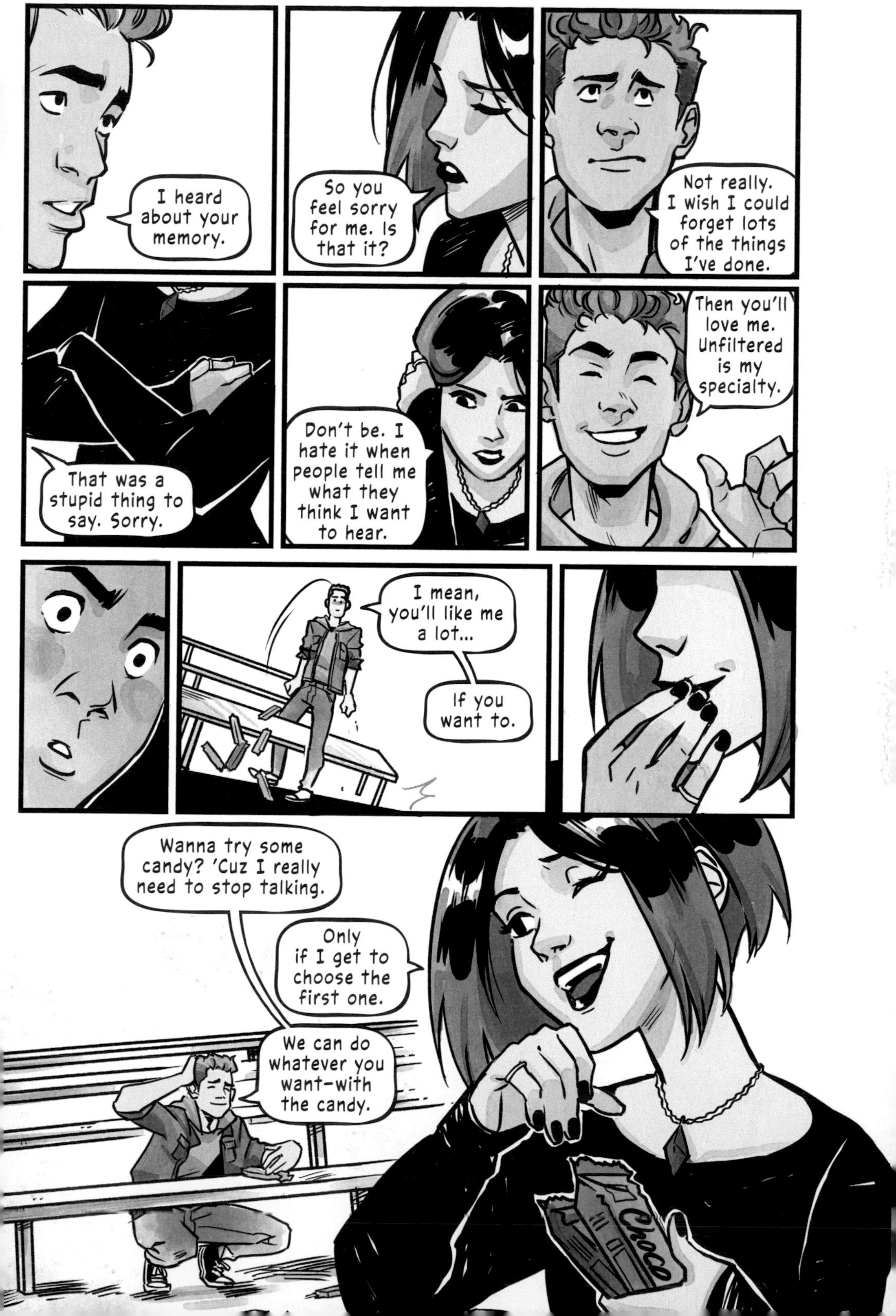
I heard about your memory.
So you feel sorry for me. Is that it?
Not really. I wish I could forget lots of the things I've done.
That was a stupid thing to say. Sorry.
Don't be. I hate it when people tell me what they think I want to hear.
Then you'll love me. Unfiltered is my specialty.
I mean, you'll like me a lot...
If you want to.
Wanna try some candy? 'Cuz I really need to stop talking.
Only if I get to choose the first one.
We can do whatever you want–with the candy.
Choco

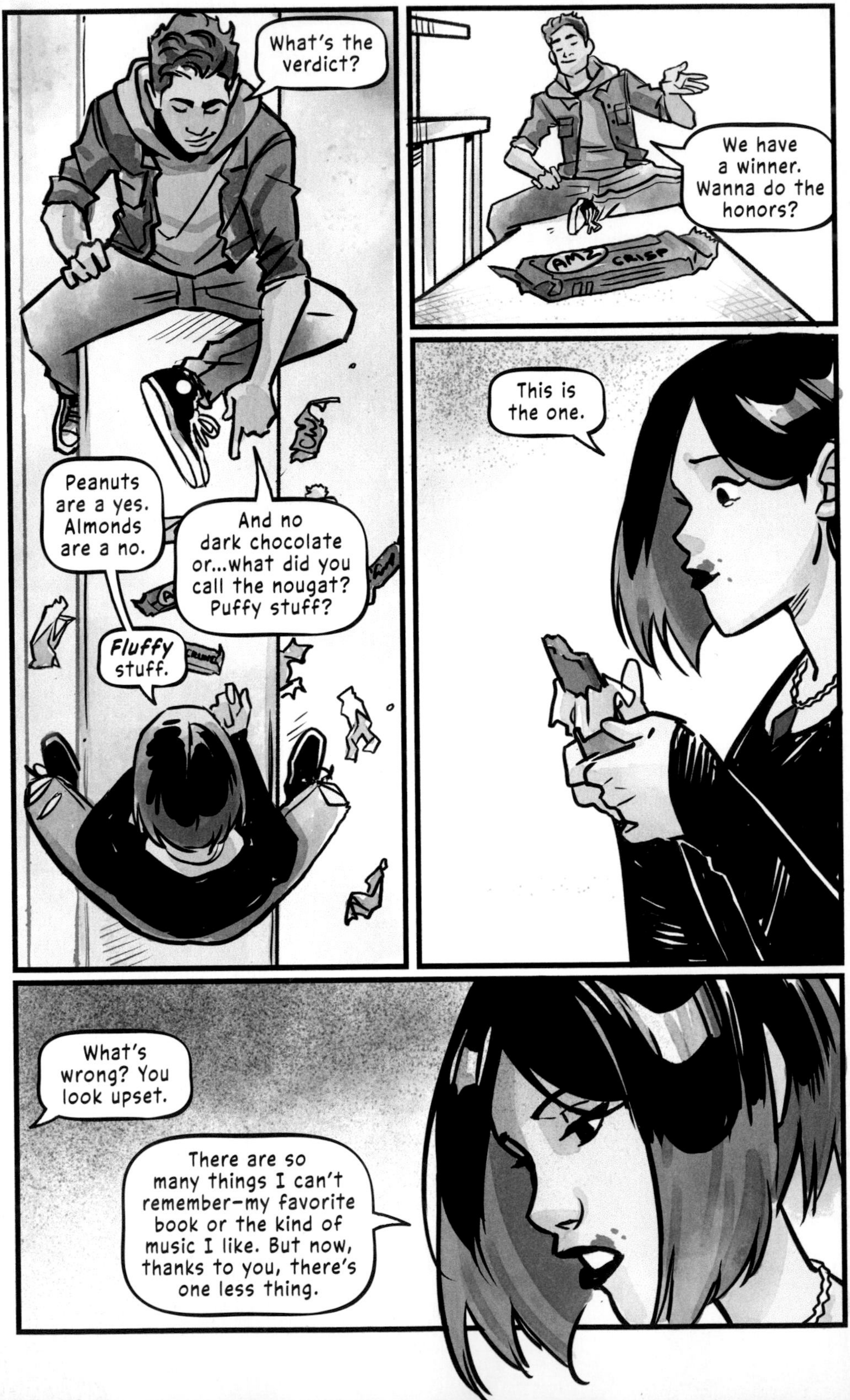
What's the verdict?
We have a winner. Wanna do the honors?
Peanuts are a yes. Almonds are a no.
And no dark chocolate or...what did you call the nougat? Puffy stuff?
Fluffy stuff.
This is the one.
What's wrong? You look upset.
There are so many things I can't remember—my favorite book or the kind of music I like. But now, thanks to you, there's one less thing.

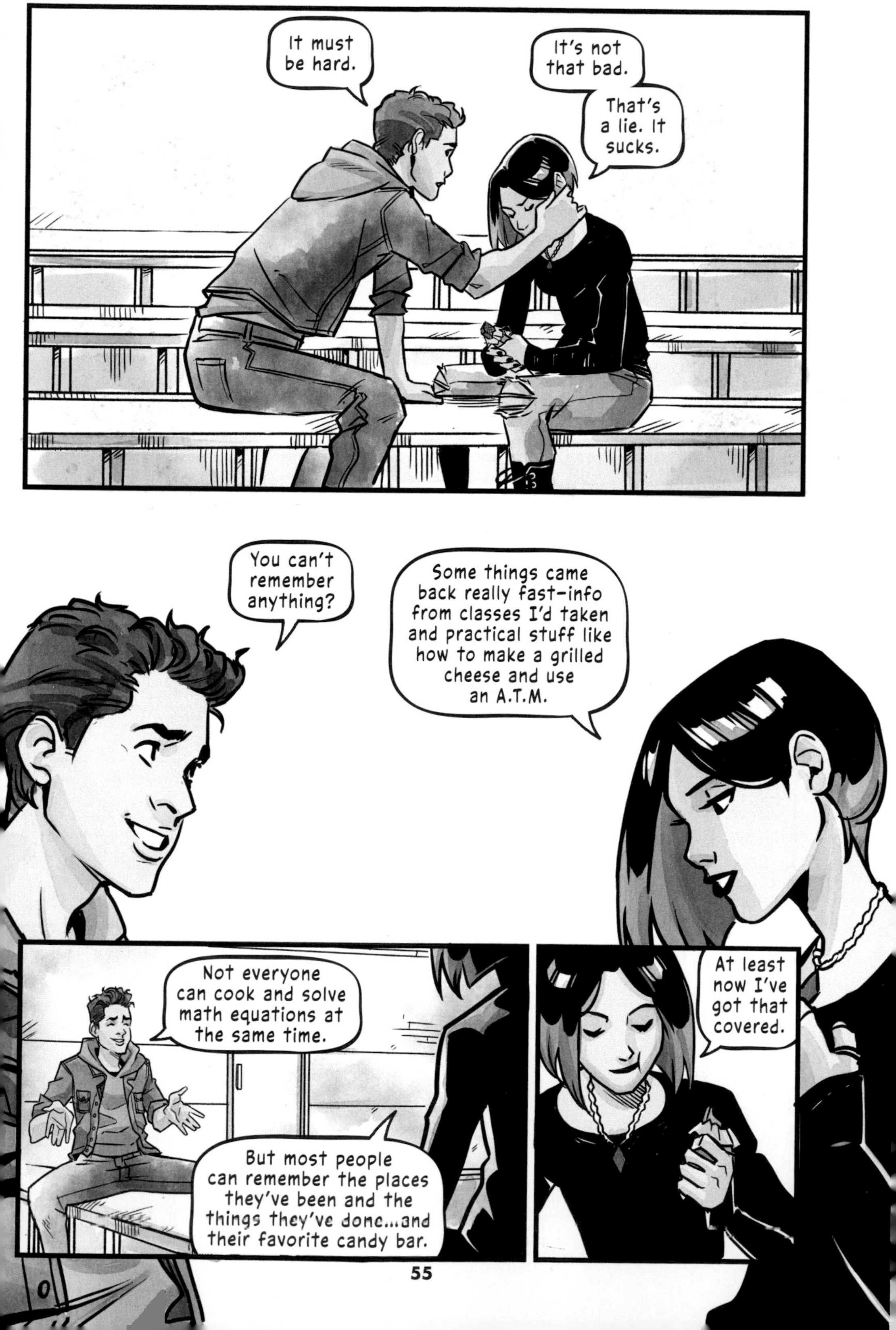
It must be hard.
It's not that bad.
That's a lie. It sucks.
You can't remember anything?
Some things came back really fast–info from classes I'd taken and practical stuff like how to make a grilled cheese and use an A.T.M.
Not everyone can cook and solve math equations at the same time.
But most people can remember the places they've been and the things they've done...and their favorite candy bar.
At least now I've got that covered.

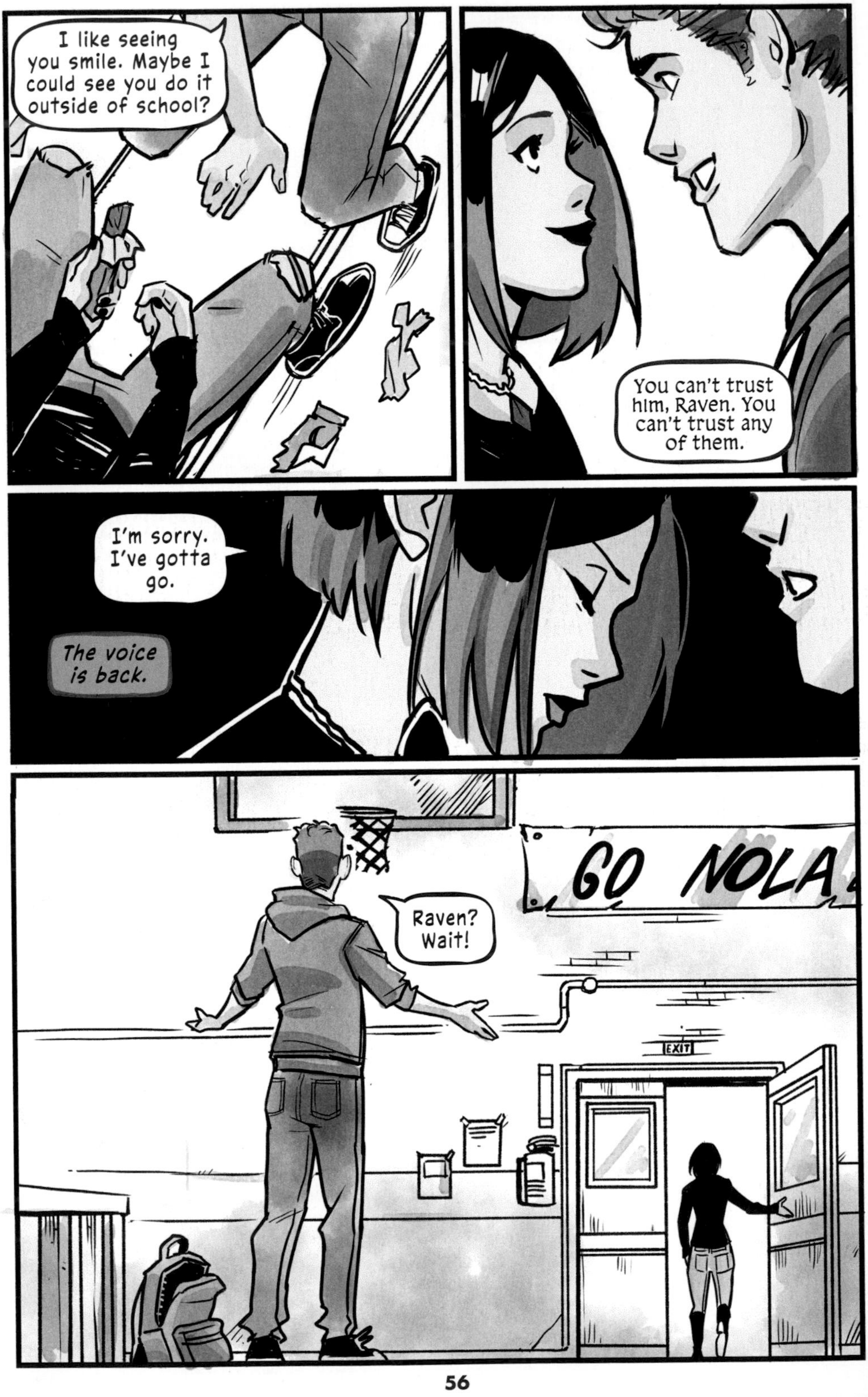
I like seeing you smile. Maybe I could see you do it outside of school?
You can't trust him, Raven. You can't trust any of them.
I'm sorry. I've gotta go.
The voice is back.
GO NOLA
Raven? Wait!
EXIT

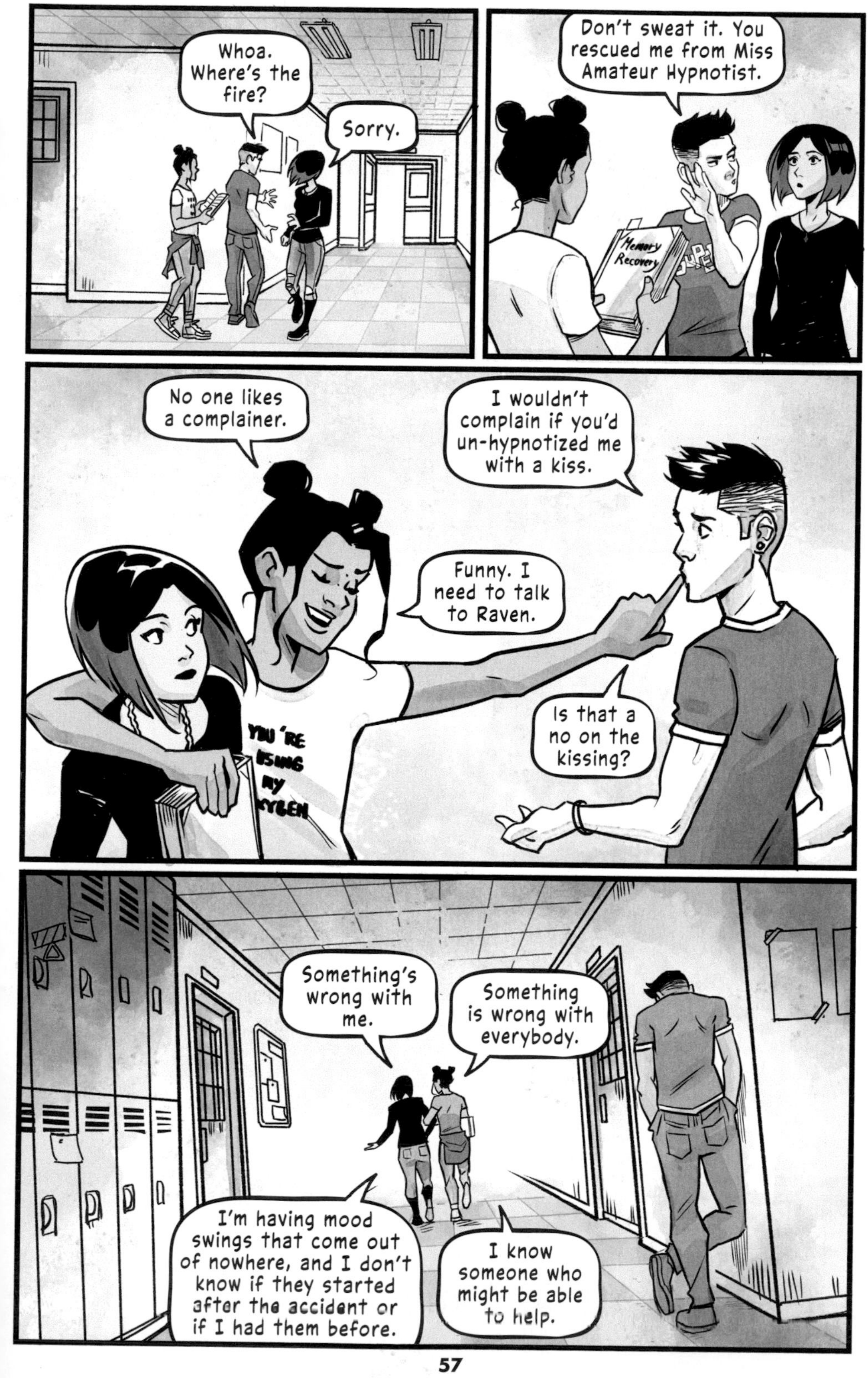
Whoa. Where's the fire?
Sorry.
Don't sweat it. You rescued me from Miss Amateur Hypnotist.
Memory Recovery
No one likes a complainer.
I wouldn't complain if you'd un-hypnotized me with a kiss.
Funny. I need to talk to Raven.
Is that a no on the kissing?
Something's wrong with me.
Something is wrong with everybody.
I'm having mood swings that come out of nowhere, and I don't know if they started after the accident or if I had them before.
I know someone who might be able to help.

CHAPTER 7: VOODOO QUEEN

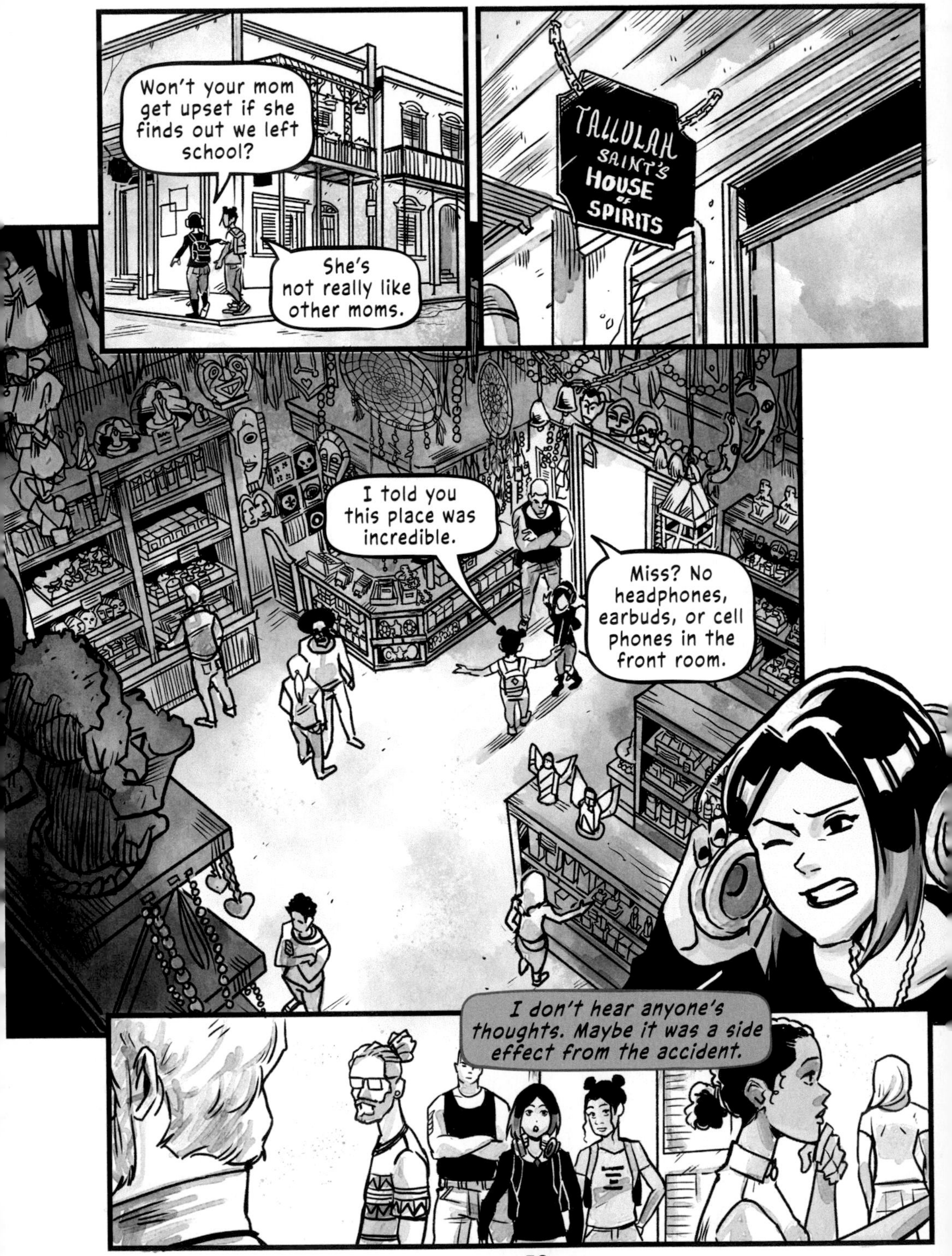

Won't your mom get upset if she finds out we left school?
She's not really like other moms.
TALLULAH SAINT'S HOUSE of SPIRITS
I told you this place was incredible.
Miss? No headphones, earbuds, or cell phones in the front room.
I don't hear anyone's thoughts. Maybe it was a side effect from the accident.

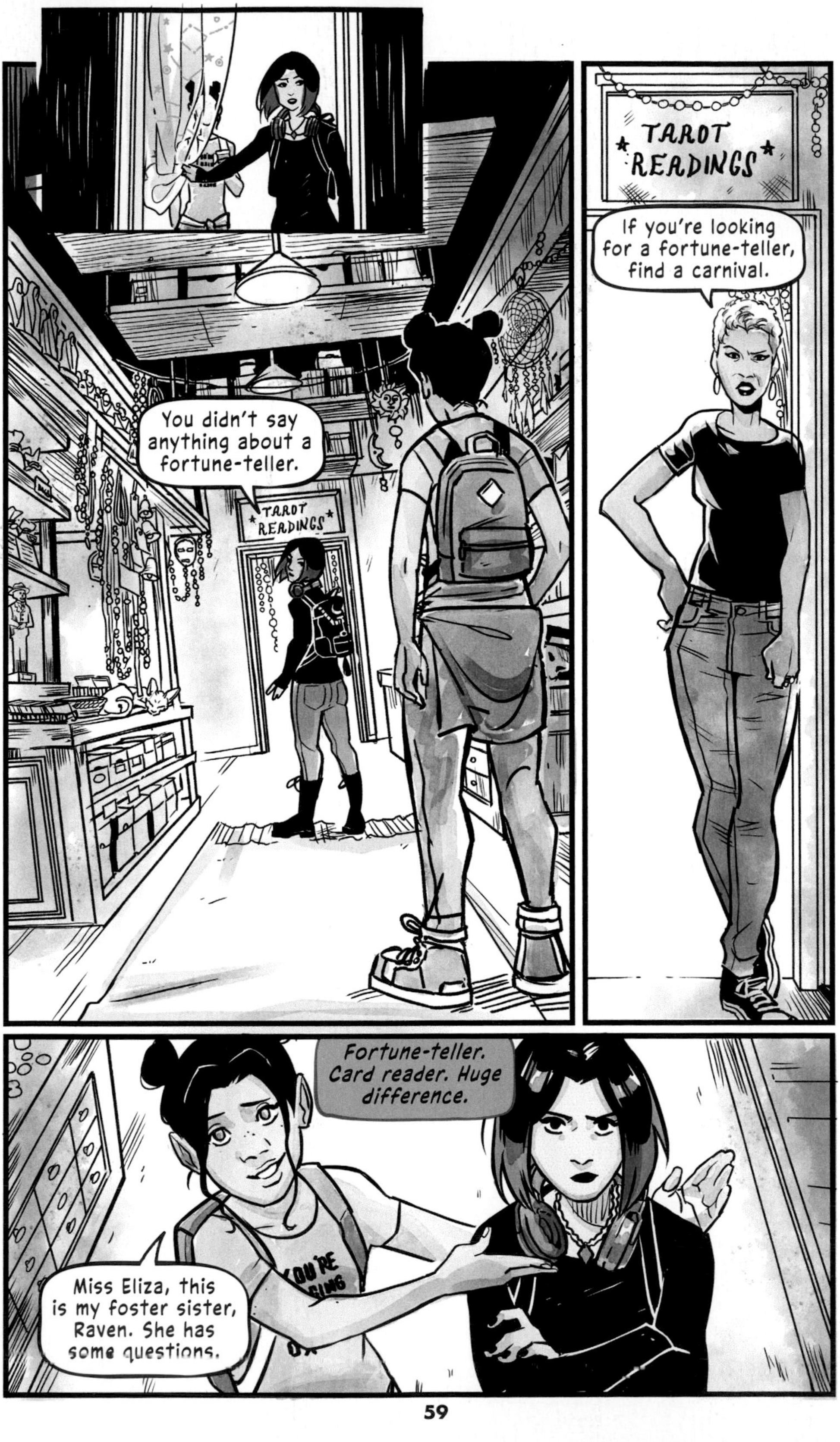
TAROT READINGS
If you're looking for a fortune-teller, find a carnival.
You didn't say anything about a fortune-teller.
TAROT READINGS
Fortune-teller. Card reader. Huge difference.
Miss Eliza, this is my foster sister, Raven. She has some questions.

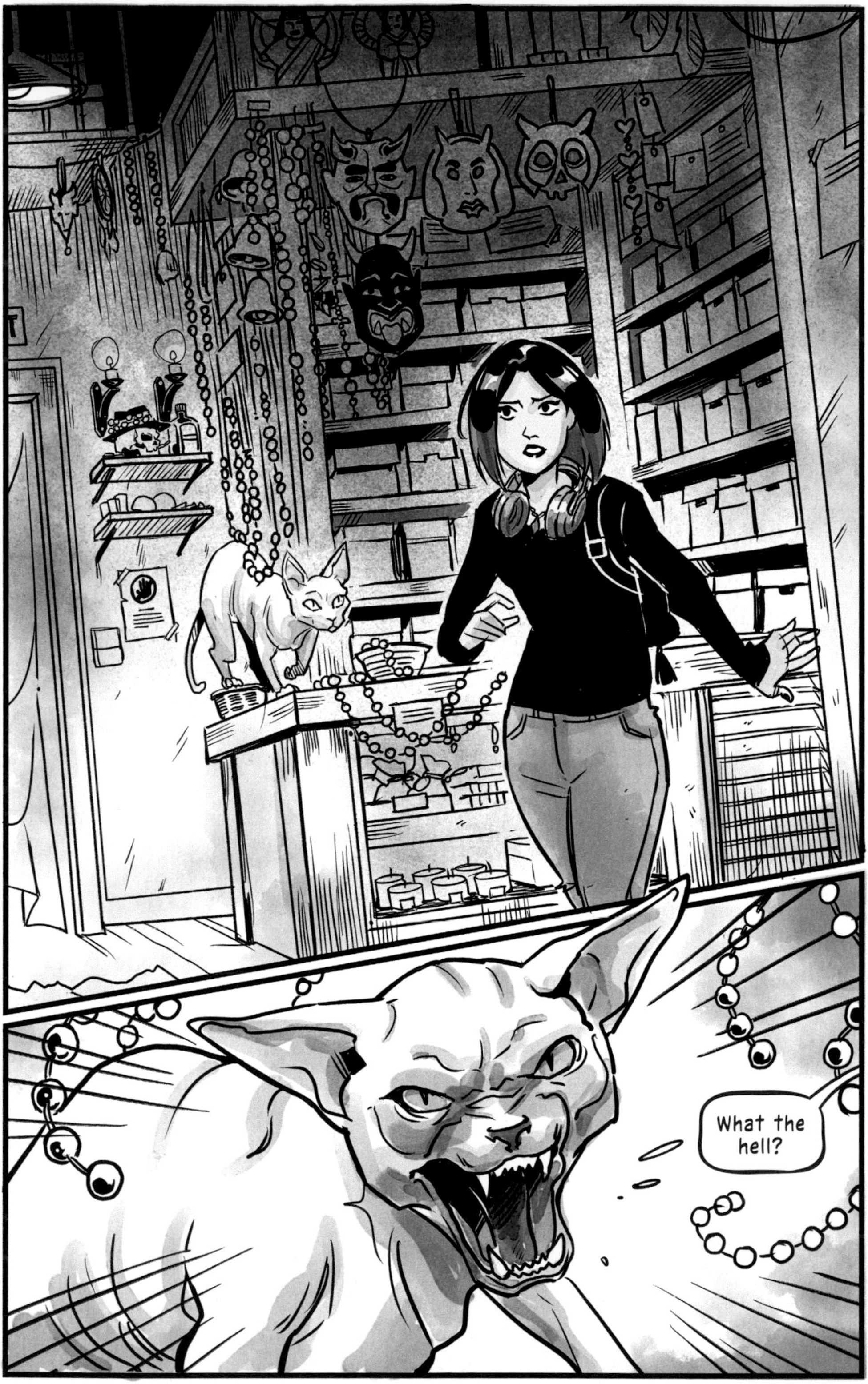
What the hell?

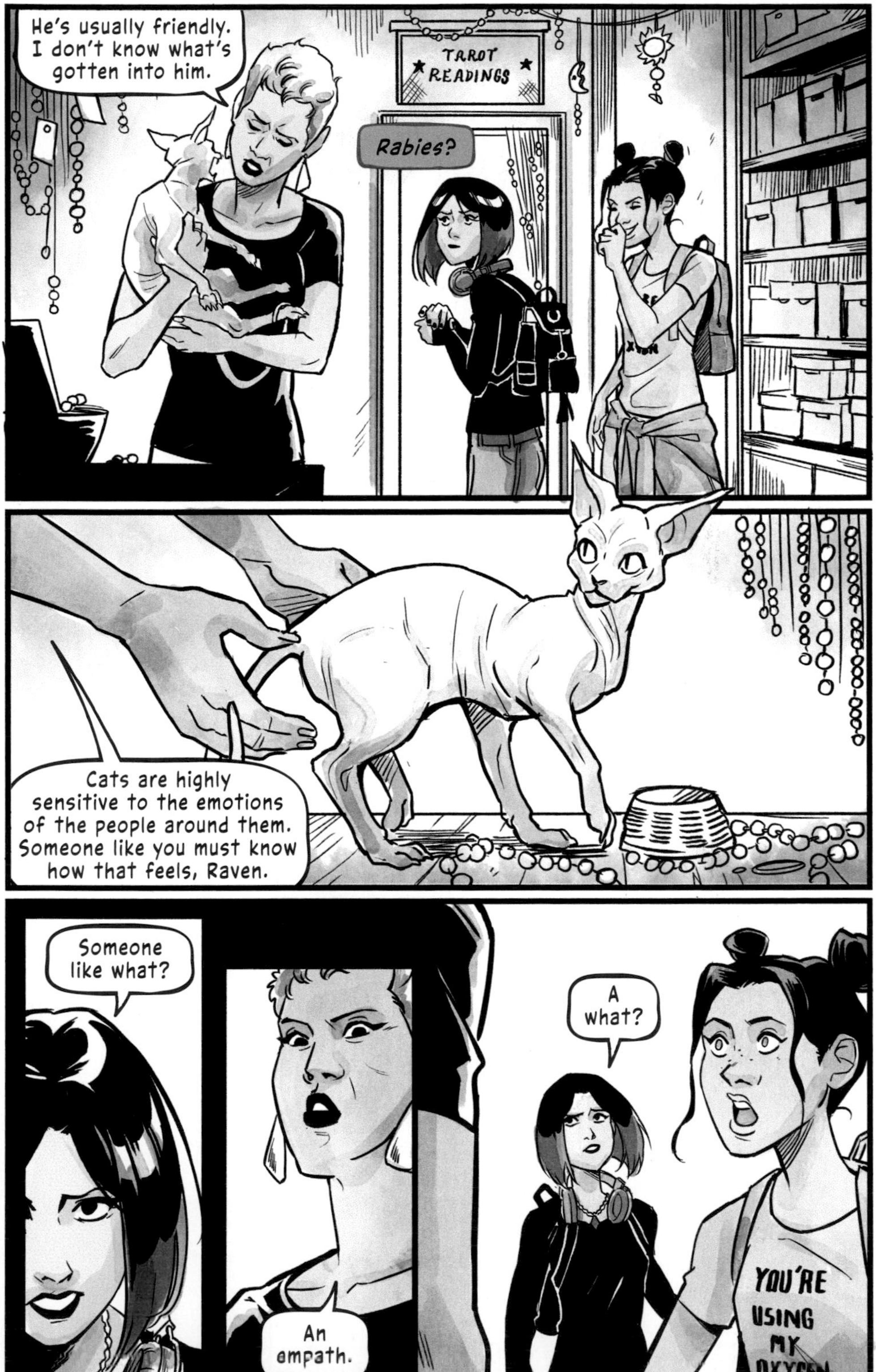
He's usually friendly. I don't know what's gotten into him.
TAROT READINGS
Rabies?
Cats are highly sensitive to the emotions of the people around them. Someone like you must know how that feels, Raven.
Someone like what?
An empath.
A what?
YOU'RE USING MY OXYGEN

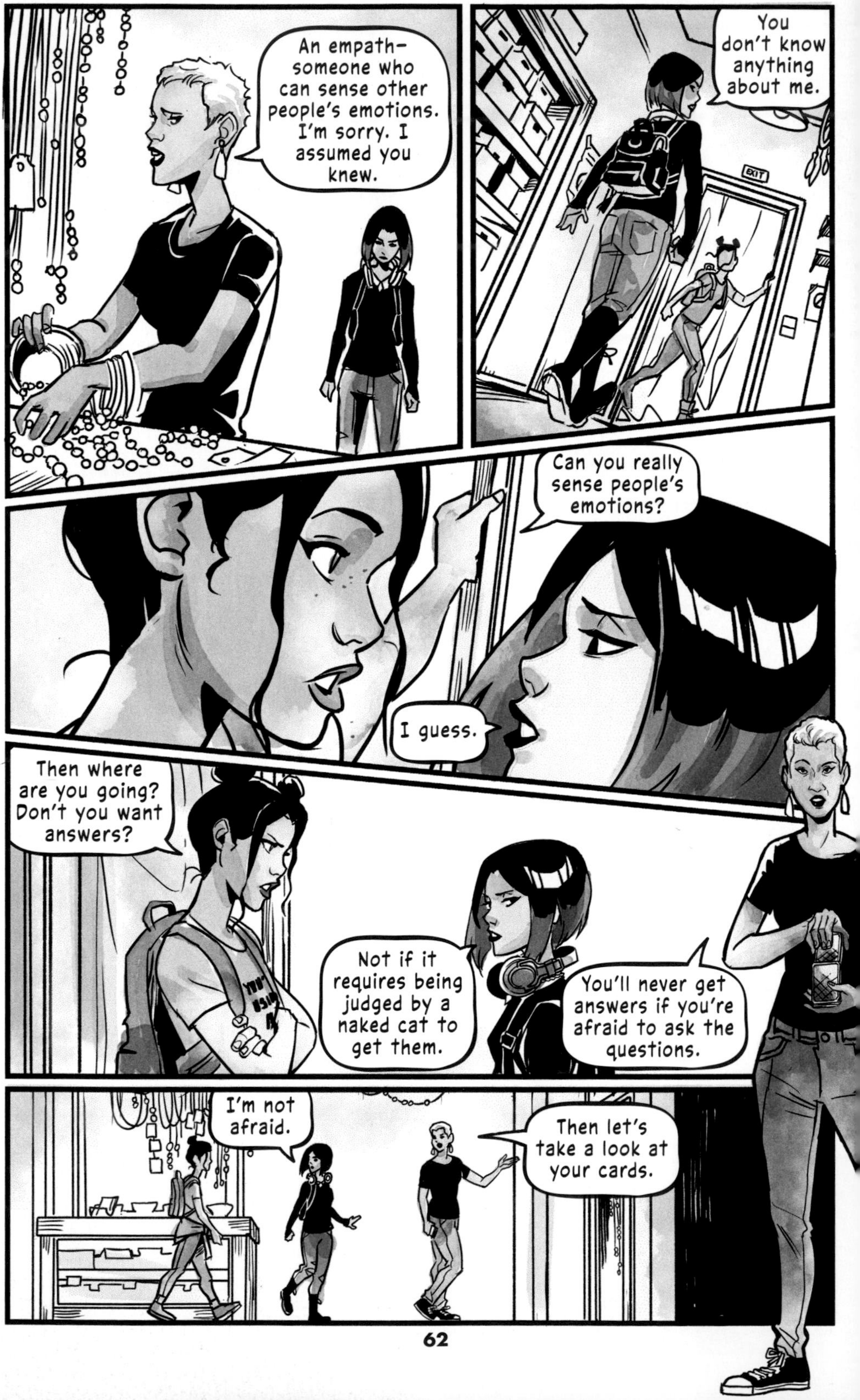
An empath—someone who can sense other people's emotions. I'm sorry. I assumed you knew.
You don't know anything about me.
Can you really sense people's emotions?
I guess.
Then where are you going? Don't you want answers?
Not if it requires being judged by a naked cat to get them.
You'll never get answers if you're afraid to ask the questions.
I'm not afraid.
Then let's take a look at your cards.

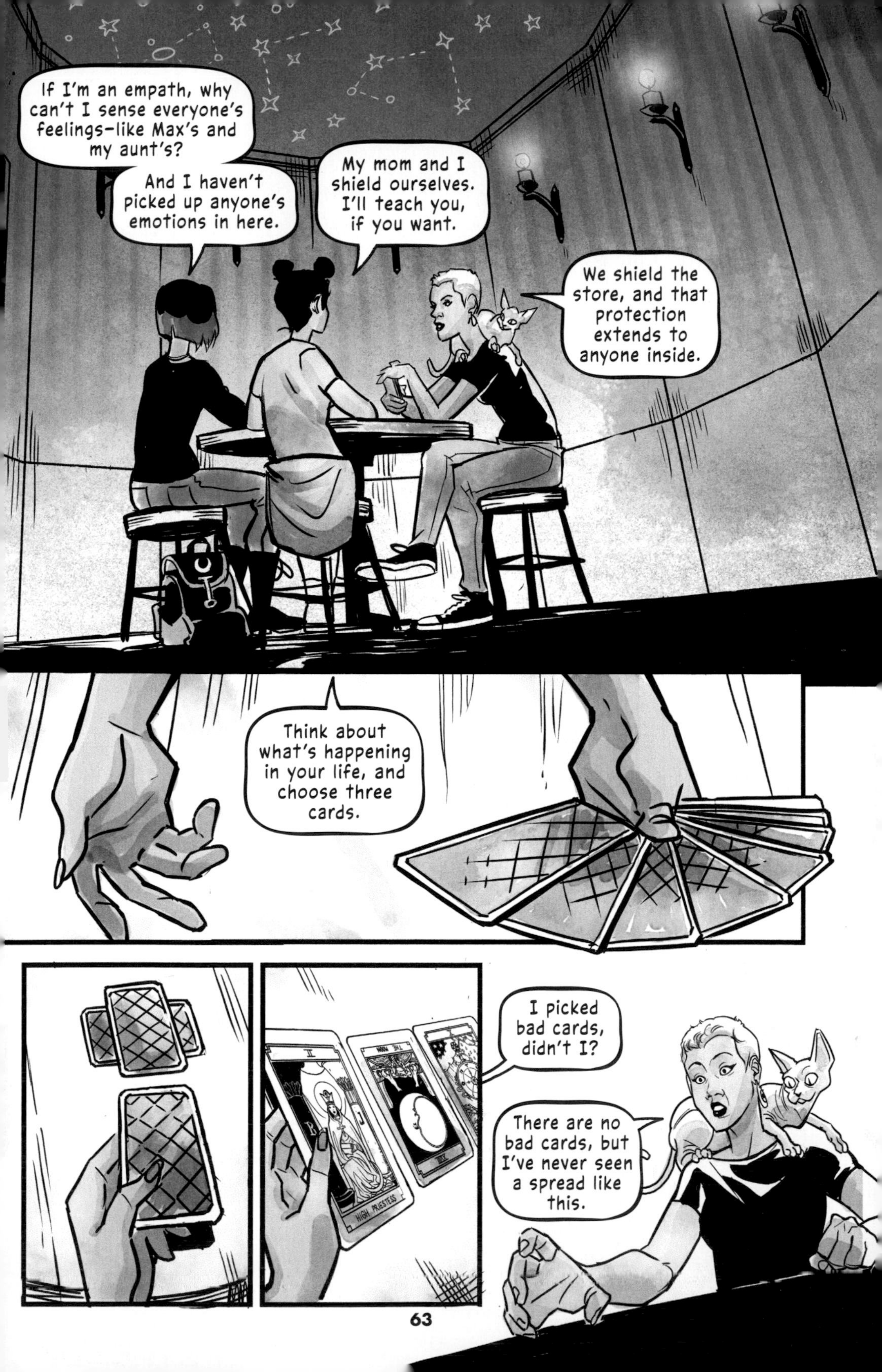

If I'm an empath, why can't I sense everyone's feelings—like Max's and my aunt's?
And I haven't picked up anyone's emotions in here.
My mom and I shield ourselves. I'll teach you, if you want.
We shield the store, and that protection extends to anyone inside.
Think about what's happening in your life, and choose three cards.
HIGH PRIESTESS
I picked bad cards, didn't I?
There are no bad cards, but I've never seen a spread like this.

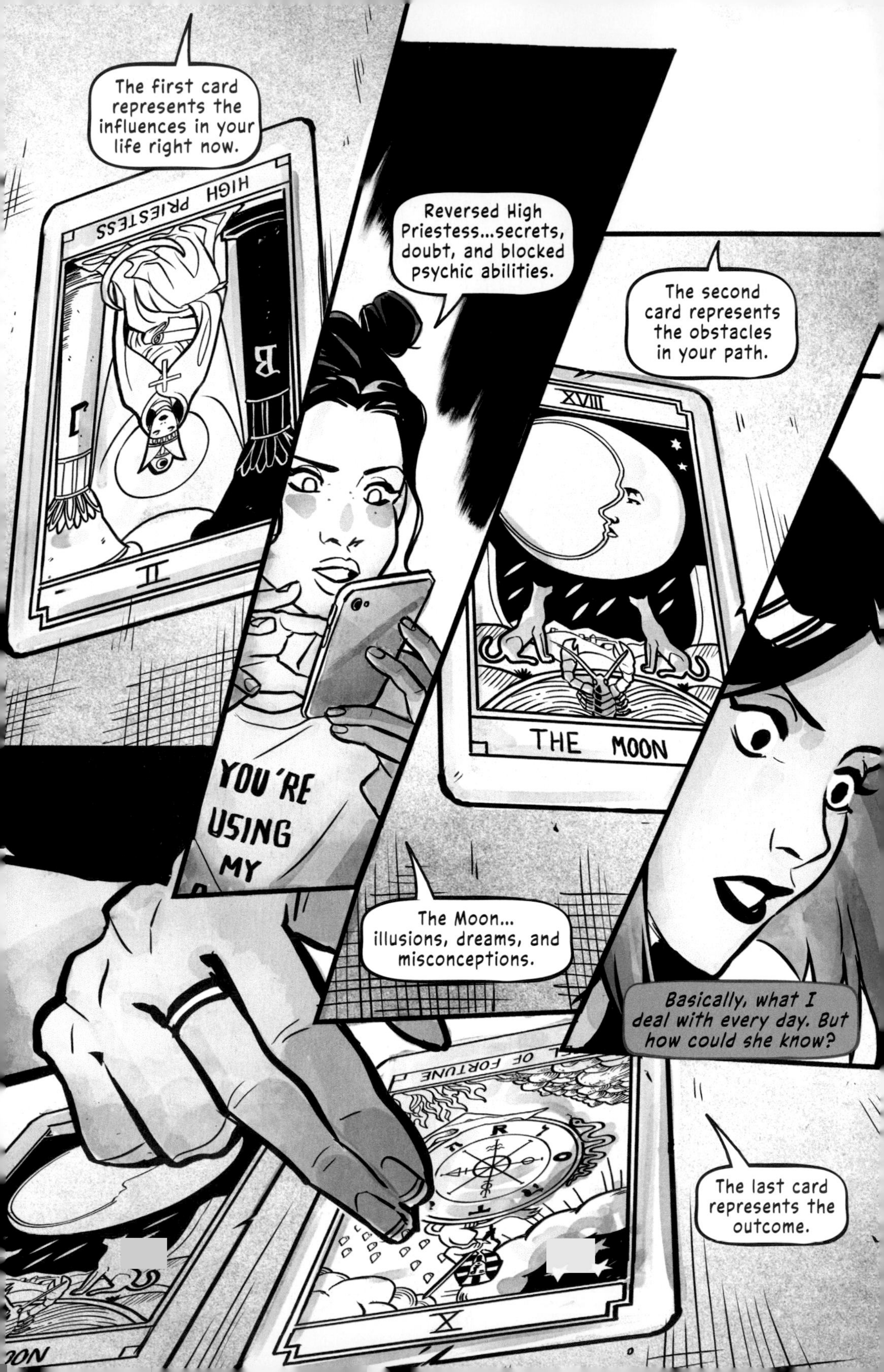

The first card represents the influences in your life right now.
HIGH PRIESTESS
Reversed High Priestess...secrets, doubt, and blocked psychic abilities.
The second card represents the obstacles in your path.
XVIII
THE MOON
YOU'RE USING MY
The Moon... illusions, dreams, and misconceptions.
Basically, what I deal with every day. But how could she know?
OF FORTUNE
The last card represents the outcome.

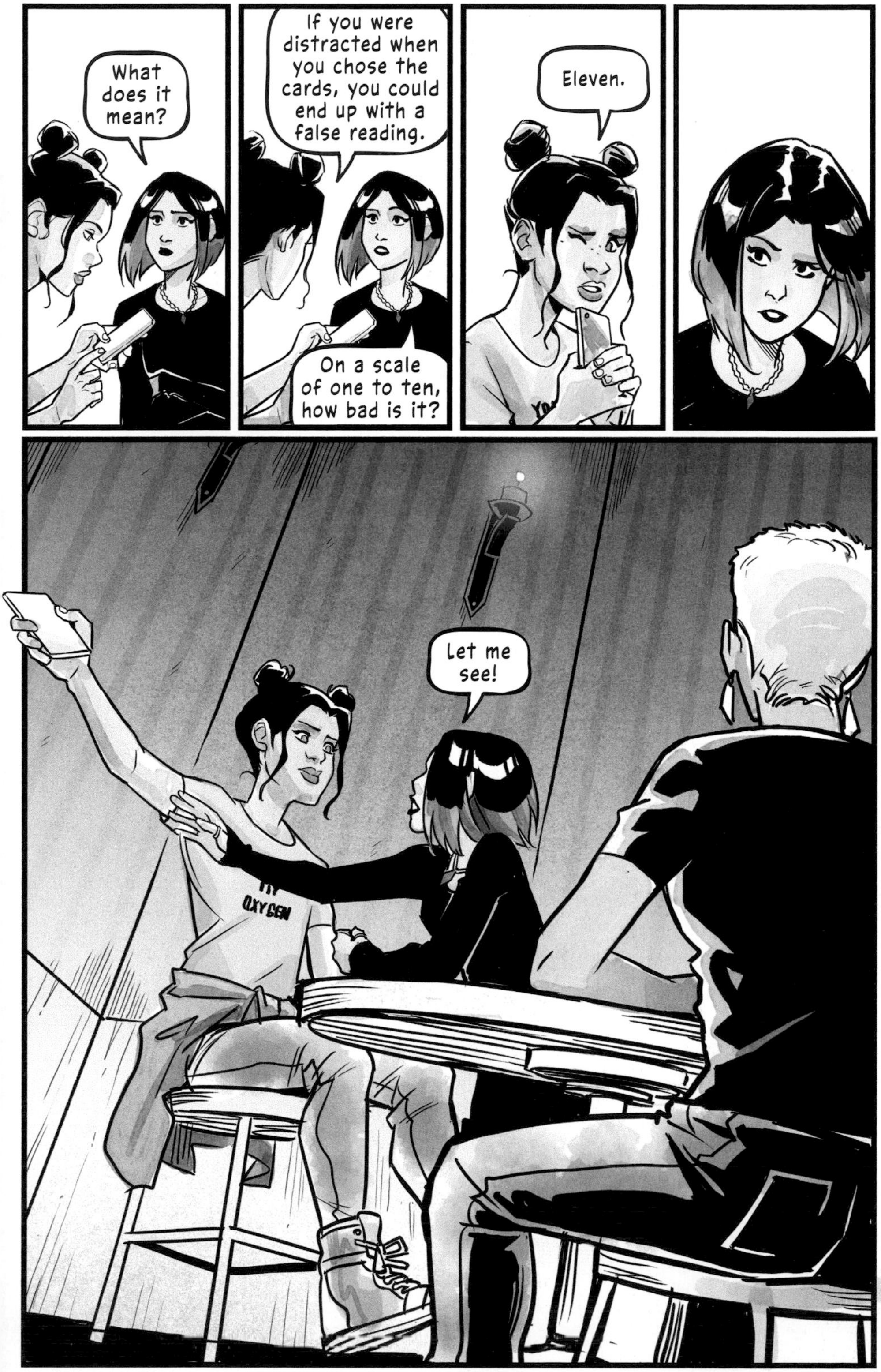
What does it mean?
If you were distracted when you chose the cards, you could end up with a false reading.
On a scale of one to ten, how bad is it?
Eleven.
Let me see!
OXYGEN

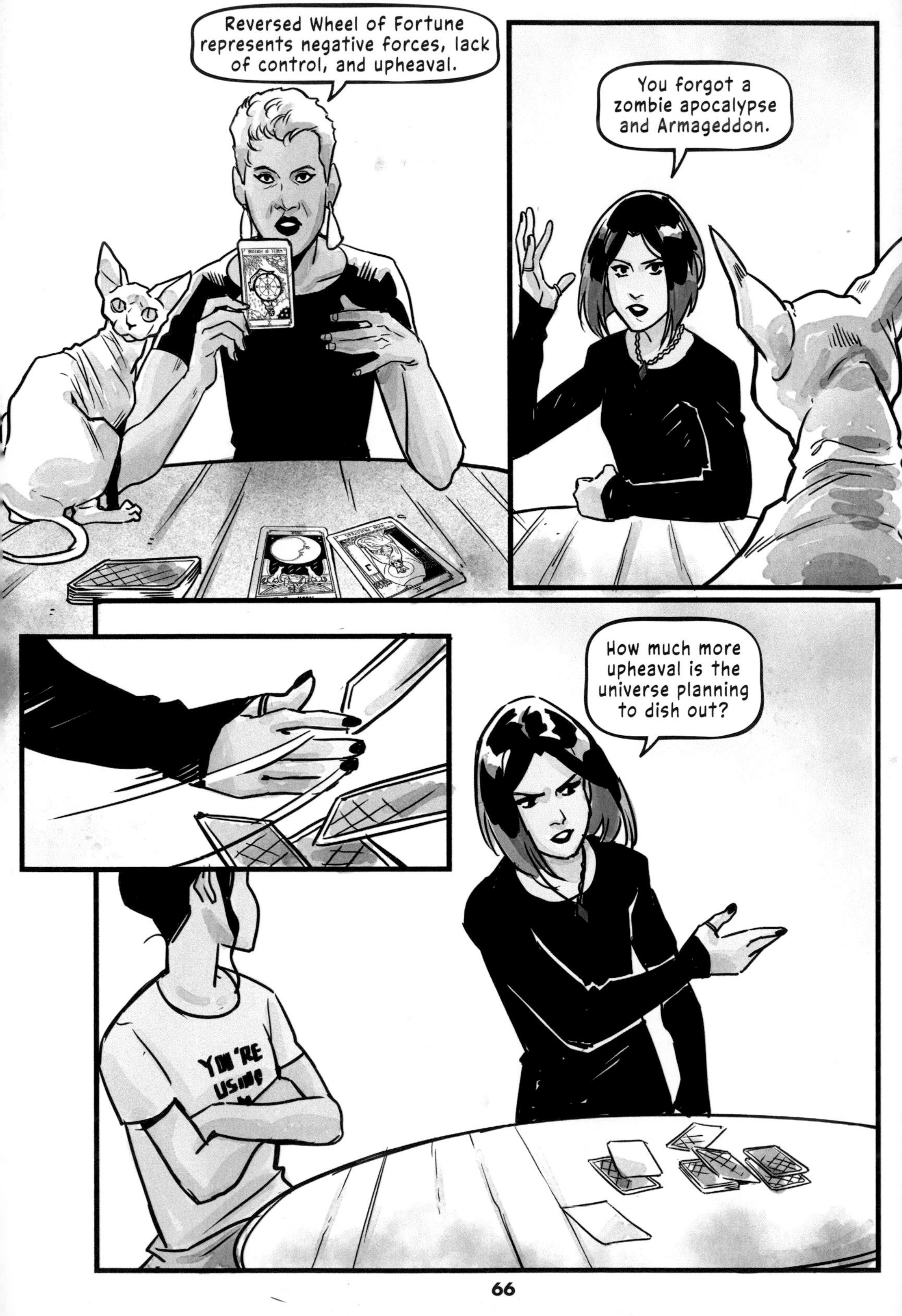
Reversed Wheel of Fortune represents negative forces, lack of control, and upheaval.
You forgot a zombie apocalypse and Armageddon.
How much more upheaval is the universe planning to dish out?
YOU'RE USING

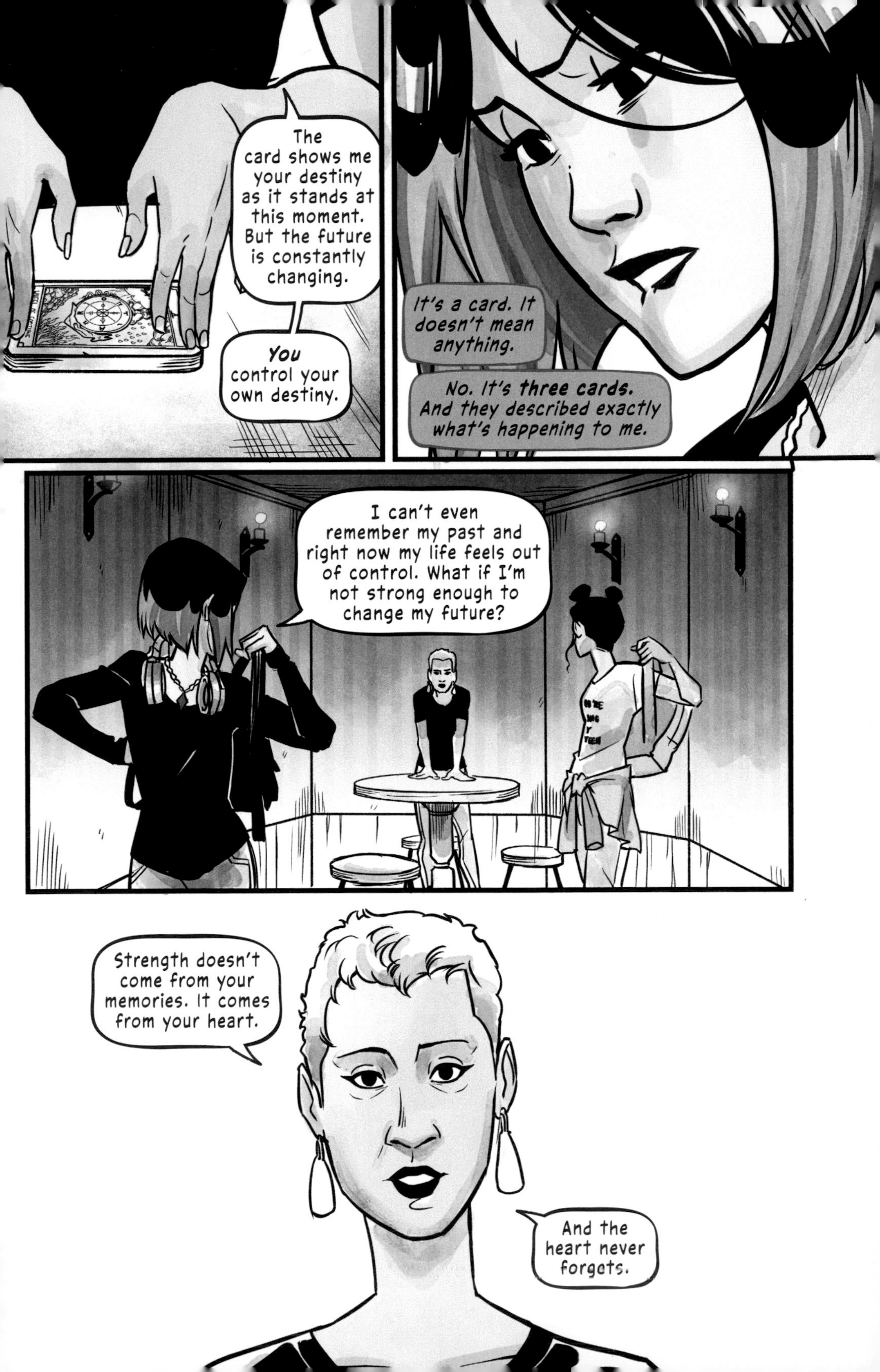
The card shows me your destiny as it stands at this moment. But the future is constantly changing.
You control your own destiny.
It's a card. It doesn't mean anything.
*No. It's **three cards.** And they described exactly what's happening to me.*
I can't even remember my past and right now my life feels out of control. What if I'm not strong enough to change my future?
Strength doesn't come from your memories. It comes from your heart.
And the heart never forgets.

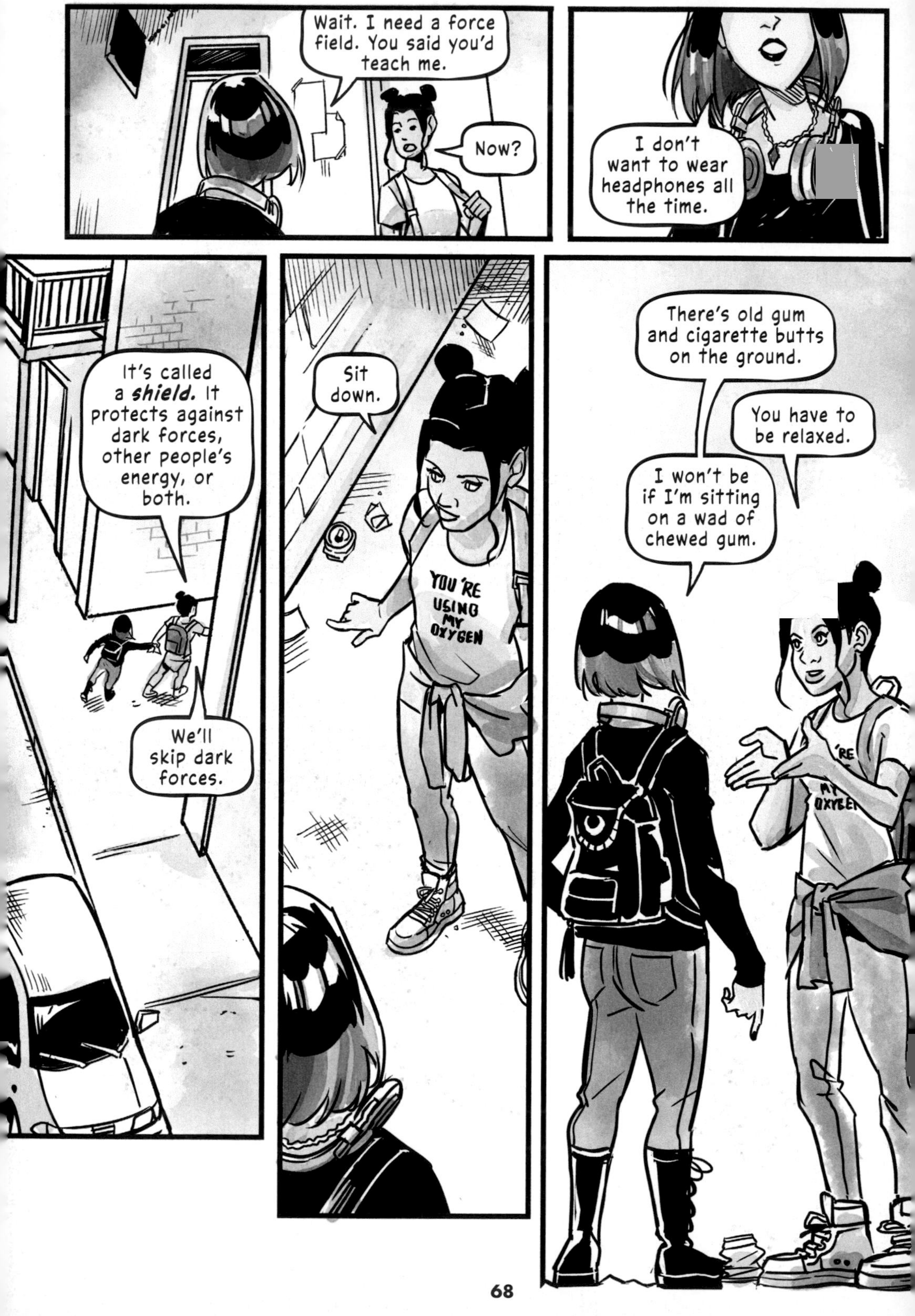

Wait. I need a force field. You said you'd teach me.
Now?
I don't want to wear headphones all the time.
It's called a ***shield.*** It protects against dark forces, other people's energy, or both.
We'll skip dark forces.
Sit down.
YOU'RE USING MY OXYGEN
There's old gum and cigarette butts on the ground.
You have to be relaxed.
I won't be if I'm sitting on a wad of chewed gum.

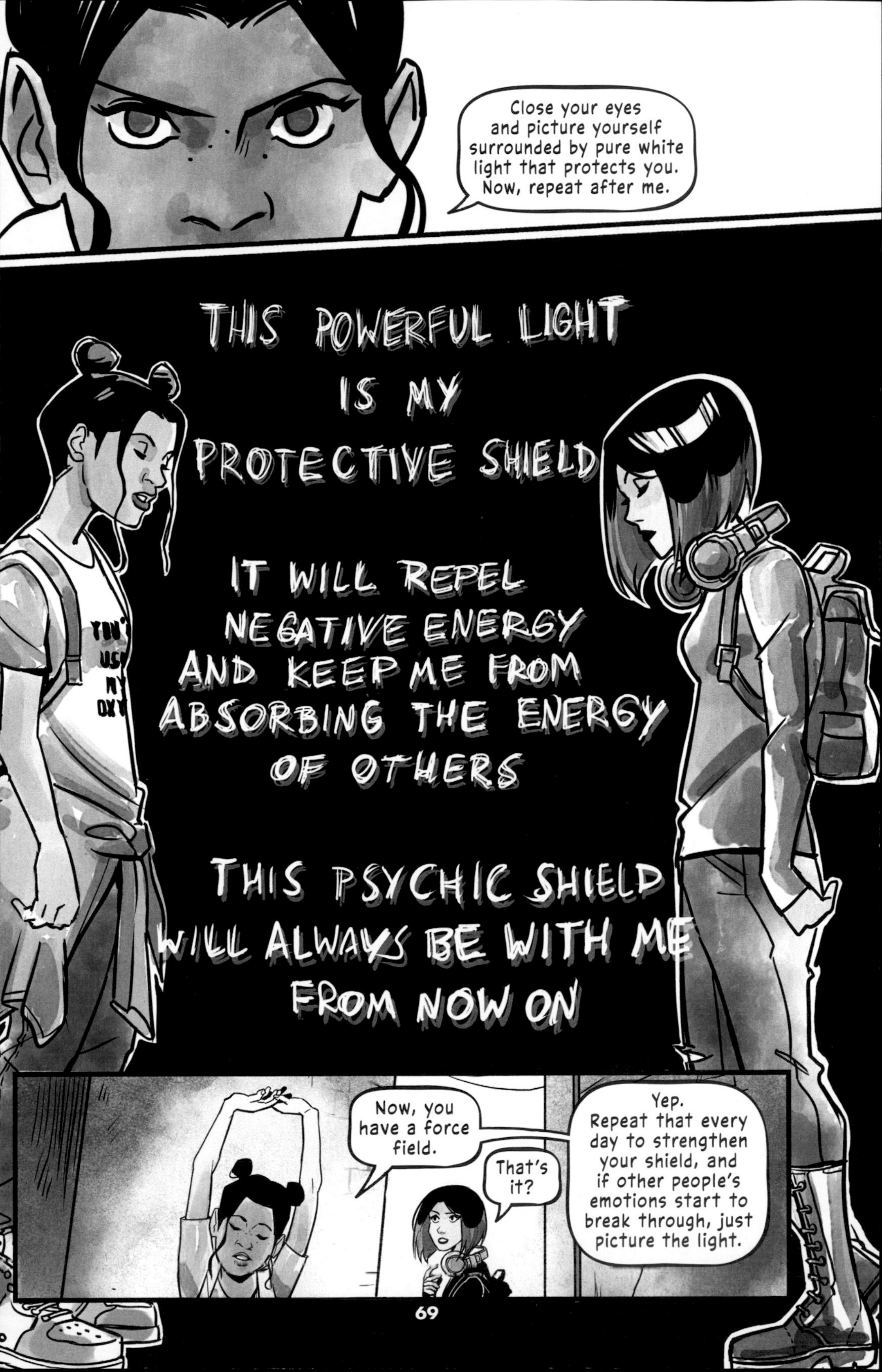
Close your eyes and picture yourself surrounded by pure white light that protects you. Now, repeat after me.
THIS POWERFUL LIGHT IS MY PROTECTIVE SHIELD
IT WILL REPEL NEGATIVE ENERGY AND KEEP ME FROM ABSORBING THE ENERGY OF OTHERS
THIS PSYCHIC SHIELD WILL ALWAYS BE WITH ME FROM NOW ON
Now, you have a force field.
That's it?
Yep. Repeat that every day to strengthen your shield, and if other people's emotions start to break through, just picture the light.

CHAPTER 8: TRUST FALL

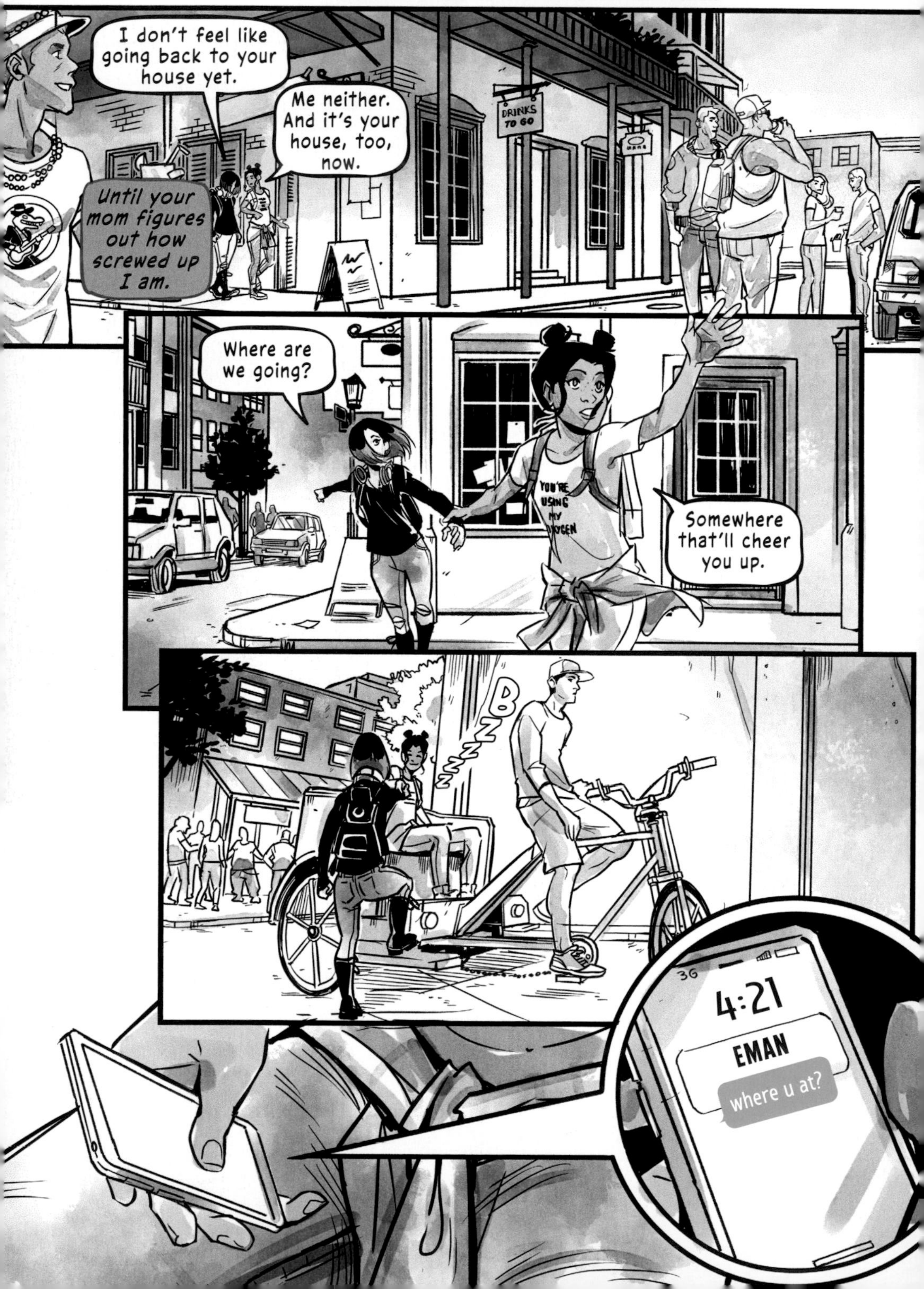

I don't feel like going back to your house yet.
Me neither. And it's your house, too, now.
Until your mom figures out how screwed up I am.
DRINKS TO GO
Where are we going?
YOU'RE USING MY OXYGEN
Somewhere that'll cheer you up.
BZZZZZ
3G
4:21
EMAN
where u at?

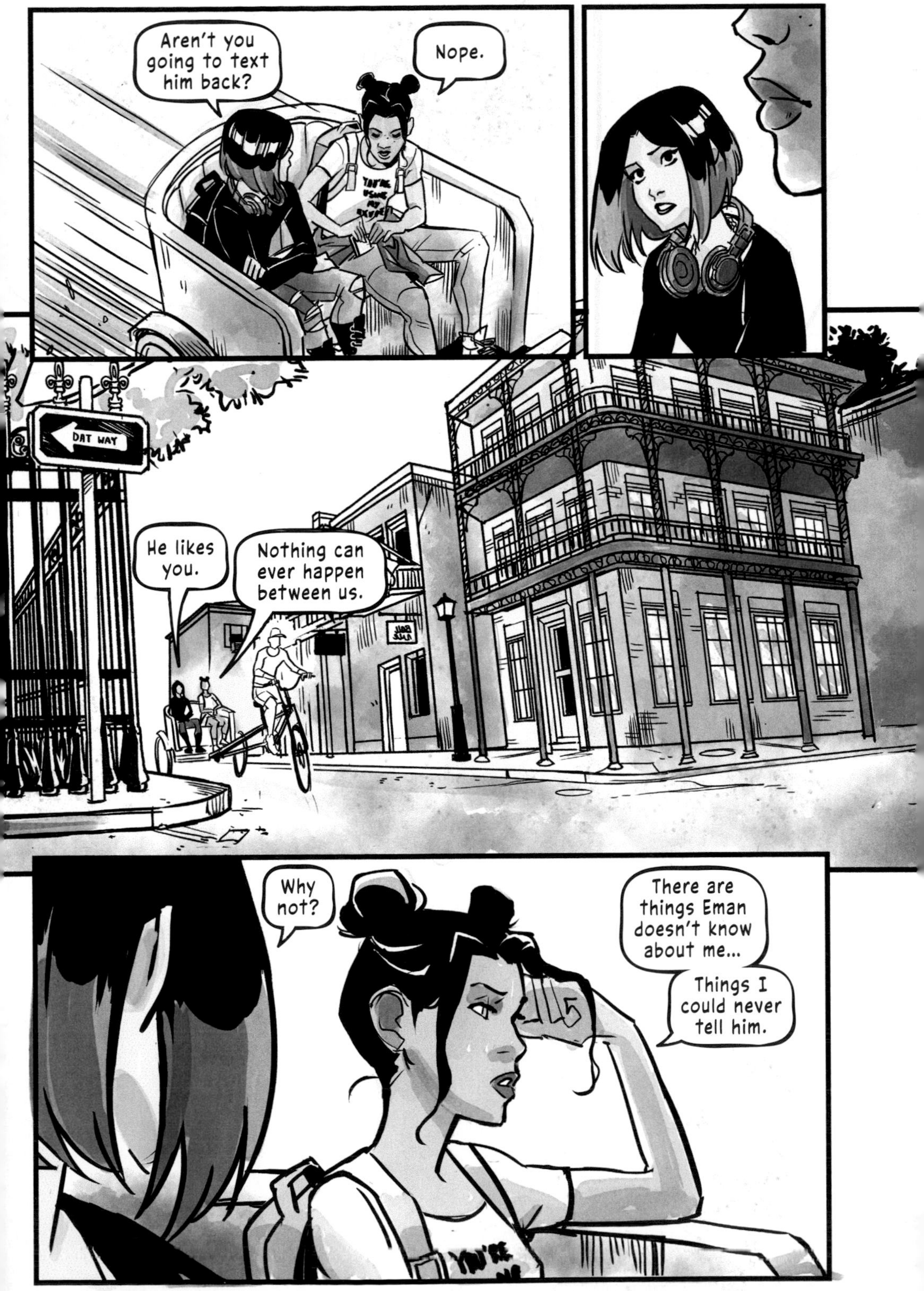
Aren't you going to text him back?
Nope.
DAT WAY
He likes you.
Nothing can ever happen between us.
Why not?
There are things Eman doesn't know about me...
Things I could never tell him.

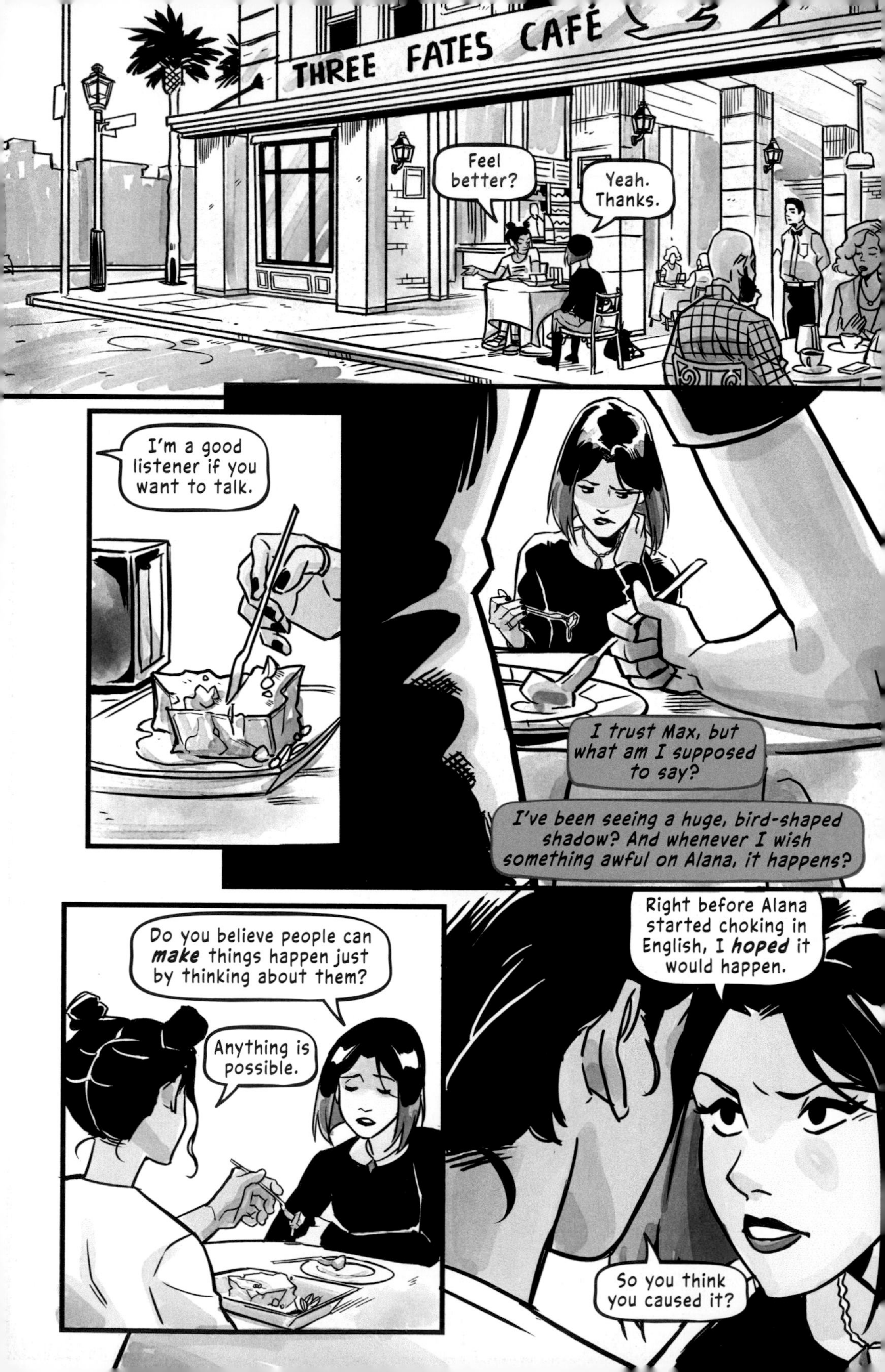
THREE FATES CAFÉ
Feel better?
Yeah. Thanks.
I'm a good listener if you want to talk.
I trust Max, but what am I supposed to say?
I've been seeing a huge, bird-shaped shadow? And whenever I wish something awful on Alana, it happens?
Do you believe people can make things happen just by thinking about them?
Anything is possible.
Right before Alana started choking in English, I hoped it would happen.
So you think you caused it?

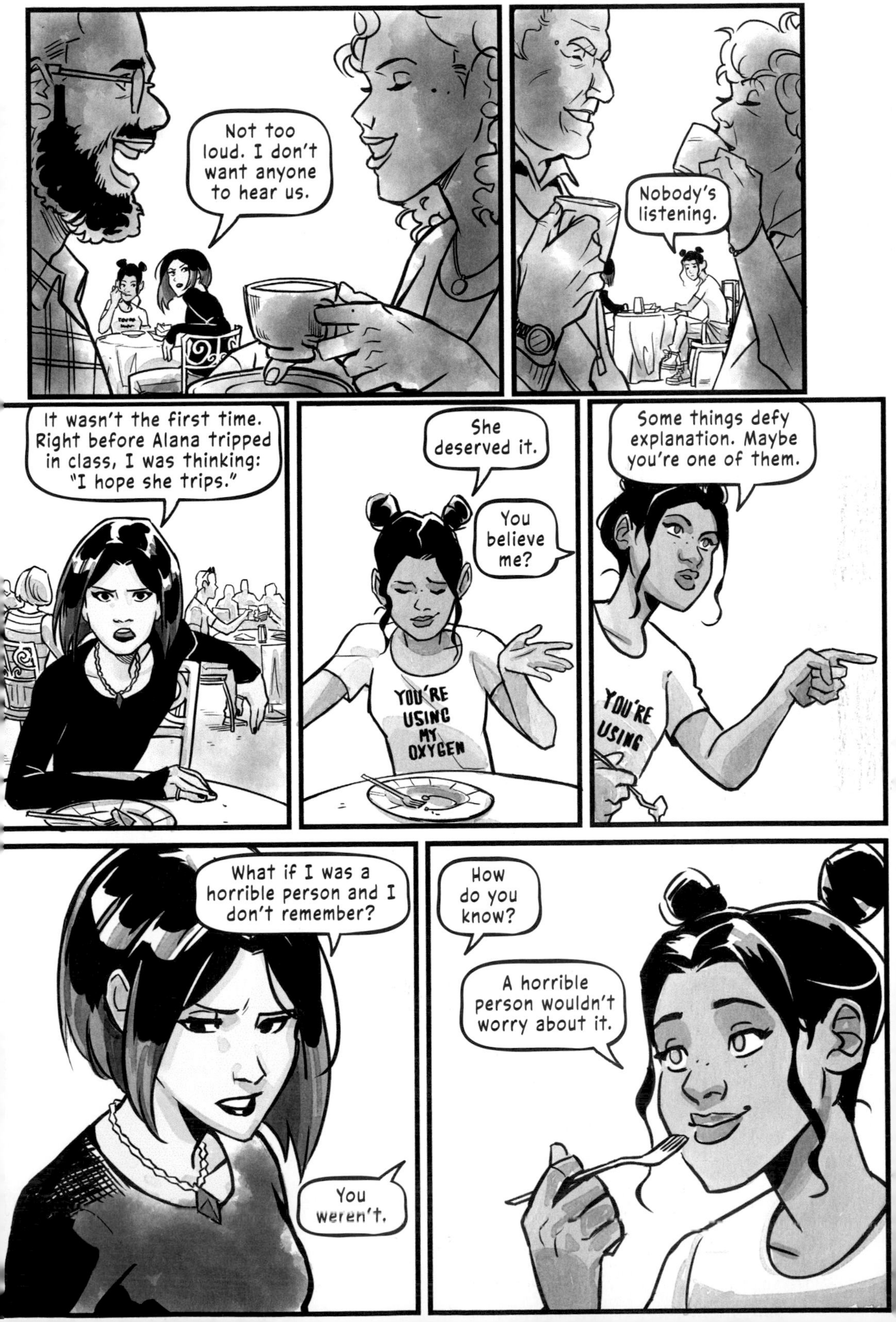
Not too loud. I don't want anyone to hear us.
Nobody's listening.
It wasn't the first time. Right before Alana tripped in class, I was thinking: "I hope she trips."
She deserved it.
You believe me?
YOU'RE USING MY OXYGEN
Some things defy explanation. Maybe you're one of them.
YOU'RE USING
What if I was a horrible person and I don't remember?
You weren't.
How do you know?
A horrible person wouldn't worry about it.

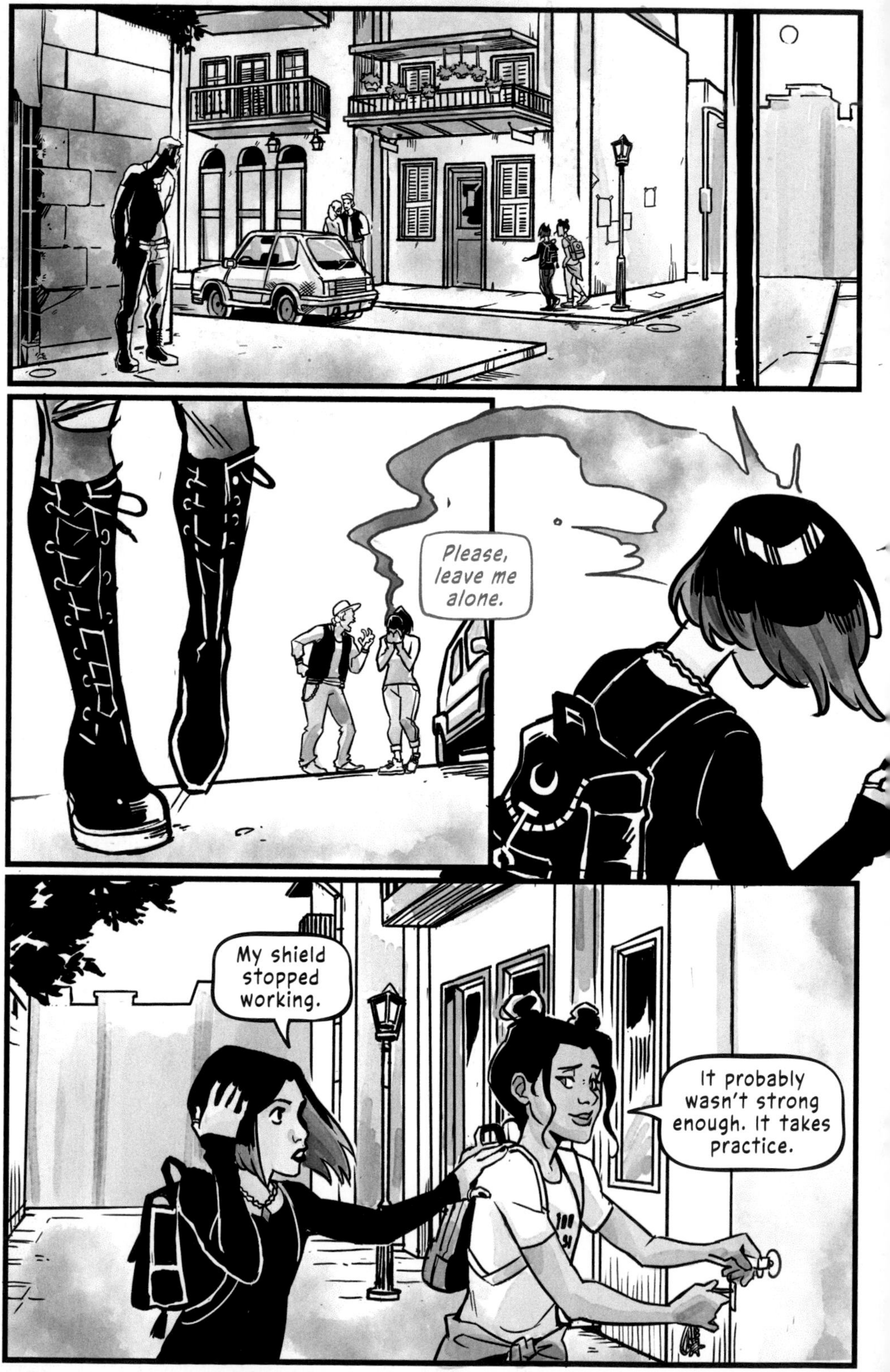
Please, leave me alone.
My shield stopped working.
It probably wasn't strong enough. It takes practice.

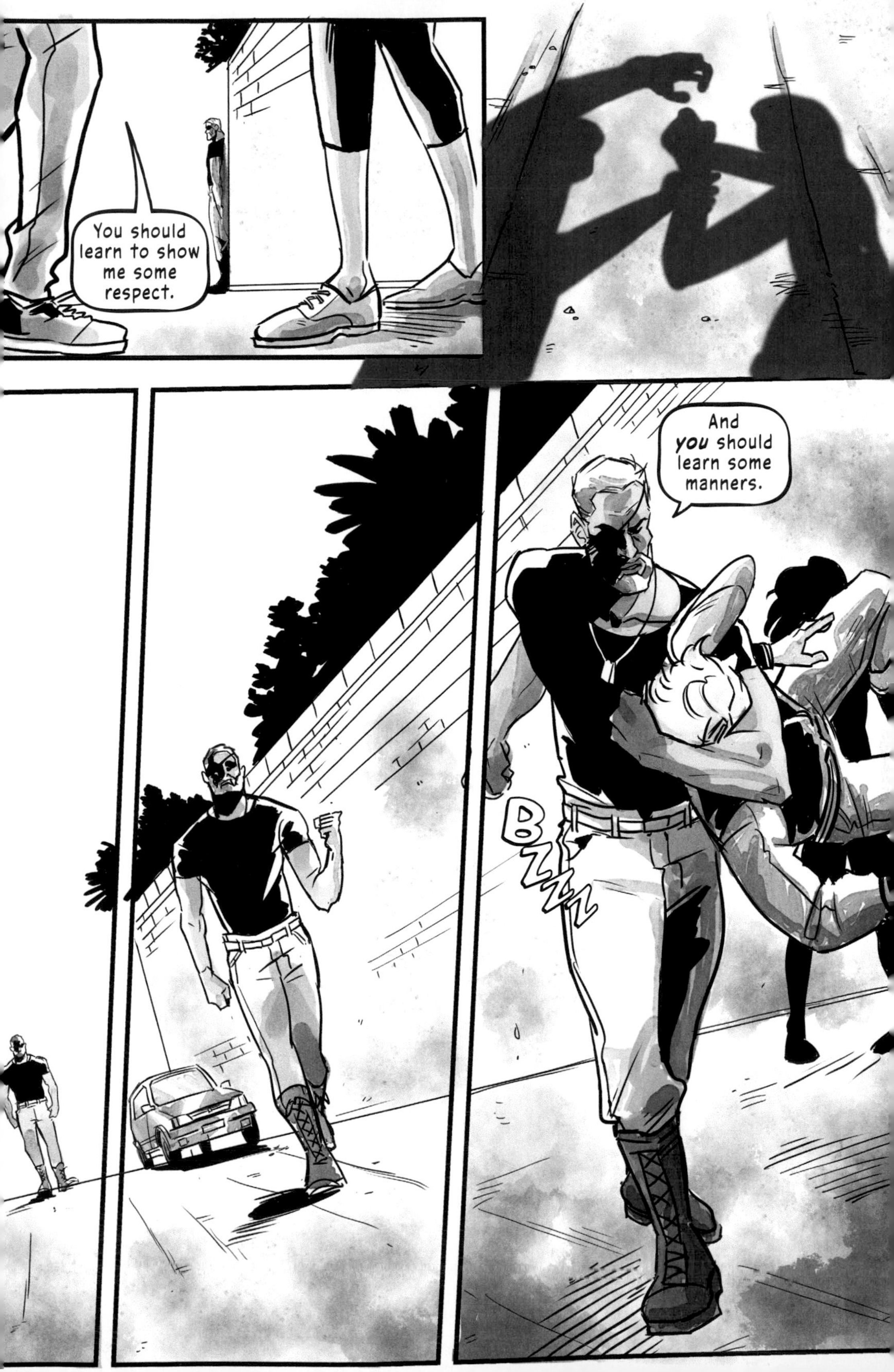
You should learn to show me some respect.
And *you* should learn some manners.
BZZZ

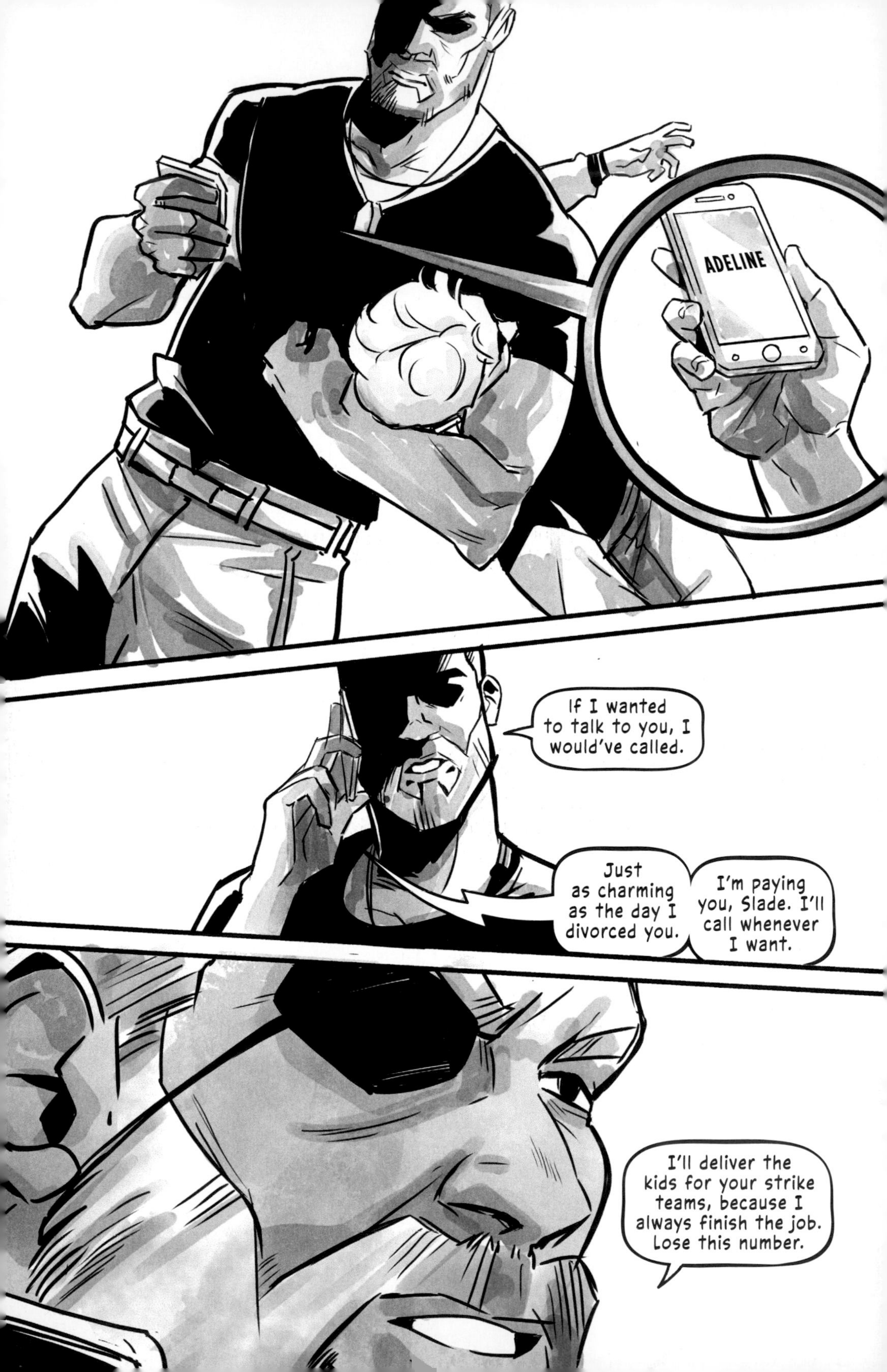
ADELINE
If I wanted to talk to you, I would've called.
Just as charming as the day I divorced you.
I'm paying you, Slade. I'll call whenever I want.
I'll deliver the kids for your strike teams, because I always finish the job. Lose this number.

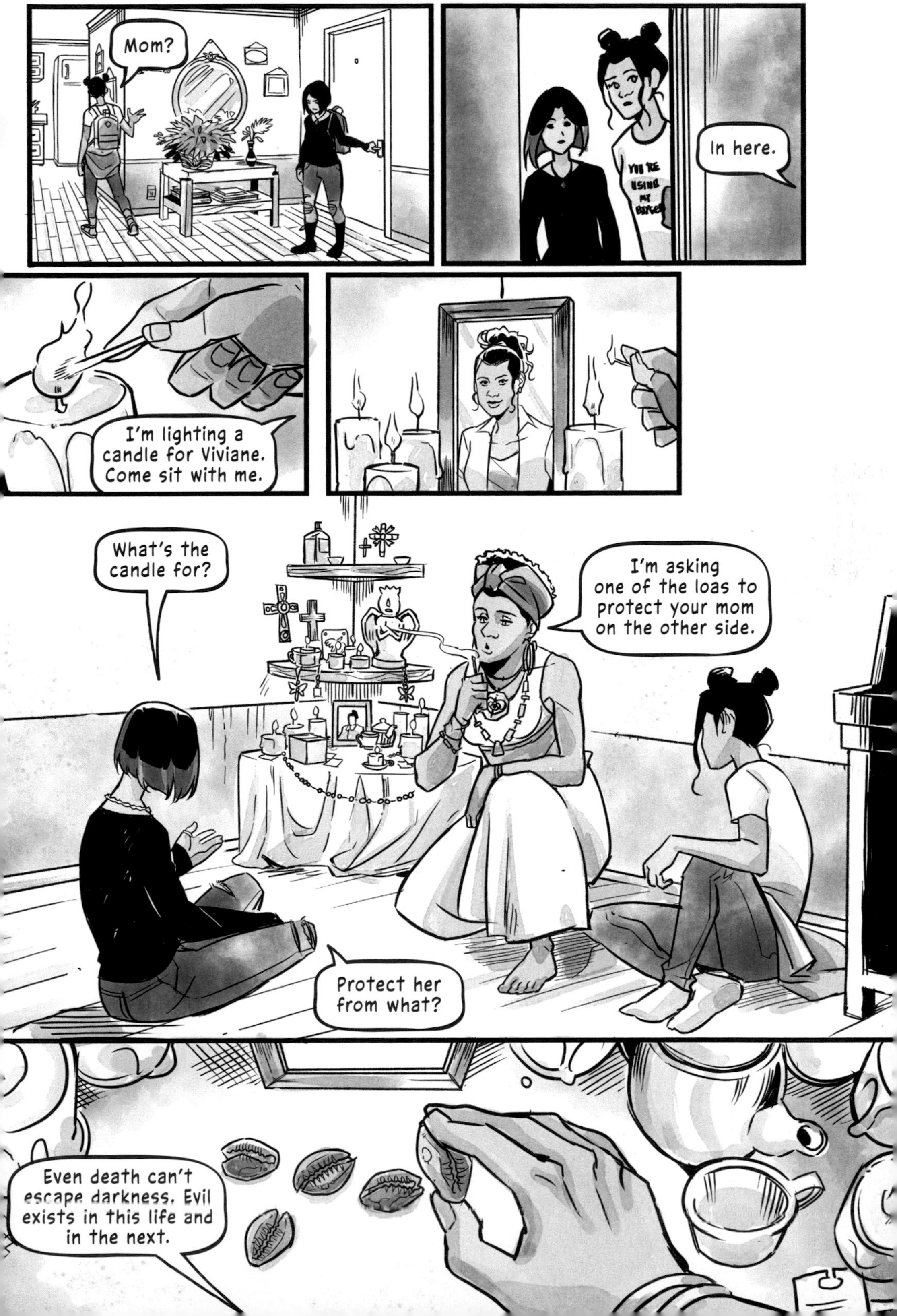
Mom?
In here.
I'm lighting a candle for Viviane. Come sit with me.
What's the candle for?
I'm asking one of the loas to protect your mom on the other side.
Protect her from what?
Even death can't escape darkness. Evil exists in this life and in the next.

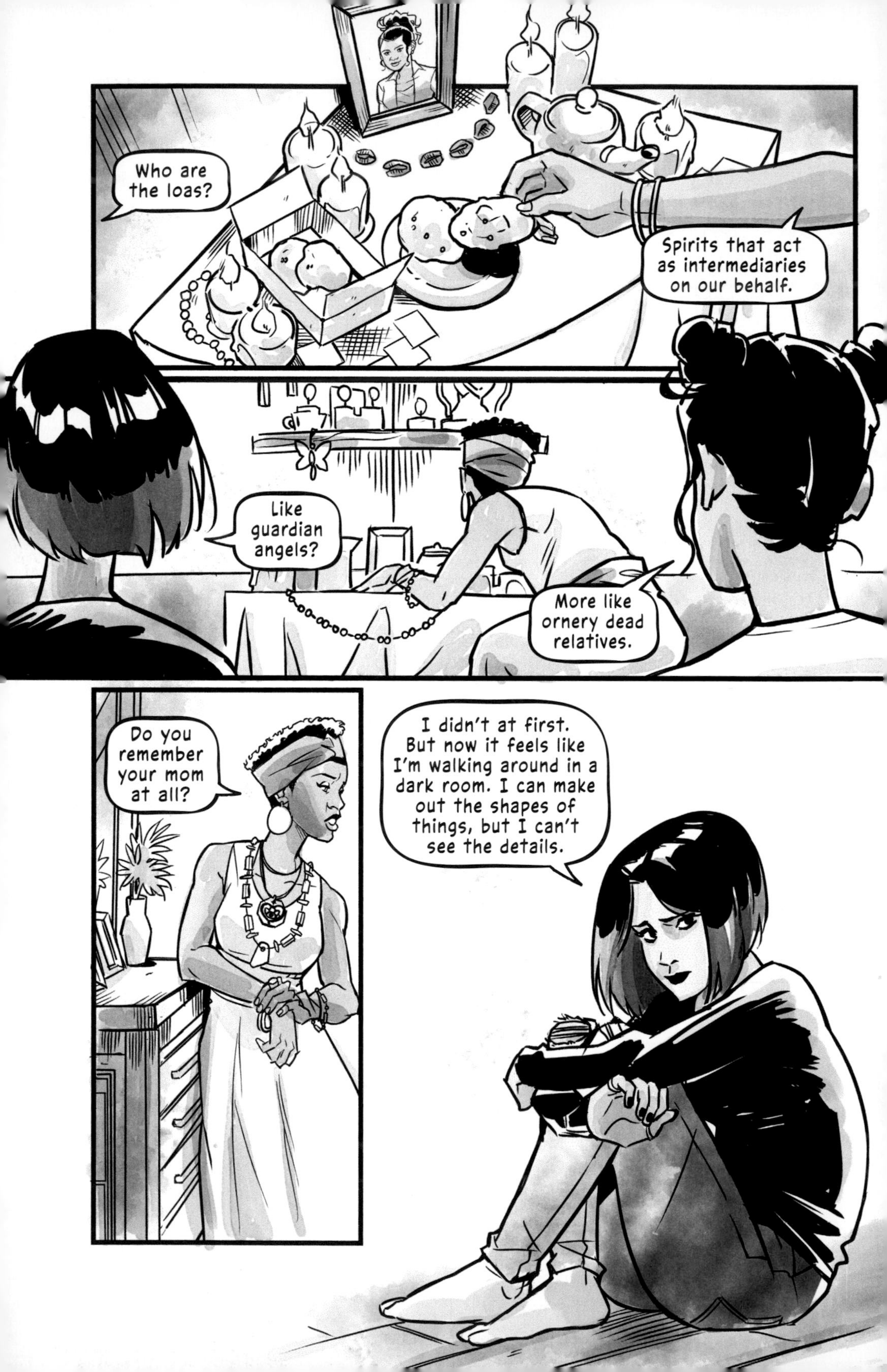
Who are the loas?
Spirits that act as intermediaries on our behalf.
Like guardian angels?
More like ornery dead relatives.
Do you remember your mom at all?
I didn't at first. But now it feels like I'm walking around in a dark room. I can make out the shapes of things, but I can't see the details.

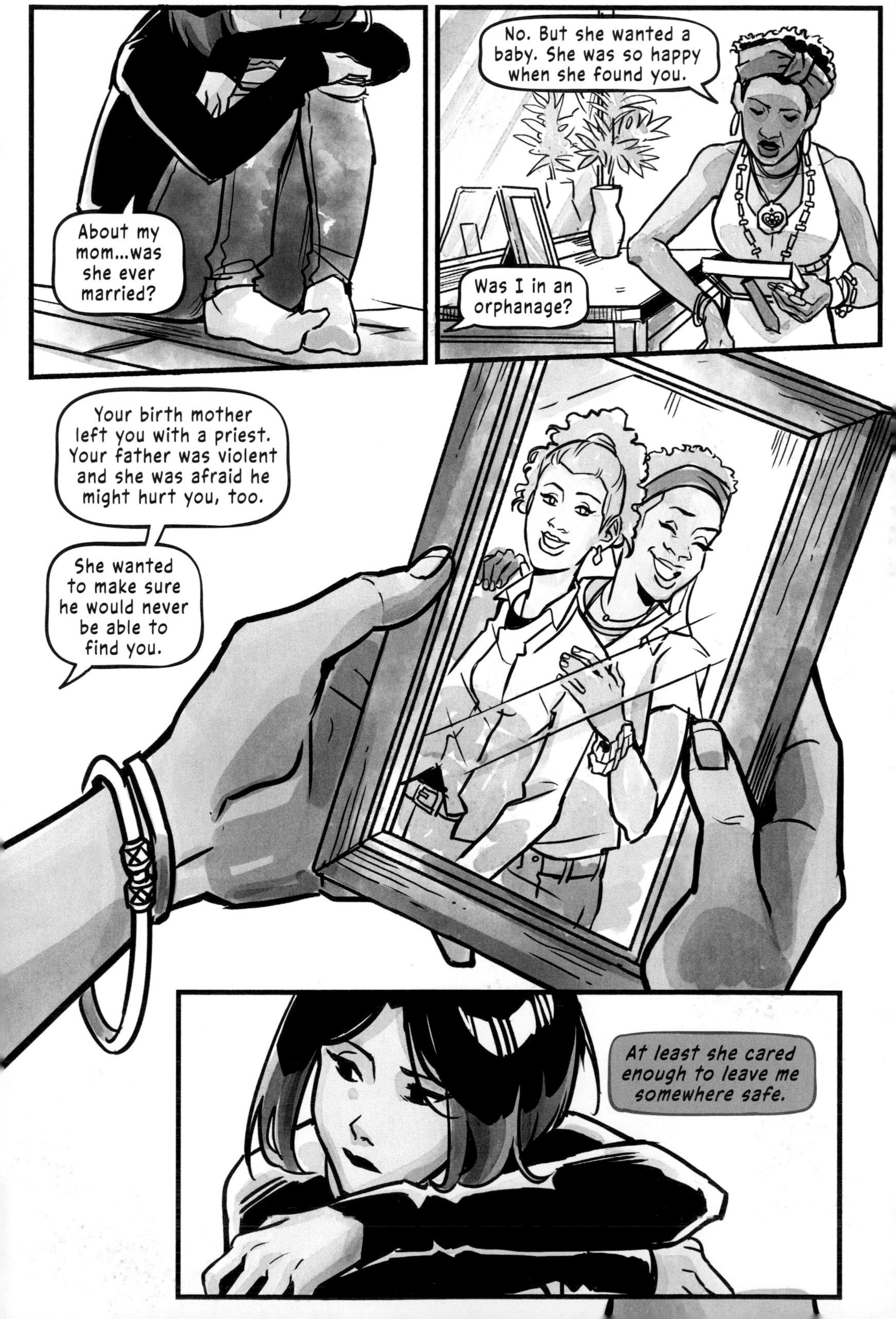
About my mom...was she ever married?
No. But she wanted a baby. She was so happy when she found you.
Was I in an orphanage?
Your birth mother left you with a priest. Your father was violent and she was afraid he might hurt you, too.
She wanted to make sure he would never be able to find you.
At least she cared enough to leave me somewhere safe.

CHAPTER 9: SWEET DREAMS

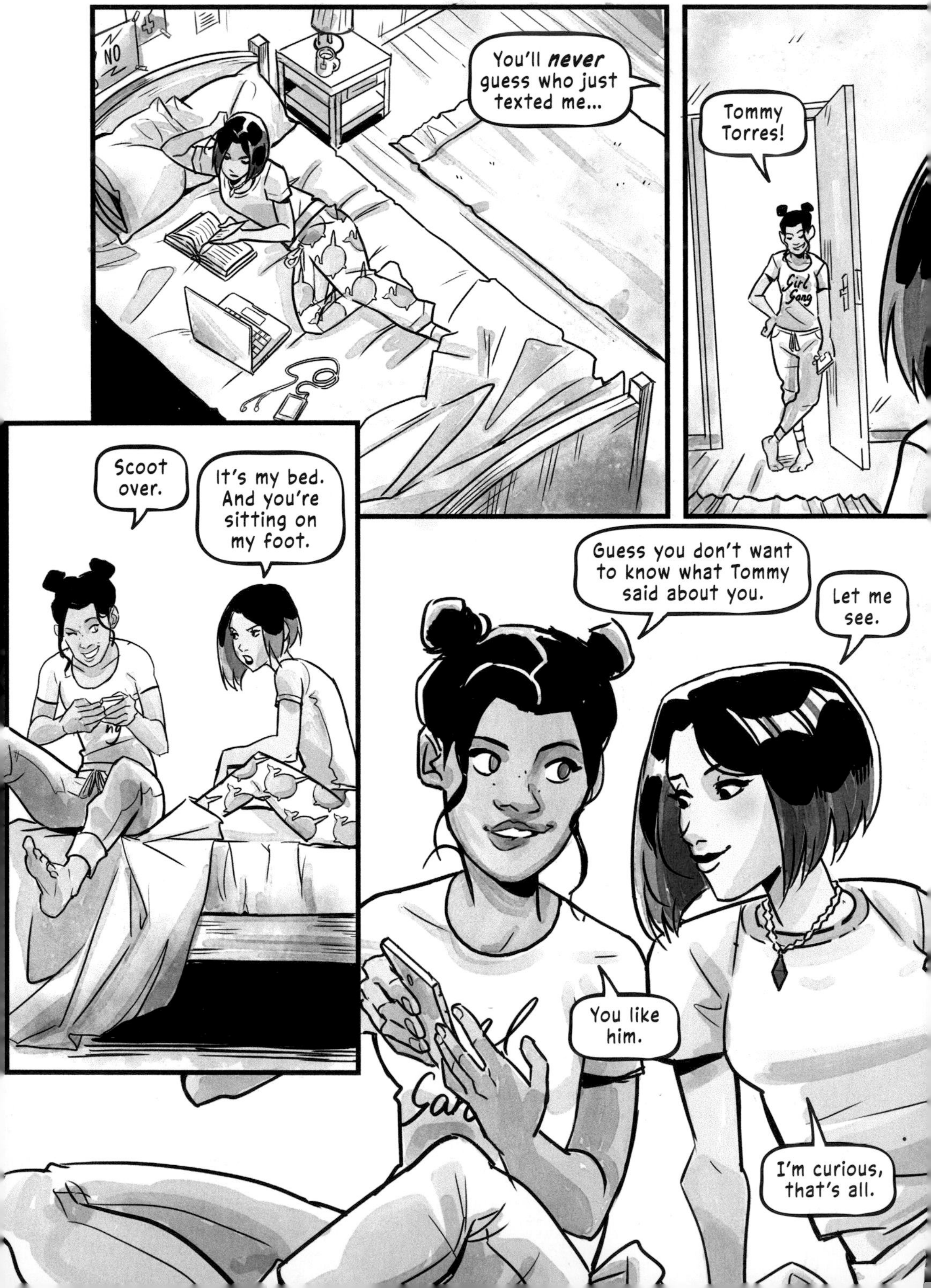
NO
You'll *never* guess who just texted me...
Tommy Torres!
Girl Gang
Scoot over.
It's my bed. And you're sitting on my foot.
Guess you don't want to know what Tommy said about you.
Let me see.
You like him.
I'm curious, that's all.

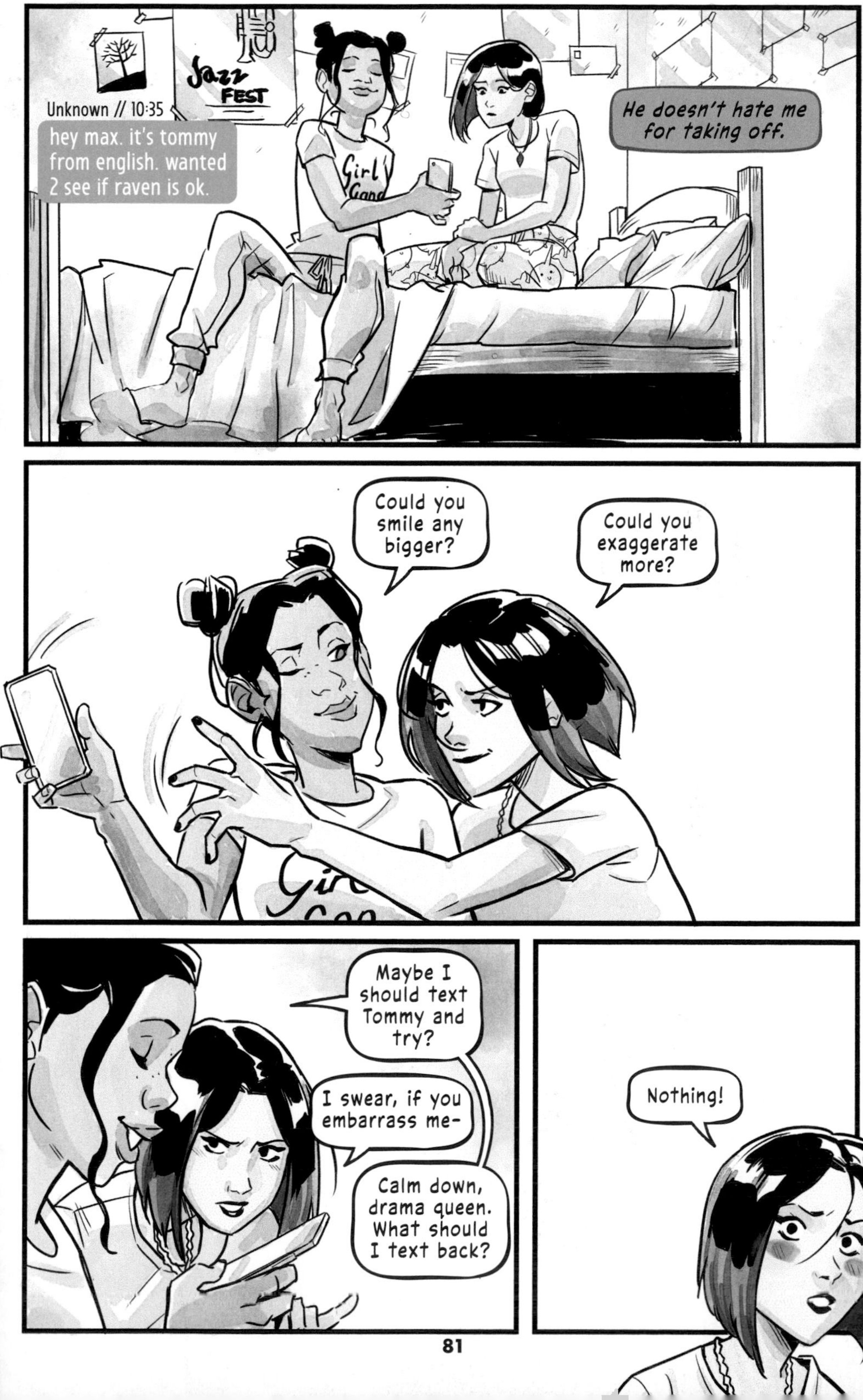
Jazz FEST
Unknown // 10:35
hey max. it's tommy from english. wanted 2 see if raven is ok.
He doesn't hate me for taking off.
Girl Gang
Could you smile any bigger?
Could you exaggerate more?
Maybe I should text Tommy and try?
I swear, if you embarrass me-
Calm down, drama queen. What should I text back?
Nothing!

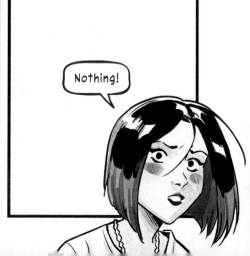

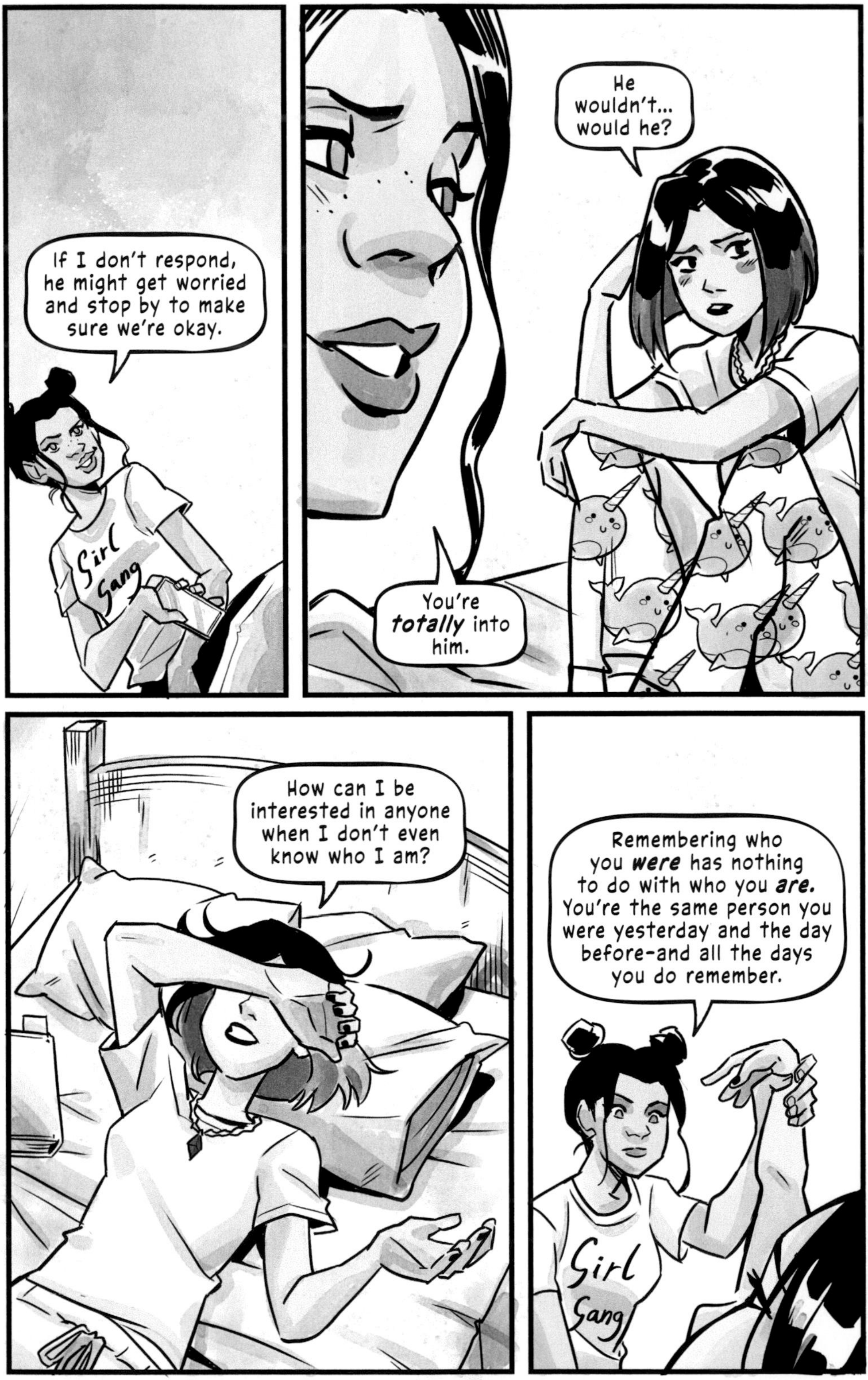
If I don't respond, he might get worried and stop by to make sure we're okay.
Girl Gang
He wouldn't... would he?
You're *totally* into him.
How can I be interested in anyone when I don't even know who I am?
Remembering who you *were* has nothing to do with who you *are.* You're the same person you were yesterday and the day before-and all the days you do remember.
Girl Gang

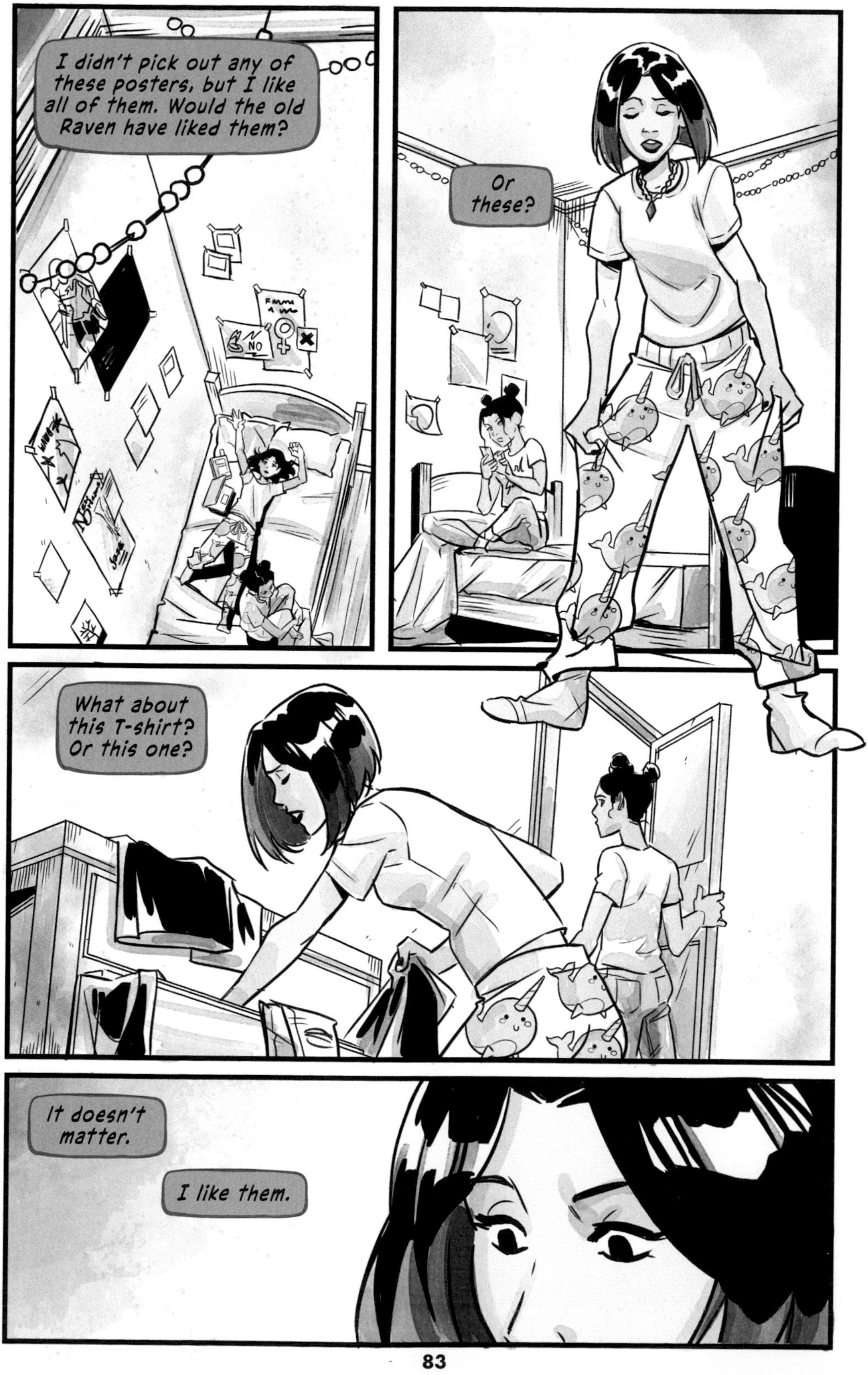
I didn't pick out any of these posters, but I like all of them. Would the old Raven have liked them?
Or these?
What about this T-shirt? Or this one?
It doesn't matter.
I like them.

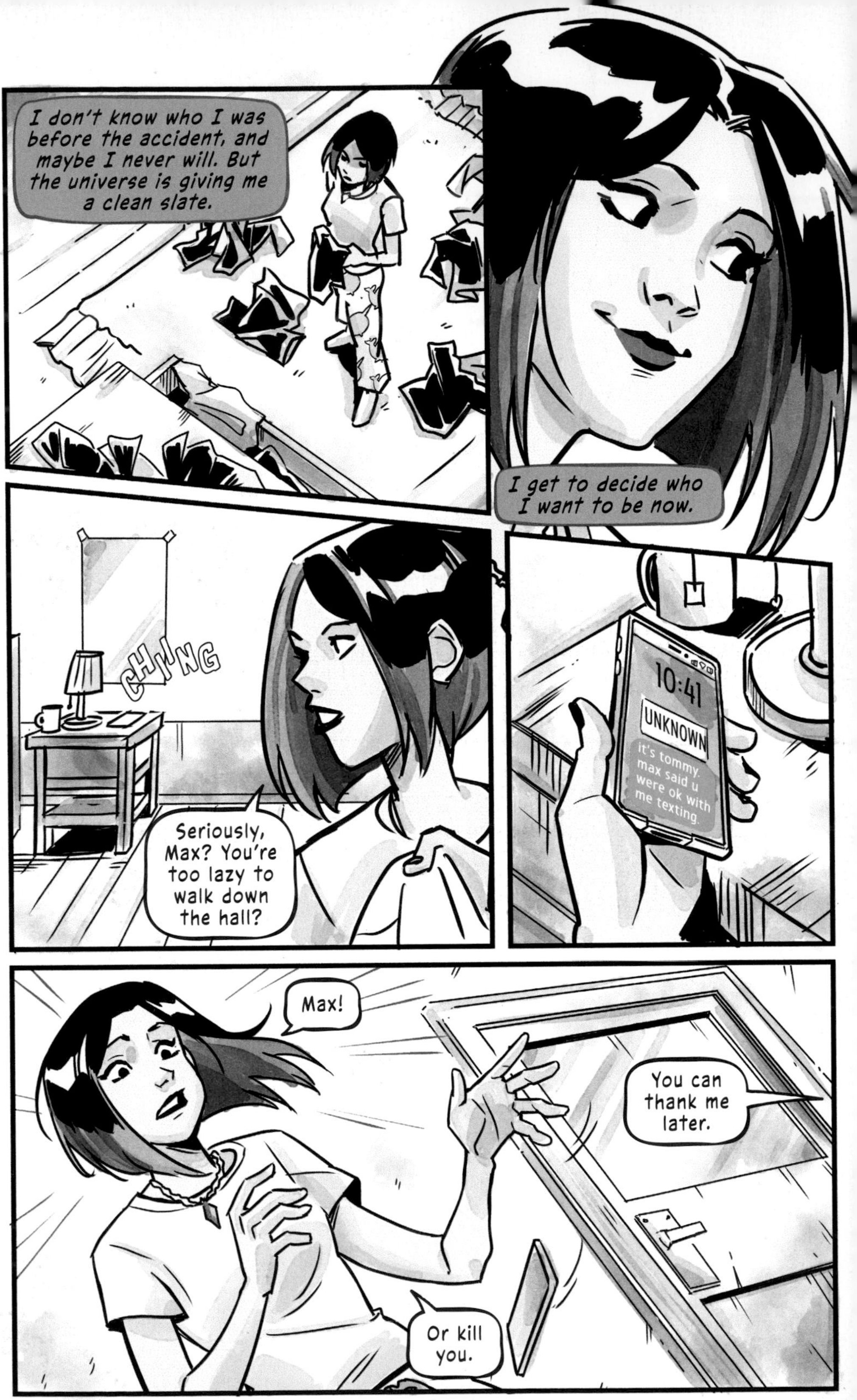
I don't know who I was before the accident, and maybe I never will. But the universe is giving me a clean slate.
I get to decide who I want to be now.
CHING
Seriously, Max? You're too lazy to walk down the hall?
10:41
UNKNOWN
it's tommy. max said u were ok with me texting.
Max!
You can thank me later.
Or kill you.

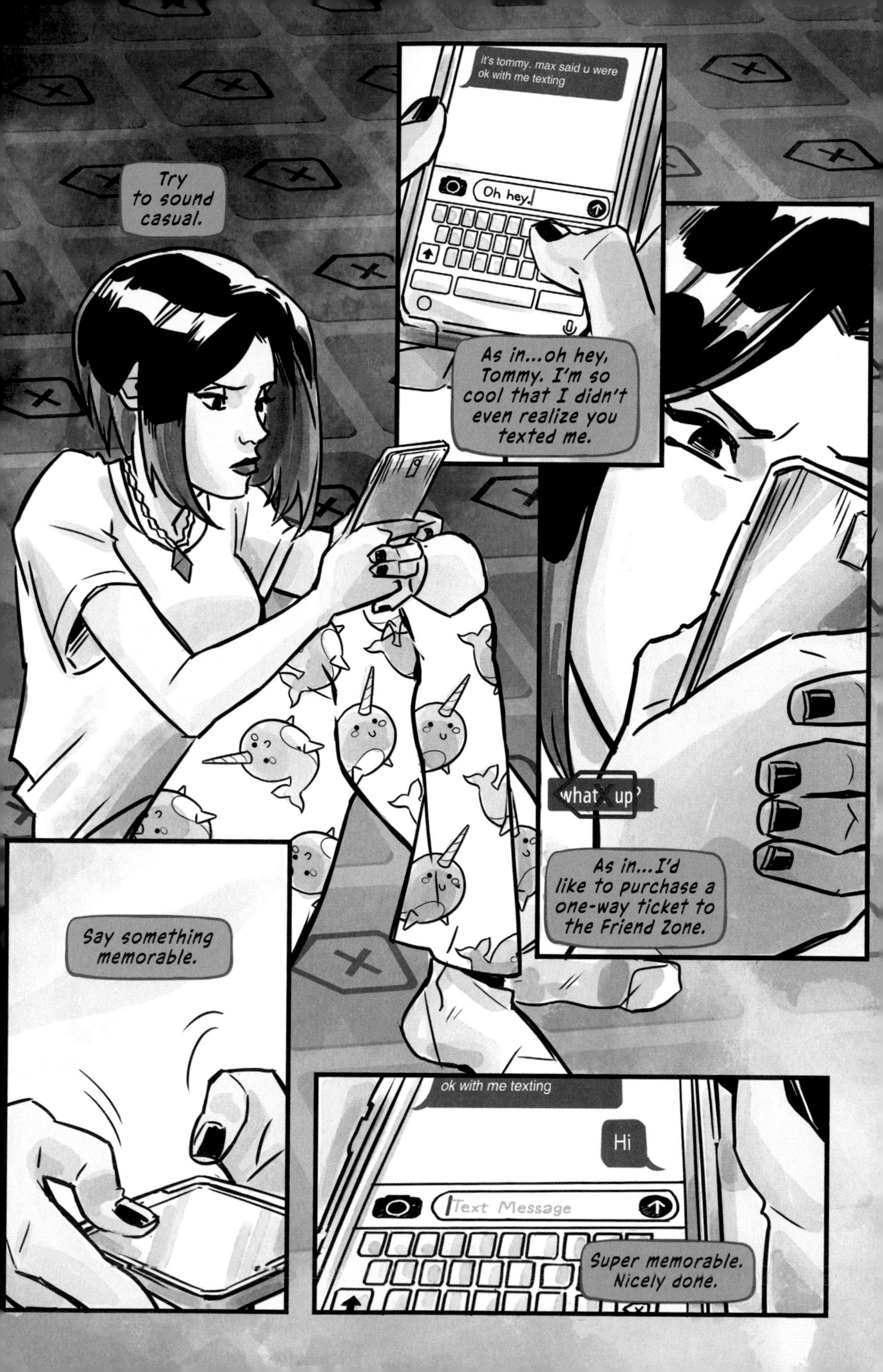
Try to sound casual.
it's tommy. max said u were ok with me texting
Oh hey.
As in...oh hey, Tommy. I'm so cool that I didn't even realize you texted me.
what up?
As in...I'd like to purchase a one-way ticket to the Friend Zone.
Say something memorable.
ok with me texting
Hi
Text Message
Super memorable. Nicely done.

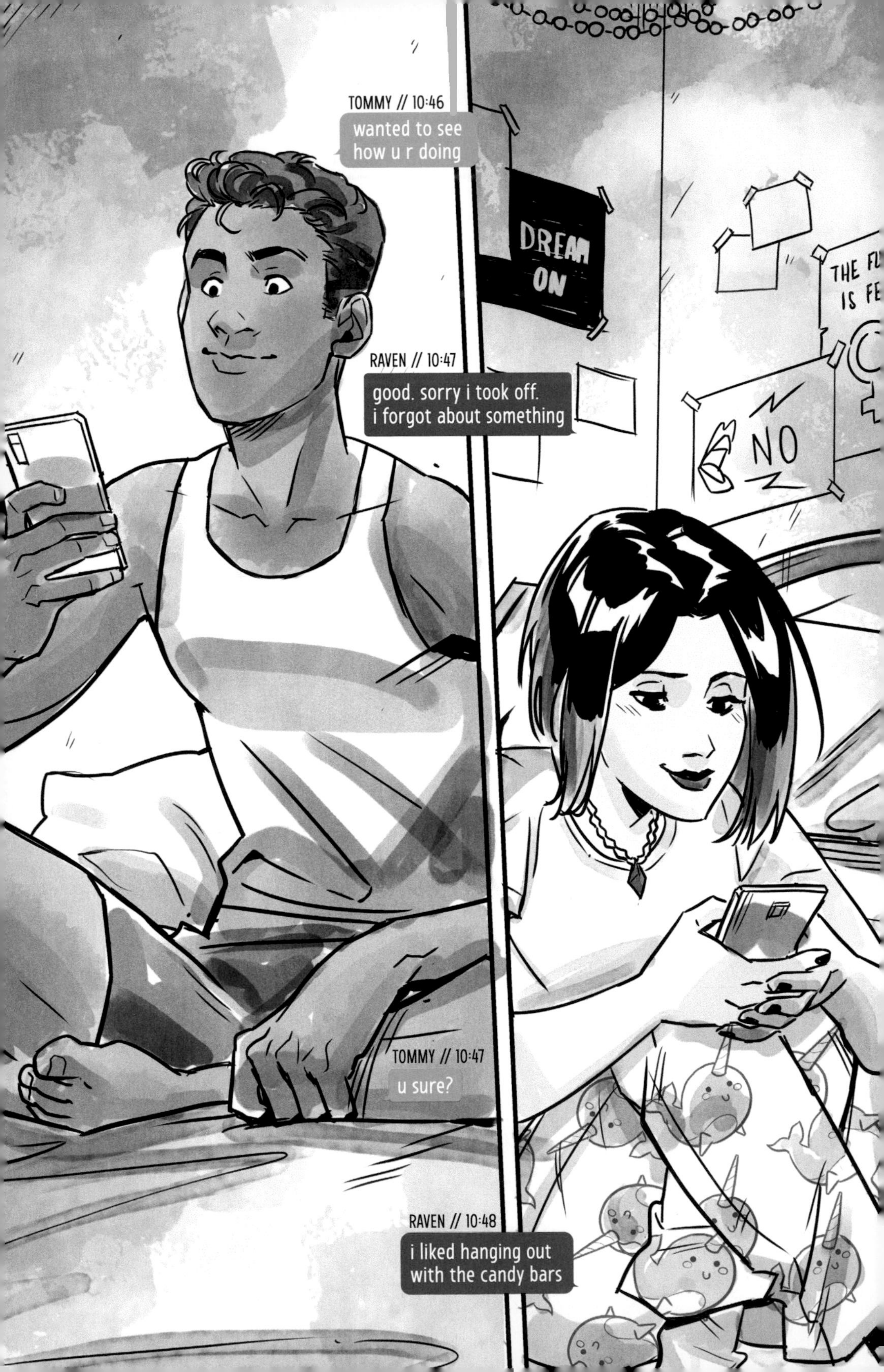
TOMMY // 10:46
wanted to see how u r doing
DREAM ON
RAVEN // 10:47
good. sorry i took off. i forgot about something
NO
TOMMY // 10:47
u sure?
RAVEN // 10:48
i liked hanging out with the candy bars

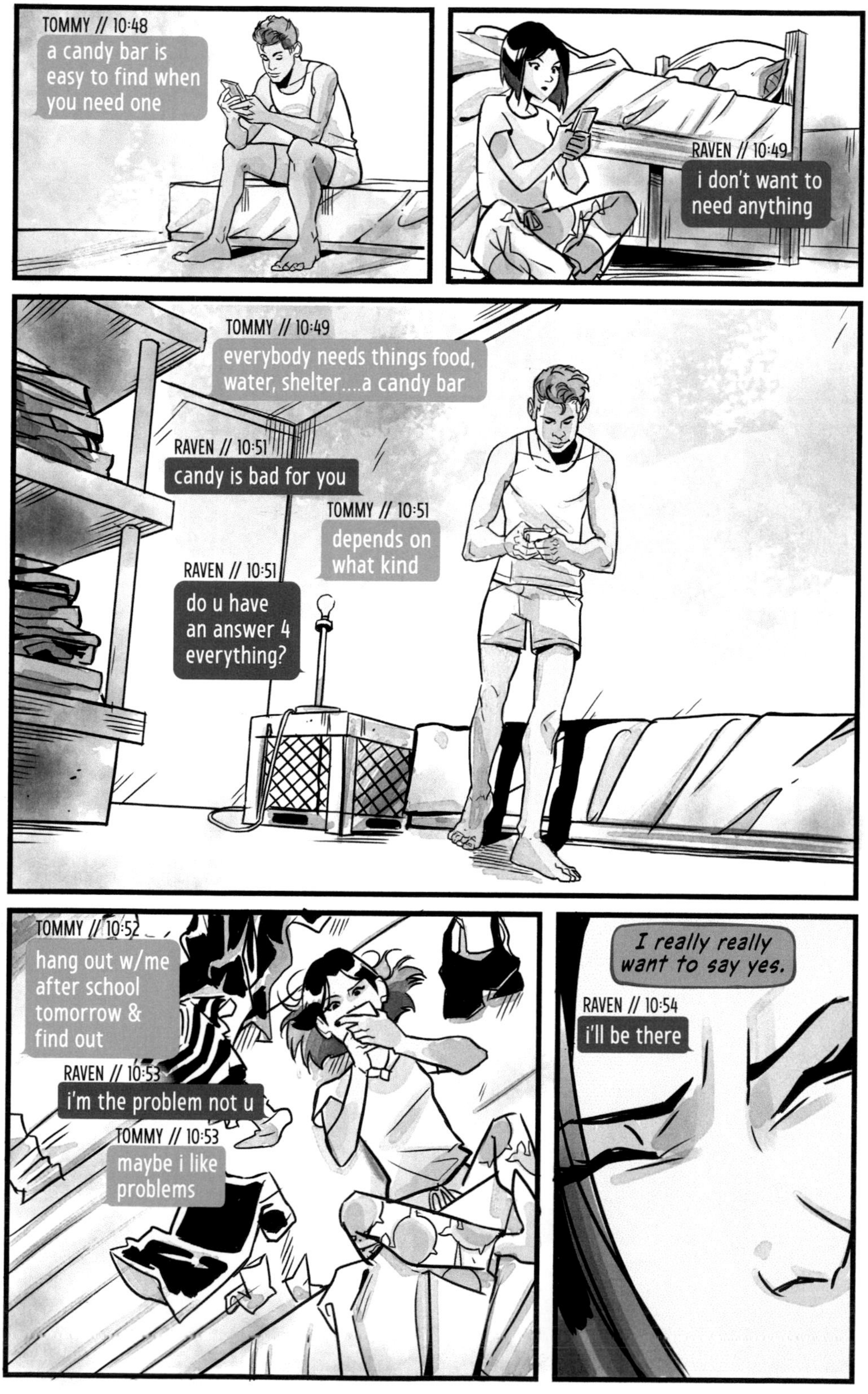
TOMMY // 10:48
a candy bar is easy to find when you need one
RAVEN // 10:49
i don't want to need anything
TOMMY // 10:49
everybody needs things food, water, shelter....a candy bar
RAVEN // 10:51
candy is bad for you
TOMMY // 10:51
depends on what kind
RAVEN // 10:51
do u have an answer 4 everything?
TOMMY // 10:52
hang out w/me after school tomorrow & find out
RAVEN // 10:53
i'm the problem not u
TOMMY // 10:53
maybe i like problems
I really really want to say yes.
RAVEN // 10:54
i'll be there

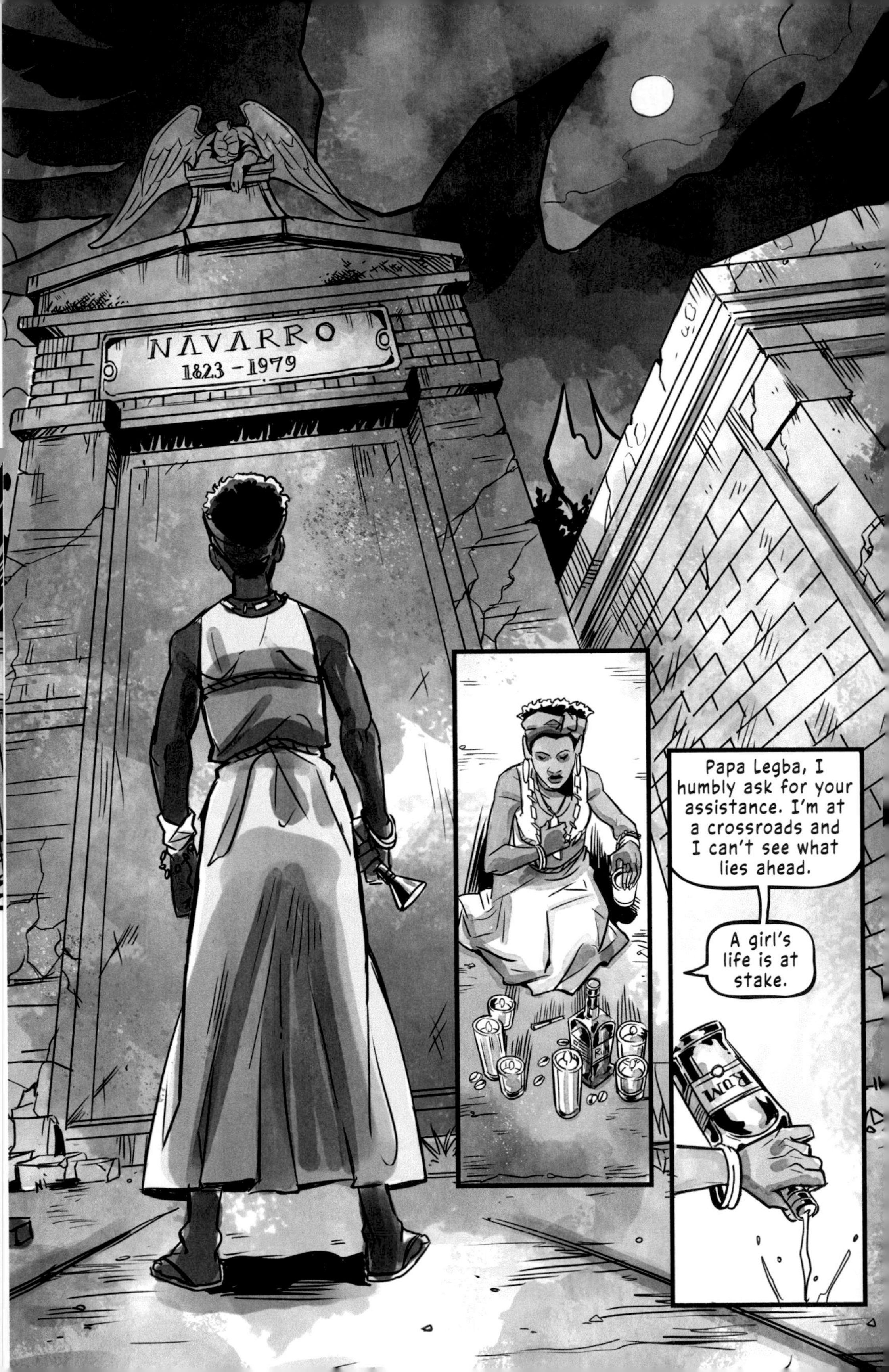
NAVARRO
1823 - 1979
Papa Legba, I humbly ask for your assistance. I'm at a crossroads and I can't see what lies ahead.
A girl's life is at stake.
RUM

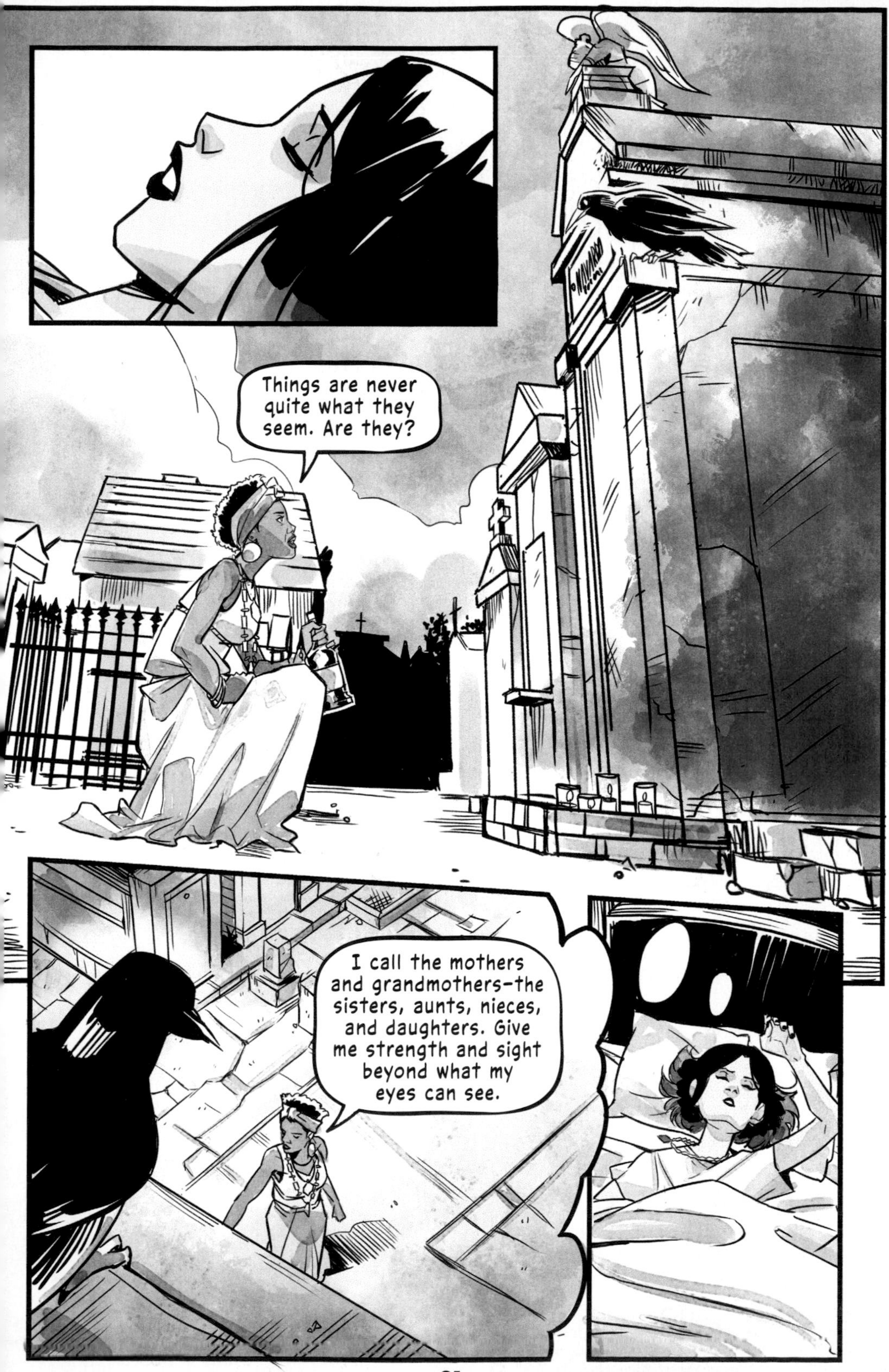
Things are never quite what they seem. Are they?
I call the mothers and grandmothers–the sisters, aunts, nieces, and daughters. Give me strength and sight beyond what my eyes can see.

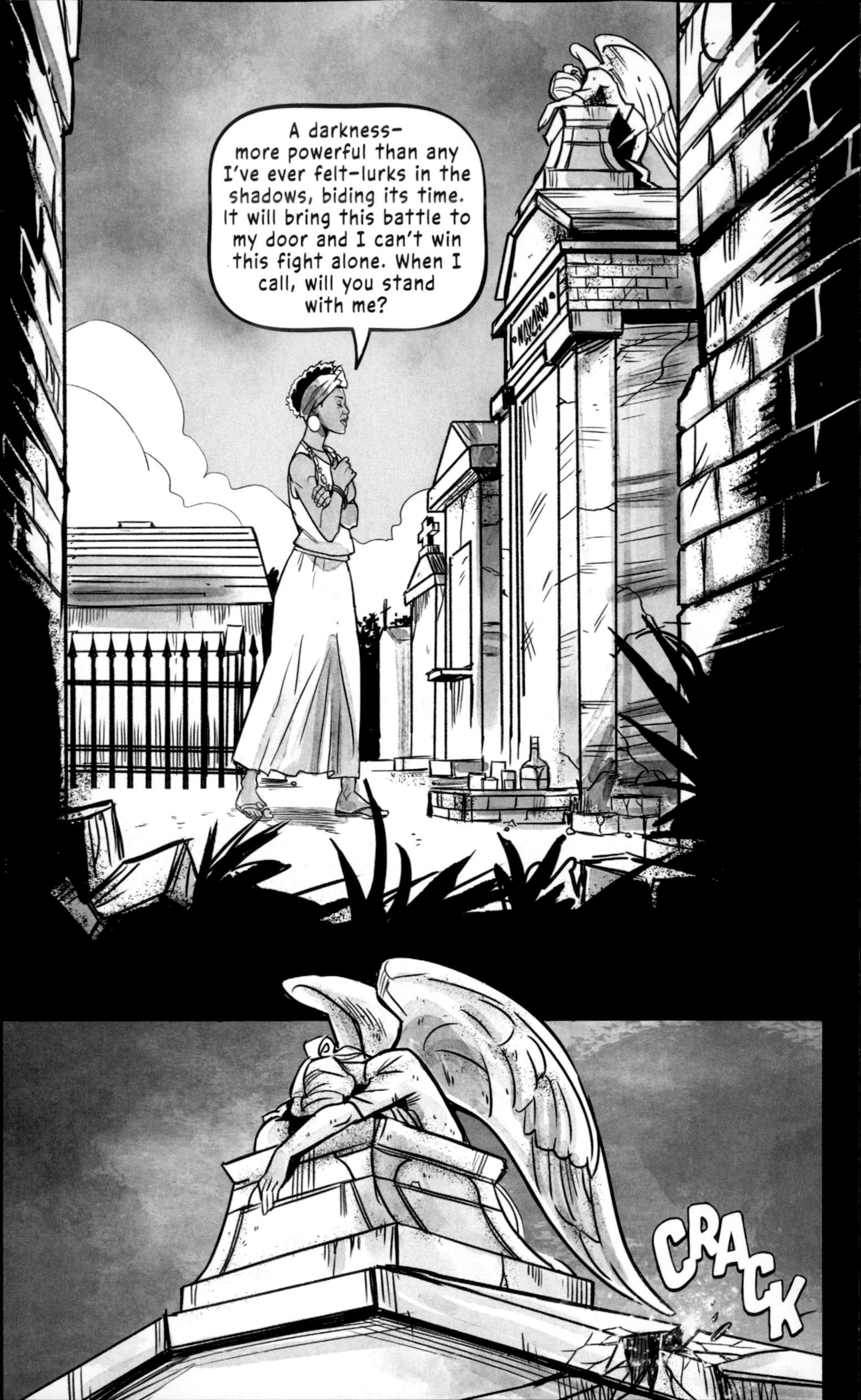
A darkness—more powerful than any I've ever felt—lurks in the shadows, biding its time. It will bring this battle to my door and I can't win this fight alone. When I call, will you stand with me?
CRACK

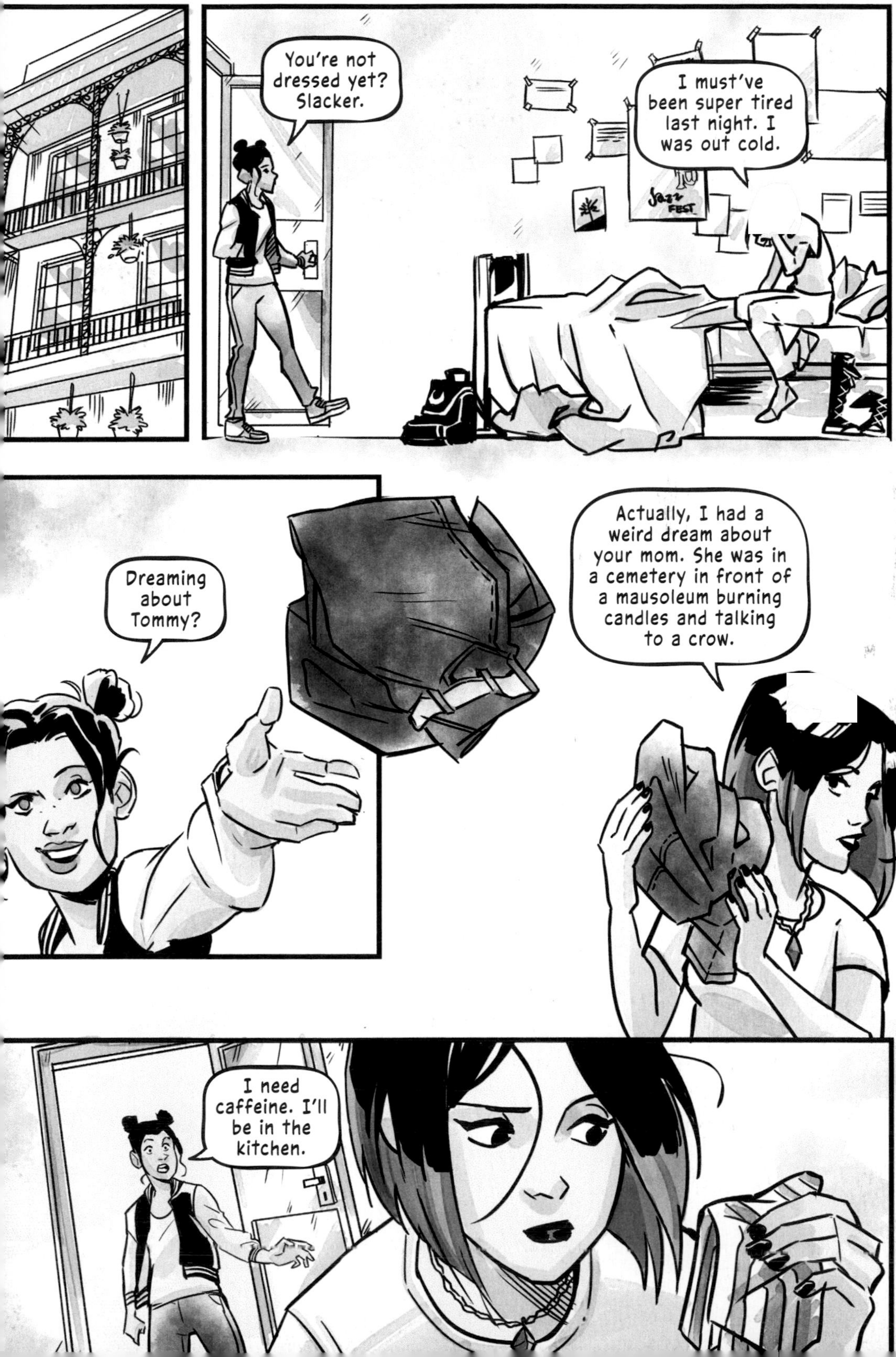
You're not dressed yet? Slacker.
I must've been super tired last night. I was out cold.
Jazz Fest
Dreaming about Tommy?
Actually, I had a weird dream about your mom. She was in a cemetery in front of a mausoleum burning candles and talking to a crow.
I need caffeine. I'll be in the kitchen.

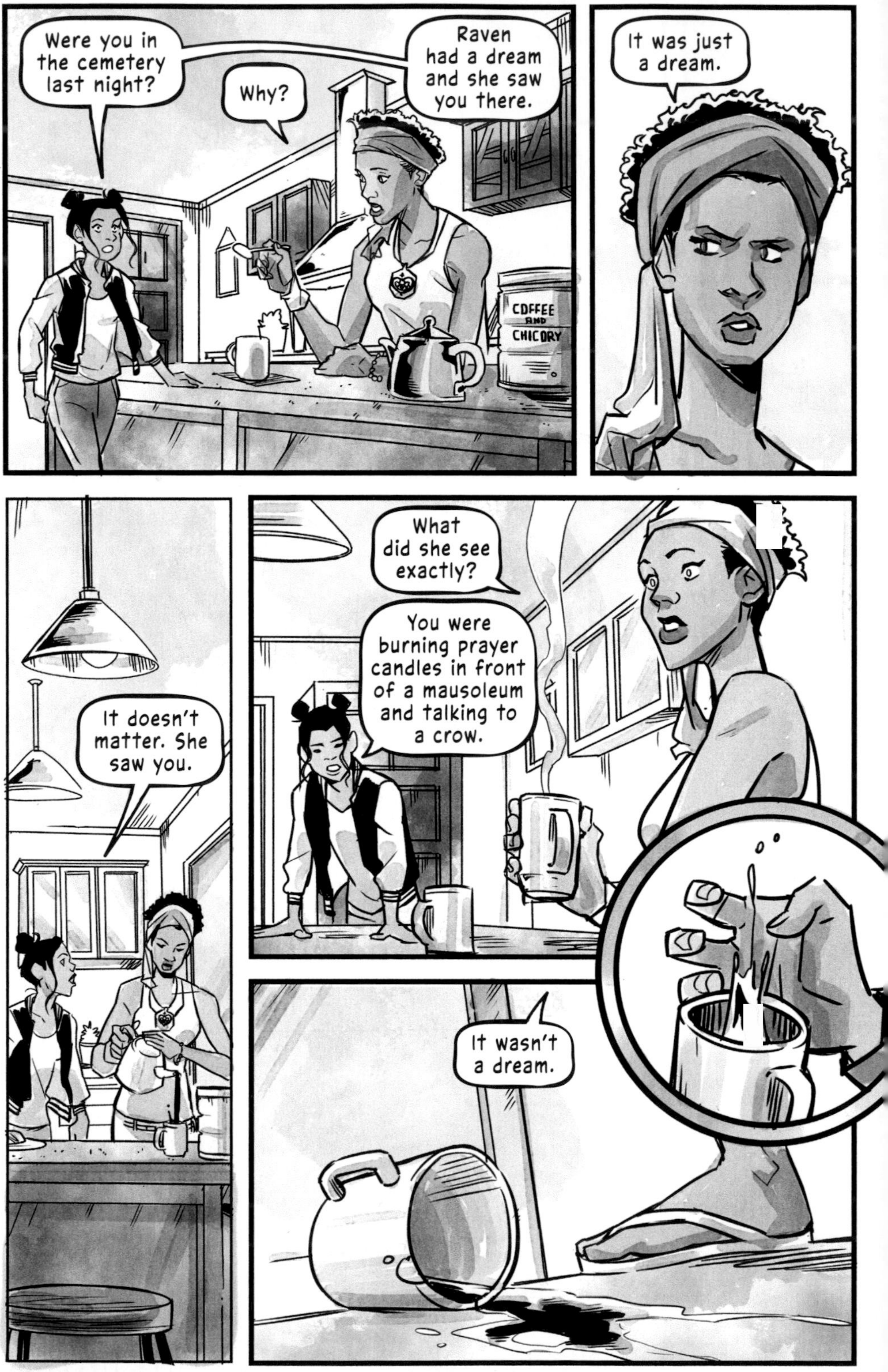
Were you in the cemetery last night?
Why?
Raven had a dream and she saw you there.
COFFEE AND CHICORY
It was just a dream.
It doesn't matter. She saw you.
What did she see exactly?
You were burning prayer candles in front of a mausoleum and talking to a crow.
It wasn't a dream.

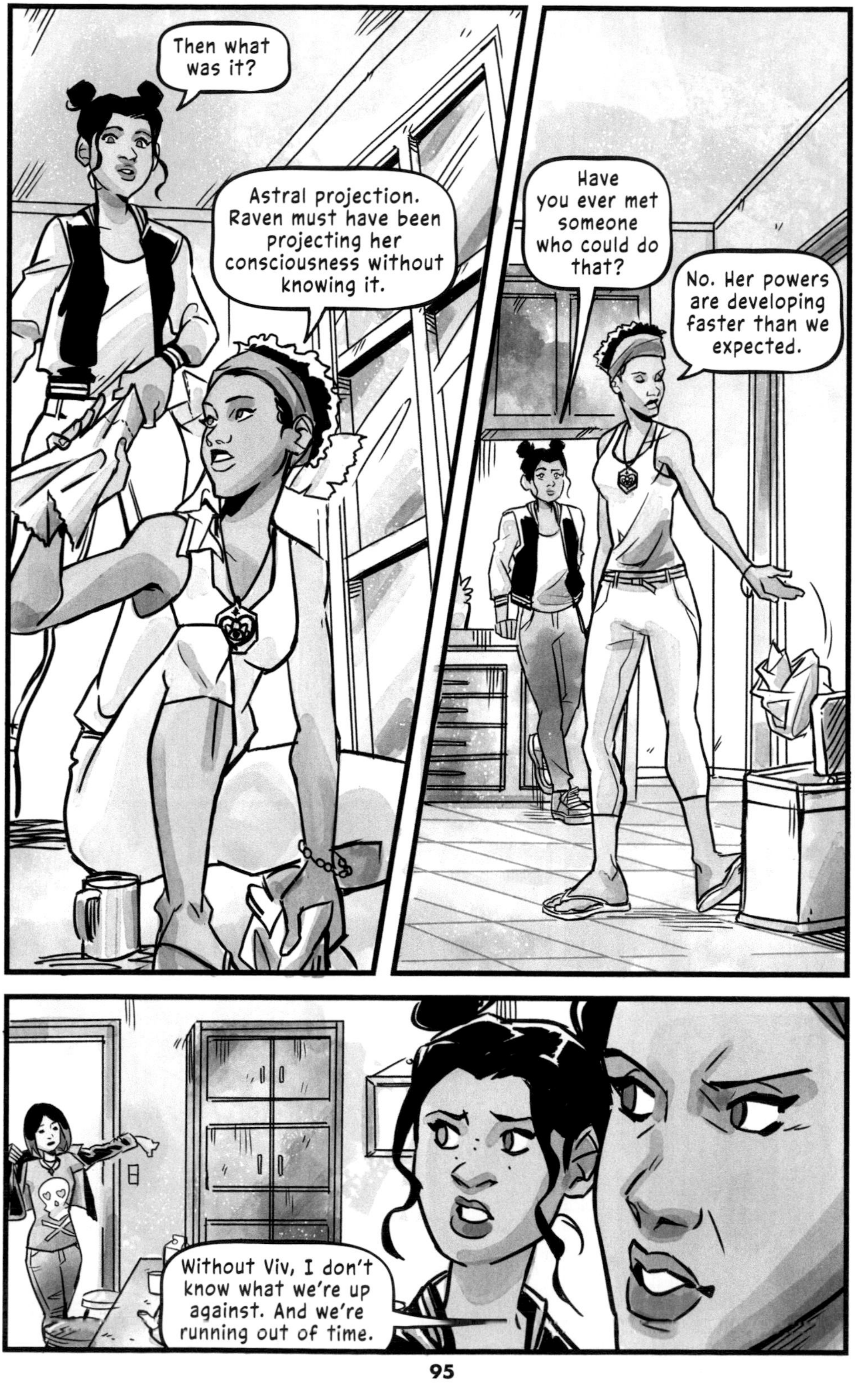
Then what was it?
Astral projection. Raven must have been projecting her consciousness without knowing it.
Have you ever met someone who could do that?
No. Her powers are developing faster than we expected.
Without Viv, I don't know what we're up against. And we're running out of time.

CHAPTER 11: ROSES ARE RED

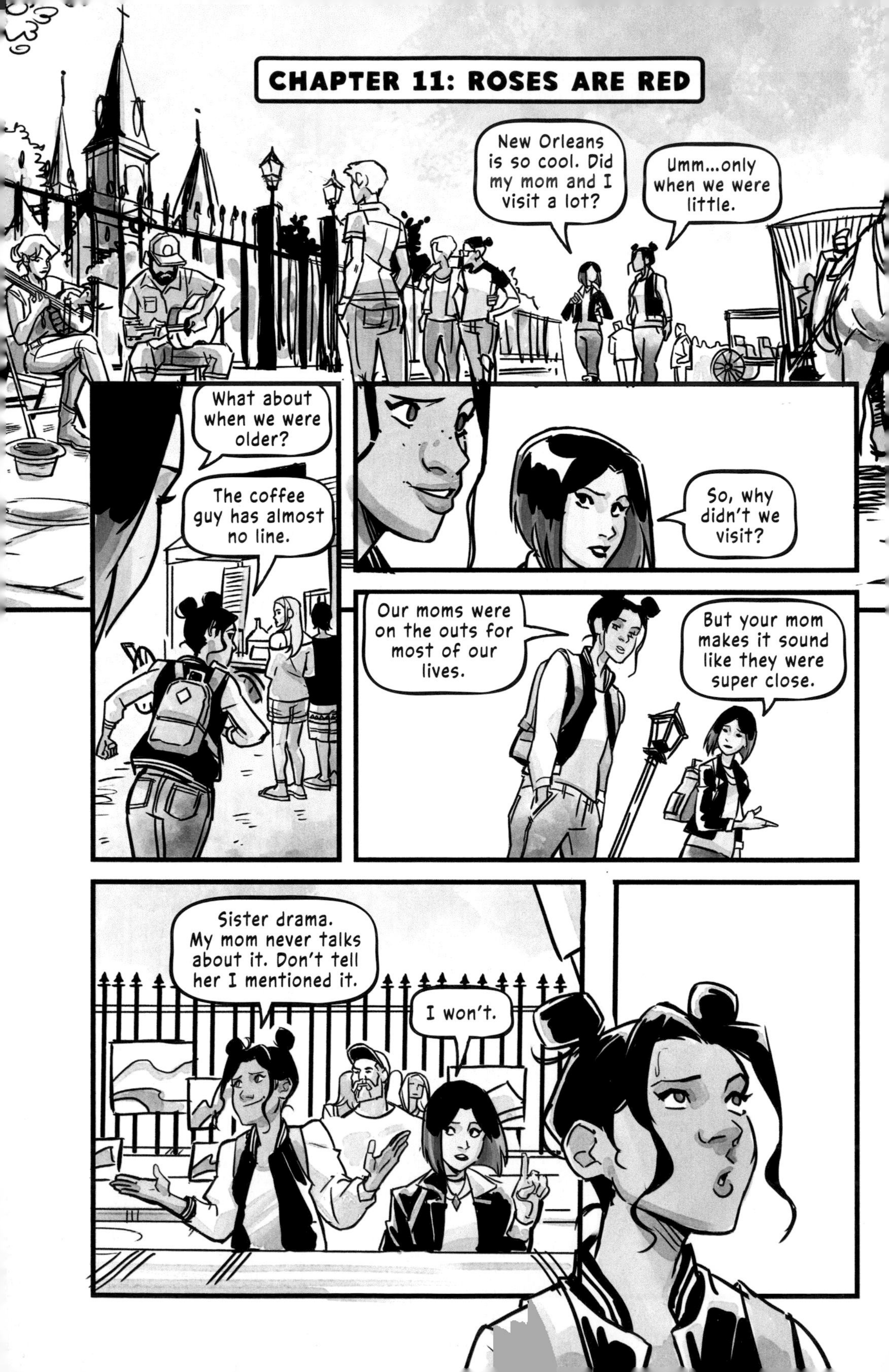
New Orleans is so cool. Did my mom and I visit a lot?
Umm...only when we were little.
What about when we were older?
The coffee guy has almost no line.
So, why didn't we visit?
Our moms were on the outs for most of our lives.
But your mom makes it sound like they were super close.
Sister drama. My mom never talks about it. Don't tell her I mentioned it.
I won't.

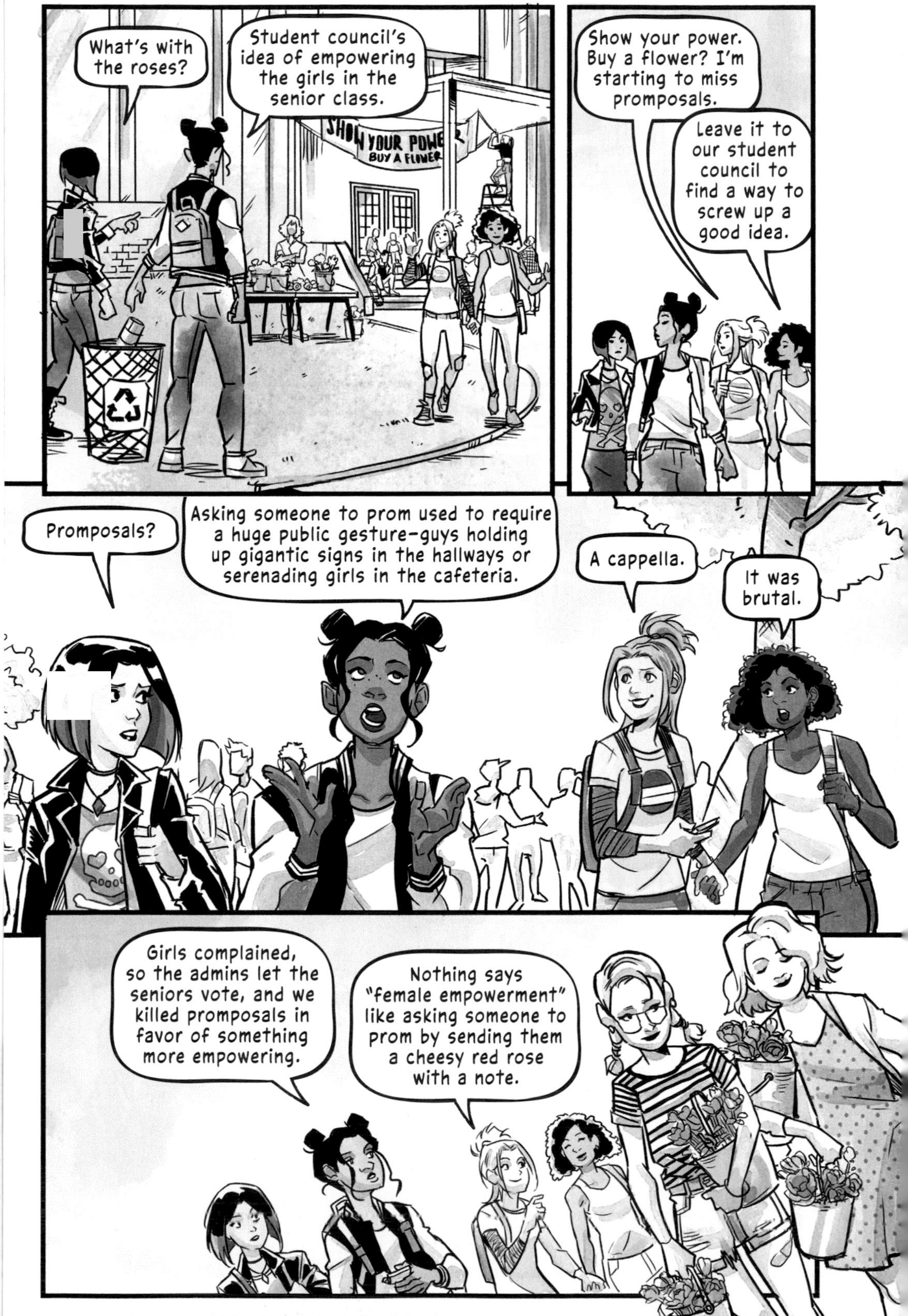
What's with the roses?
Student council's idea of empowering the girls in the senior class.
SHOW YOUR POWE
BUY A FLOWER
Show your power. Buy a flower? I'm starting to miss promposals.
Leave it to our student council to find a way to screw up a good idea.
Promposals?
Asking someone to prom used to require a huge public gesture—guys holding up gigantic signs in the hallways or serenading girls in the cafeteria.
A cappella.
It was brutal.
Girls complained, so the admins let the seniors vote, and we killed promposals in favor of something more empowering.
Nothing says "female empowerment" like asking someone to prom by sending them a cheesy red rose with a note.

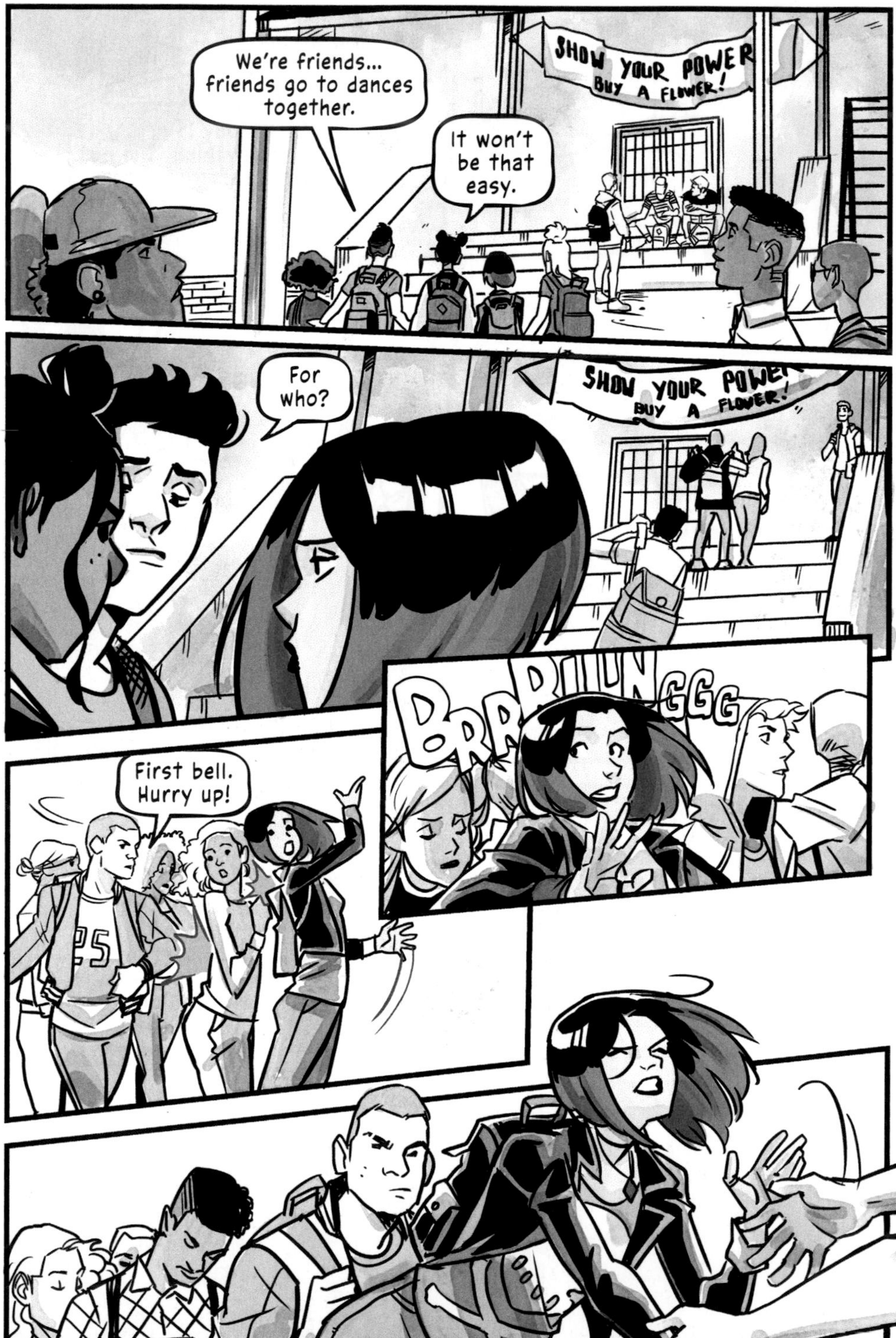

SHOW YOUR POWER
BUY A FLOWER!
We're friends... friends go to dances together.
It won't be that easy.
SHOW YOUR POWER
BUY A FLOWER!
For who?
BRRRIIINGGG
First bell. Hurry up!

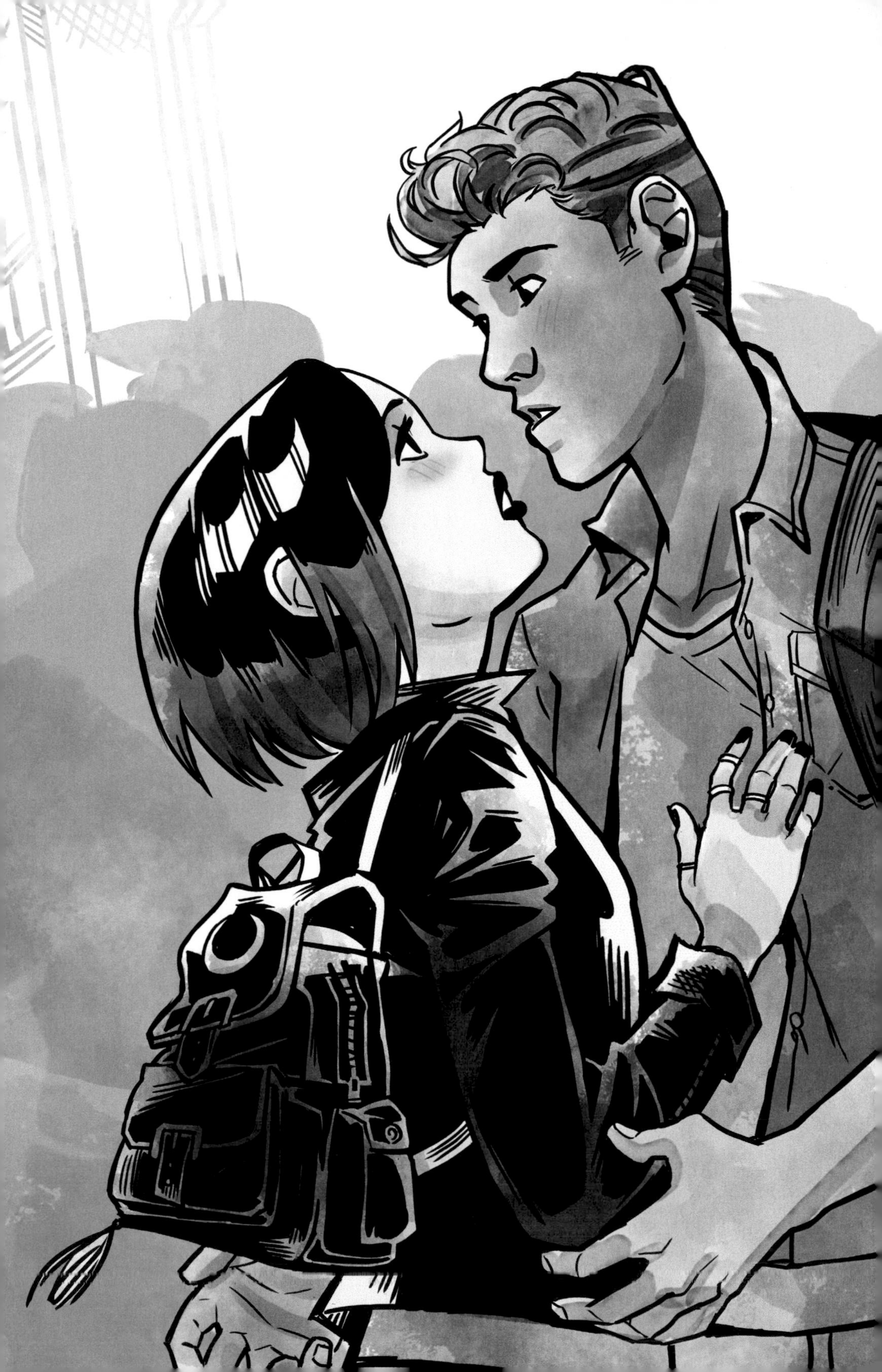

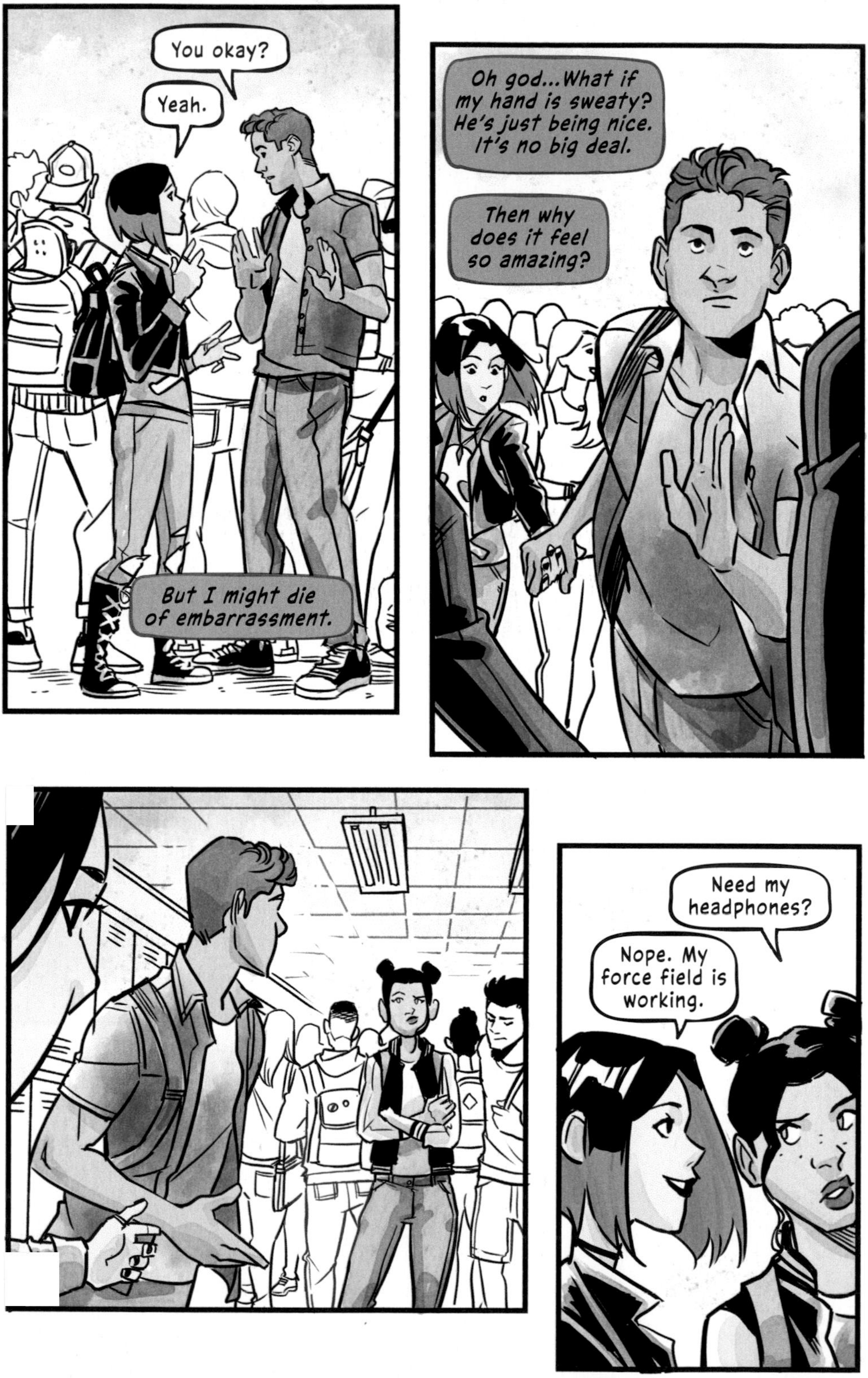
You okay?
Yeah.
But I might die of embarrassment.
Oh god...What if my hand is sweaty? He's just being nice. It's no big deal.
Then why does it feel so amazing?
Need my headphones?
Nope. My force field is working.

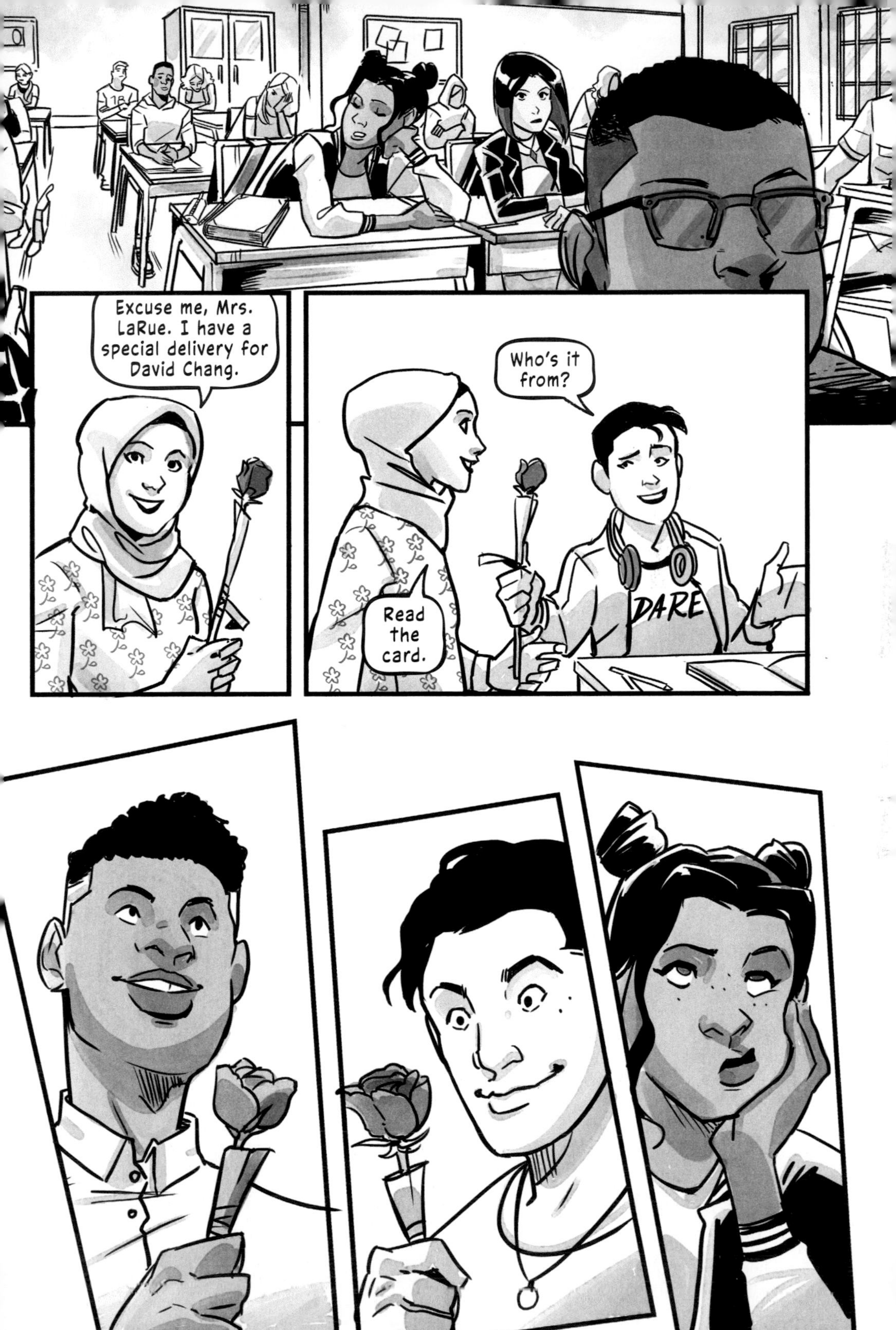
Excuse me, Mrs. LaRue. I have a special delivery for David Chang.
Who's it from?
DARE
Read the card.

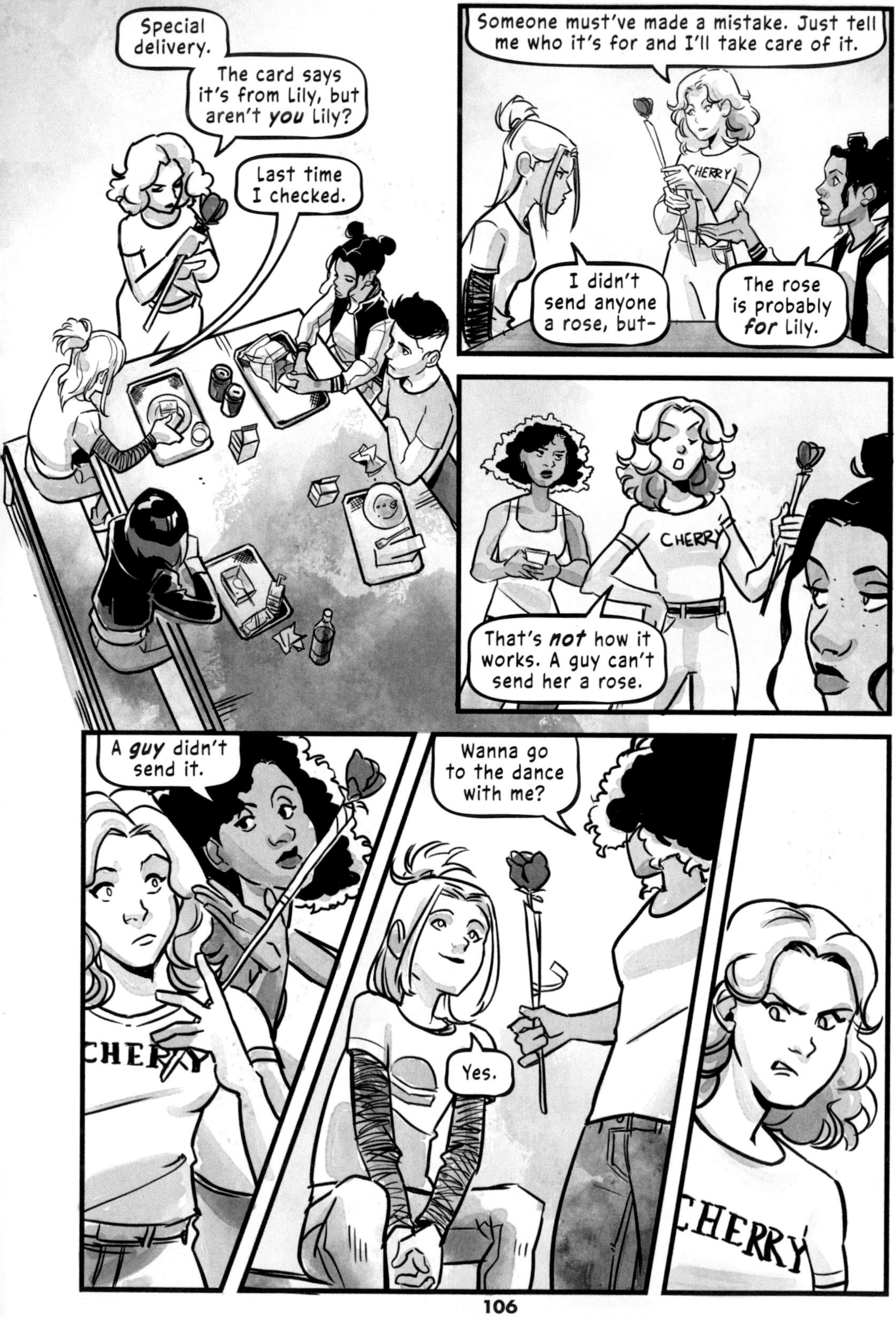

Special delivery.
The card says it's from Lily, but aren't *you* Lily?
Last time I checked.
Someone must've made a mistake. Just tell me who it's for and I'll take care of it.
CHERRY
I didn't send anyone a rose, but-
The rose is probably *for* Lily.
CHERRY
That's *not* how it works. A guy can't send her a rose.
A *guy* didn't send it.
CHERRY
Wanna go to the dance with me?
Yes.
CHERRY

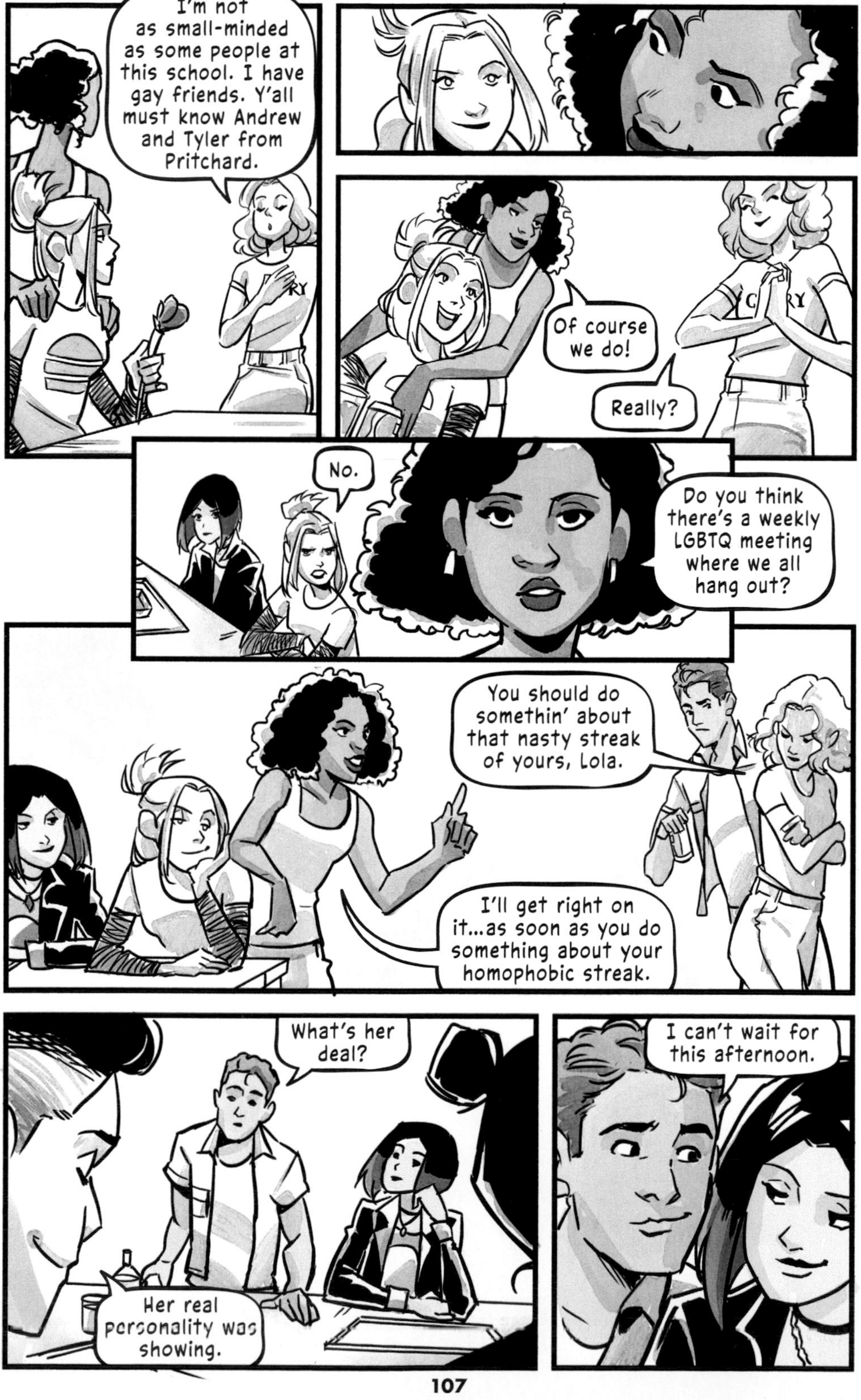
I'm not as small-minded as some people at this school. I have gay friends. Y'all must know Andrew and Tyler from Pritchard.
Of course we do!
Really?
No.
Do you think there's a weekly LGBTQ meeting where we all hang out?
You should do somethin' about that nasty streak of yours, Lola.
I'll get right on it...as soon as you do something about your homophobic streak.
What's her deal?
Her real personality was showing.
I can't wait for this afternoon.

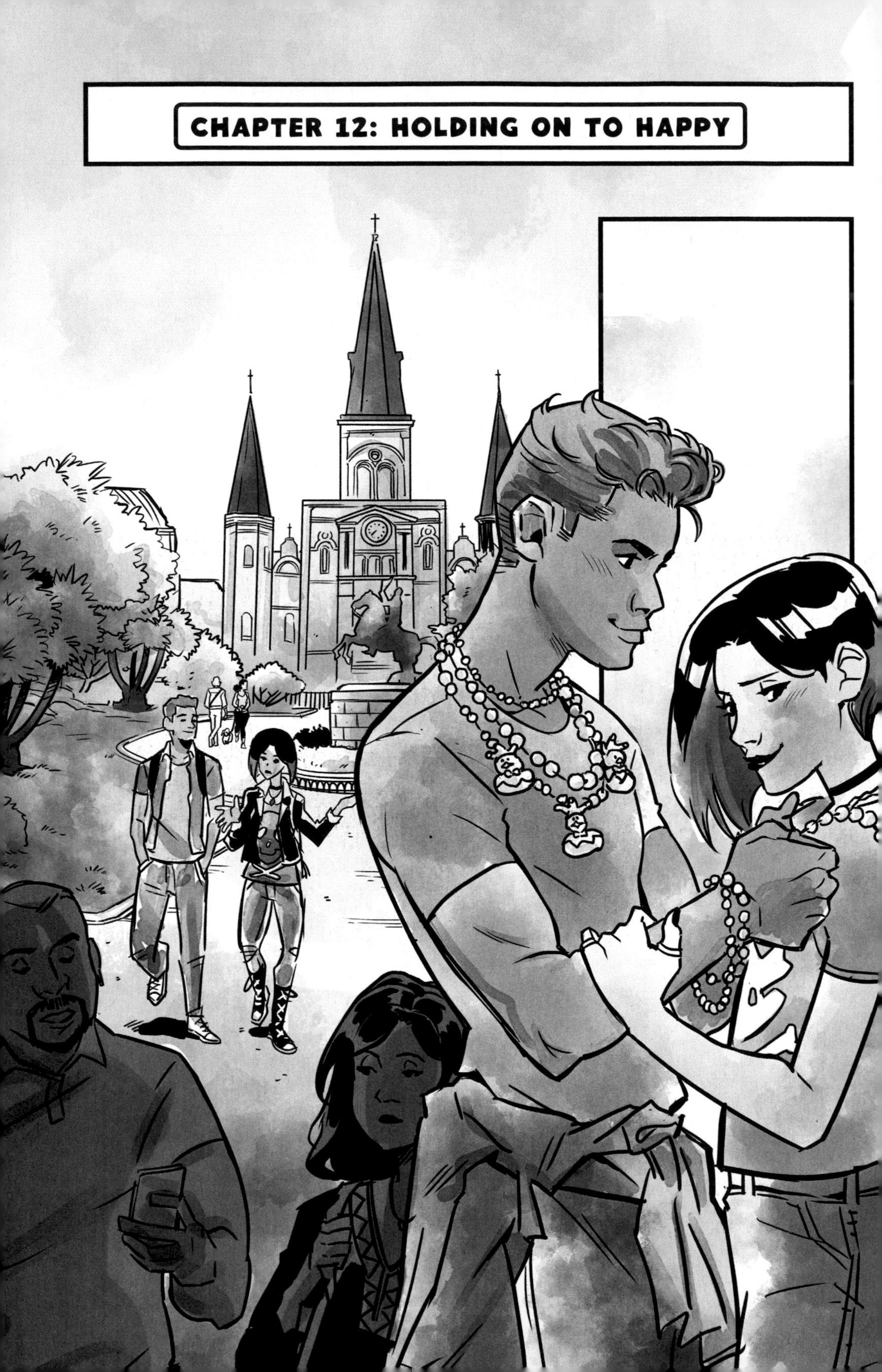
CHAPTER 12: HOLDING ON TO HAPPY

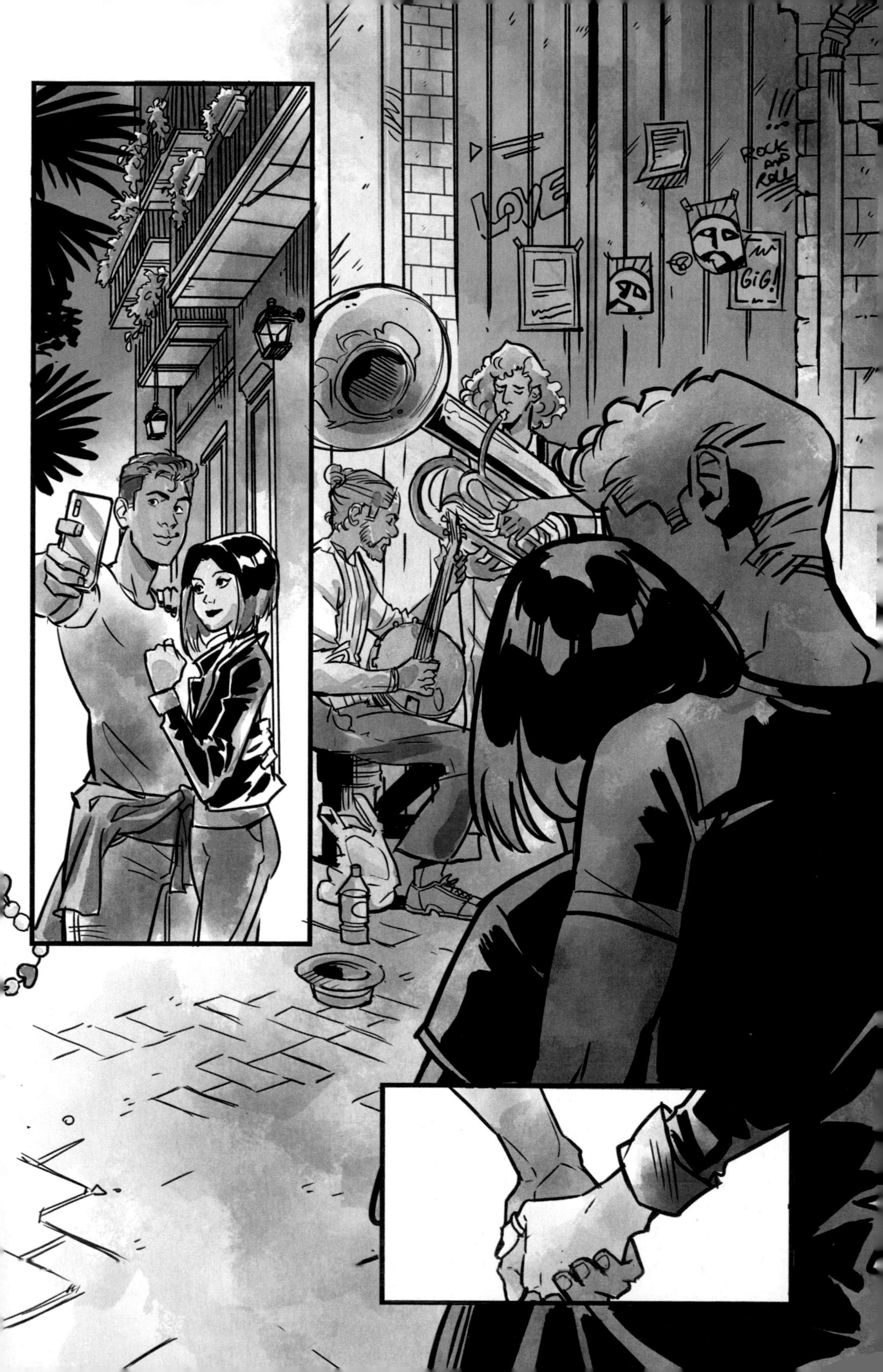

LOVE
ROCK AND ROLL
GIG!

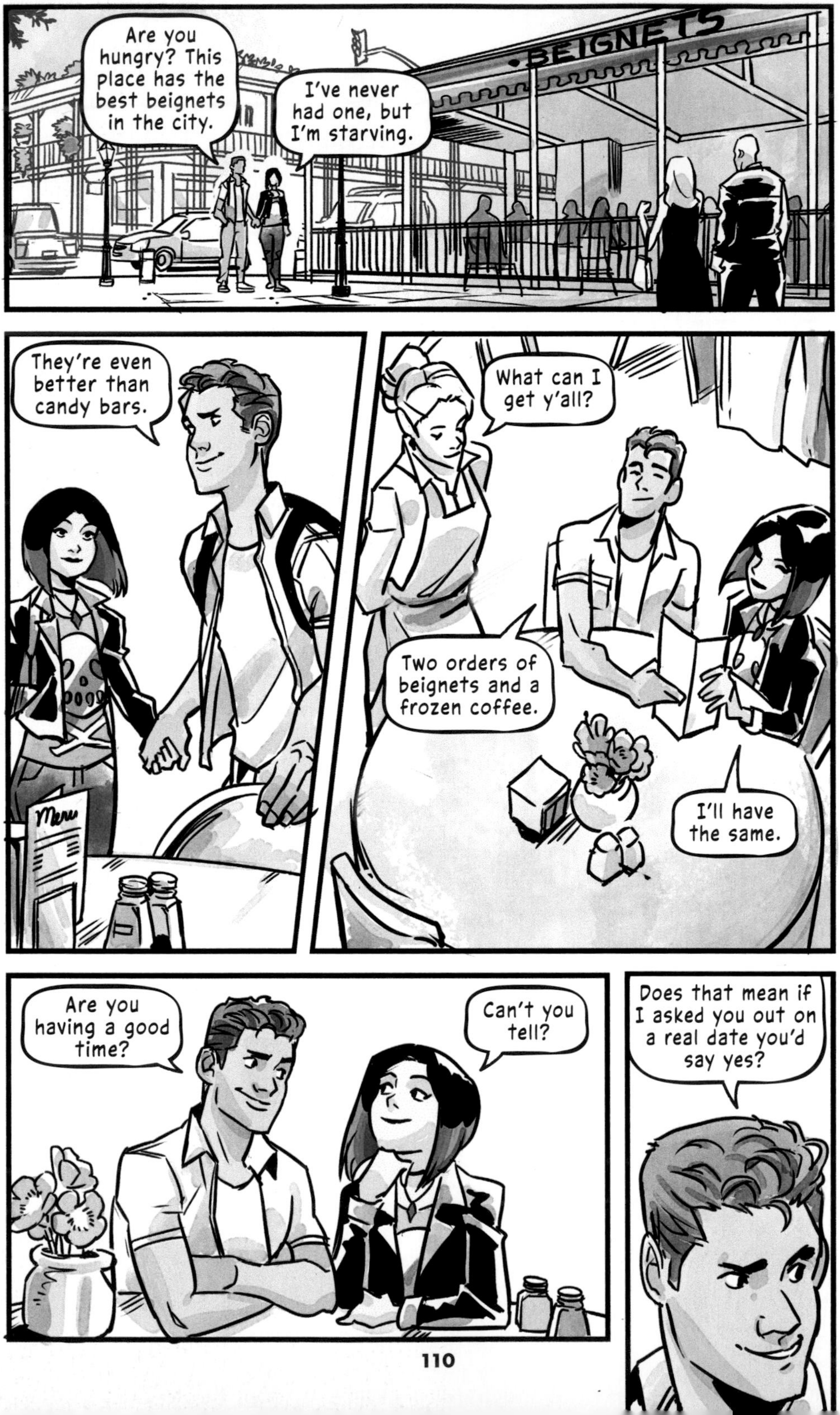
BEIGNETS
Are you hungry? This place has the best beignets in the city.
I've never had one, but I'm starving.
They're even better than candy bars.
Menu
What can I get y'all?
Two orders of beignets and a frozen coffee.
I'll have the same.
Are you having a good time?
Can't you tell?
Does that mean if I asked you out on a real date you'd say yes?

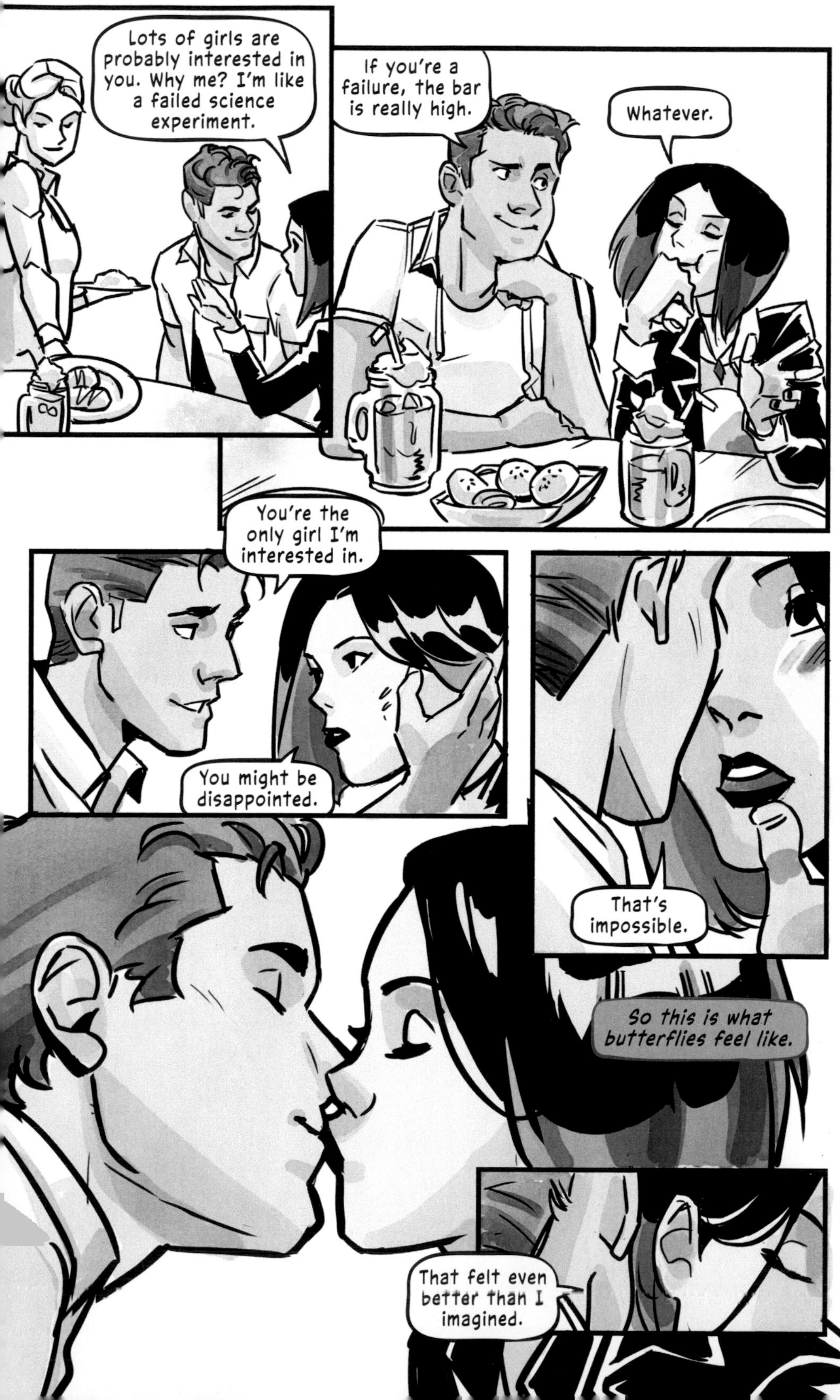
Lots of girls are probably interested in you. Why me? I'm like a failed science experiment.
If you're a failure, the bar is really high.
Whatever.
You're the only girl I'm interested in.
You might be disappointed.
That's impossible.
So this is what butterflies feel like.
That felt even better than I imagined.

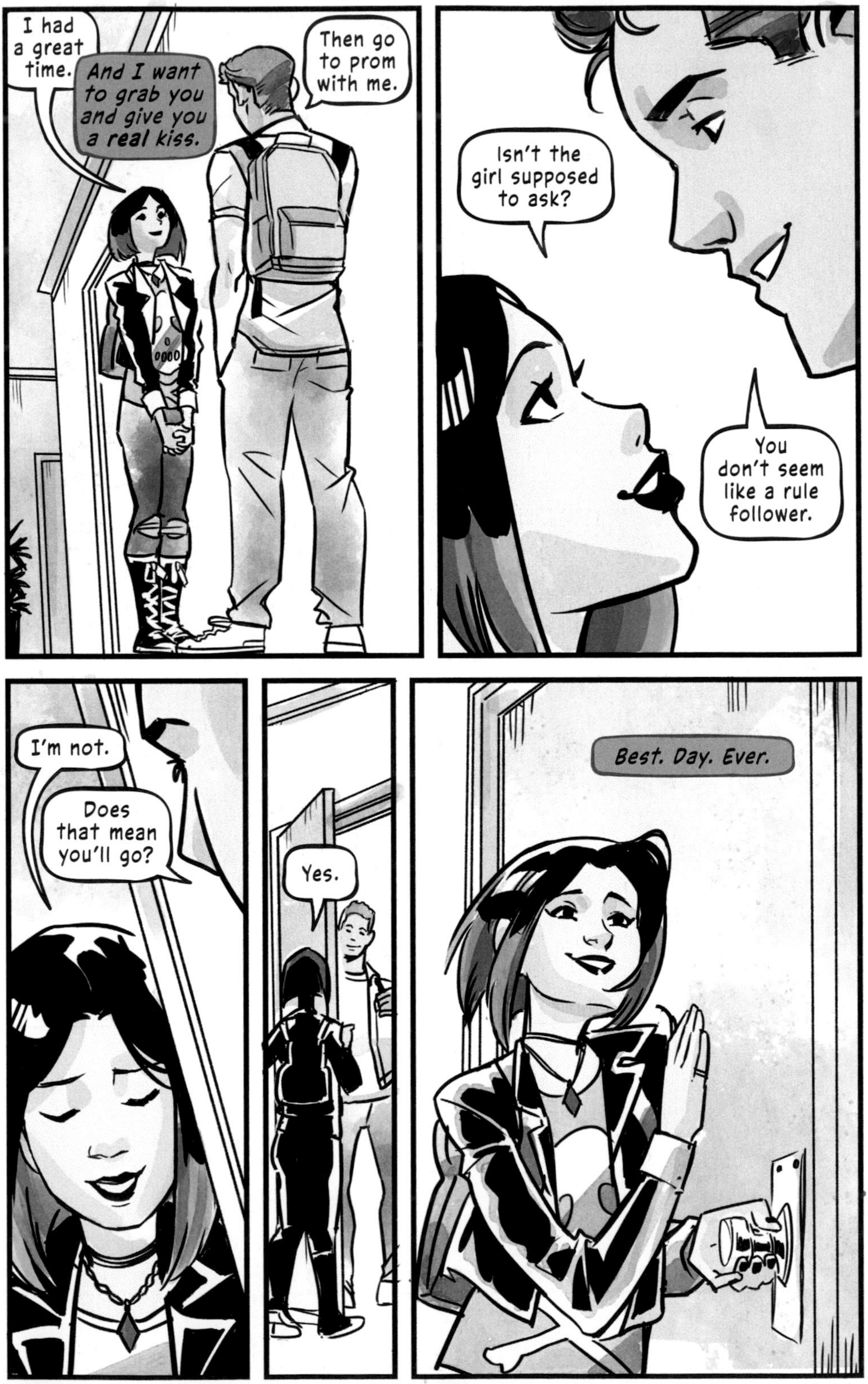
I had a great time.
And I want to grab you and give you a real kiss.
Then go to prom with me.
Isn't the girl supposed to ask?
You don't seem like a rule follower.
I'm not.
Does that mean you'll go?
Yes.
Best. Day. Ever.

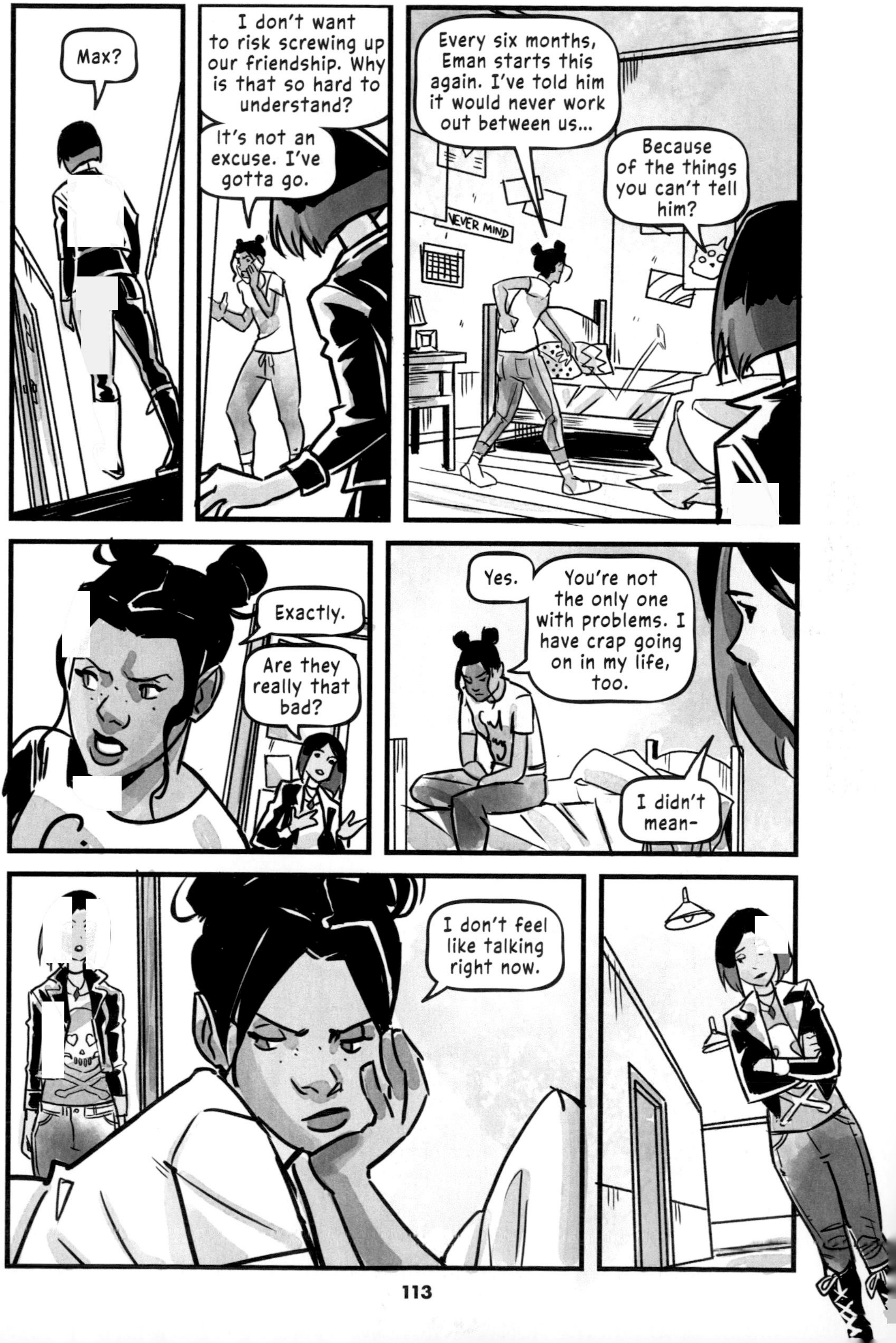
Max?
I don't want to risk screwing up our friendship. Why is that so hard to understand?
It's not an excuse. I've gotta go.
Every six months, Eman starts this again. I've told him it would never work out between us...
NEVER MIND
Because of the things you can't tell him?
Exactly.
Are they really that bad?
Yes.
You're not the only one with problems. I have crap going on in my life, too.
I didn't mean-
I don't feel like talking right now.

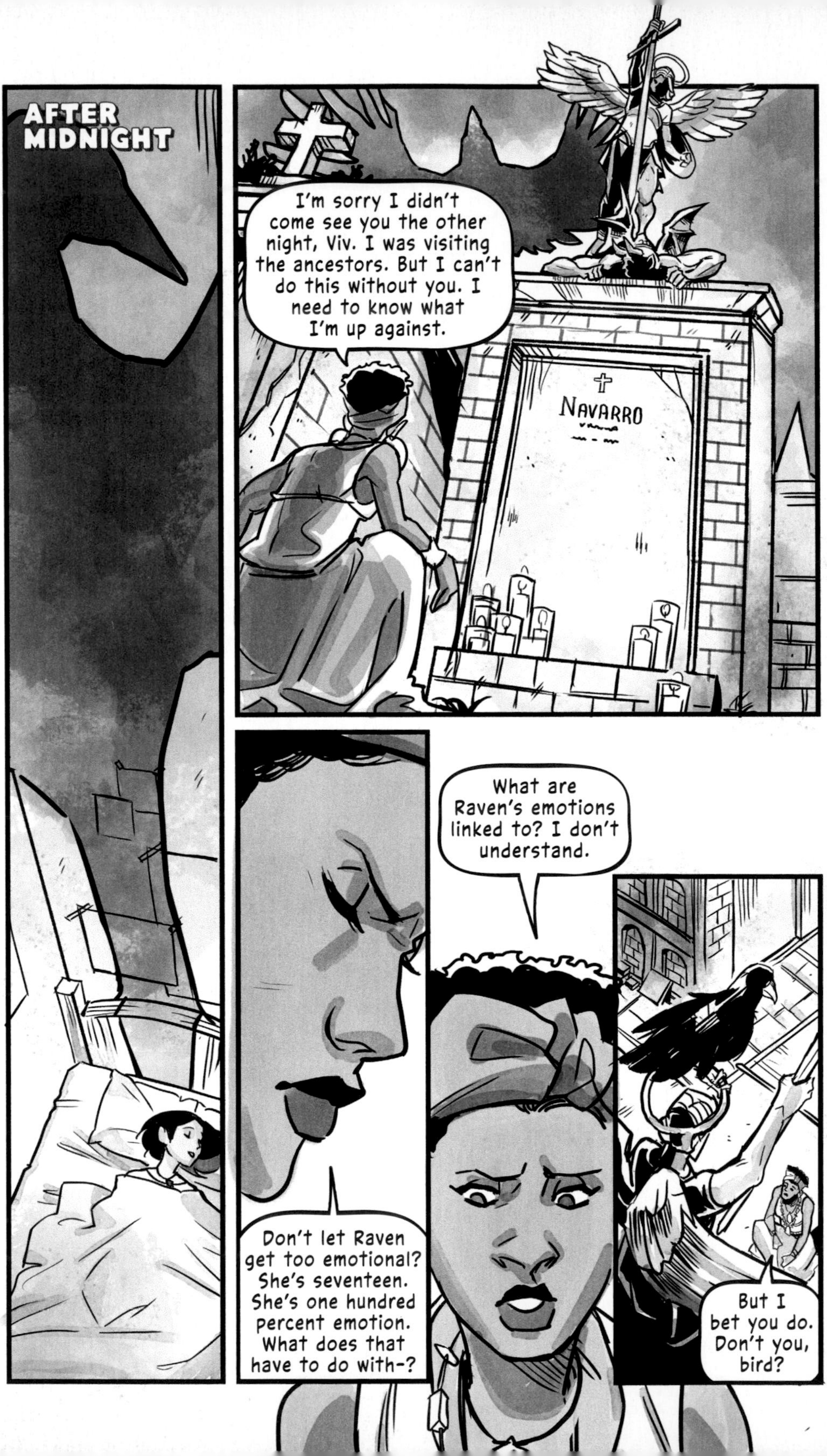
AFTER MIDNIGHT
I'm sorry I didn't come see you the other night, Viv. I was visiting the ancestors. But I can't do this without you. I need to know what I'm up against.
NAVARRO
Don't let Raven get too emotional? She's seventeen. She's one hundred percent emotion. What does that have to do with-?
What are Raven's emotions linked to? I don't understand.
But I bet you do. Don't you, bird?

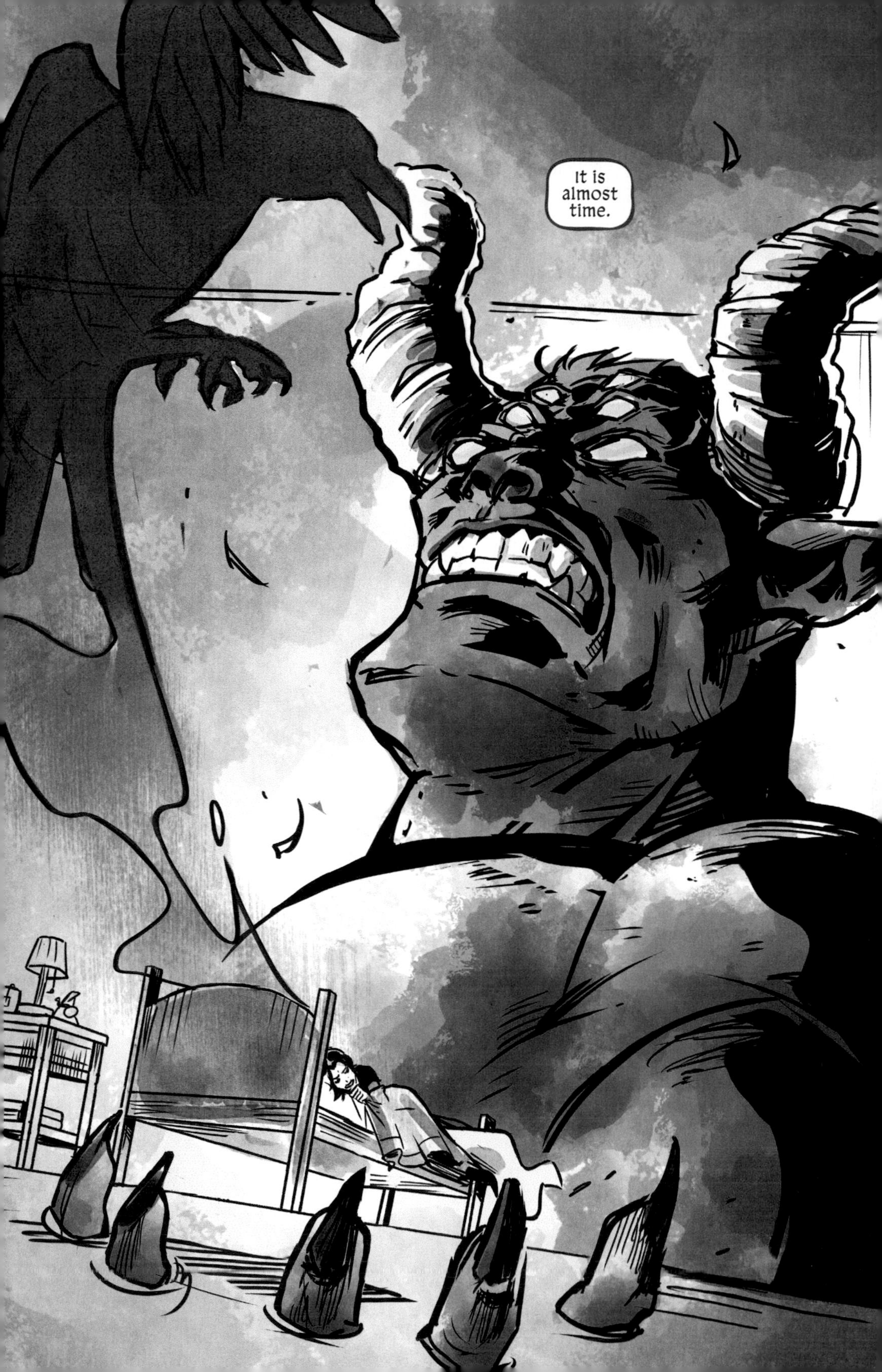
It is almost time.

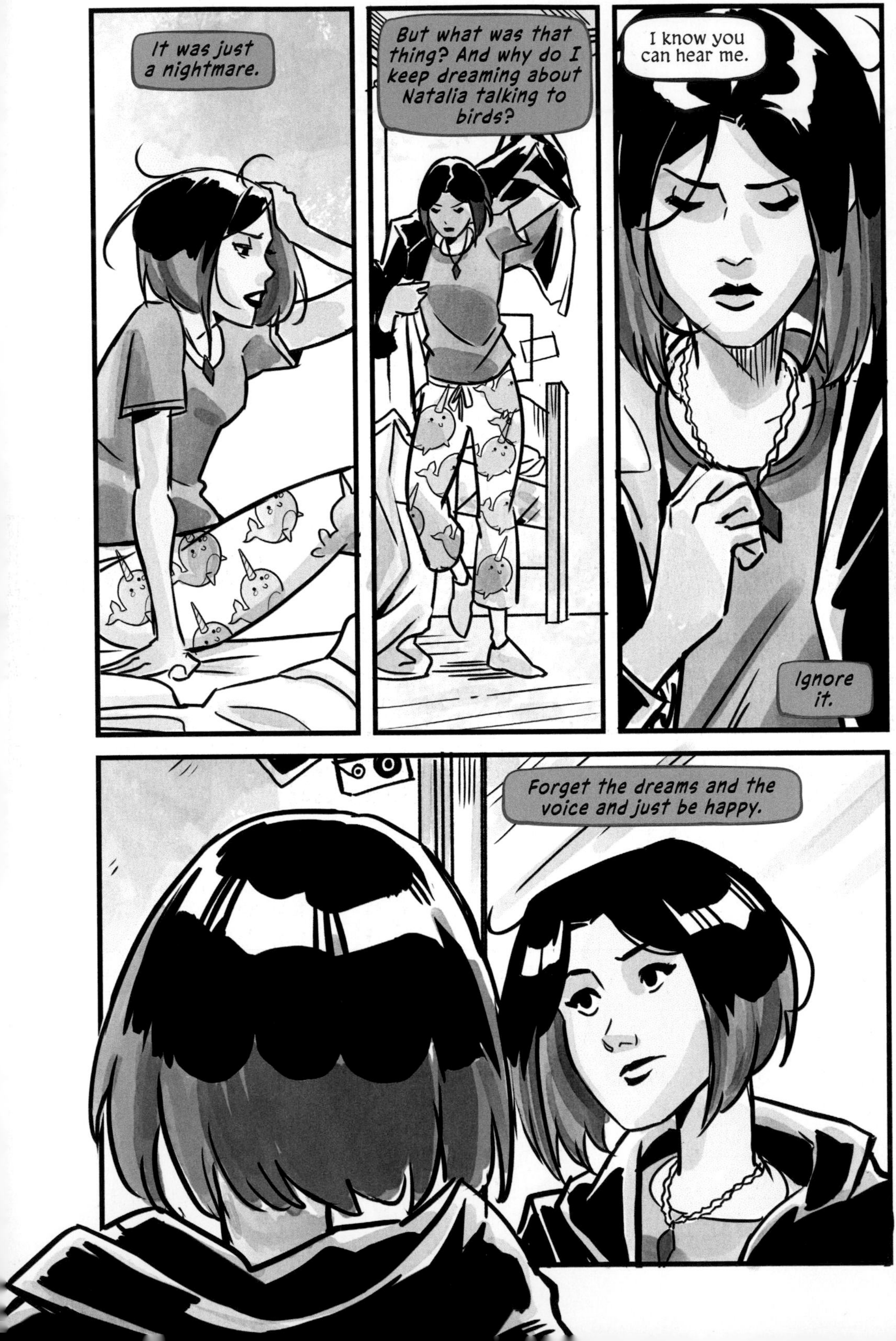
It was just a nightmare.
But what was that thing? And why do I keep dreaming about Natalia talking to birds?
I know you can hear me.
Ignore it.
Forget the dreams and the voice and just be happy.

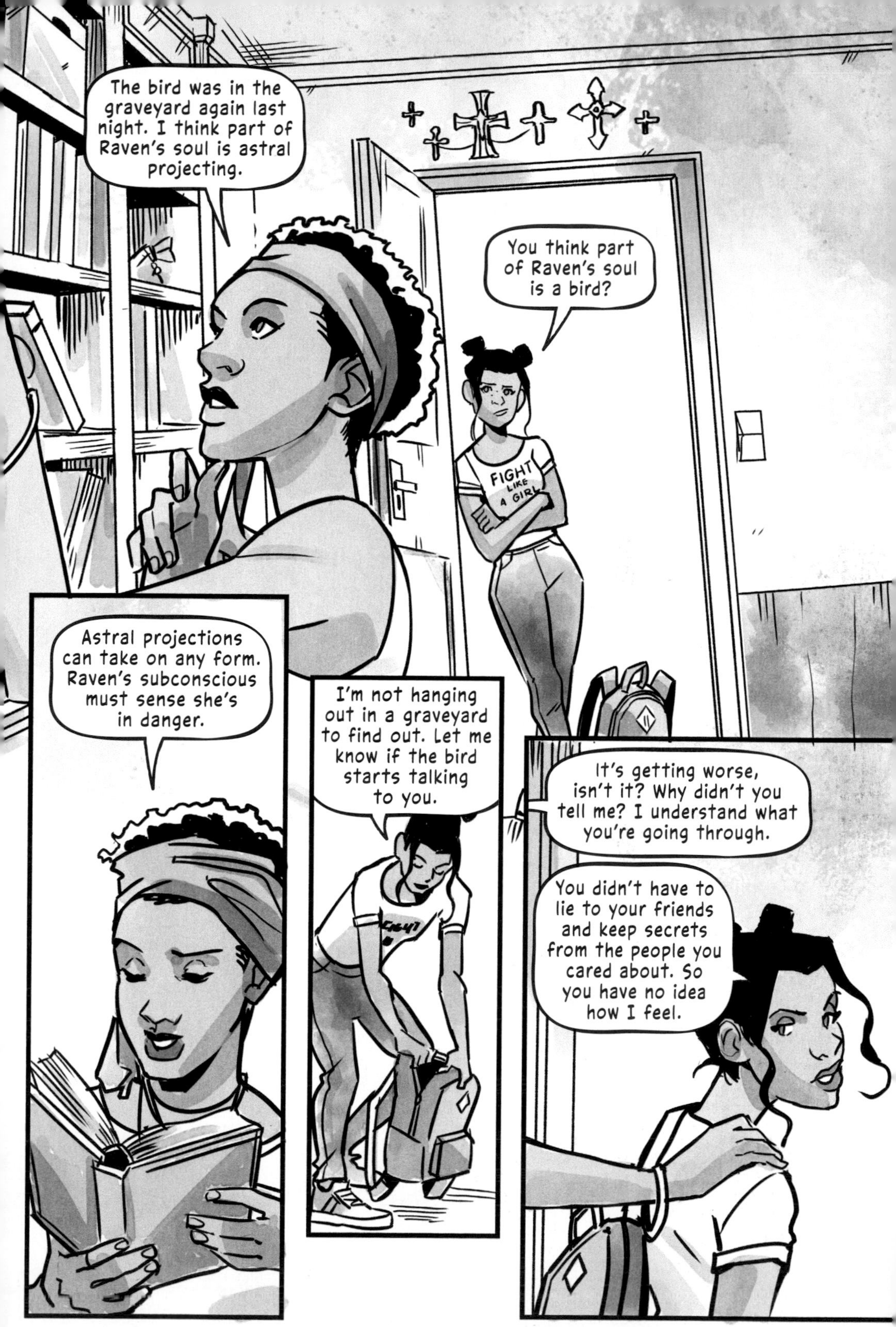
The bird was in the graveyard again last night. I think part of Raven's soul is astral projecting.
You think part of Raven's soul is a bird?
FIGHT LIKE A GIRL
Astral projections can take on any form. Raven's subconscious must sense she's in danger.
I'm not hanging out in a graveyard to find out. Let me know if the bird starts talking to you.
It's getting worse, isn't it? Why didn't you tell me? I understand what you're going through.
You didn't have to lie to your friends and keep secrets from the people you cared about. So you have no idea how I feel.

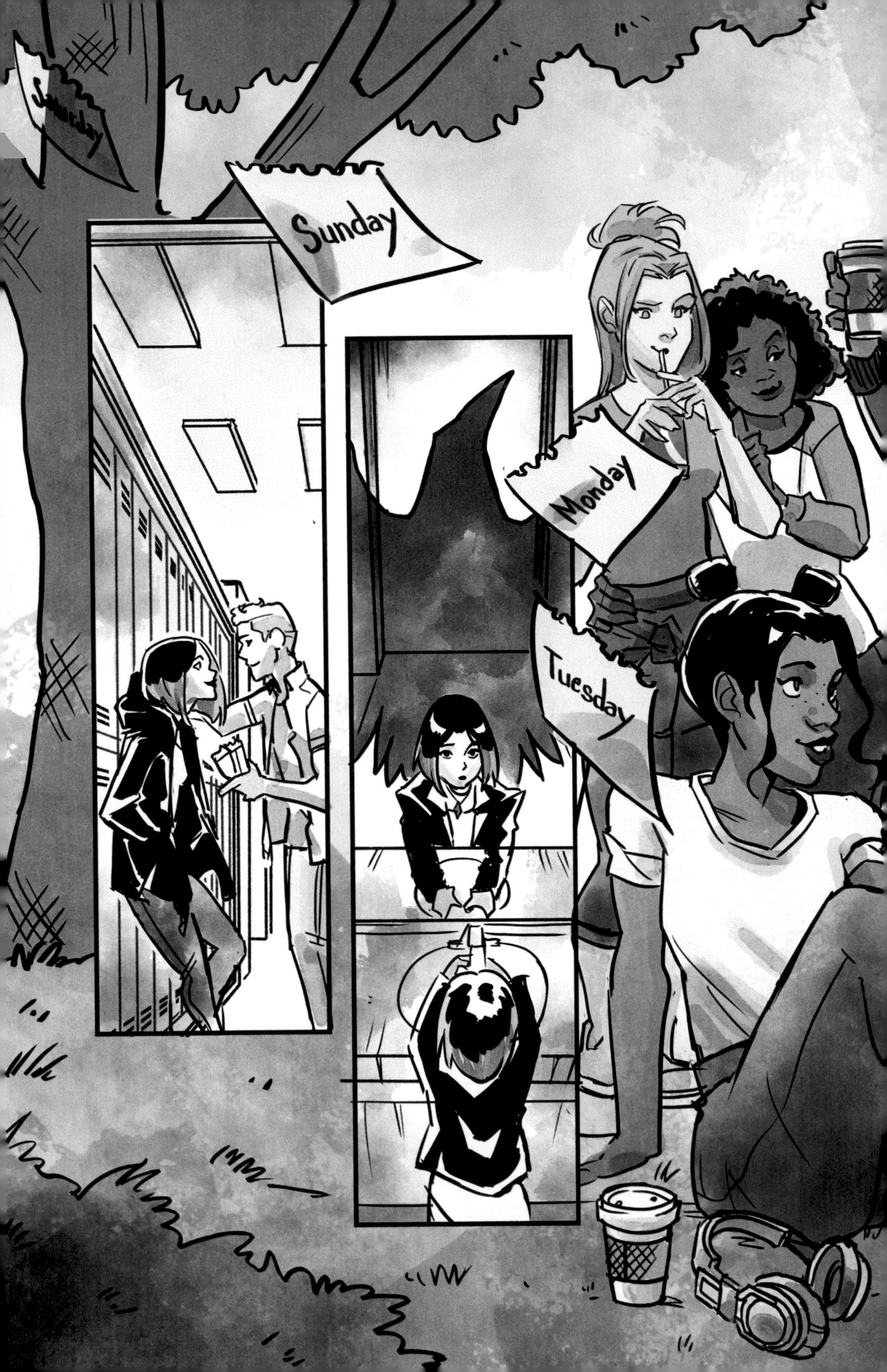

Saturday
Sunday
Monday
Tuesday

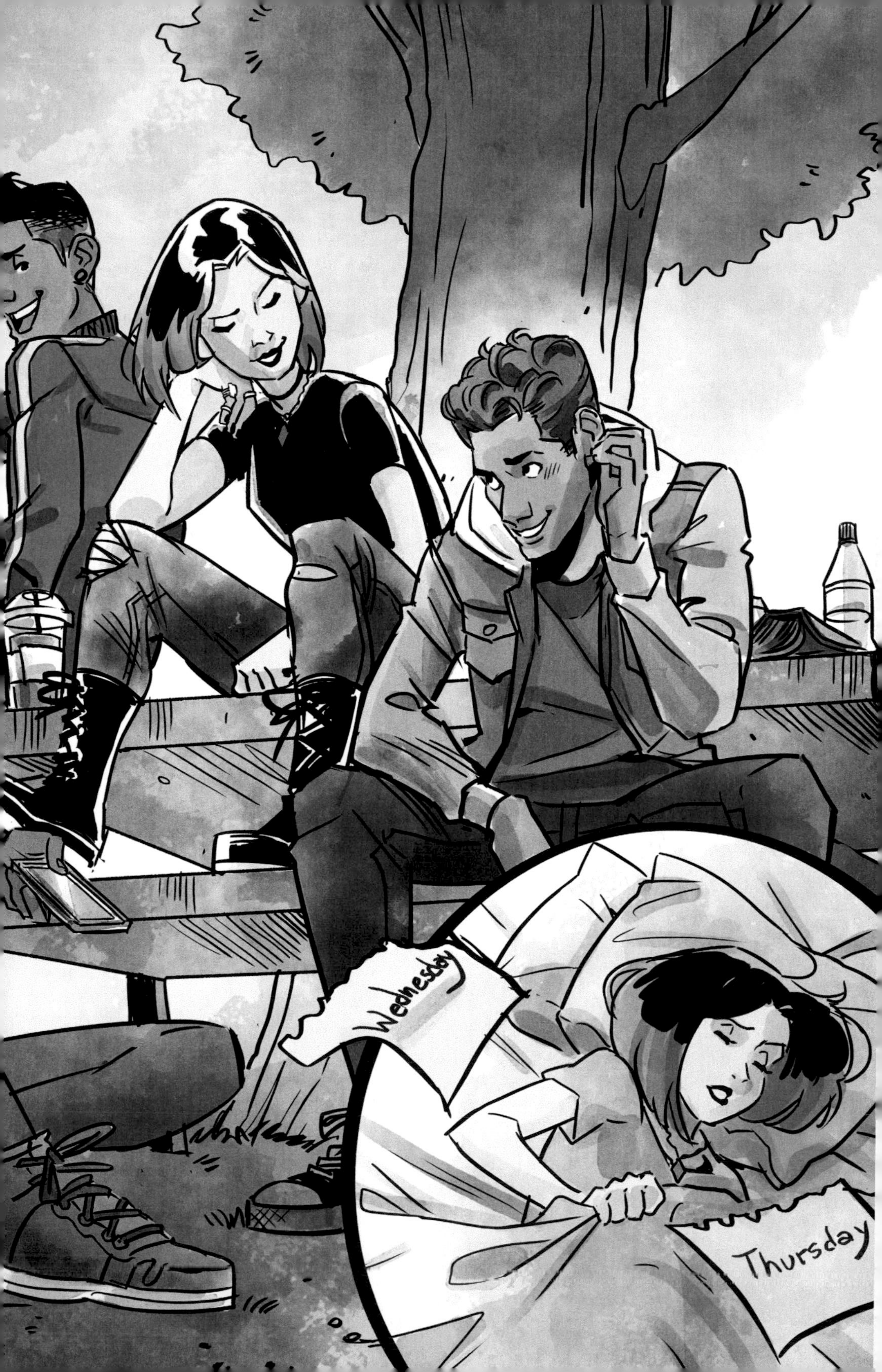

Wednesday
Thursday

CHAPTER 13: PROM NIGHT, PLASTIC RINGS, AND PROMISES

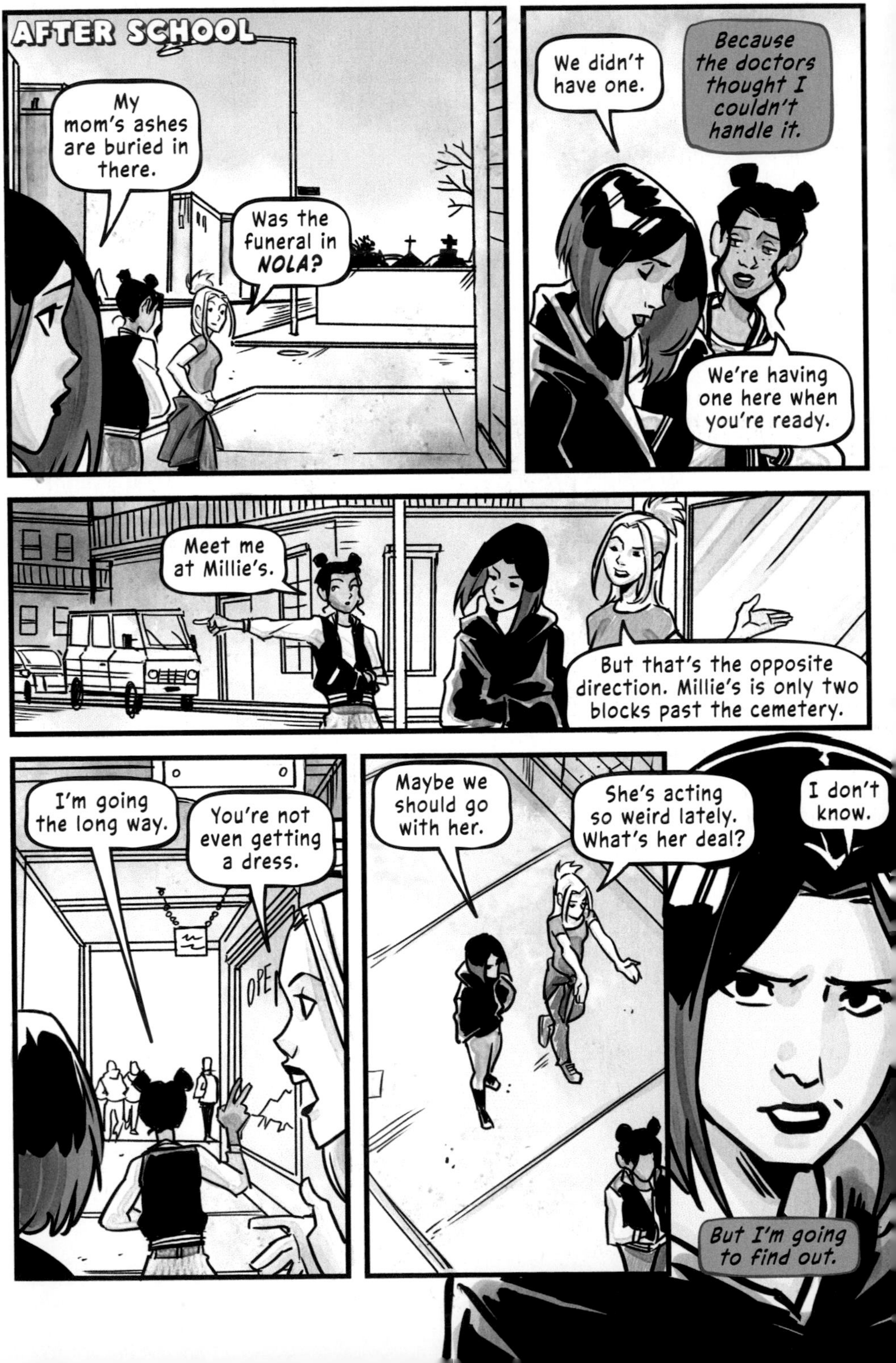

AFTER SCHOOL
My mom's ashes are buried in there.
Was the funeral in NOLA?
We didn't have one.
Because the doctors thought I couldn't handle it.
We're having one here when you're ready.
Meet me at Millie's.
But that's the opposite direction. Millie's is only two blocks past the cemetery.
I'm going the long way.
You're not even getting a dress.
OPEN
Maybe we should go with her.
She's acting so weird lately. What's her deal?
I don't know.
But I'm going to find out.

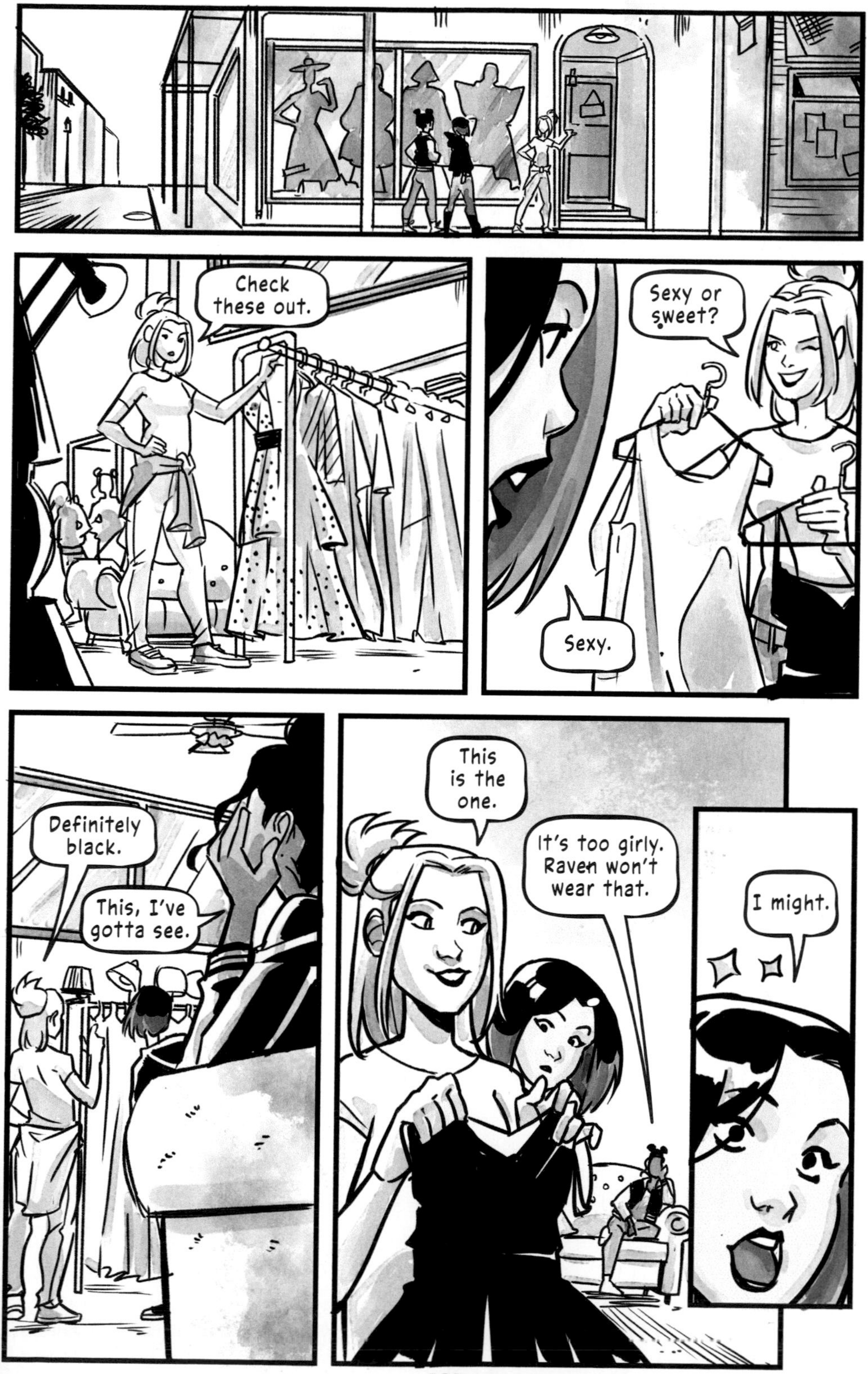
Check these out.
Sexy or sweet?
Sexy.
Definitely black.
This, I've gotta see.
This is the one.
It's too girly. Raven won't wear that.
I might.

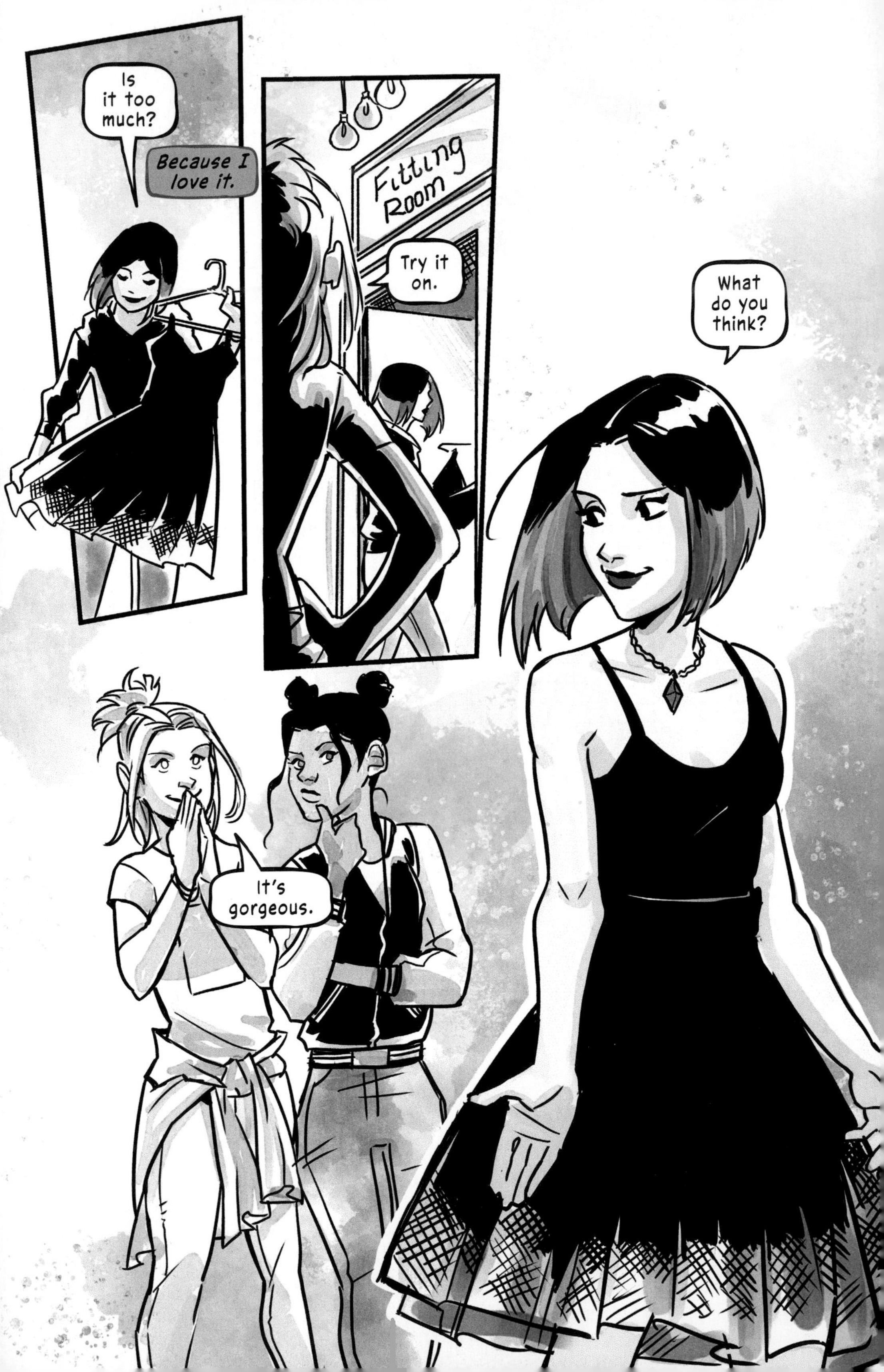
Is it too much?
Because I love it.
Fitting Room
Try it on.
What do you think?
It's gorgeous.

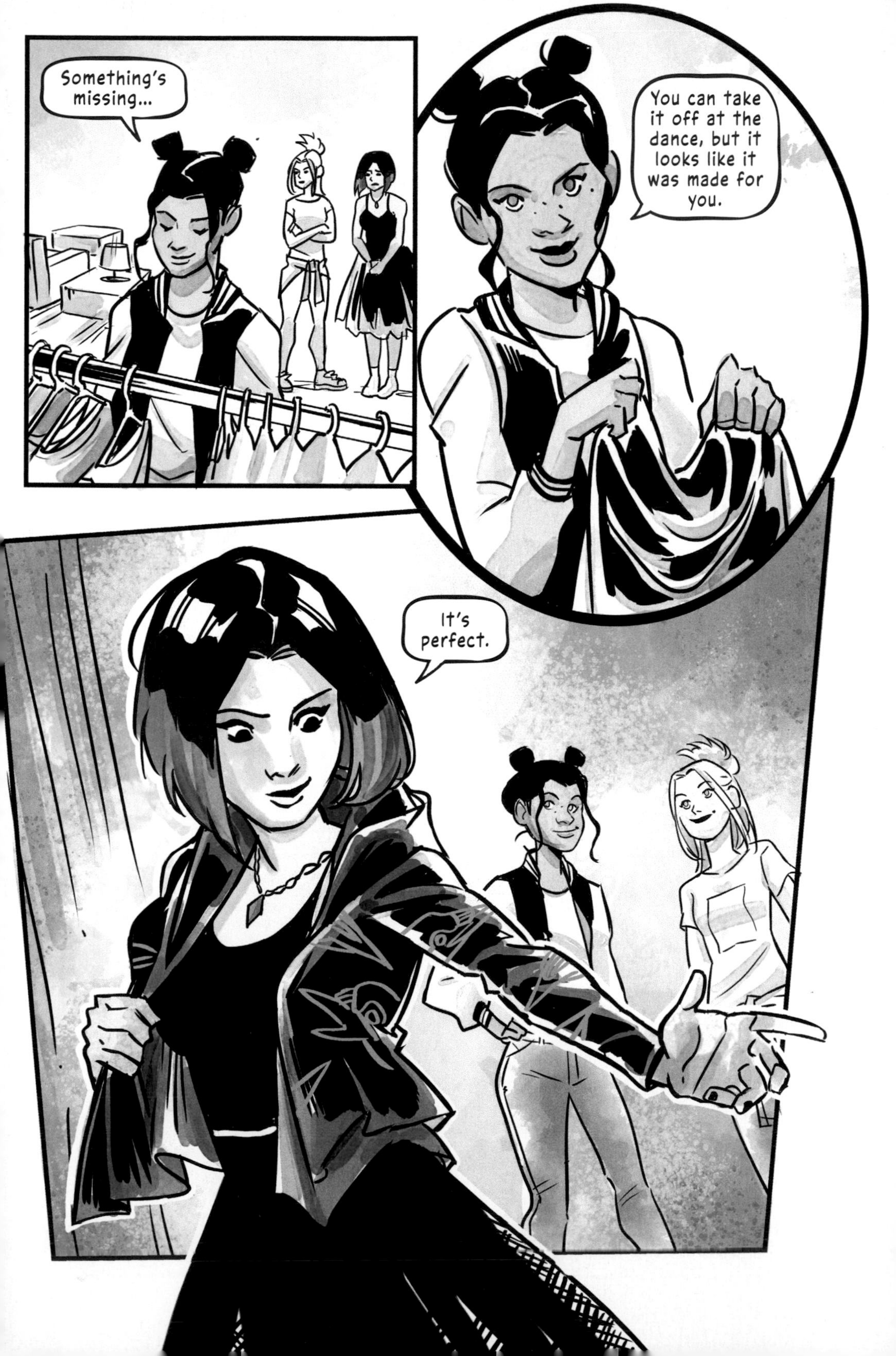
Something's missing...
You can take it off at the dance, but it looks like it was made for you.
It's perfect.

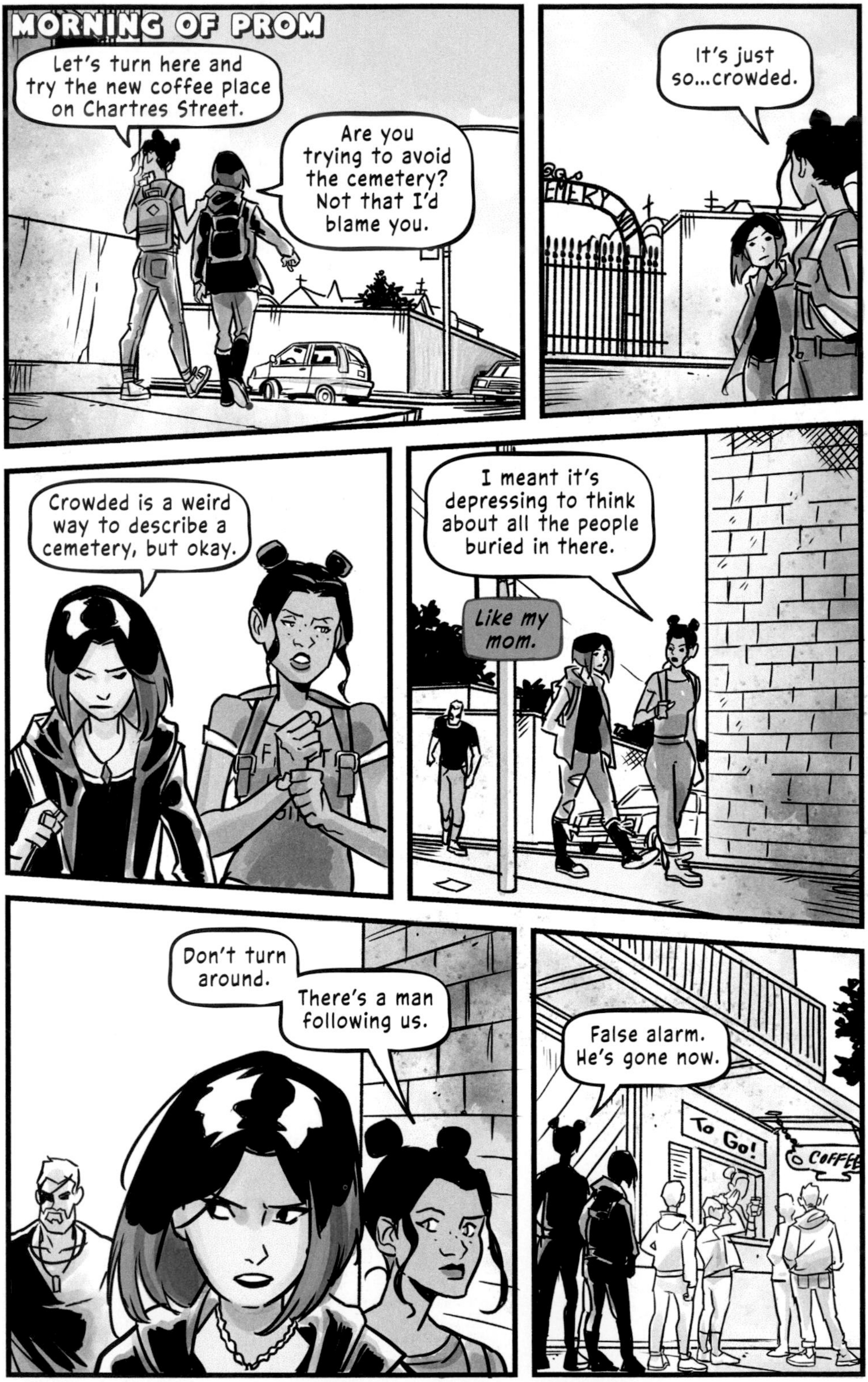
MORNING OF PROM
Let's turn here and try the new coffee place on Chartres Street.
Are you trying to avoid the cemetery? Not that I'd blame you.
It's just so...crowded.
Crowded is a weird way to describe a cemetery, but okay.
I meant it's depressing to think about all the people buried in there.
Like my mom.
Don't turn around.
There's a man following us.
False alarm. He's gone now.
To Go!
COFFEE

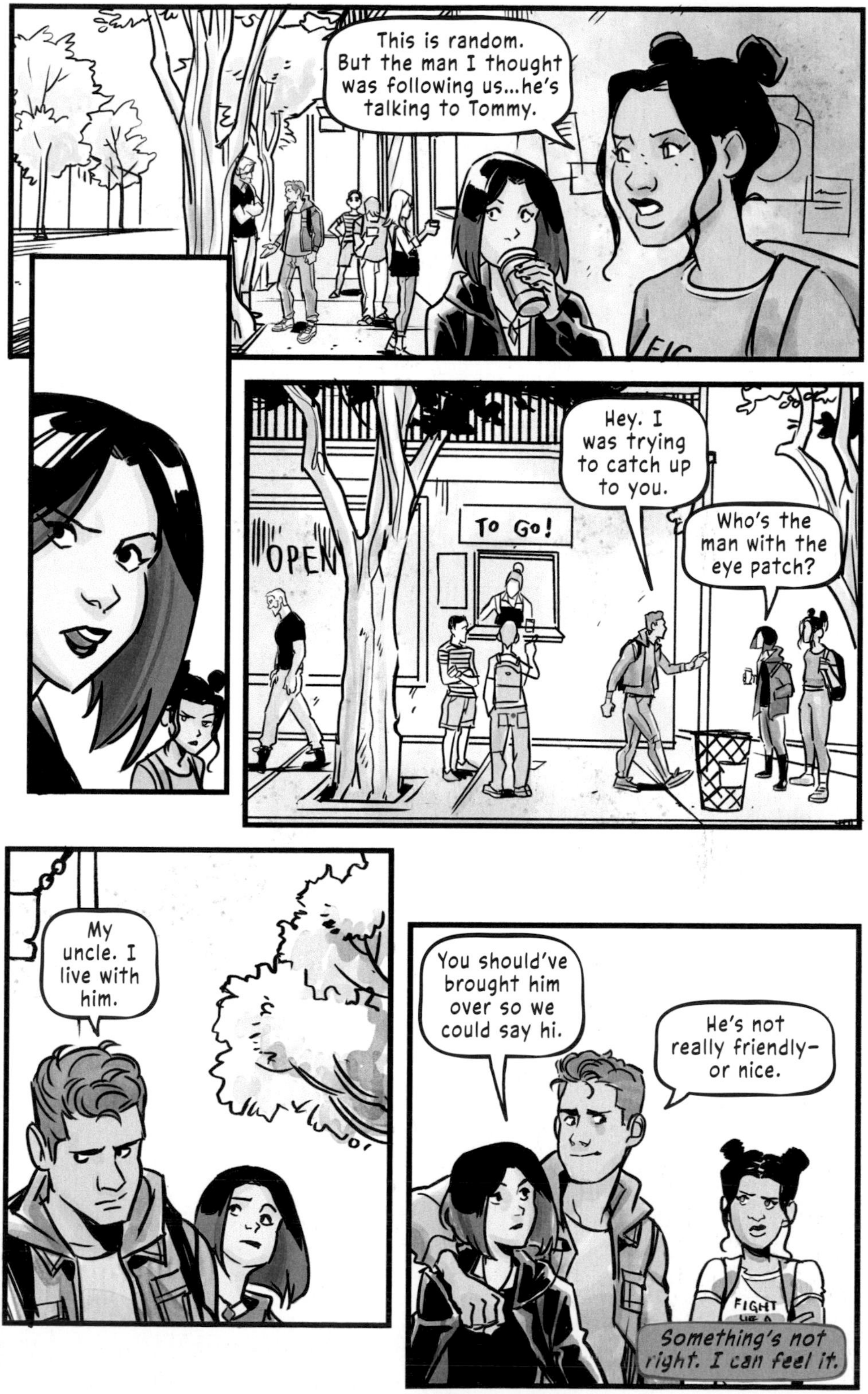

This is random. But the man I thought was following us...he's talking to Tommy.
OPEN
TO GO!
Hey. I was trying to catch up to you.
Who's the man with the eye patch?
My uncle. I live with him.
You should've brought him over so we could say hi.
He's not really friendly—or nice.
FIGHT
Something's not right. I can feel it.

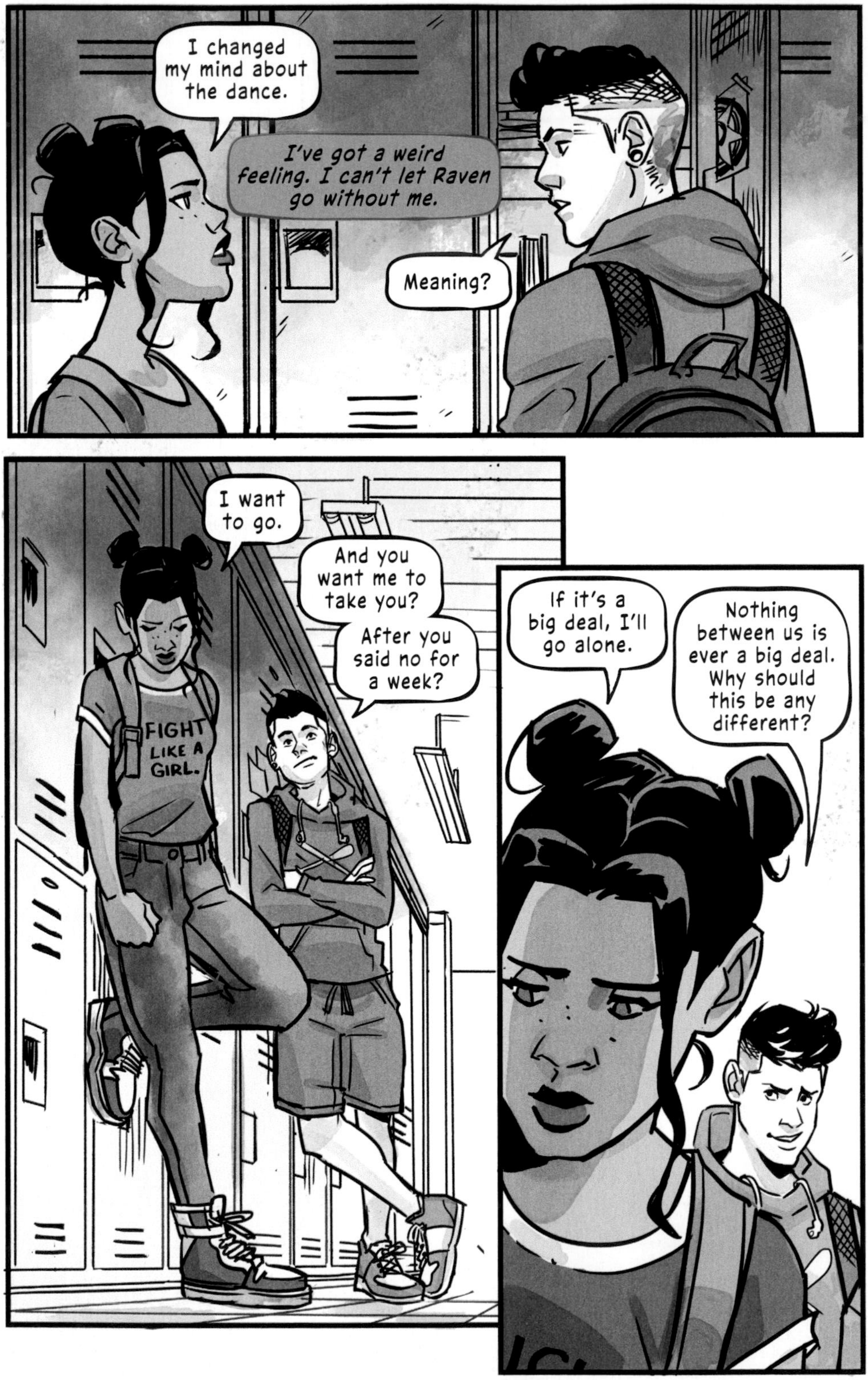
I changed my mind about the dance.
I've got a weird feeling. I can't let Raven go without me.
Meaning?
I want to go.
And you want me to take you?
After you said no for a week?
FIGHT LIKE A GIRL.
If it's a big deal, I'll go alone.
Nothing between us is ever a big deal. Why should this be any different?

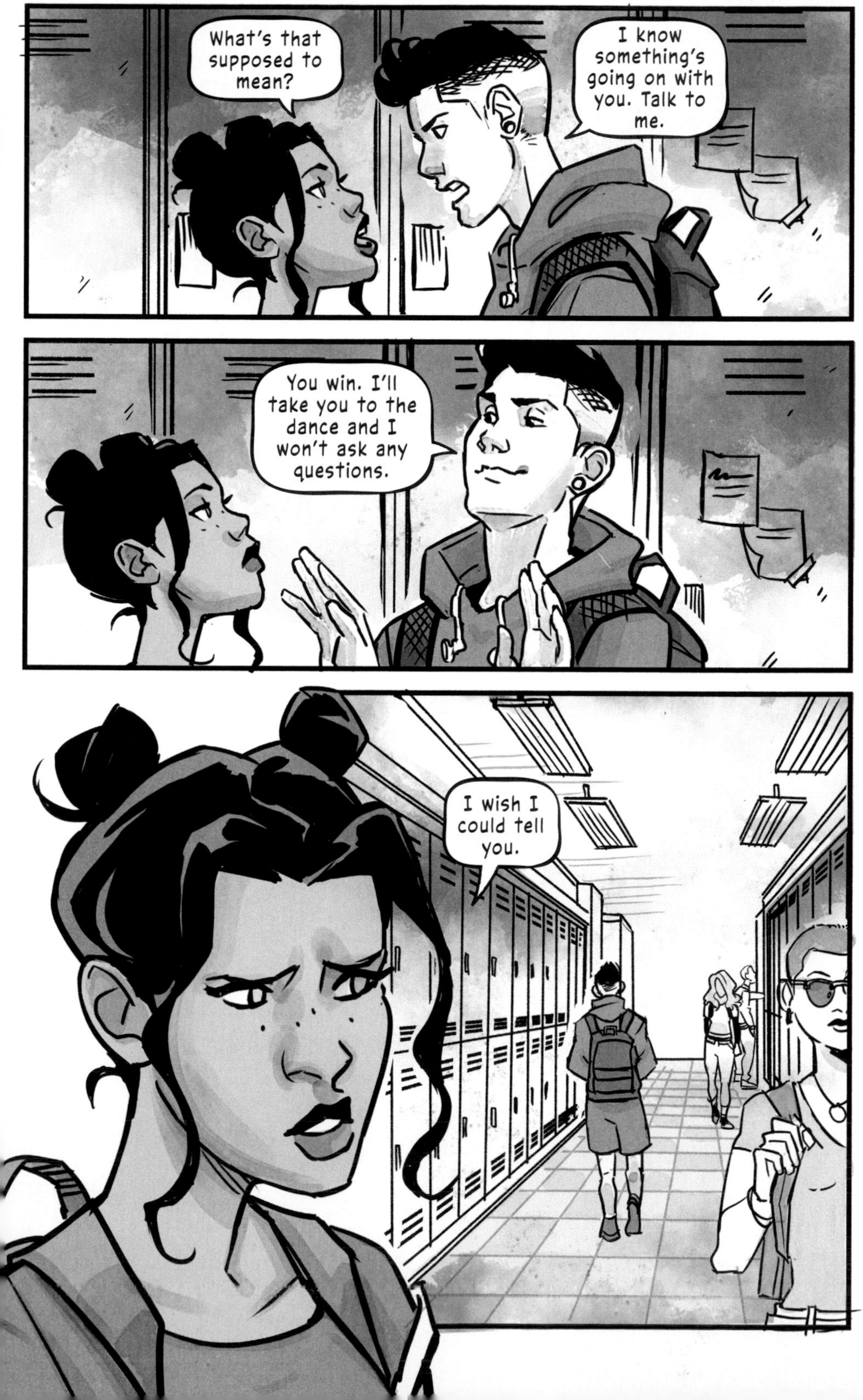
What's that supposed to mean?
I know something's going on with you. Talk to me.
You win. I'll take you to the dance and I won't ask any questions.
I wish I could tell you.

CHAPTER 14: PERFECT AND DAMAGED ARE BOTH FOUR-LETTER WORDS

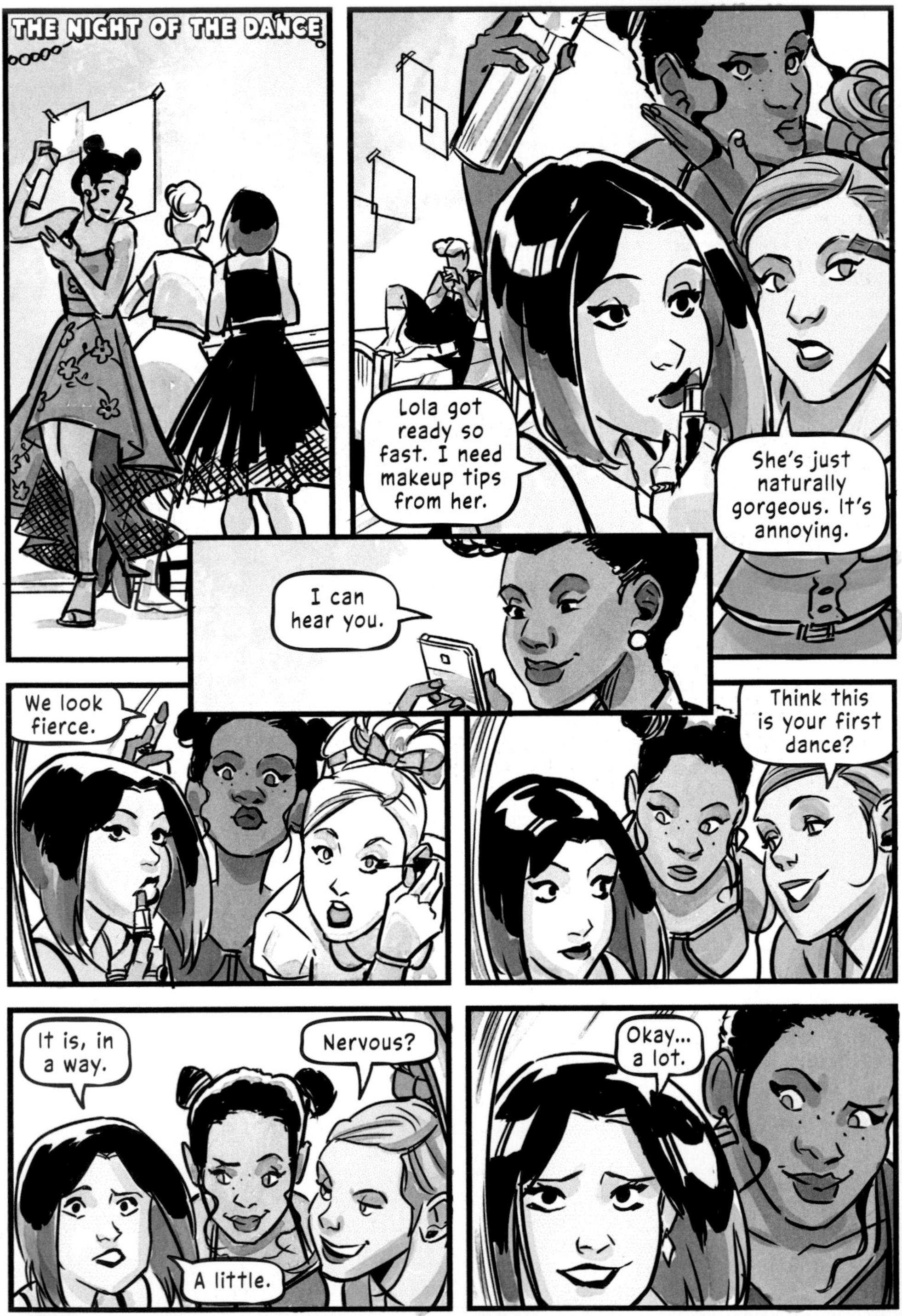
THE NIGHT OF THE DANCE
Lola got ready so fast. I need makeup tips from her.
She's just naturally gorgeous. It's annoying.
I can hear you.
We look fierce.
Think this is your first dance?
It is, in a way.
Nervous?
A little.
Okay... a lot.

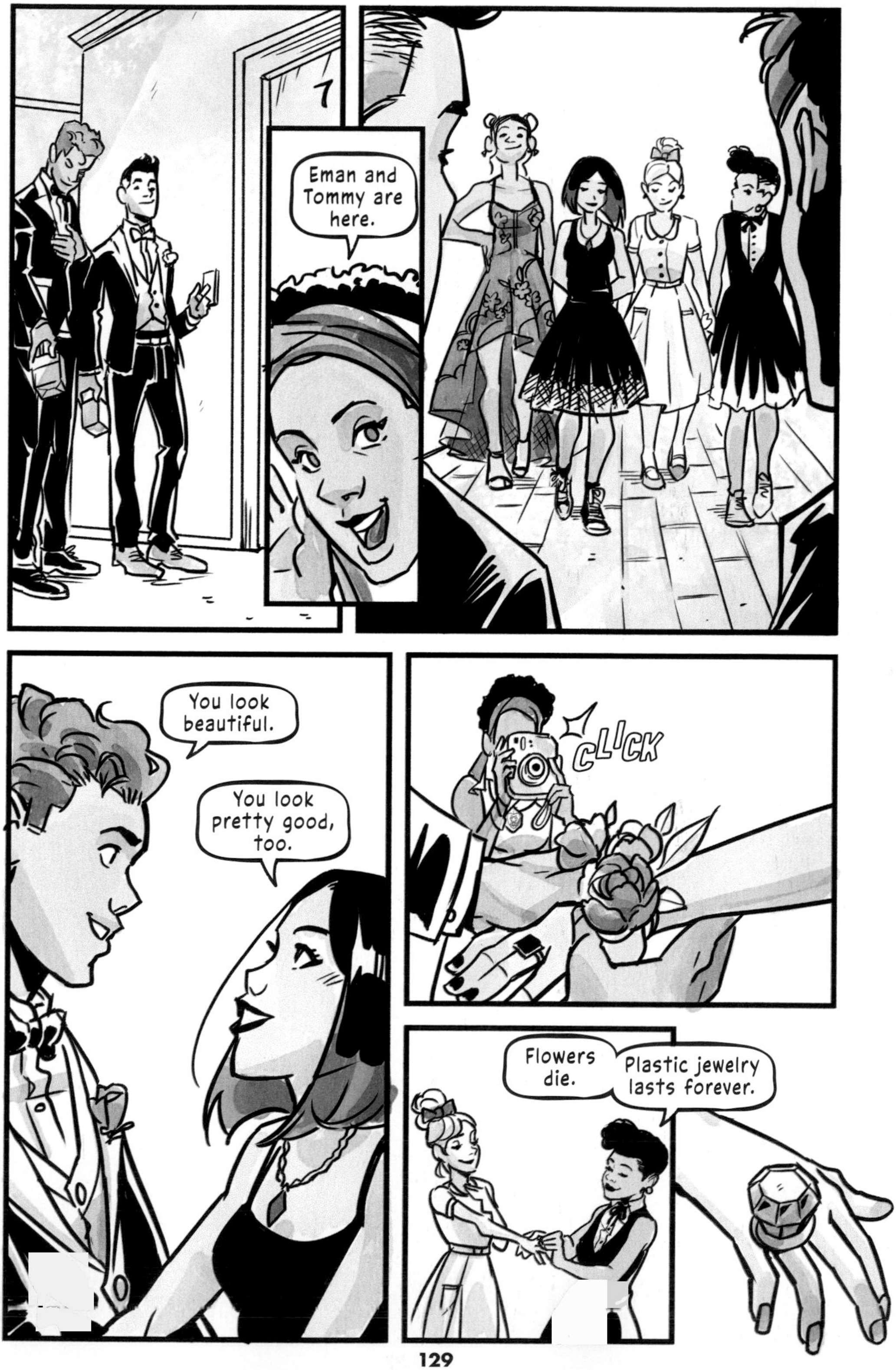
7
Eman and Tommy are here.
You look beautiful.
You look pretty good, too.
CLICK
Flowers die.
Plastic jewelry lasts forever.

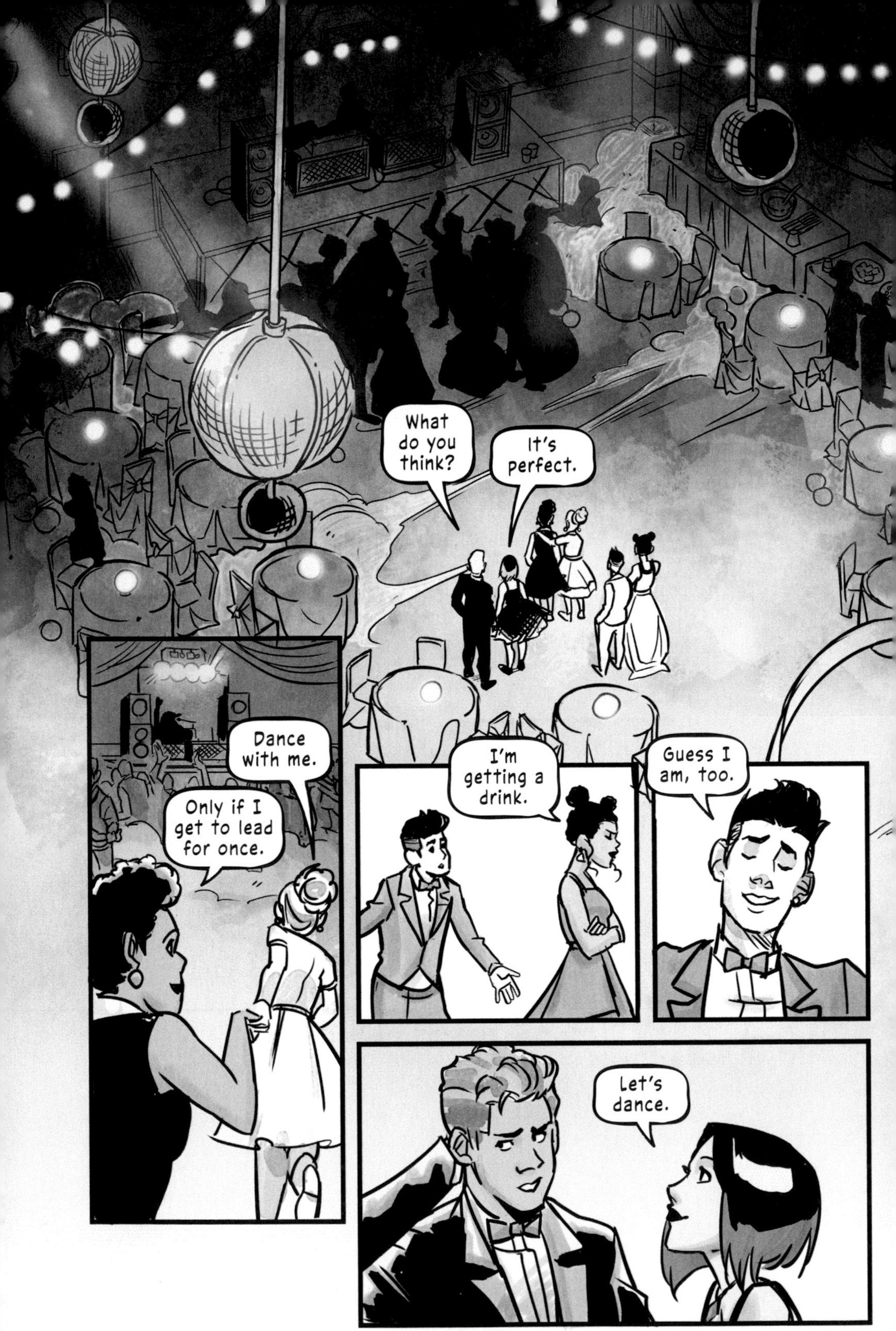
What do you think?
It's perfect.
Dance with me.
Only if I get to lead for once.
I'm getting a drink.
Guess I am, too.
Let's dance.

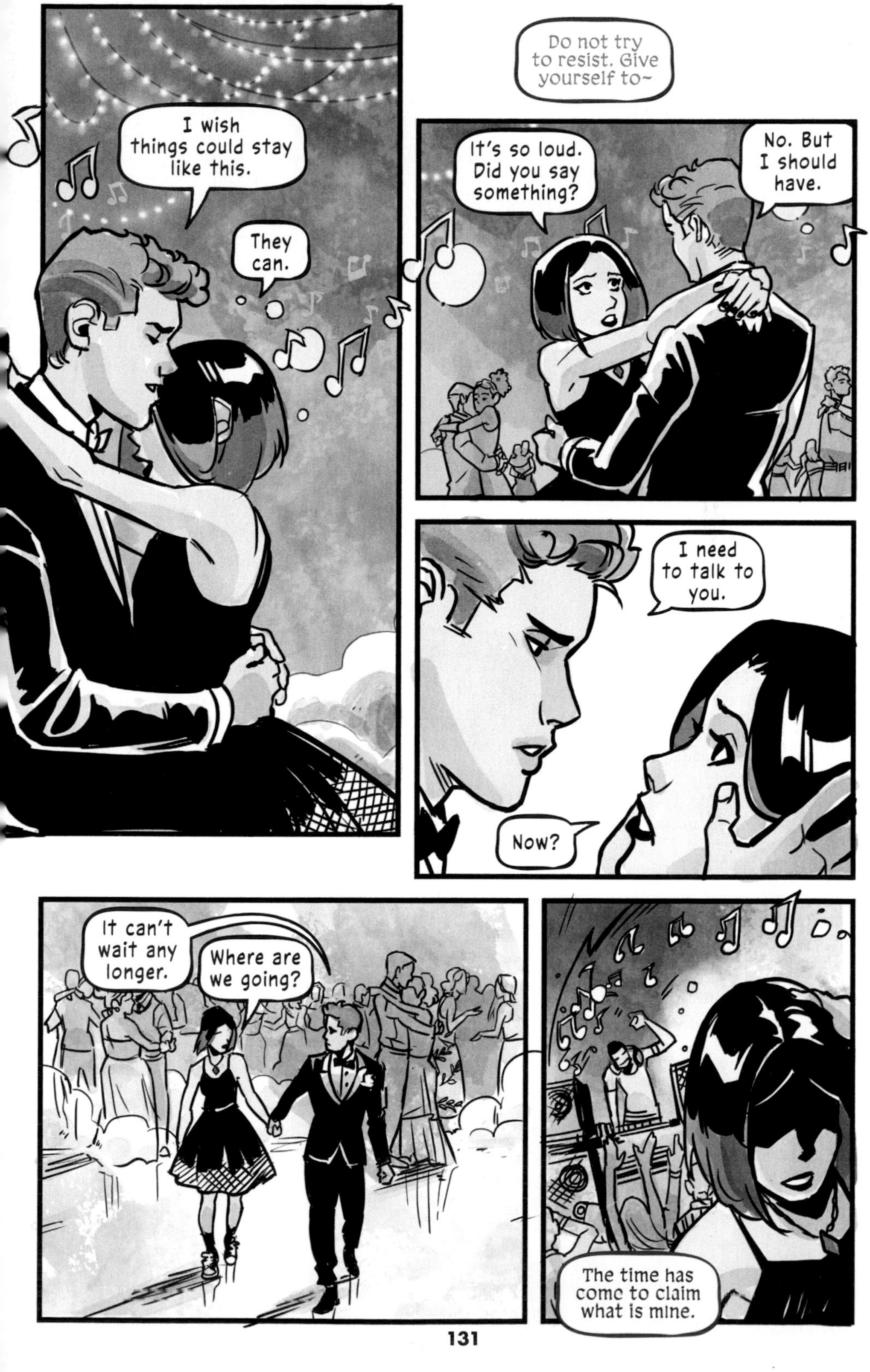

I wish things could stay like this.
They can.
Do not try to resist. Give yourself to~
It's so loud. Did you say something?
No. But I should have.
I need to talk to you.
Now?
It can't wait any longer.
Where are we going?
The time has come to claim what is mine.

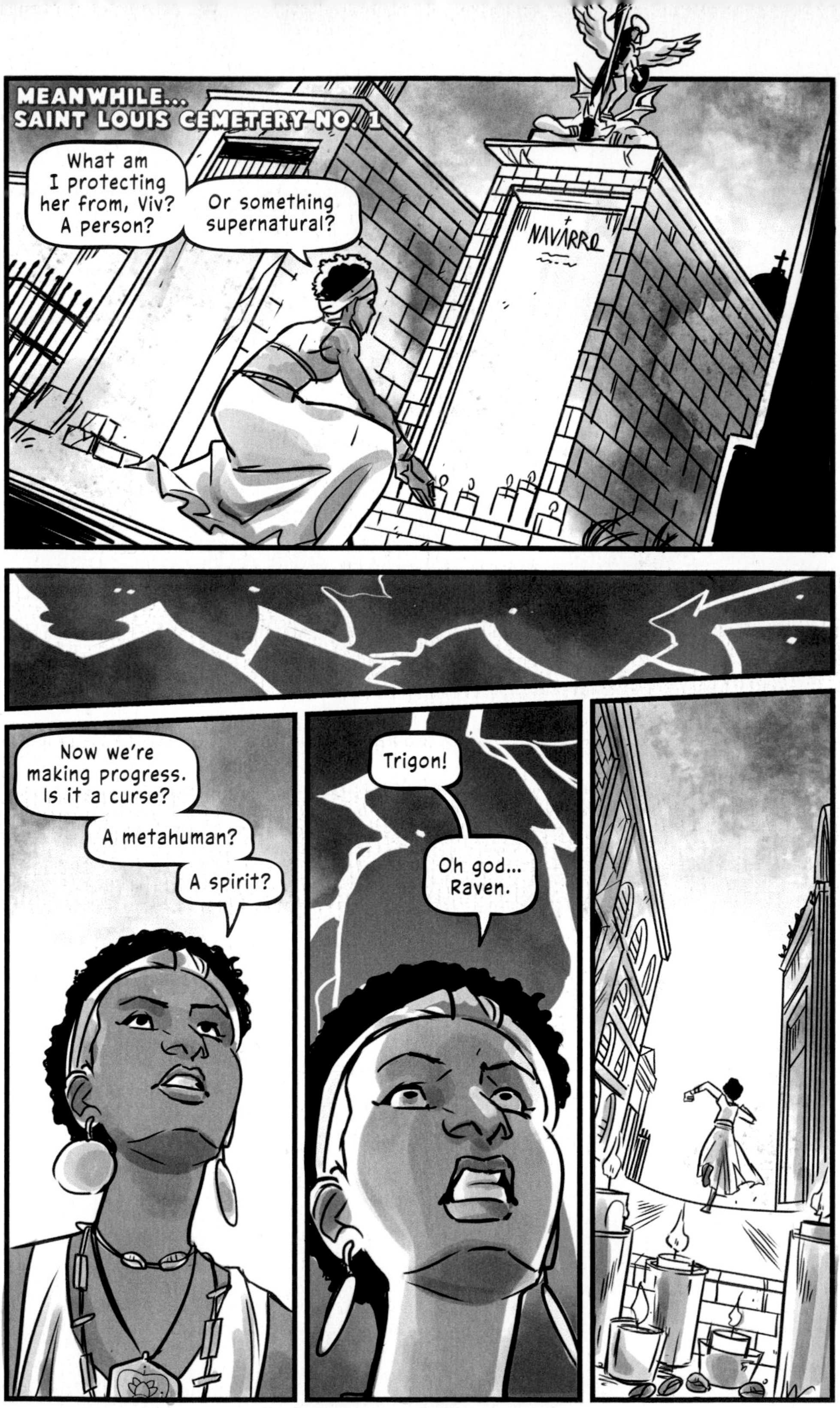
MEANWHILE...
SAINT LOUIS CEMETERY NO. 1
What am I protecting her from, Viv? A person?
Or something supernatural?
NAVARRO
Now we're making progress. Is it a curse?
A metahuman?
A spirit?
Trigon!
Oh god... Raven.

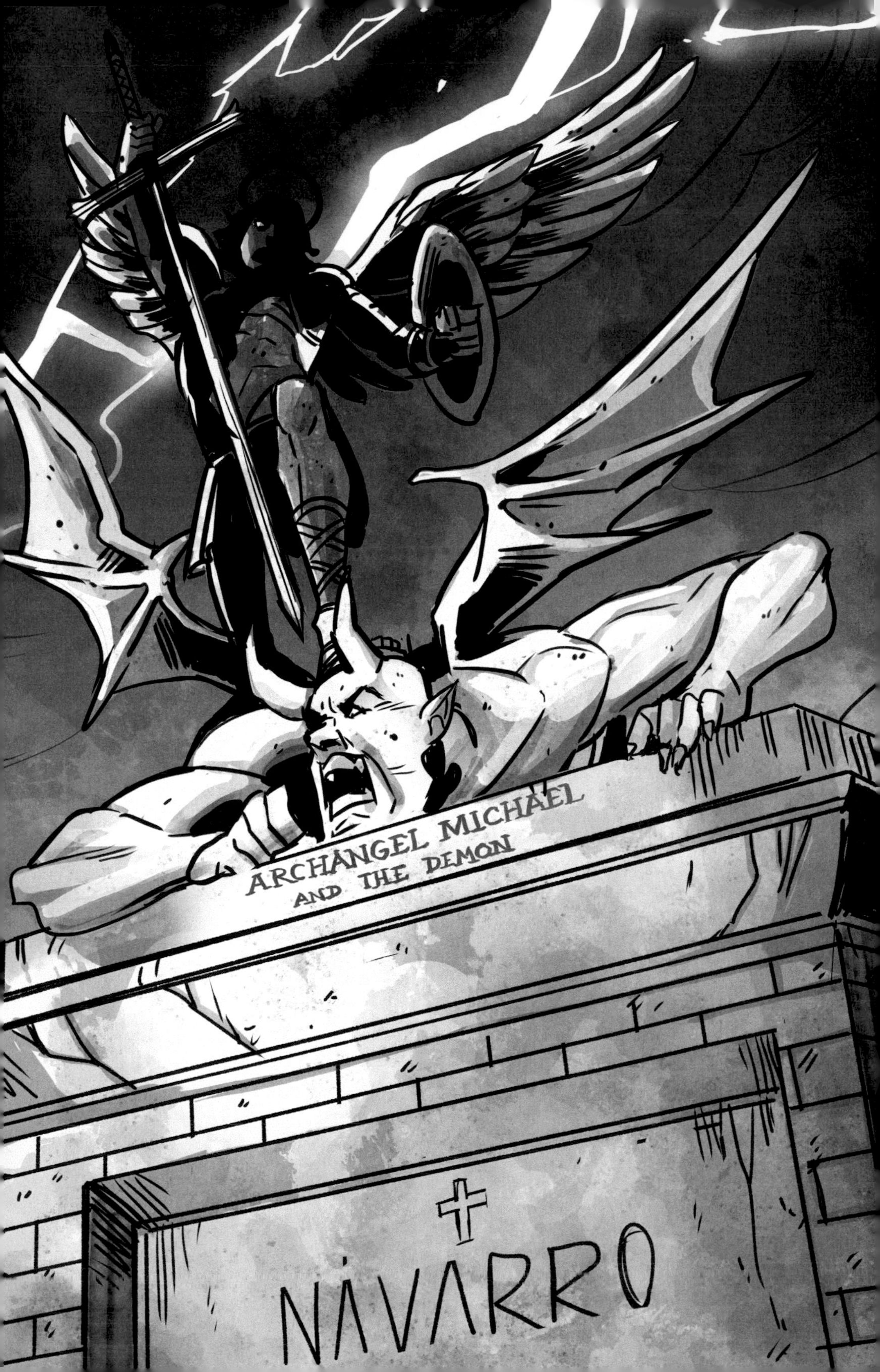
ARCHANGEL MICHAEL
AND THE DEMON
NAVARRO

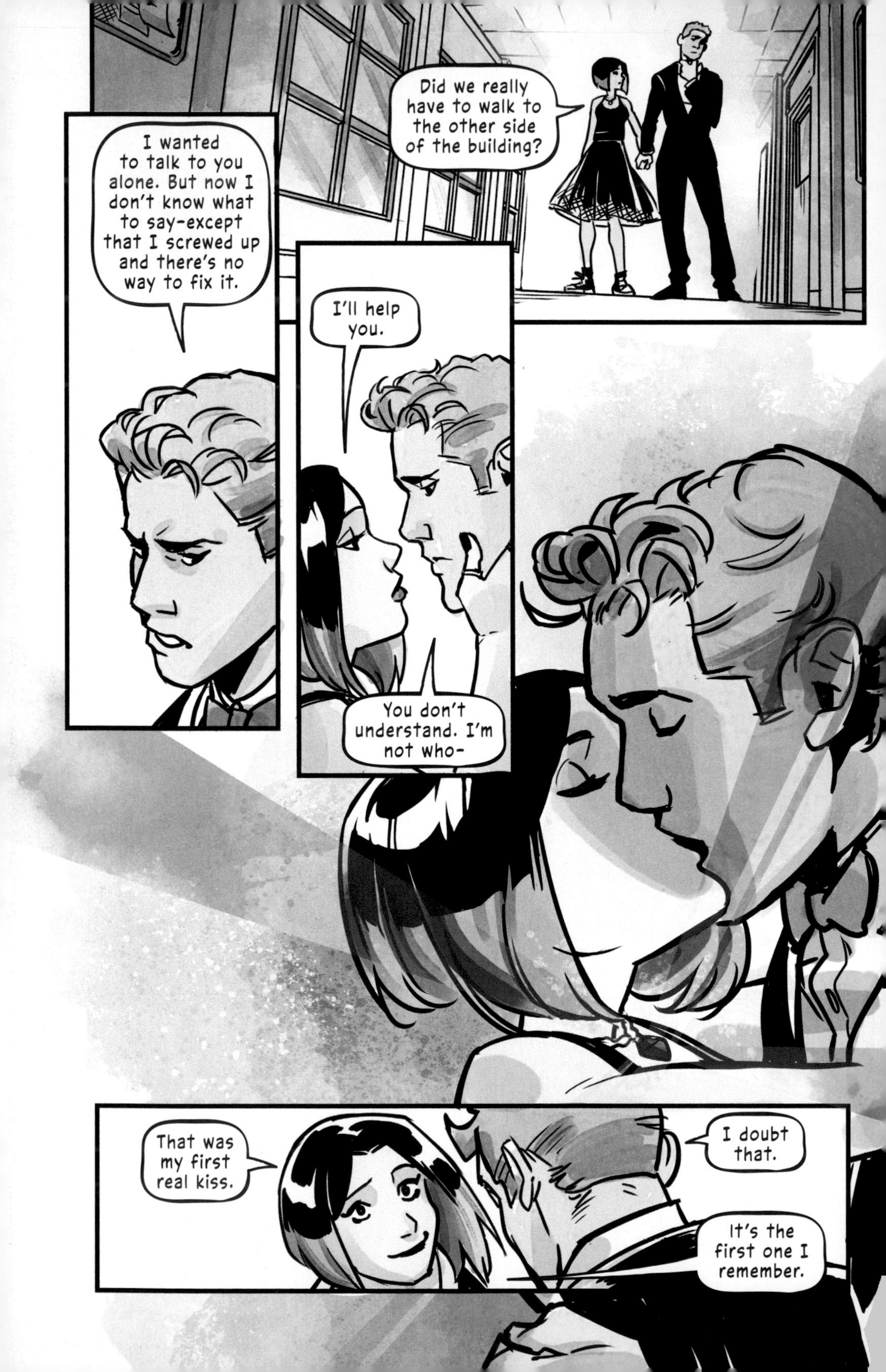
Did we really have to walk to the other side of the building?
I wanted to talk to you alone. But now I don't know what to say-except that I screwed up and there's no way to fix it.
I'll help you.
You don't understand. I'm not who-
That was my first real kiss.
I doubt that.
It's the first one I remember.

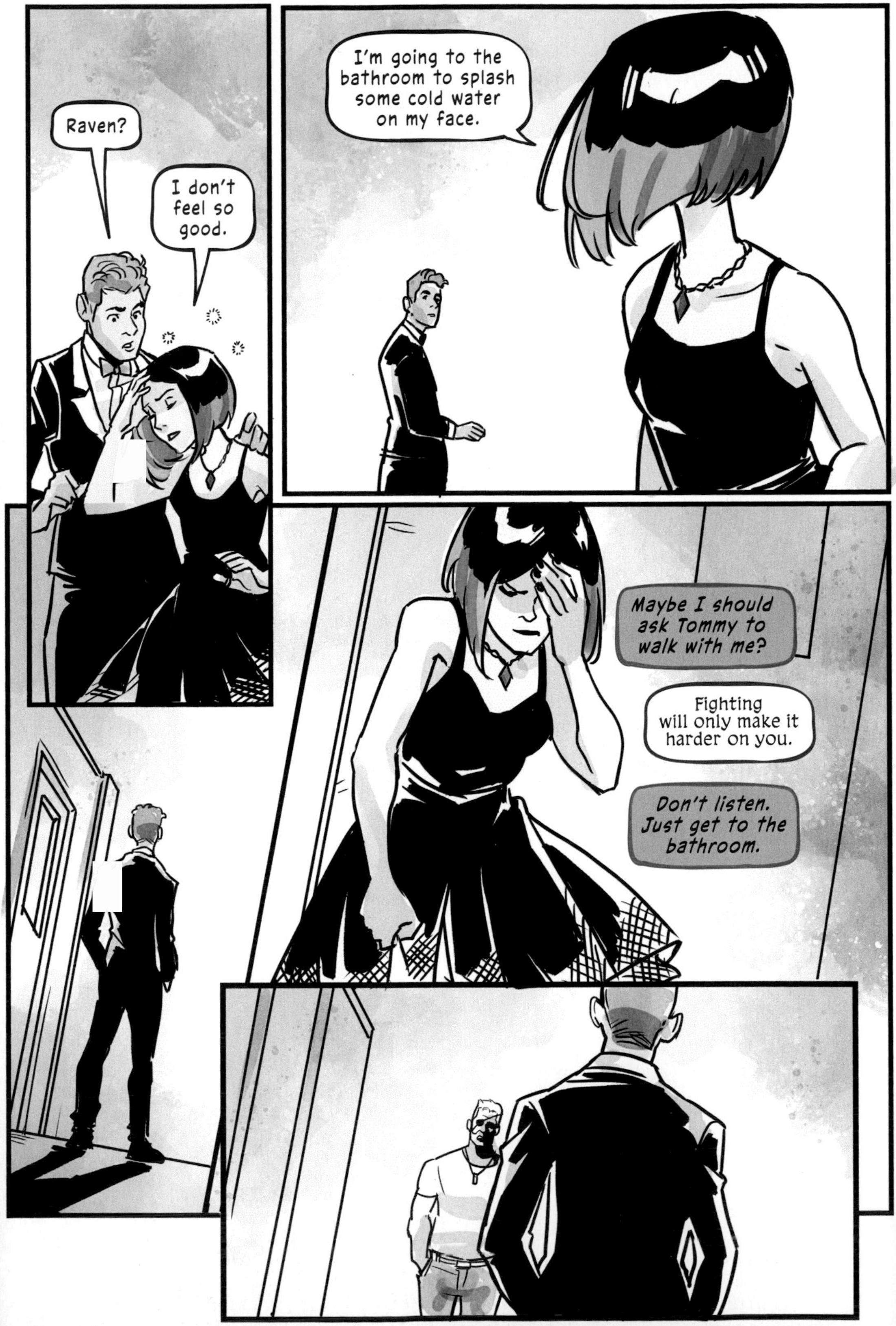
Raven?
I don't feel so good.
I'm going to the bathroom to splash some cold water on my face.
Maybe I should ask Tommy to walk with me?
Fighting will only make it harder on you.
Don't listen. Just get to the bathroom.

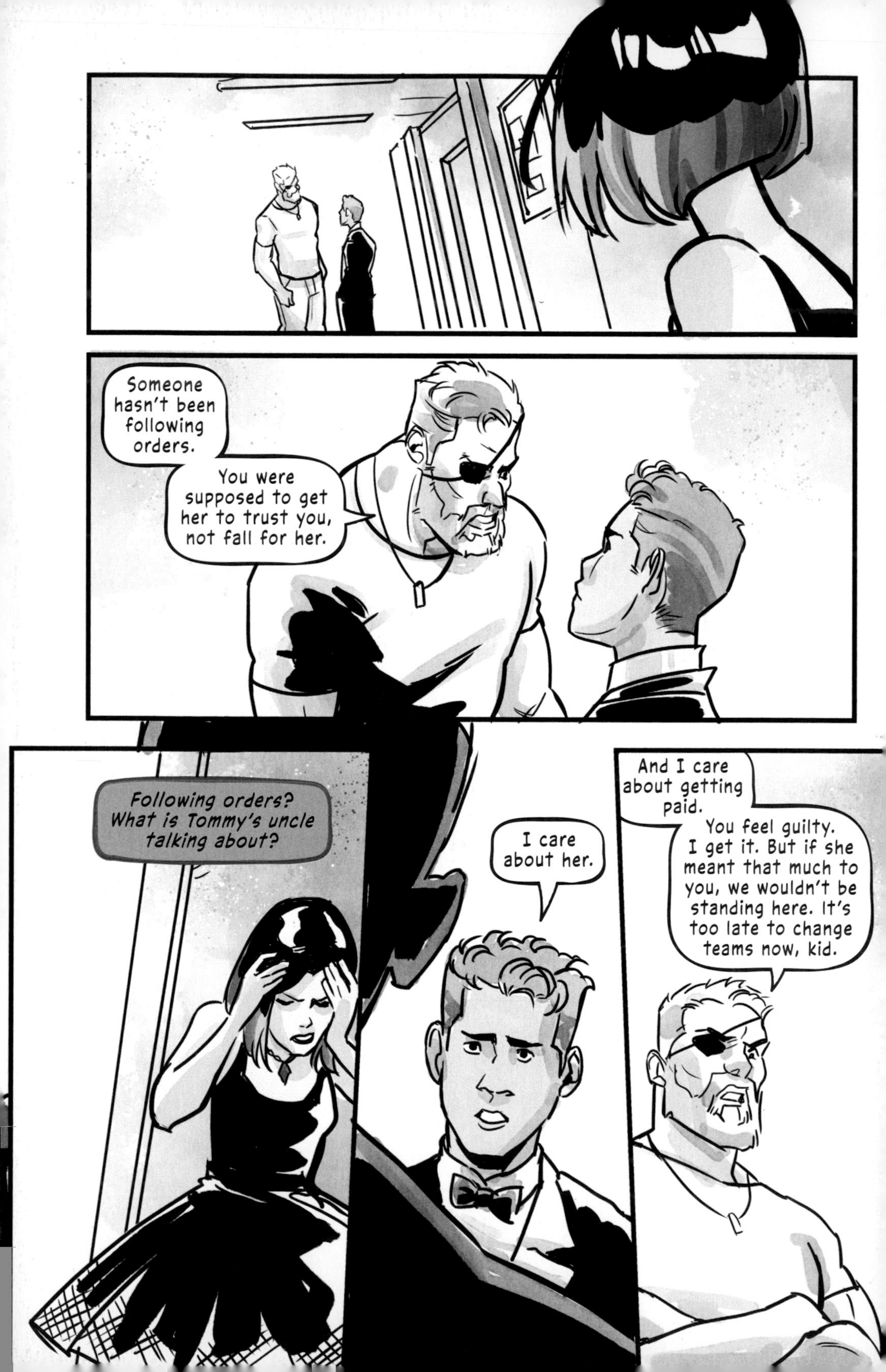
Someone hasn't been following orders.
You were supposed to get her to trust you, not fall for her.
Following orders? What is Tommy's uncle talking about?
I care about her.
And I care about getting paid.
You feel guilty. I get it. But if she meant that much to you, we wouldn't be standing here. It's too late to change teams now, kid.

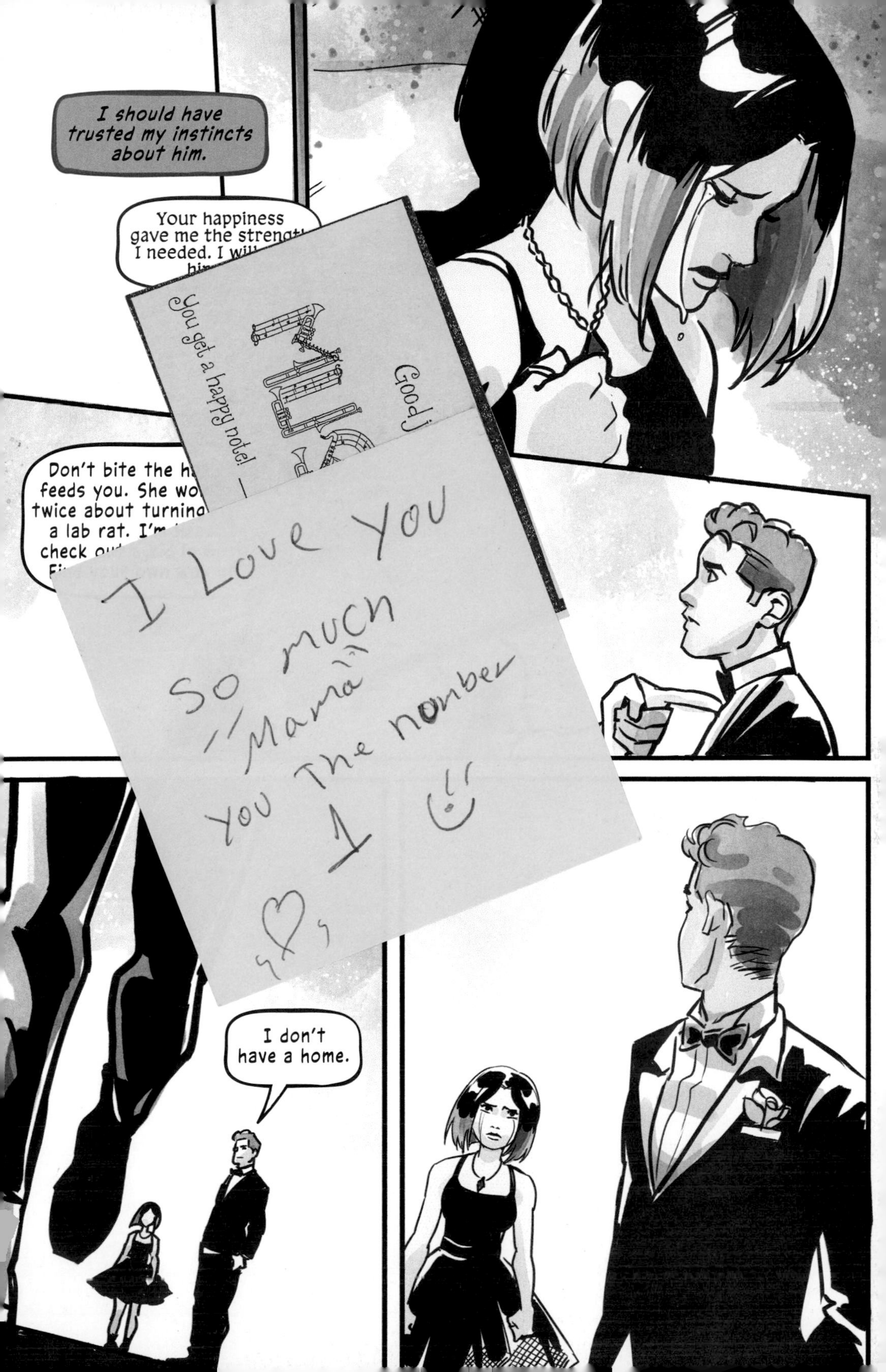
I should have trusted my instincts about him.
Your happiness gave me the strengt
I needed. I wil
Don't bite the h
feeds you. She wo
twice about turning
a lab rat. I'm
check ou
Good j
You get a happy note!
I Love You So much Mama You The number 1
I don't have a home.

CHAPTER 15: SINS OF THE FATHER

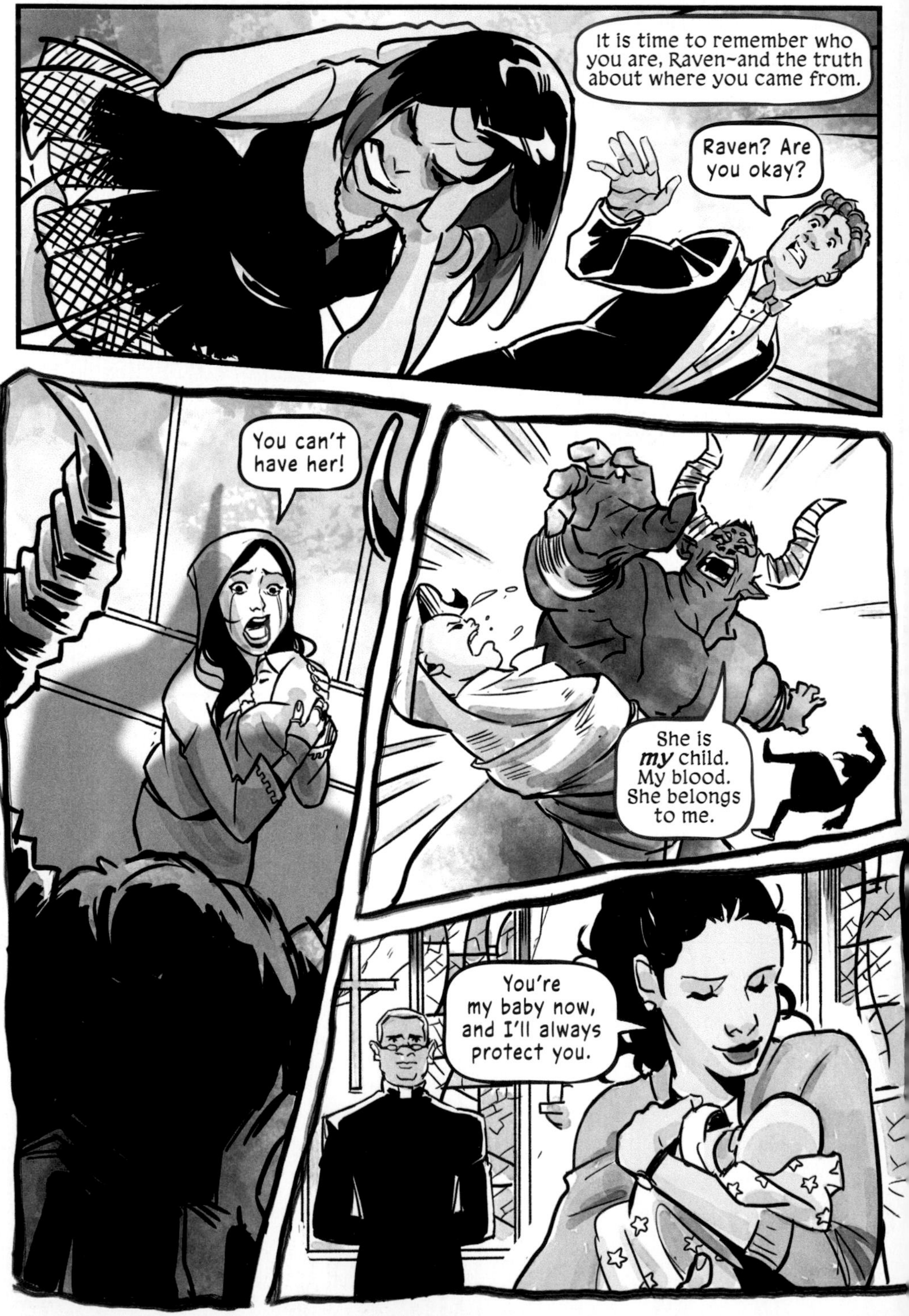

It is time to remember who you are, Raven~and the truth about where you came from.
Raven? Are you okay?
You can't have her!
She is *my* child. My blood. She belongs to me.
You're my baby now, and I'll always protect you.

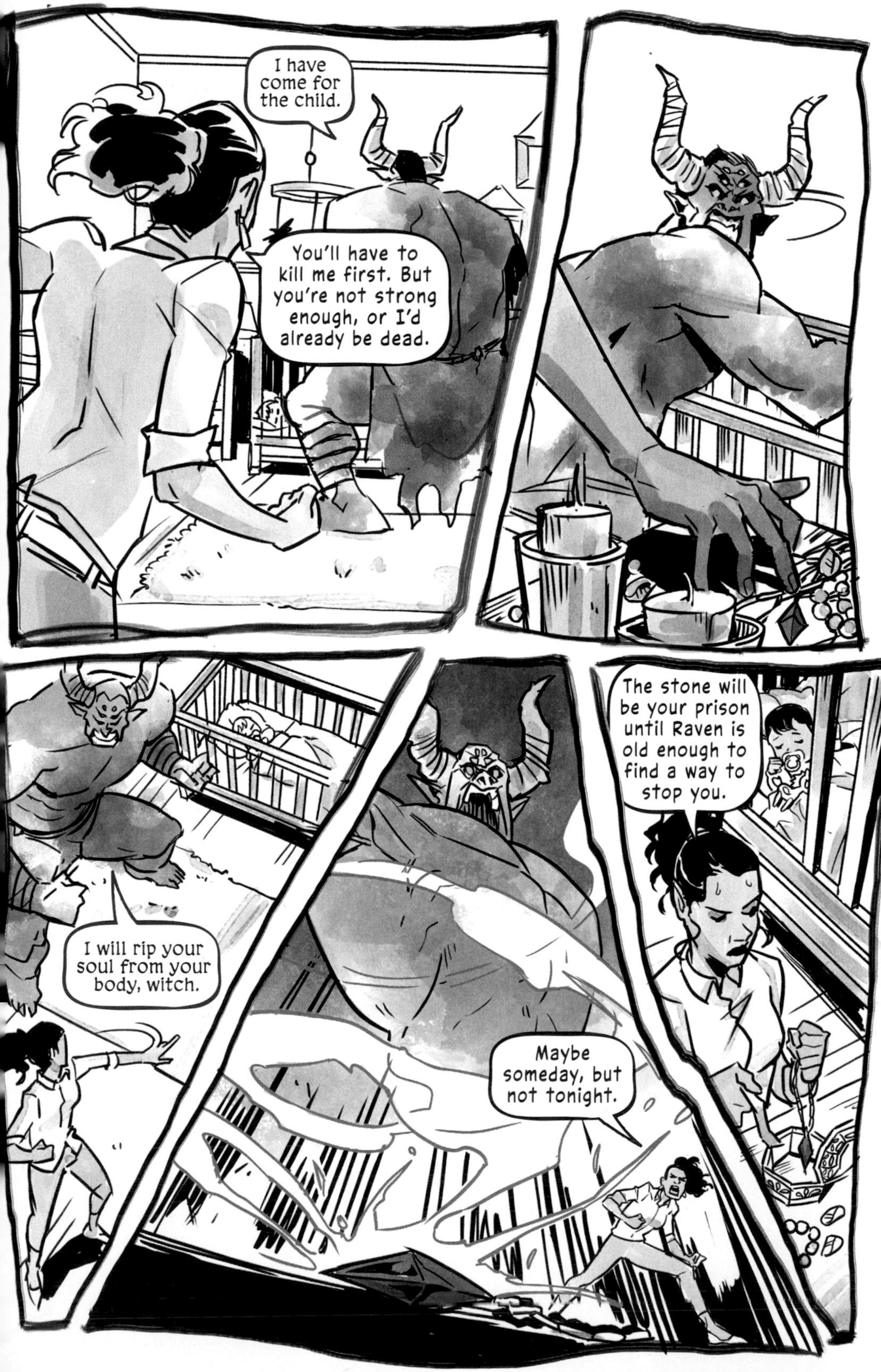
I have come for the child.
You'll have to kill me first. But you're not strong enough, or I'd already be dead.
I will rip your soul from your body, witch.
Maybe someday, but not tonight.
The stone will be your prison until Raven is old enough to find a way to stop you.

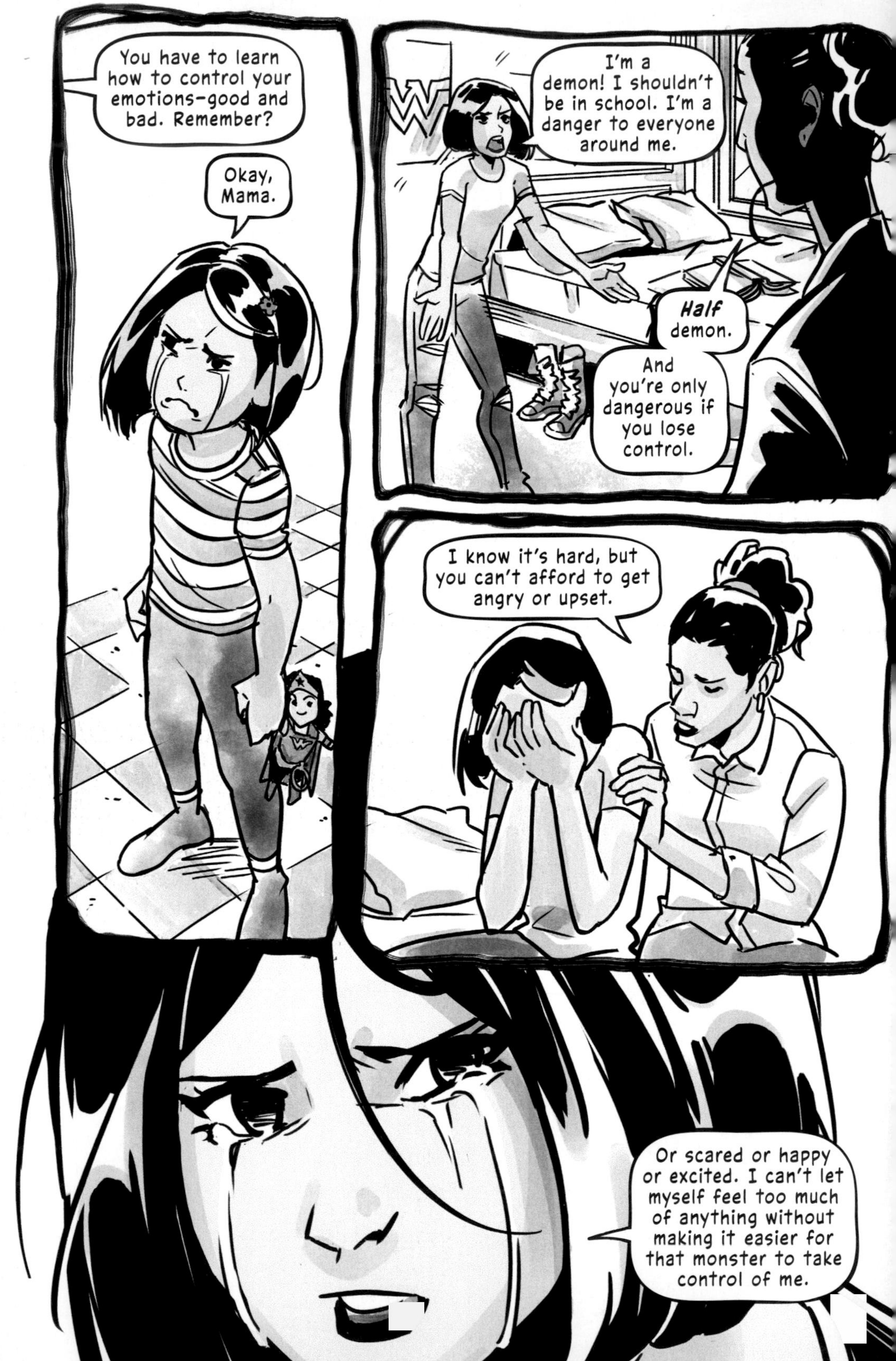
You have to learn how to control your emotions—good and bad. Remember?
Okay, Mama.
I'm a demon! I shouldn't be in school. I'm a danger to everyone around me.
Half demon.
And you're only dangerous if you lose control.
I know it's hard, but you can't afford to get angry or upset.
Or scared or happy or excited. I can't let myself feel too much of anything without making it easier for that monster to take control of me.

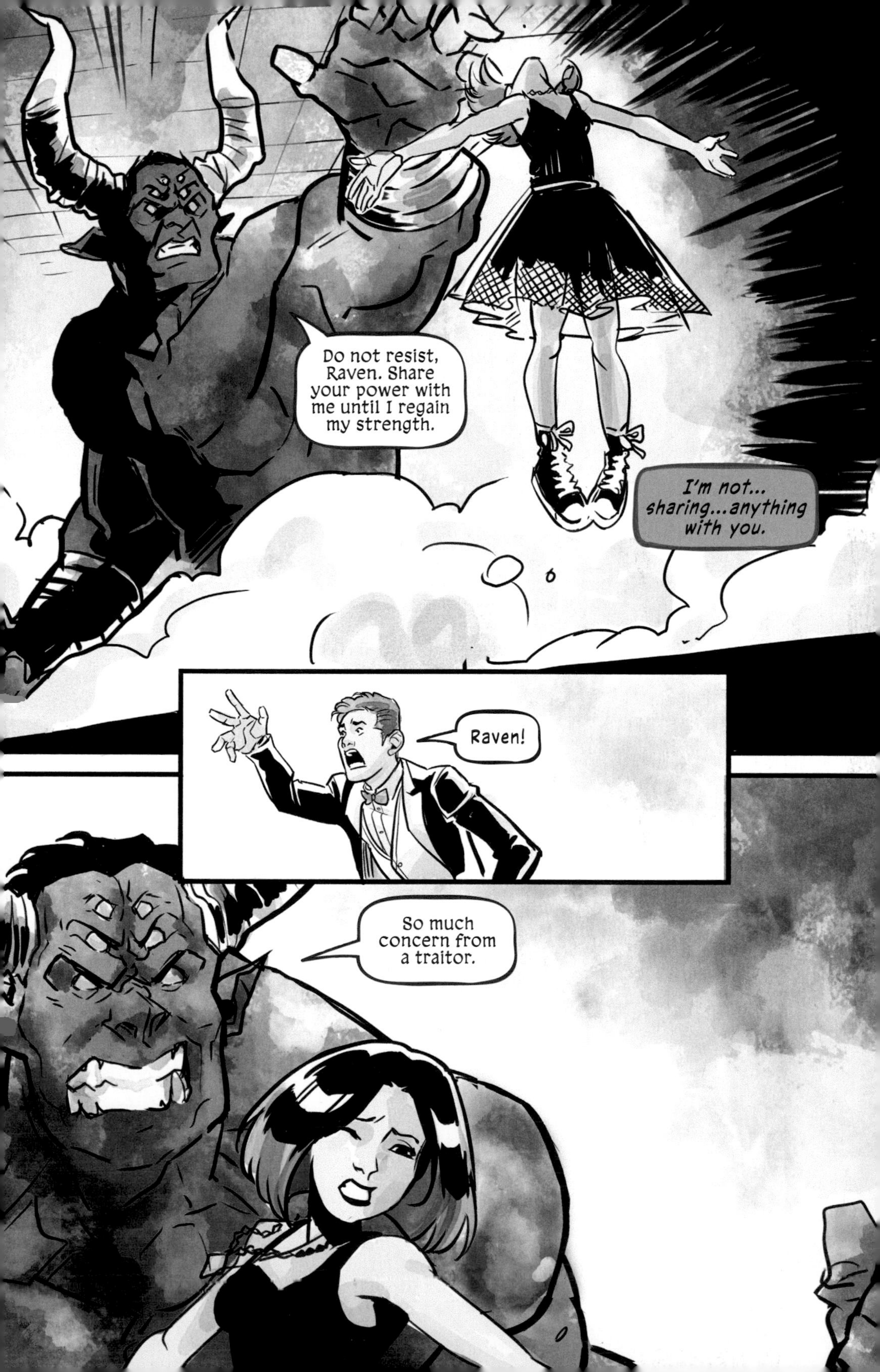
Do not resist, Raven. Share your power with me until I regain my strength.
I'm not... sharing...anything with you.
Raven!
So much concern from a traitor.

CHAPTER 16: SOULSTORM

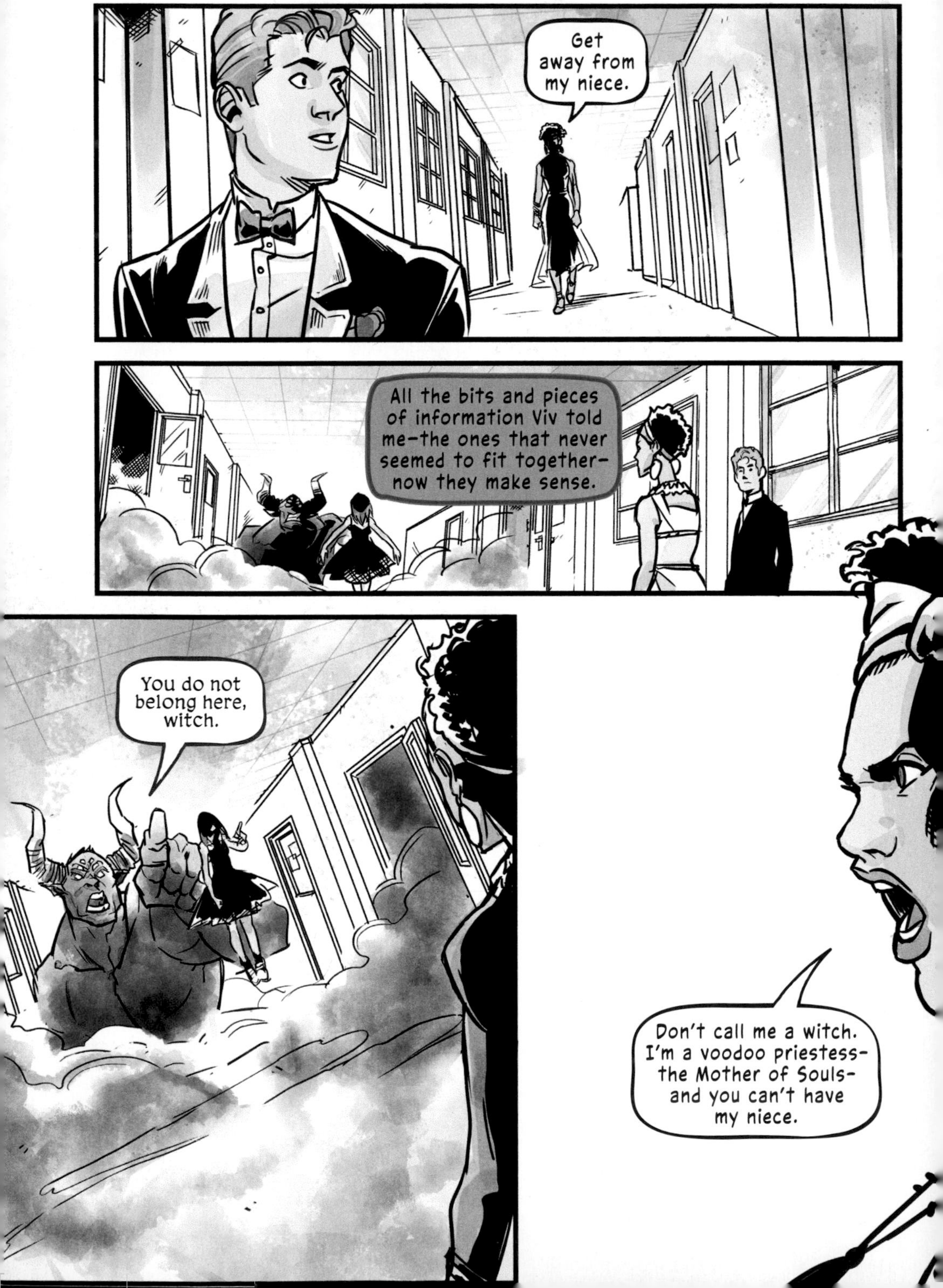
Get away from my niece.
All the bits and pieces of information Viv told me—the ones that never seemed to fit together—now they make sense.
You do not belong here, witch.
Don't call me a witch. I'm a voodoo priestess—the Mother of Souls—and you can't have my niece.

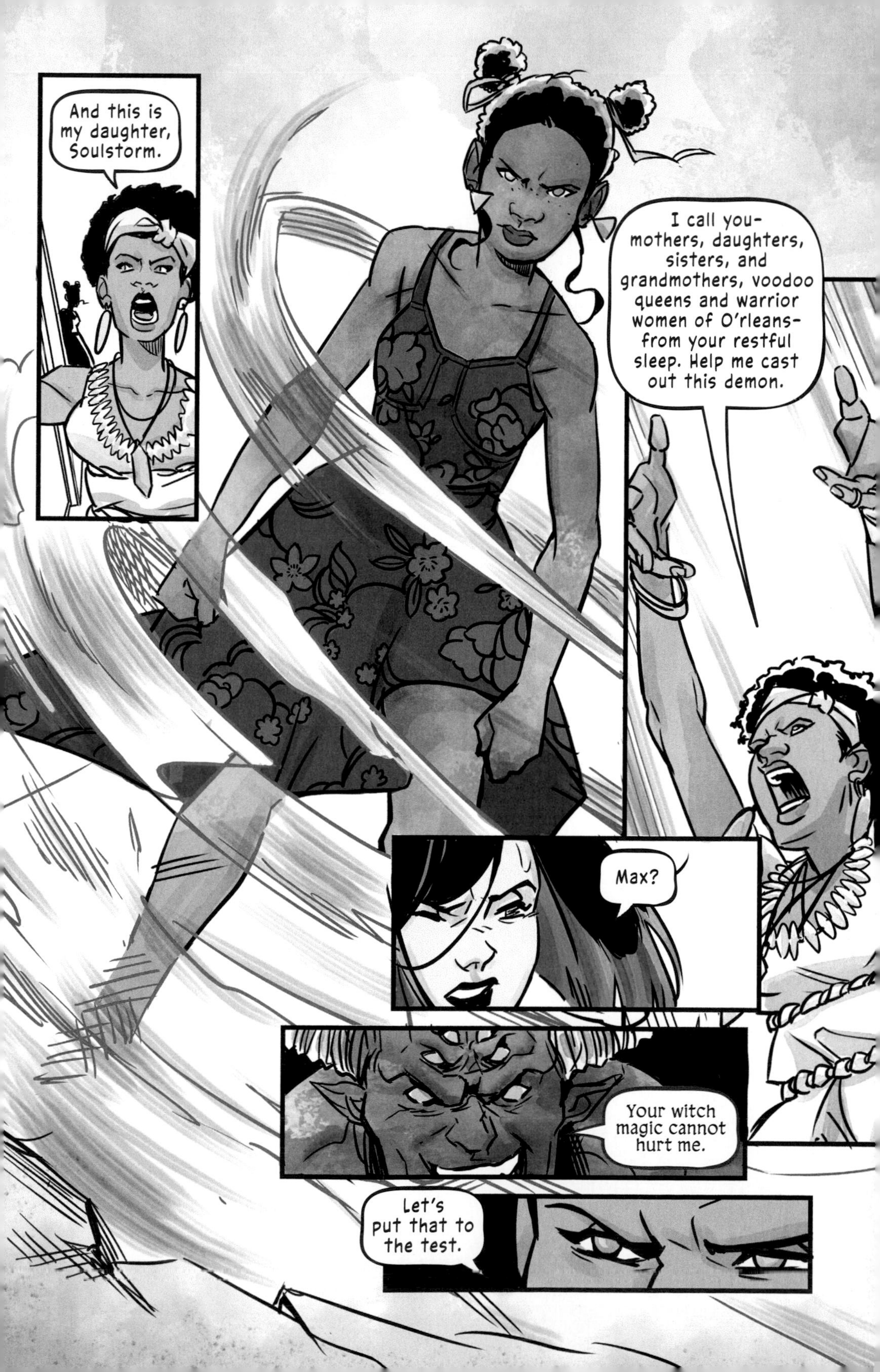
And this is my daughter, Soulstorm.
I call you- mothers, daughters, sisters, and grandmothers, voodoo queens and warrior women of O'rleans- from your restful sleep. Help me cast out this demon.
Max?
Your witch magic cannot hurt me.
Let's put that to the test.

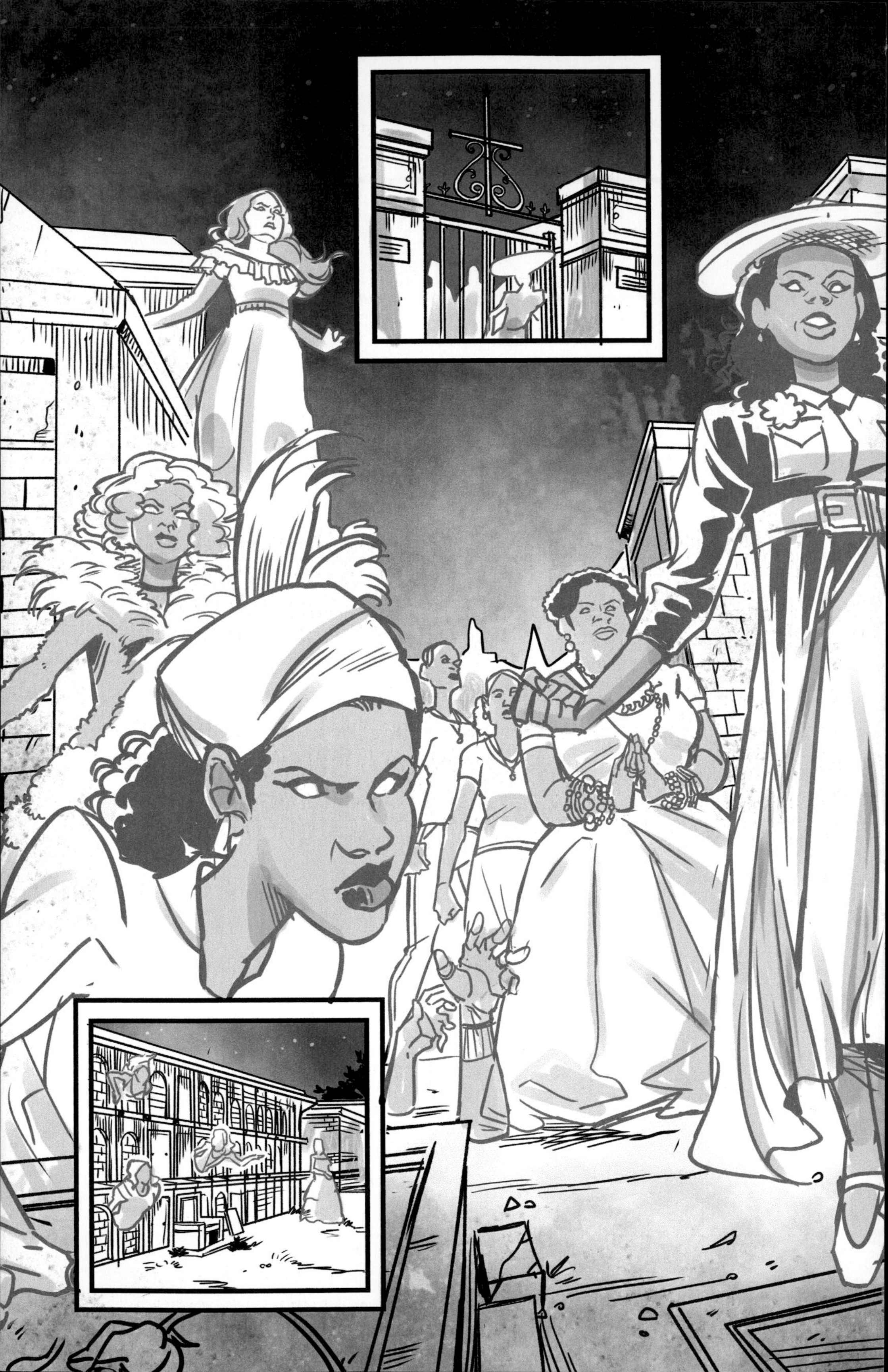

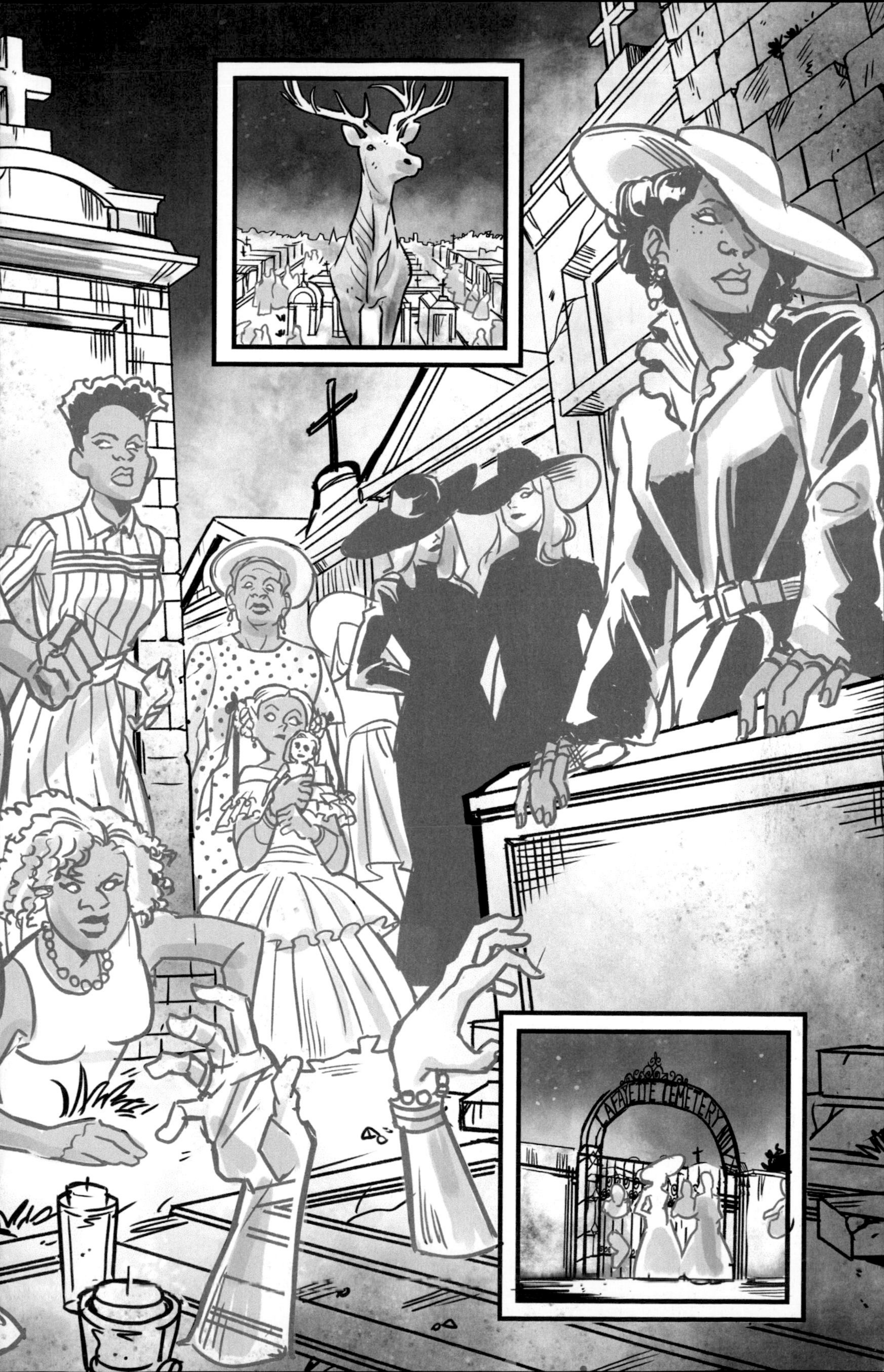
LAFAYETTE CEMETERY

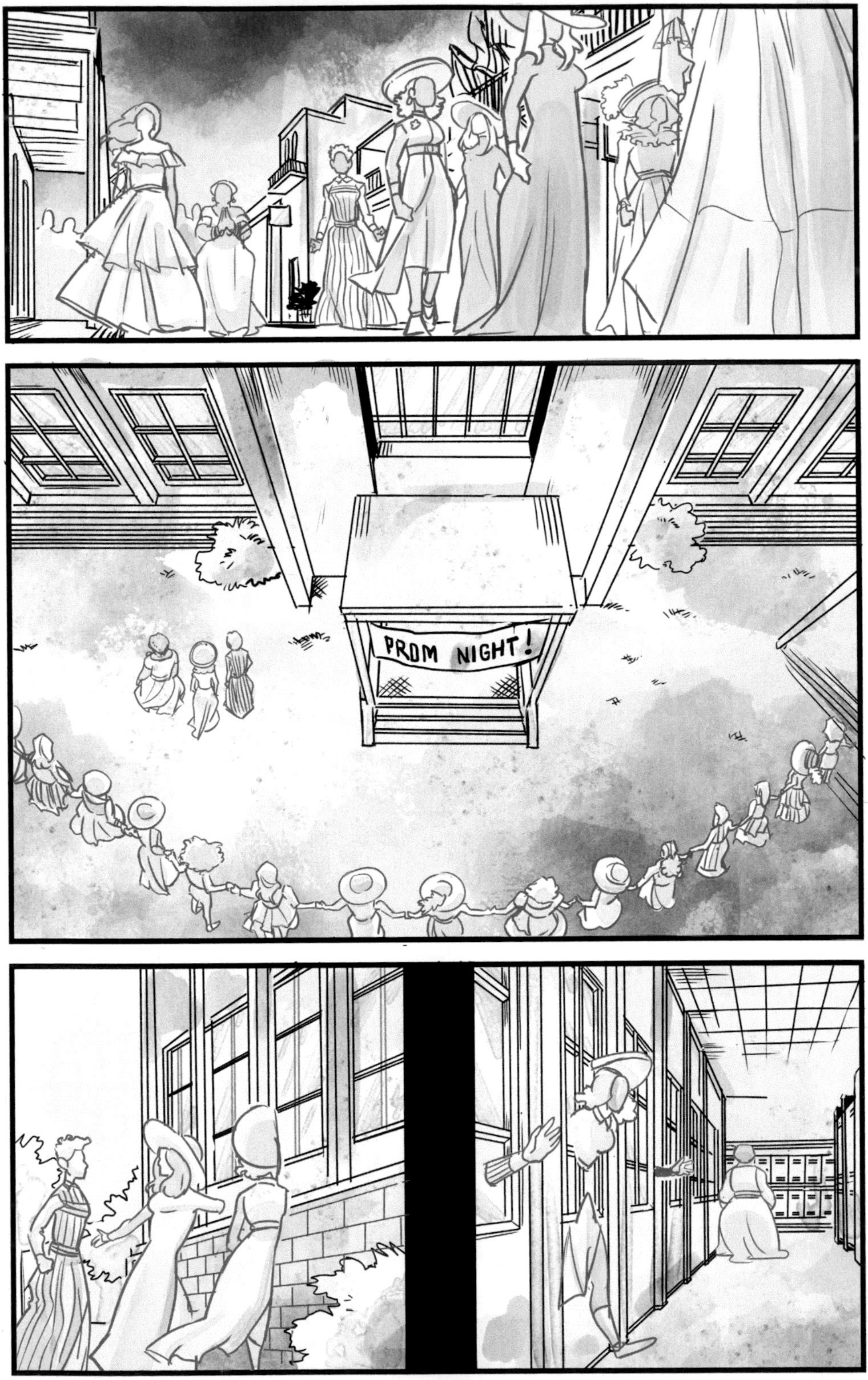
PROM NIGHT!

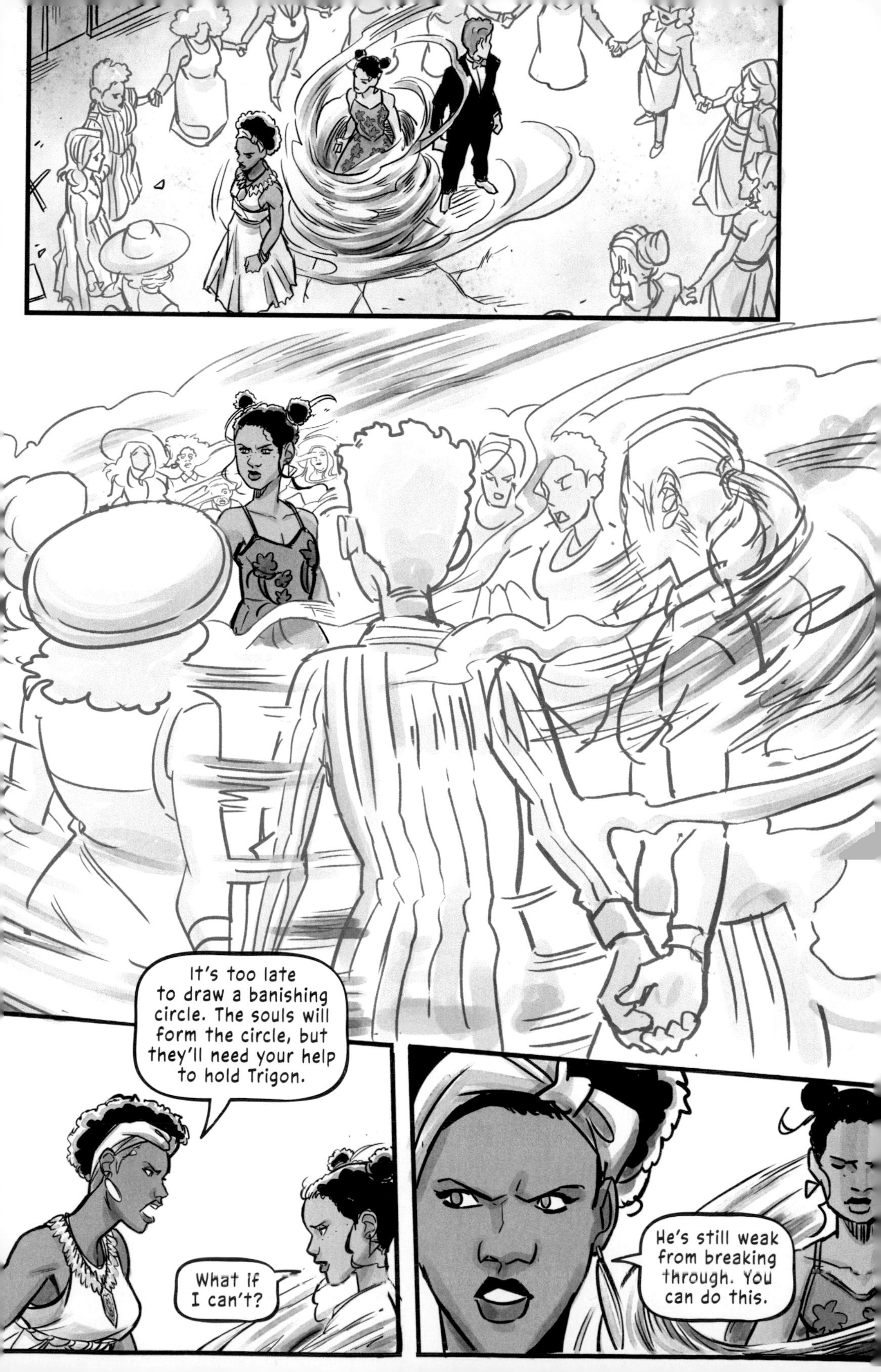
It's too late to draw a banishing circle. The souls will form the circle, but they'll need your help to hold Trigon.
What if I can't?
He's still weak from breaking through. You can do this.

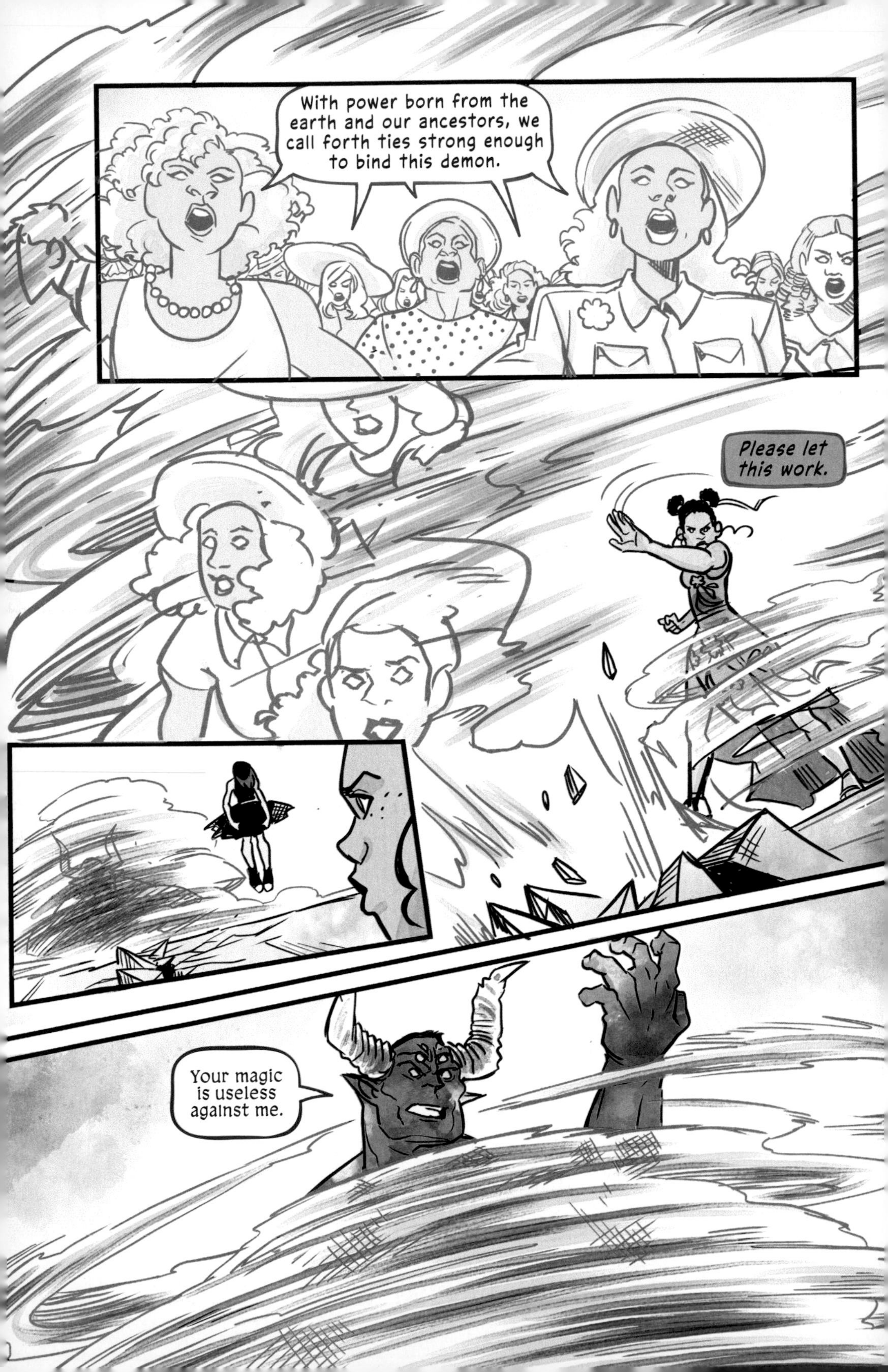
With power born from the earth and our ancestors, we call forth ties strong enough to bind this demon.
Please let this work.
Your magic is useless against me.

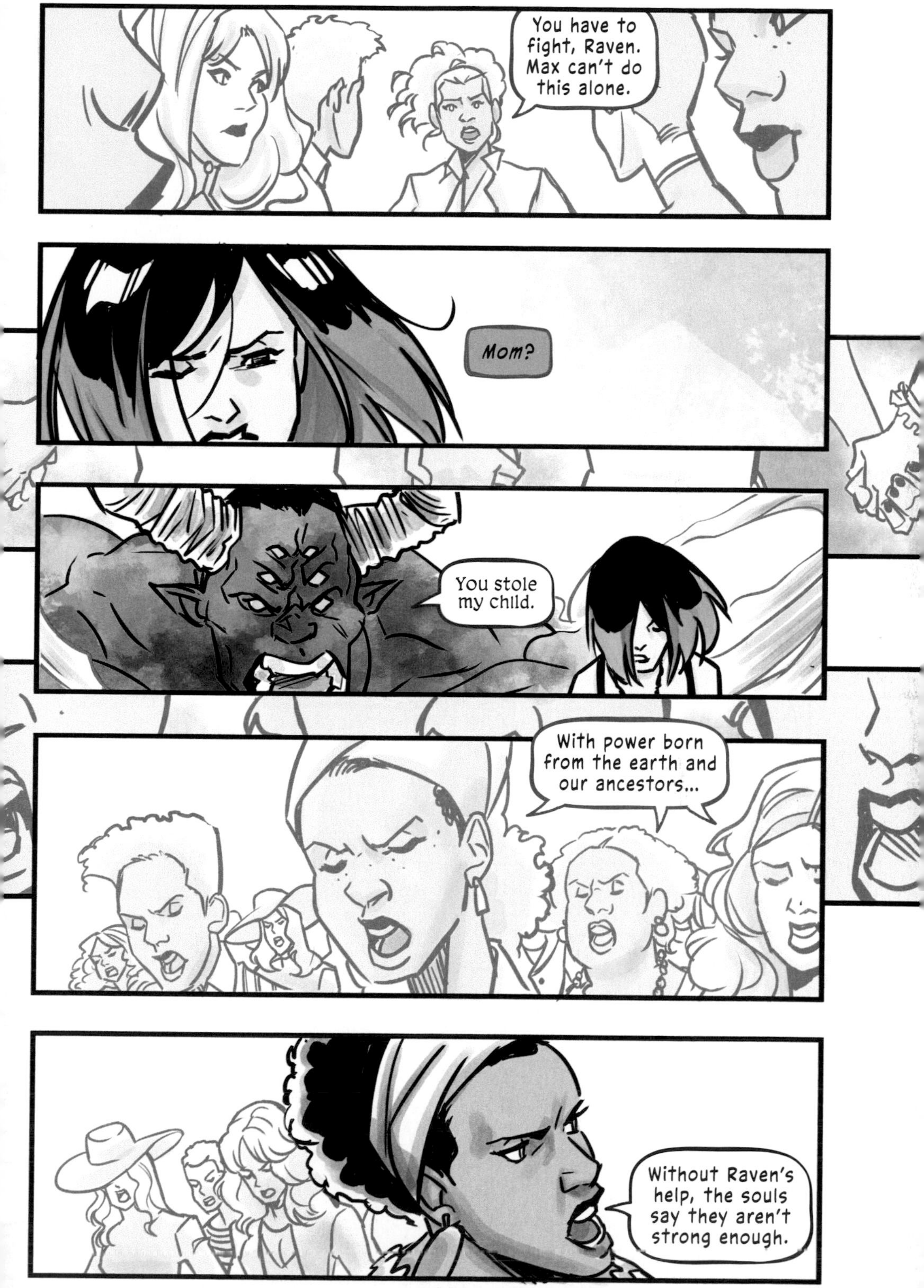
You have to fight, Raven. Max can't do this alone.
Mom?
You stole my child.
With power born from the earth and our ancestors...
Without Raven's help, the souls say they aren't strong enough.

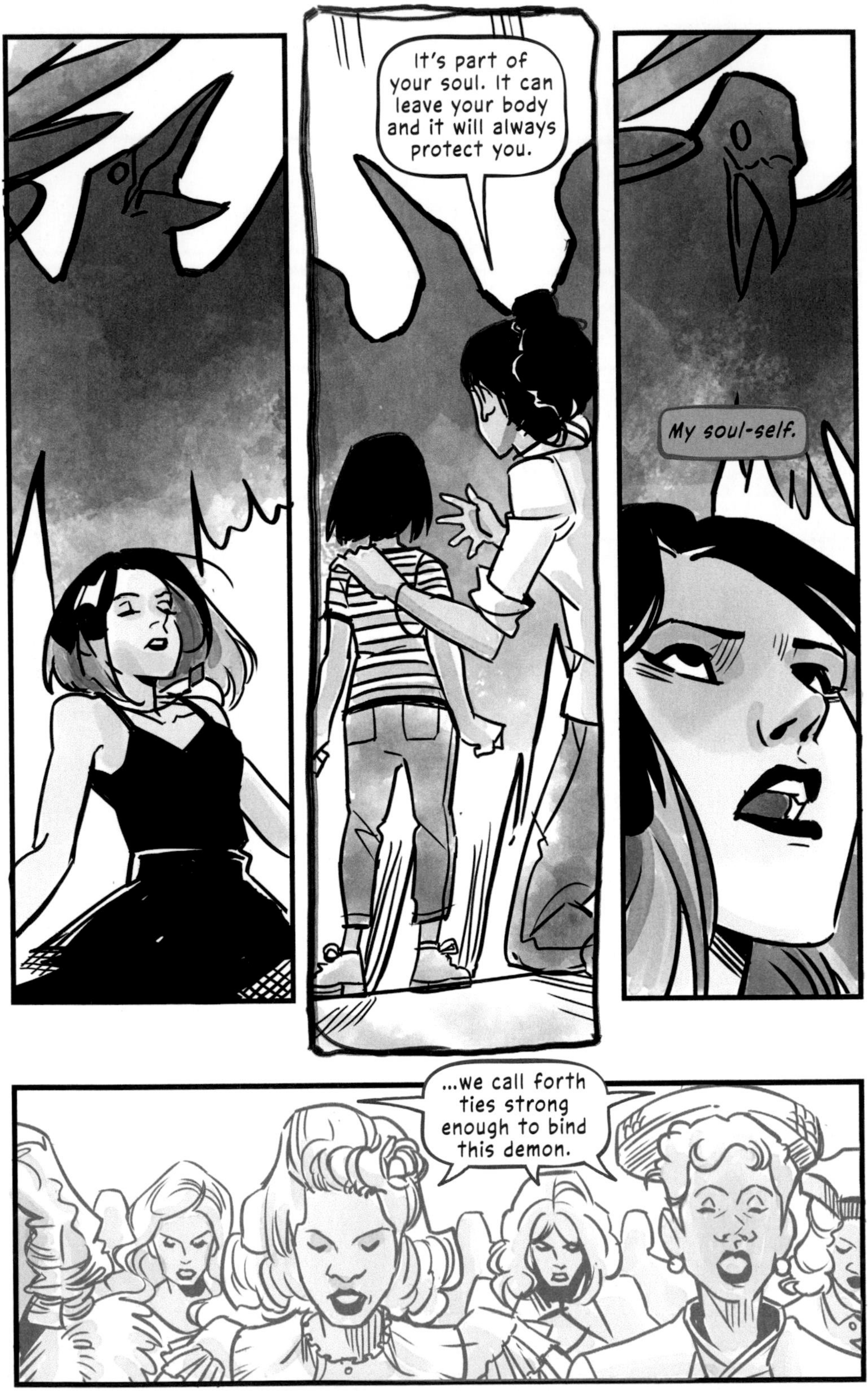
It's part of your soul. It can leave your body and it will always protect you.
My soul-self.
...we call forth ties strong enough to bind this demon.

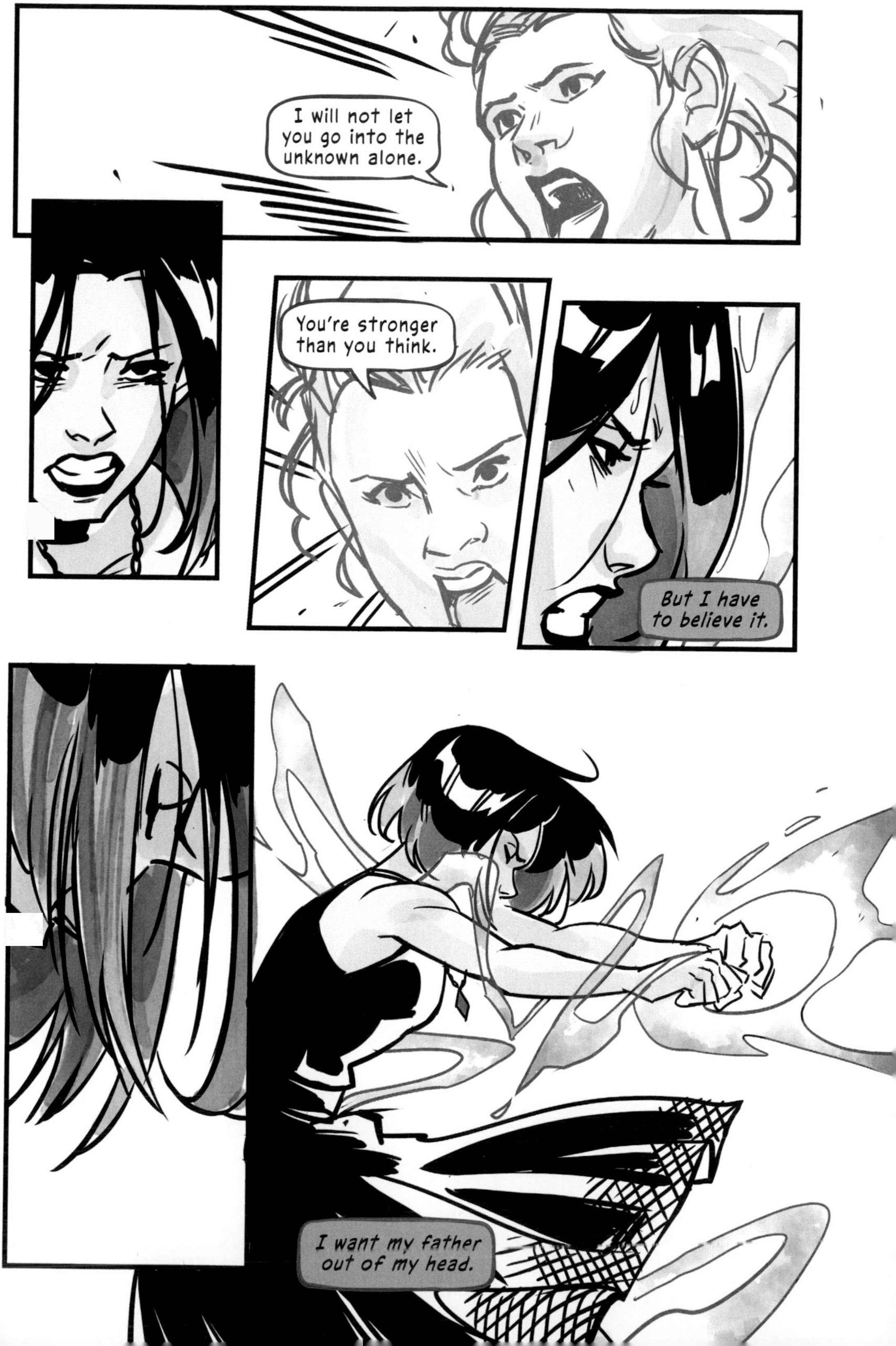
I will not let you go into the unknown alone.
You're stronger than you think.
But I have to believe it.
I want my father out of my head.

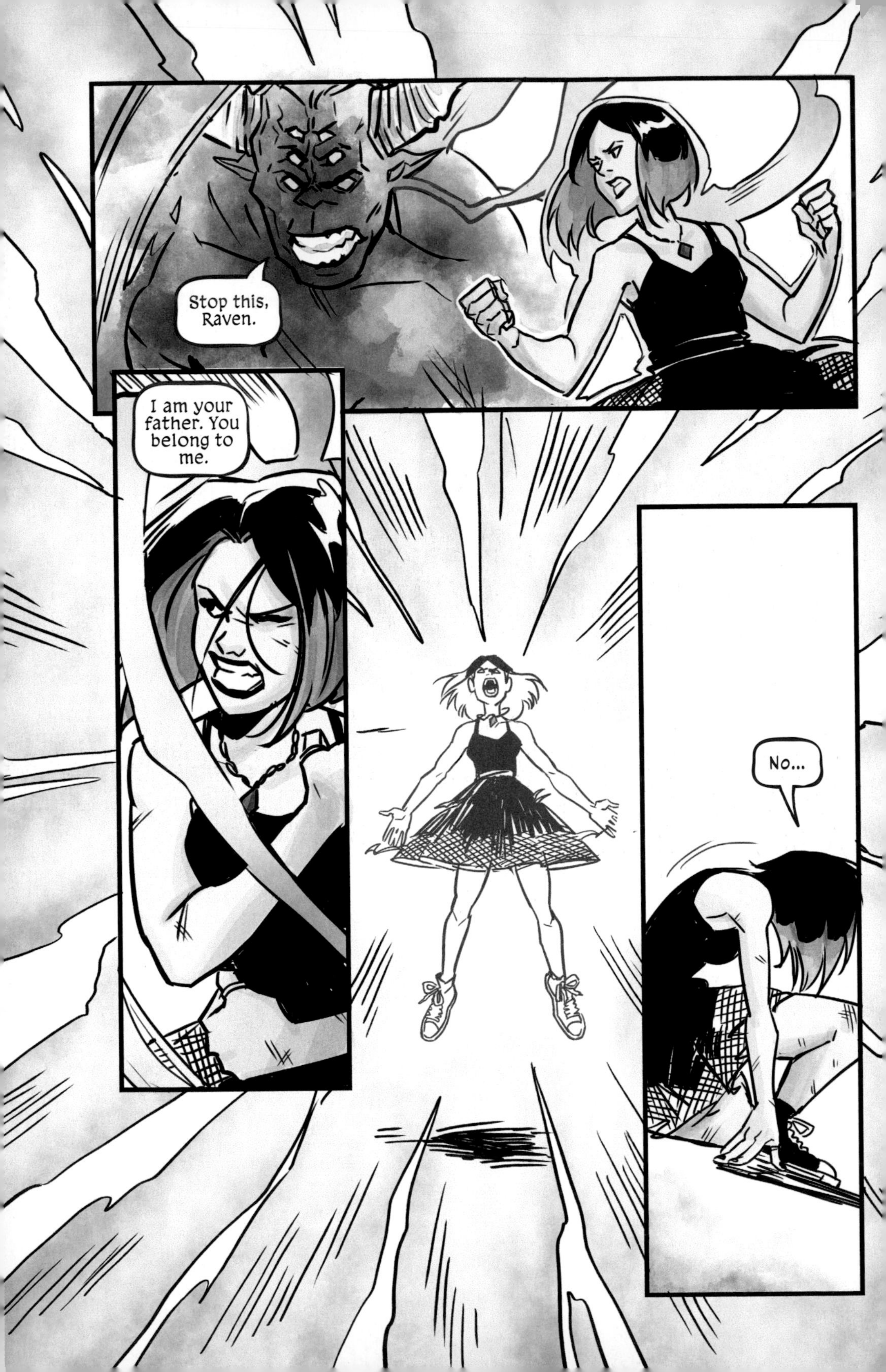
Stop this, Raven.
I am your father. You belong to me.
No...

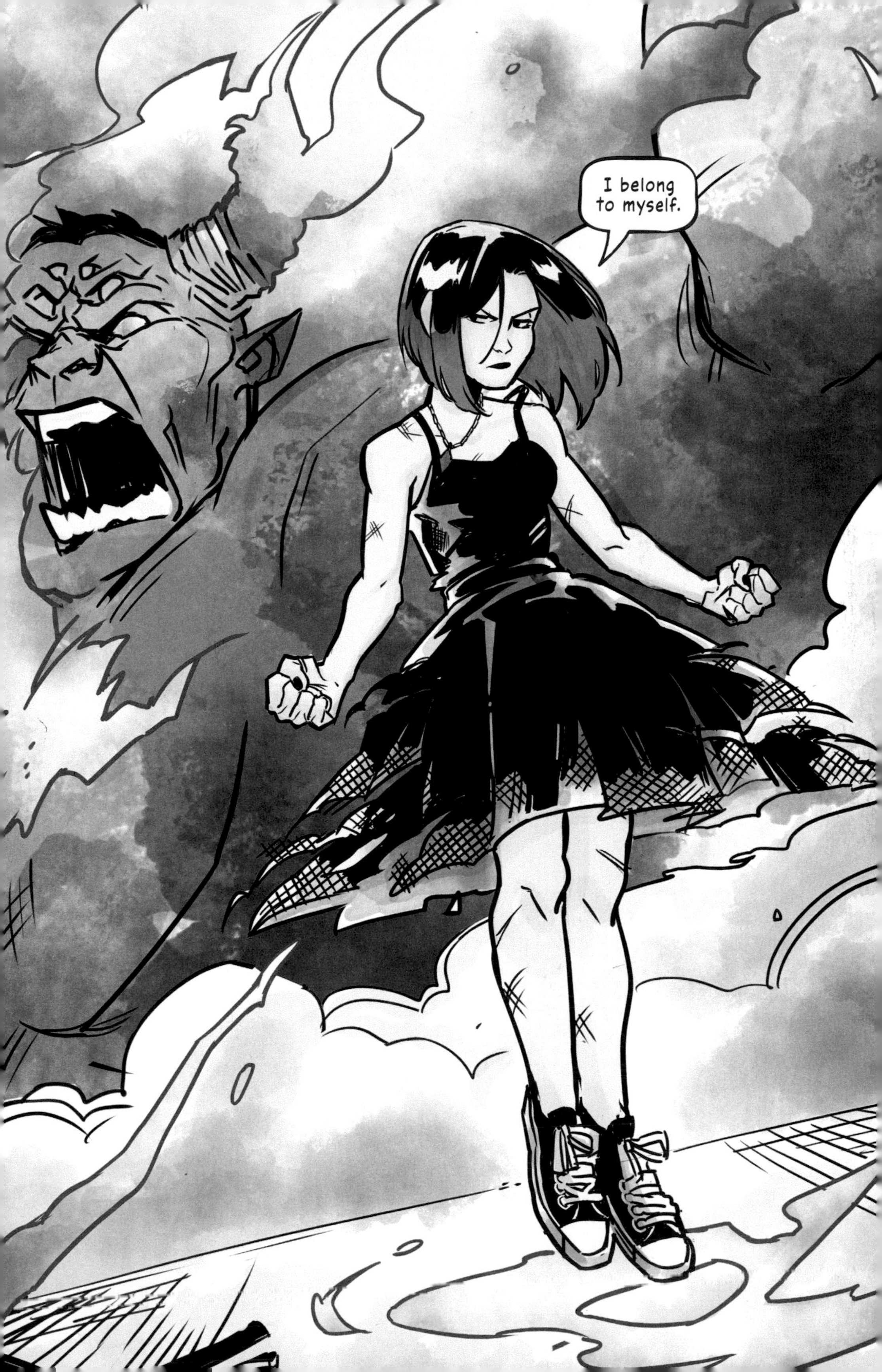
I belong to myself.

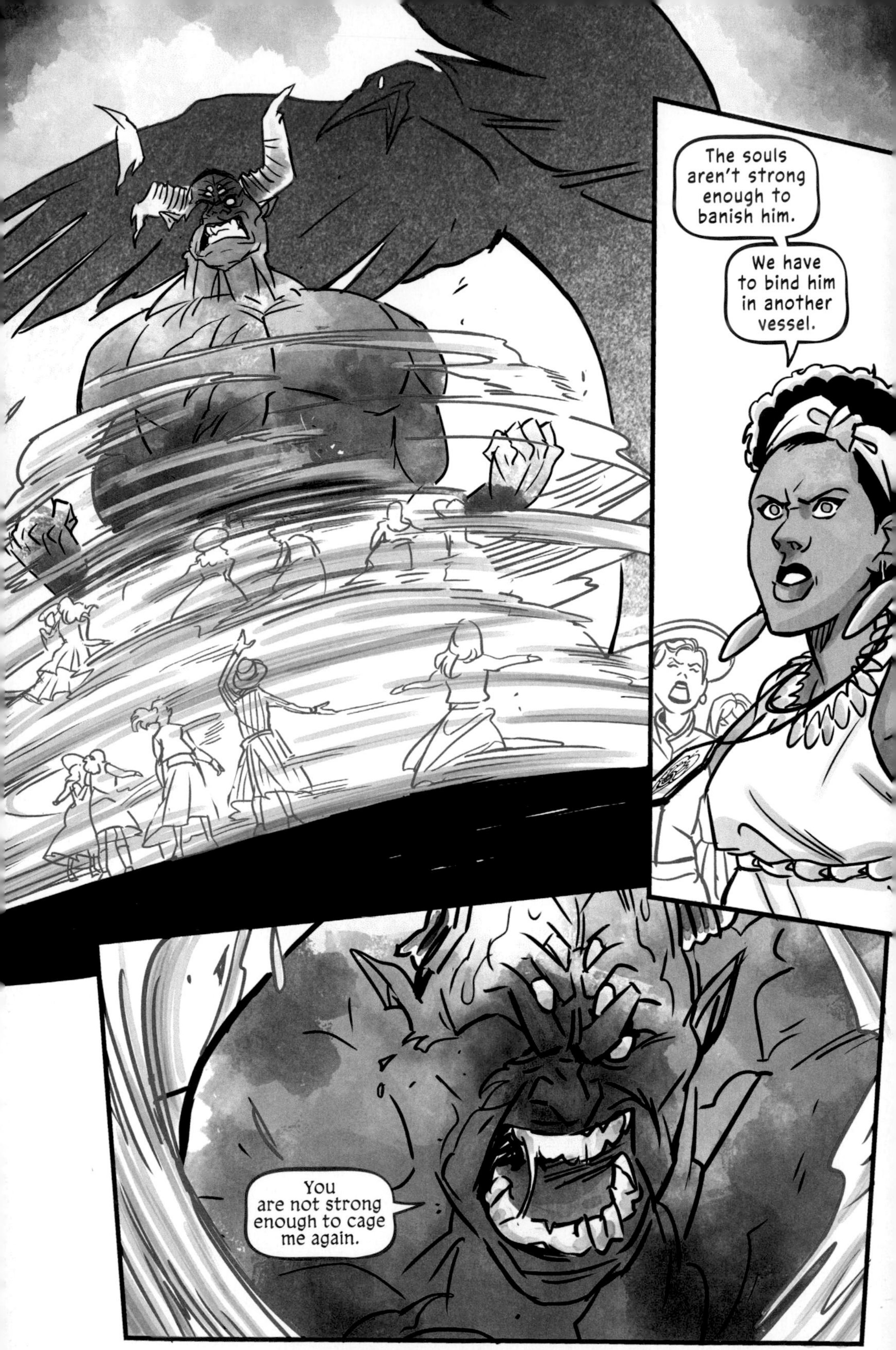
The souls aren't strong enough to banish him.
We have to bind him in another vessel.
You are not strong enough to cage me again.

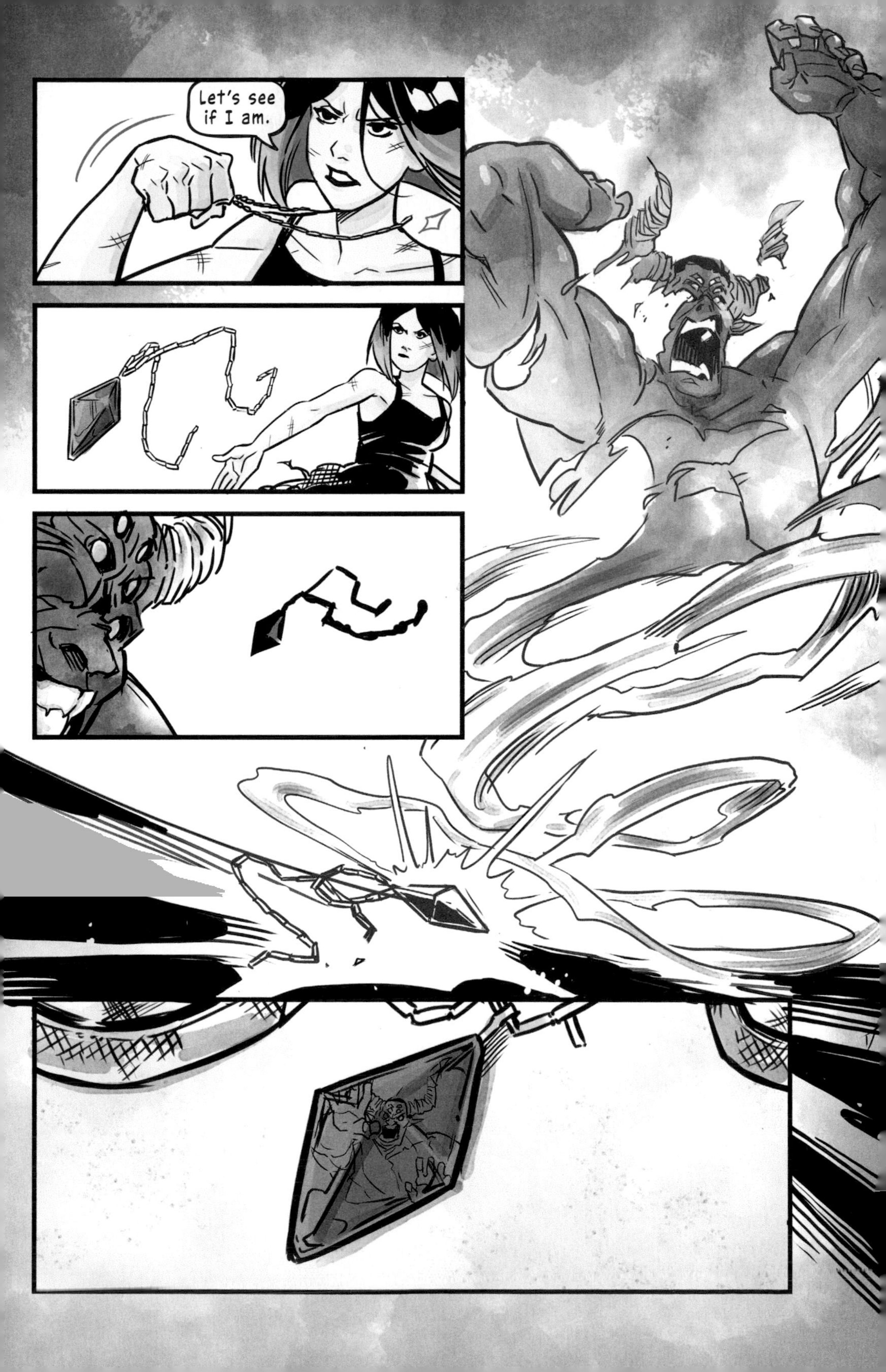
Let's see if I am.

CHAPTER 17: FORGET ME NOT

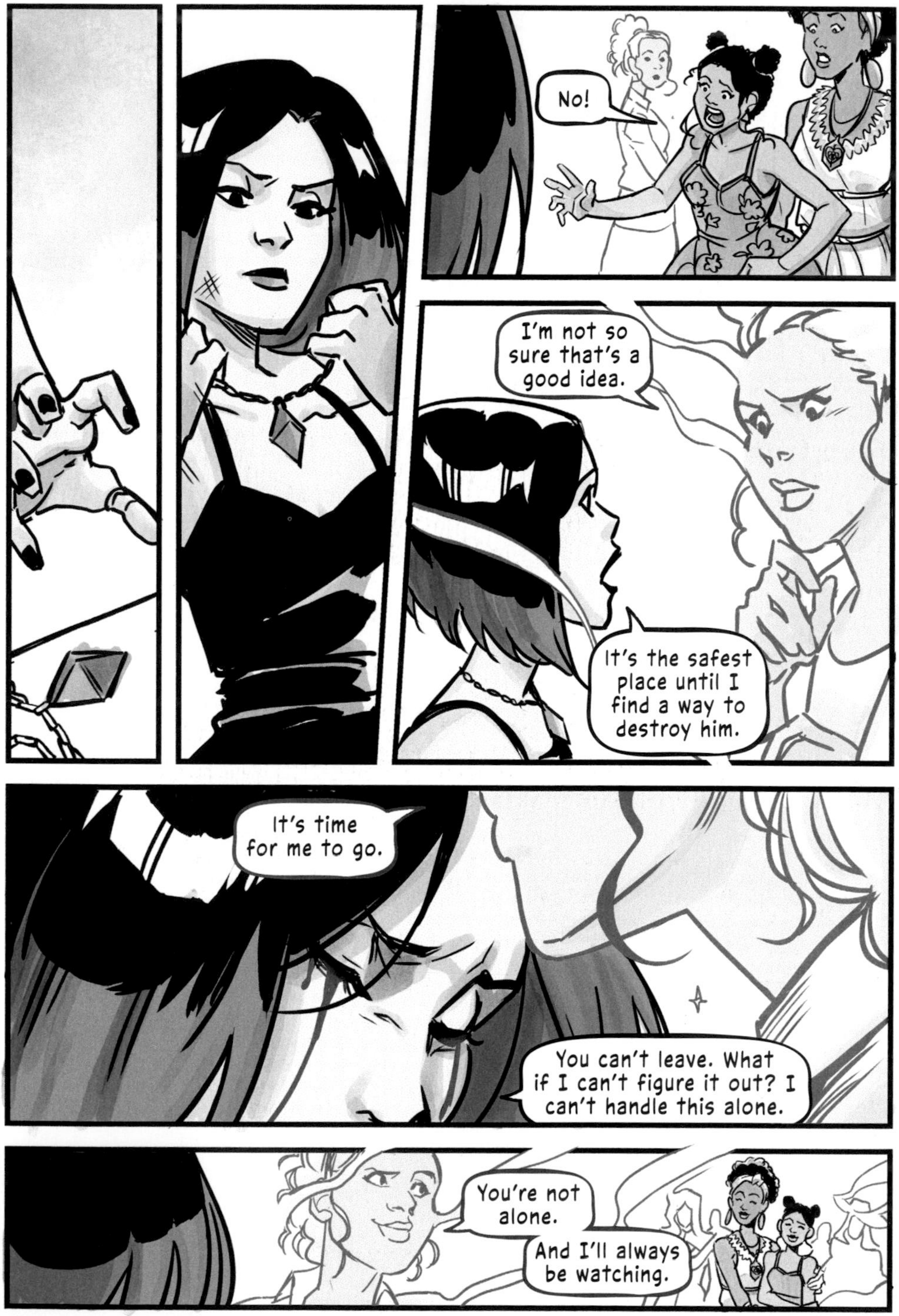
No!
I'm not so sure that's a good idea.
It's the safest place until I find a way to destroy him.
It's time for me to go.
You can't leave. What if I can't figure it out? I can't handle this alone.
You're not alone.
And I'll always be watching.

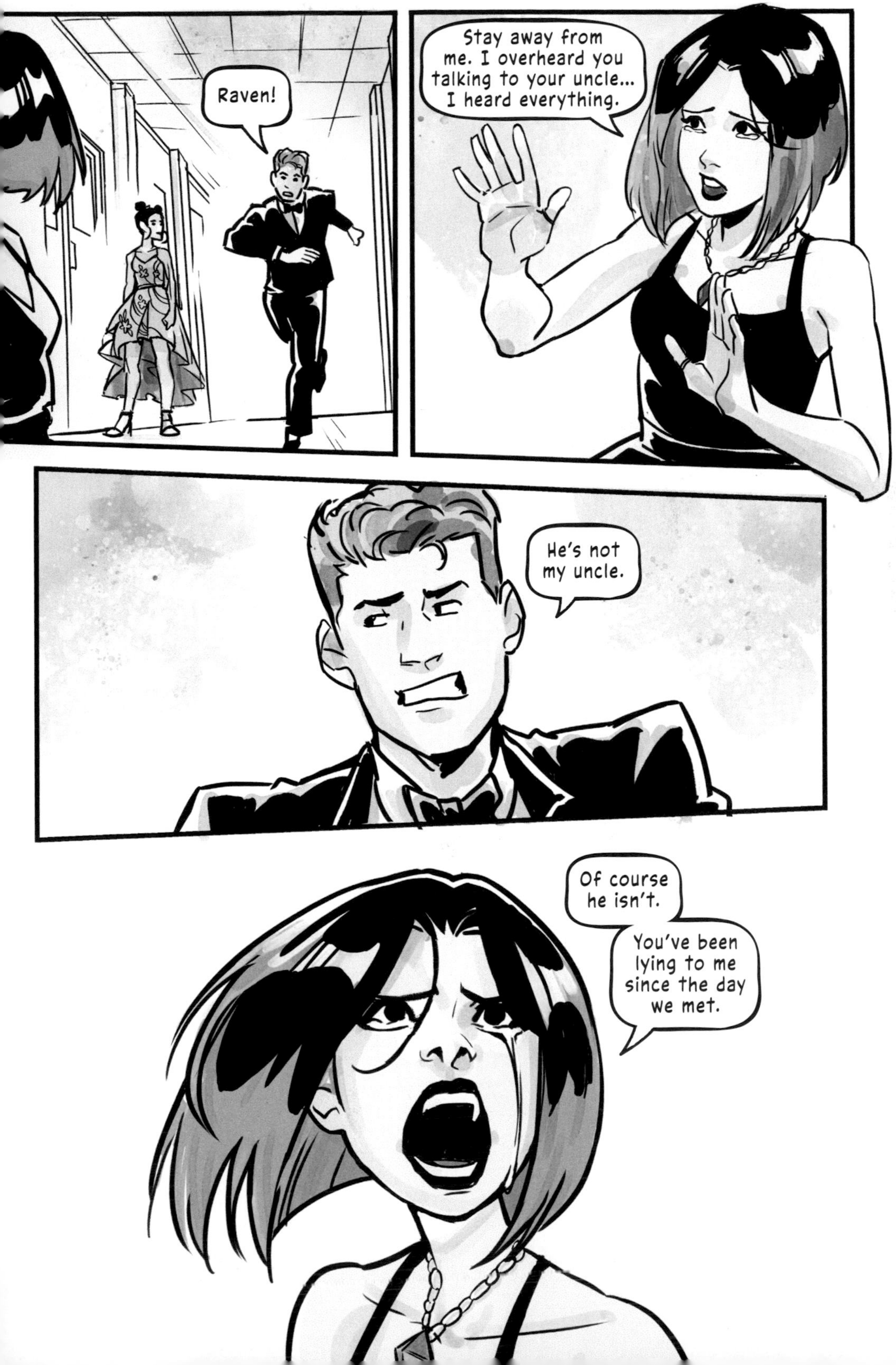
Raven!
Stay away from me. I overheard you talking to your uncle... I heard everything.
He's not my uncle.
Of course he isn't.
You've been lying to me since the day we met.

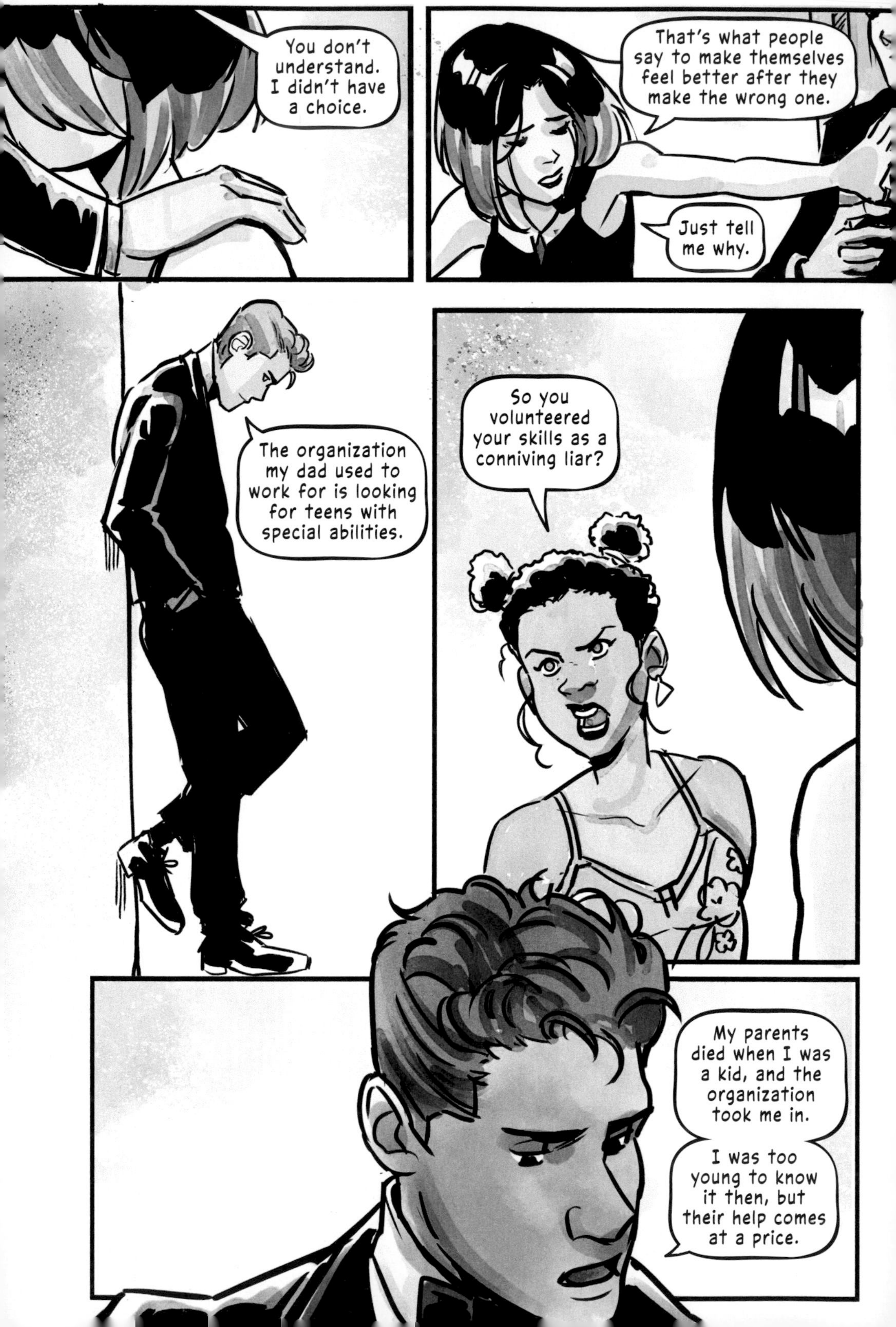
You don't understand. I didn't have a choice.
That's what people say to make themselves feel better after they make the wrong one.
Just tell me why.
The organization my dad used to work for is looking for teens with special abilities.
So you volunteered your skills as a conniving liar?
My parents died when I was a kid, and the organization took me in.
I was too young to know it then, but their help comes at a price.

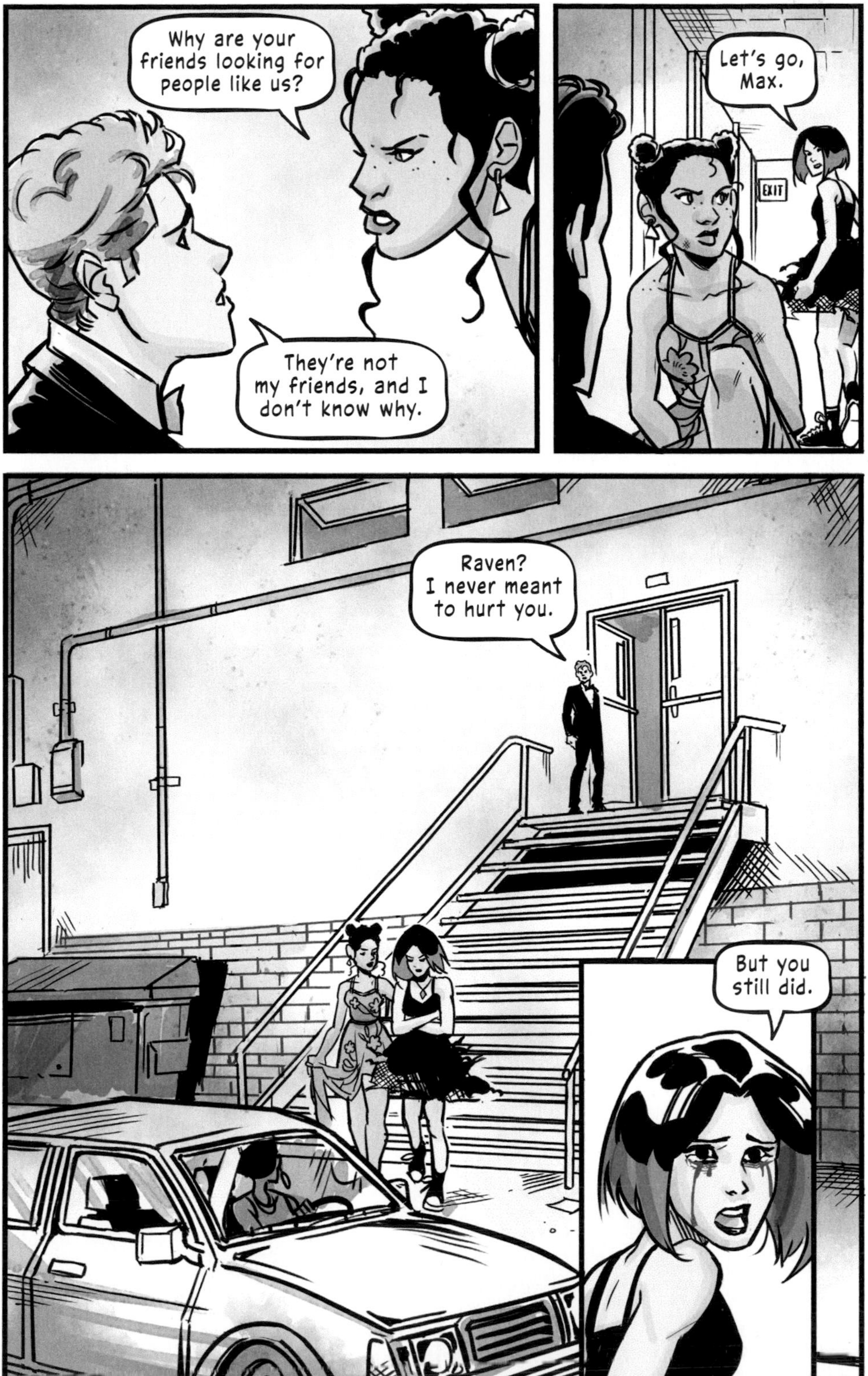
Why are your friends looking for people like us?
They're not my friends, and I don't know why.
Let's go, Max.
EXIT
Raven? I never meant to hurt you.
But you still did.

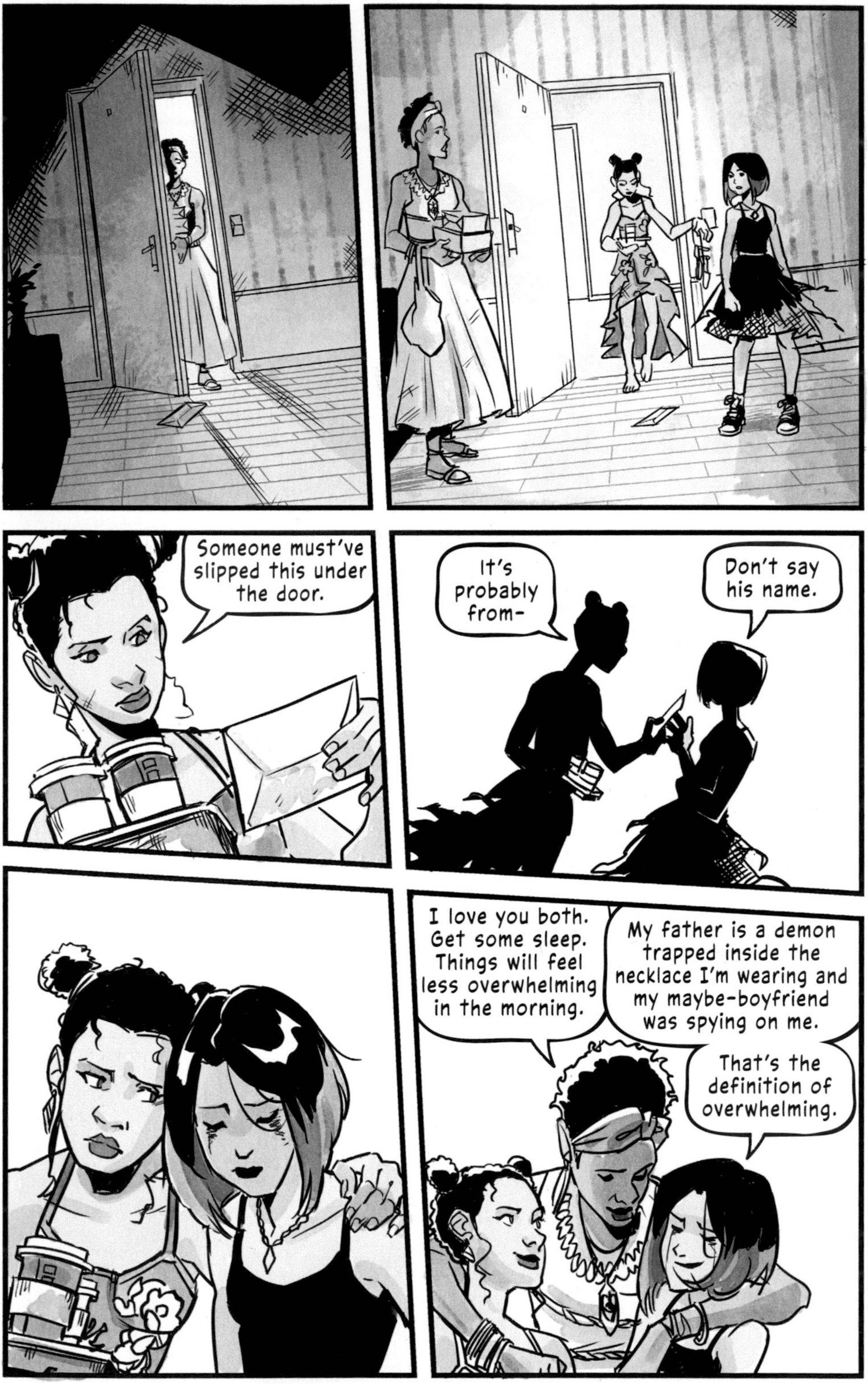
Someone must've slipped this under the door.
It's probably from-
Don't say his name.
I love you both. Get some sleep. Things will feel less overwhelming in the morning.
My father is a demon trapped inside the necklace I'm wearing and my maybe-boyfriend was spying on me.
That's the definition of overwhelming.

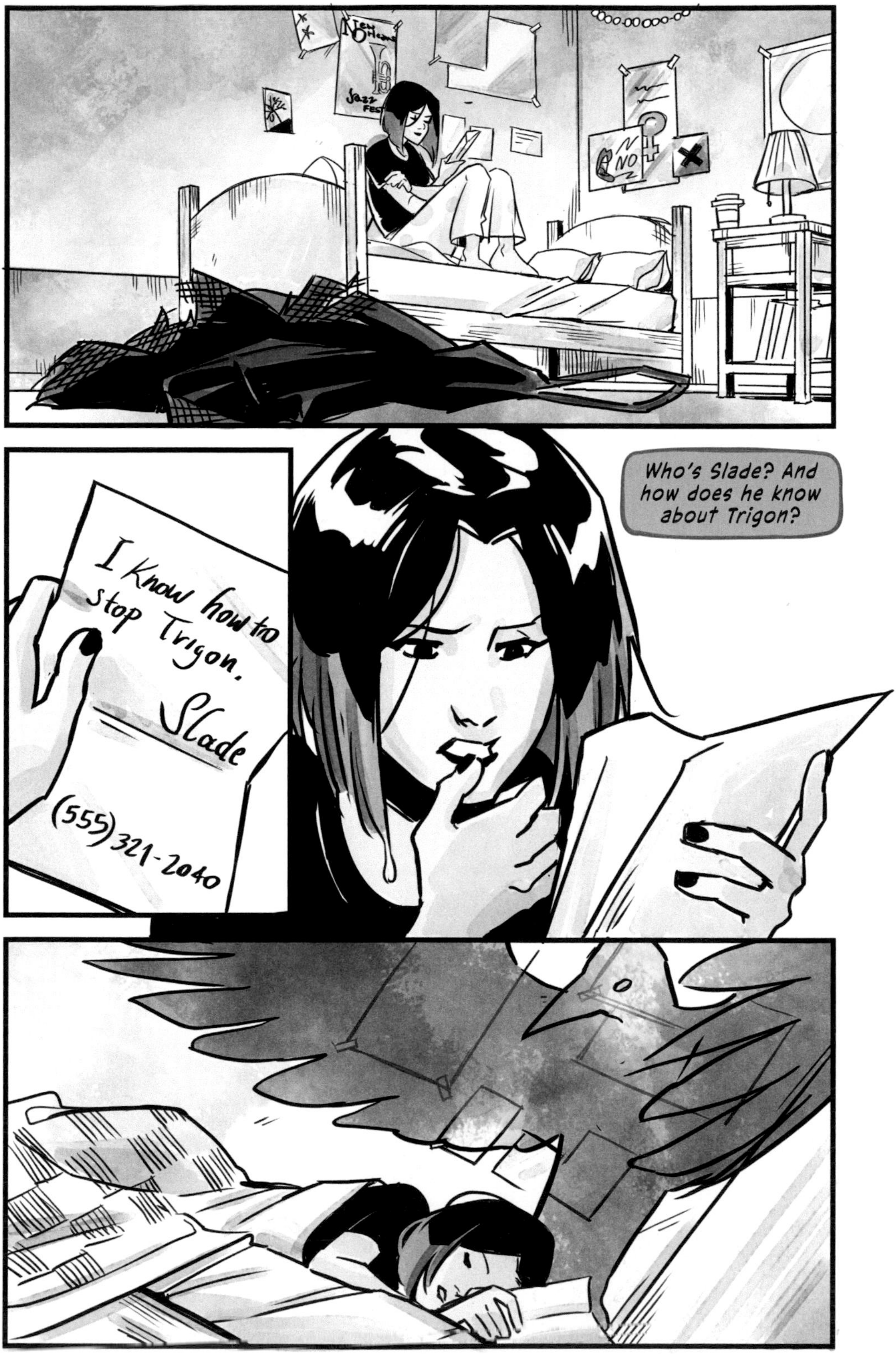

New Orleans
Jazz Fest
Who's Slade? And how does he know about Trigon?
I know how to stop Trigon.
Slade
(555) 321-2040

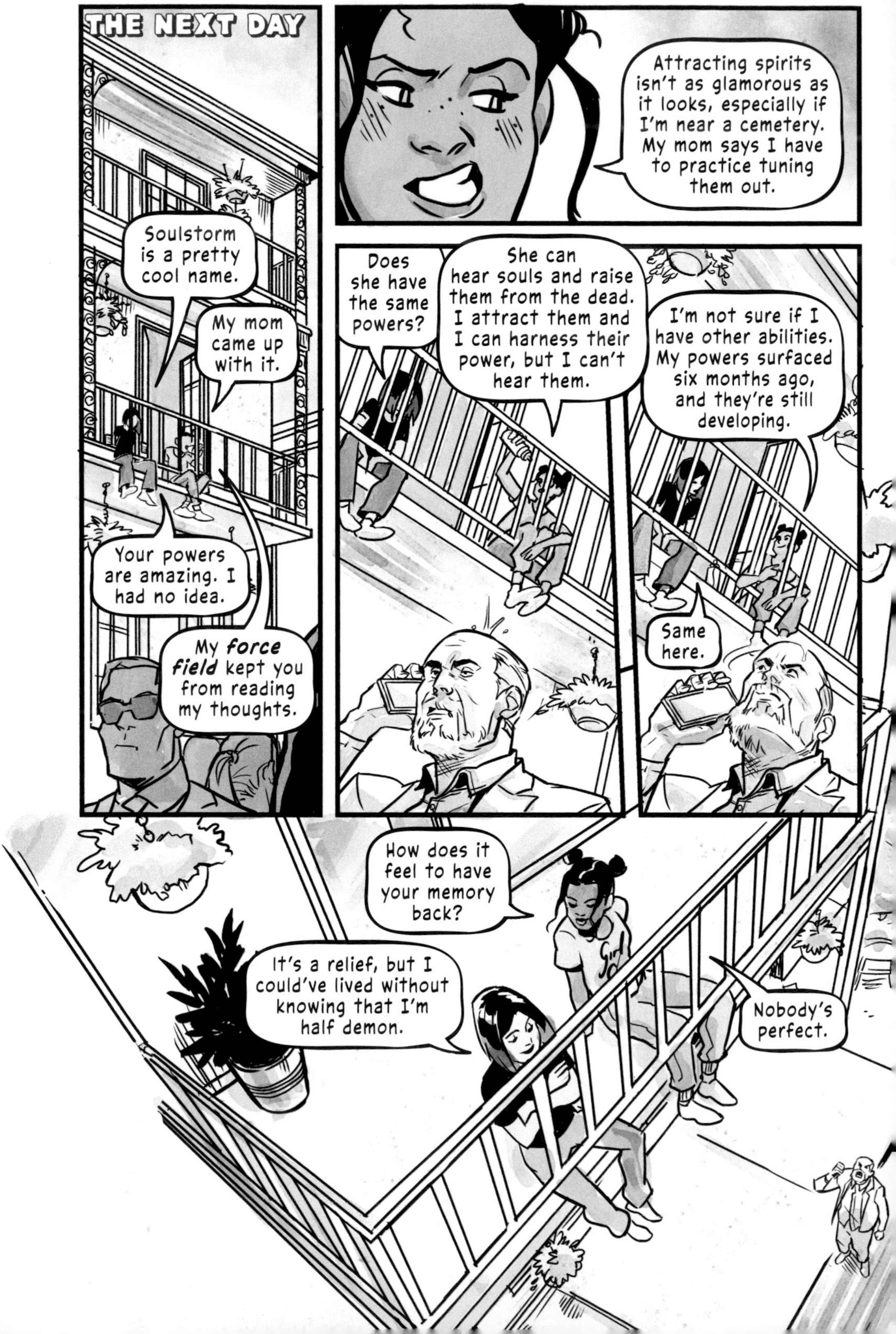
THE NEXT DAY
Soulstorm is a pretty cool name.
My mom came up with it.
Your powers are amazing. I had no idea.
My force field kept you from reading my thoughts.
Attracting spirits isn't as glamorous as it looks, especially if I'm near a cemetery. My mom says I have to practice tuning them out.
Does she have the same powers?
She can hear souls and raise them from the dead. I attract them and I can harness their power, but I can't hear them.
I'm not sure if I have other abilities. My powers surfaced six months ago, and they're still developing.
Same here.
How does it feel to have your memory back?
It's a relief, but I could've lived without knowing that I'm half demon.
Nobody's perfect.

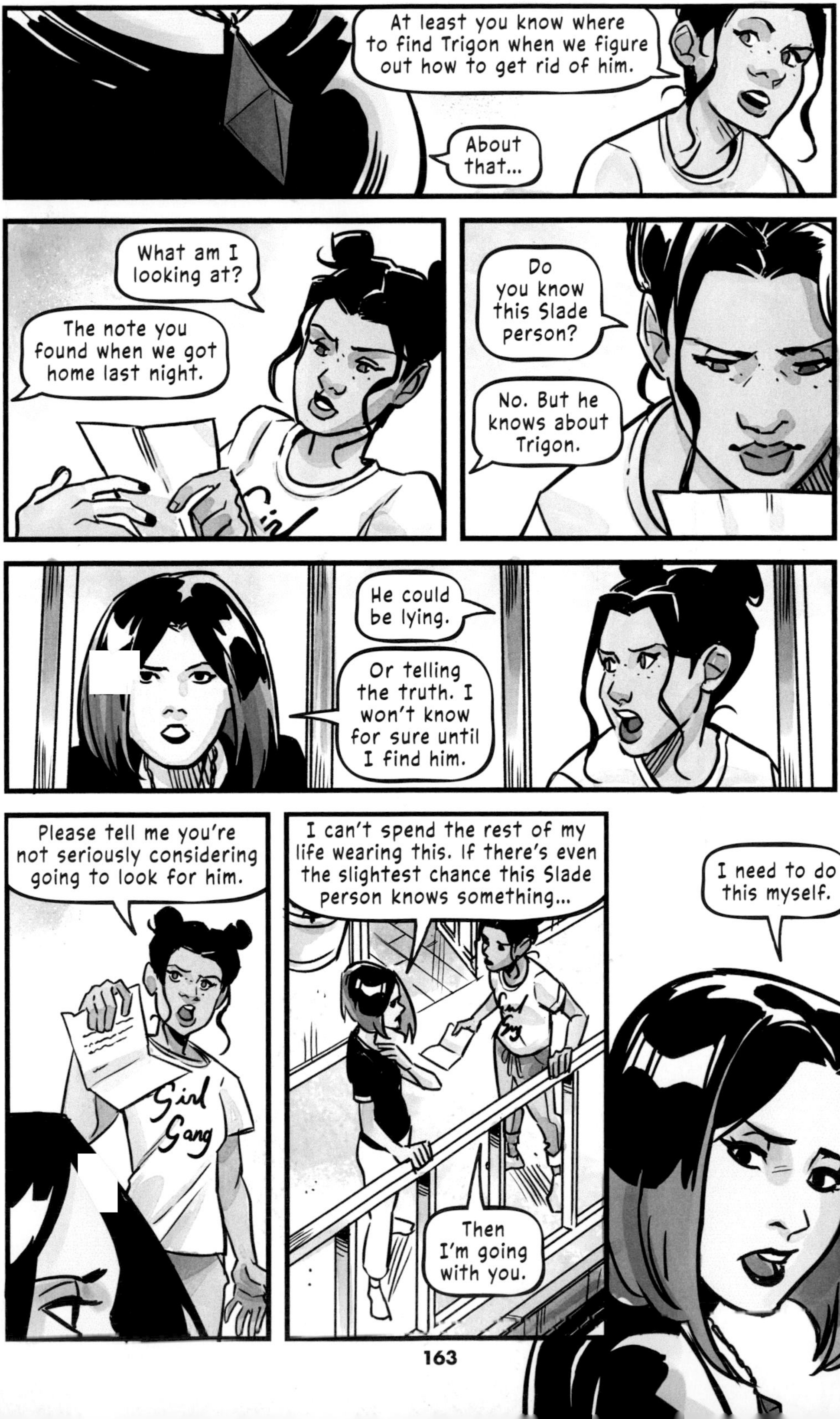

At least you know where to find Trigon when we figure out how to get rid of him.
About that...
What am I looking at?
The note you found when we got home last night.
Do you know this Slade person?
No. But he knows about Trigon.
He could be lying.
Or telling the truth. I won't know for sure until I find him.
Please tell me you're not seriously considering going to look for him.
I can't spend the rest of my life wearing this. If there's even the slightest chance this Slade person knows something...
Then I'm going with you.
I need to do this myself.

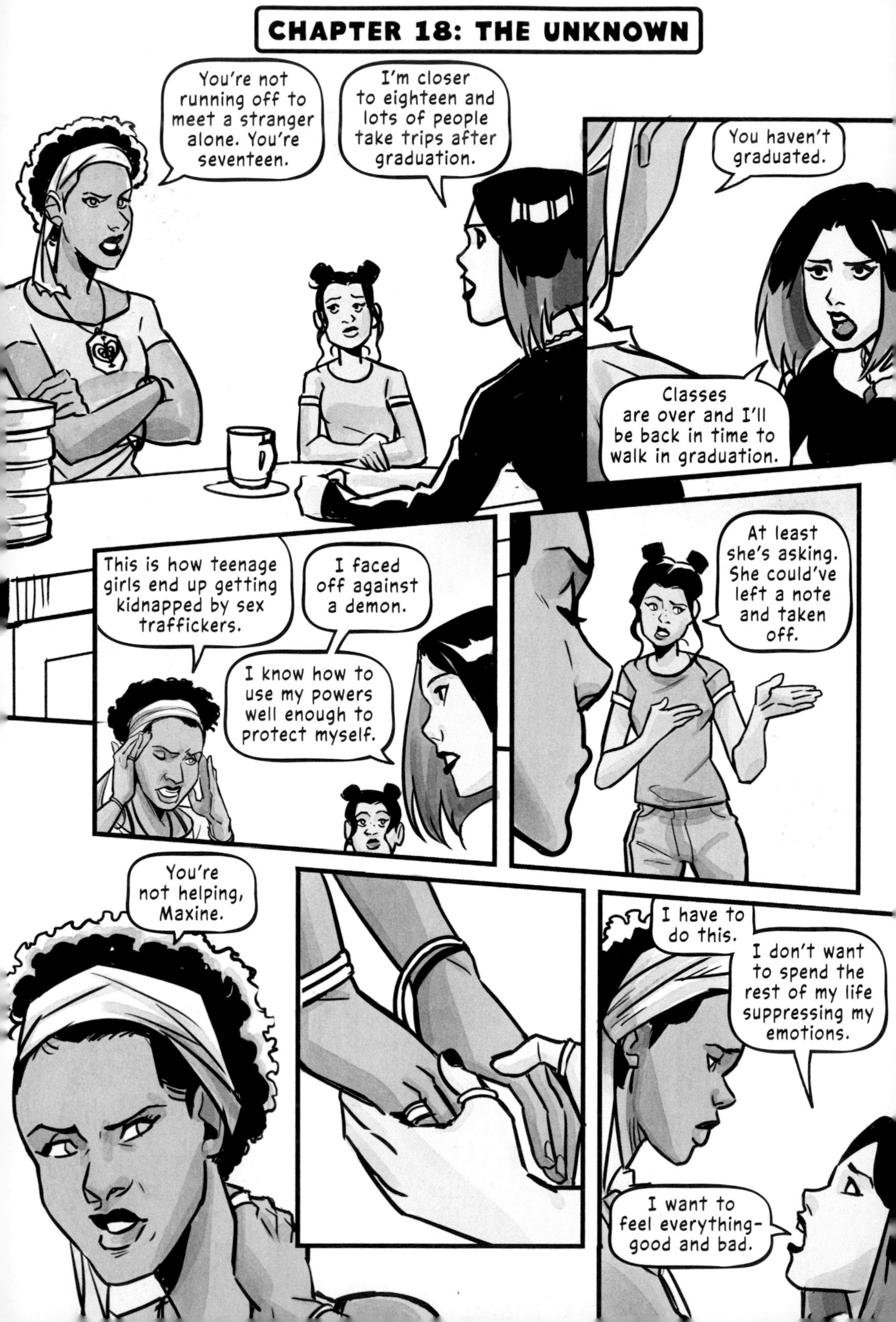
CHAPTER 18: THE UNKNOWN
You're not running off to meet a stranger alone. You're seventeen.
I'm closer to eighteen and lots of people take trips after graduation.
You haven't graduated.
Classes are over and I'll be back in time to walk in graduation.
This is how teenage girls end up getting kidnapped by sex traffickers.
I faced off against a demon.
I know how to use my powers well enough to protect myself.
At least she's asking. She could've left a note and taken off.
You're not helping, Maxine.
I have to do this.
I don't want to spend the rest of my life suppressing my emotions.
I want to feel everything-good and bad.

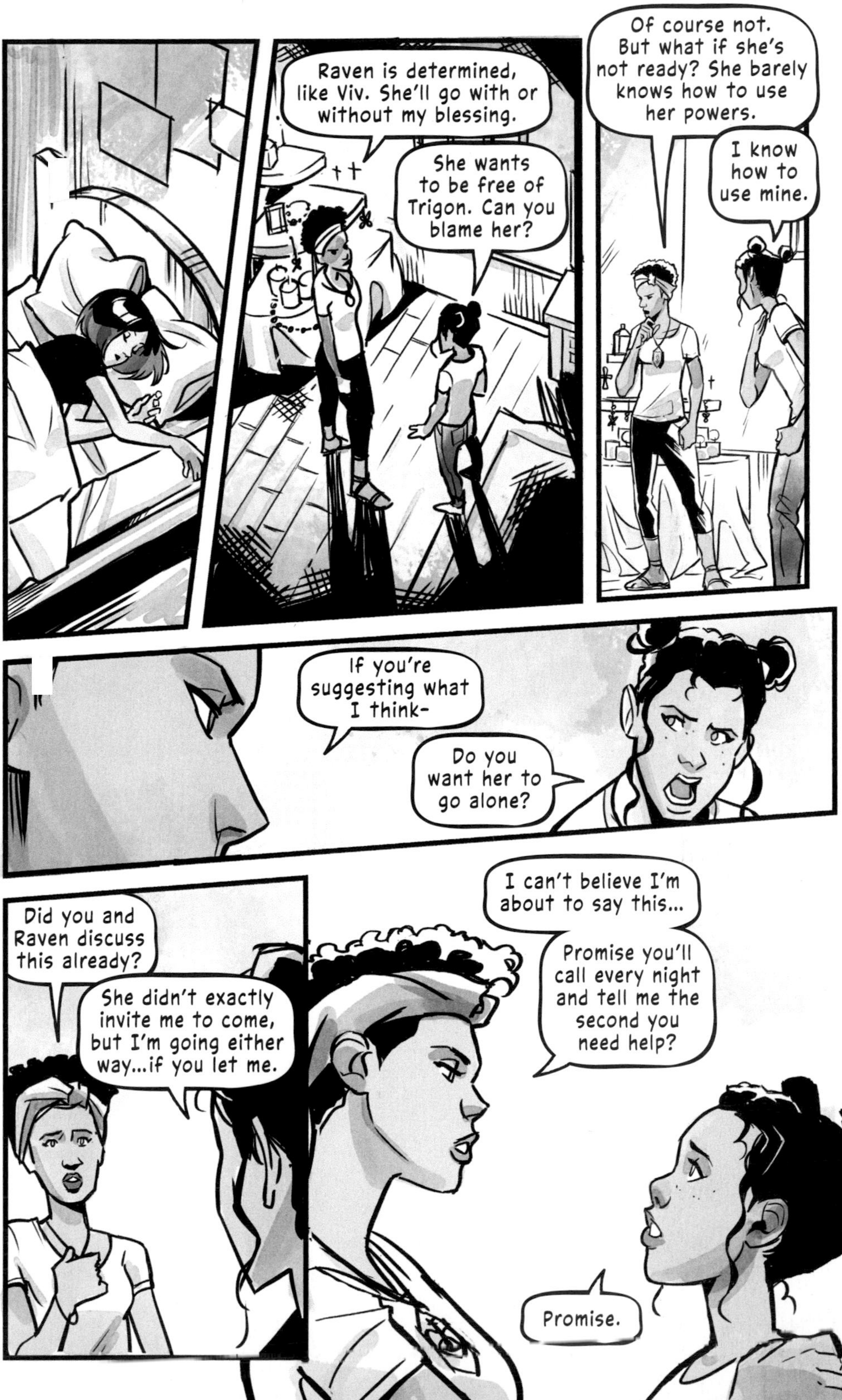
Raven is determined, like Viv. She'll go with or without my blessing.
She wants to be free of Trigon. Can you blame her?
Of course not. But what if she's not ready? She barely knows how to use her powers.
I know how to use mine.
If you're suggesting what I think-
Do you want her to go alone?
Did you and Raven discuss this already?
She didn't exactly invite me to come, but I'm going either way...if you let me.
I can't believe I'm about to say this...
Promise you'll call every night and tell me the second you need help?
Promise.

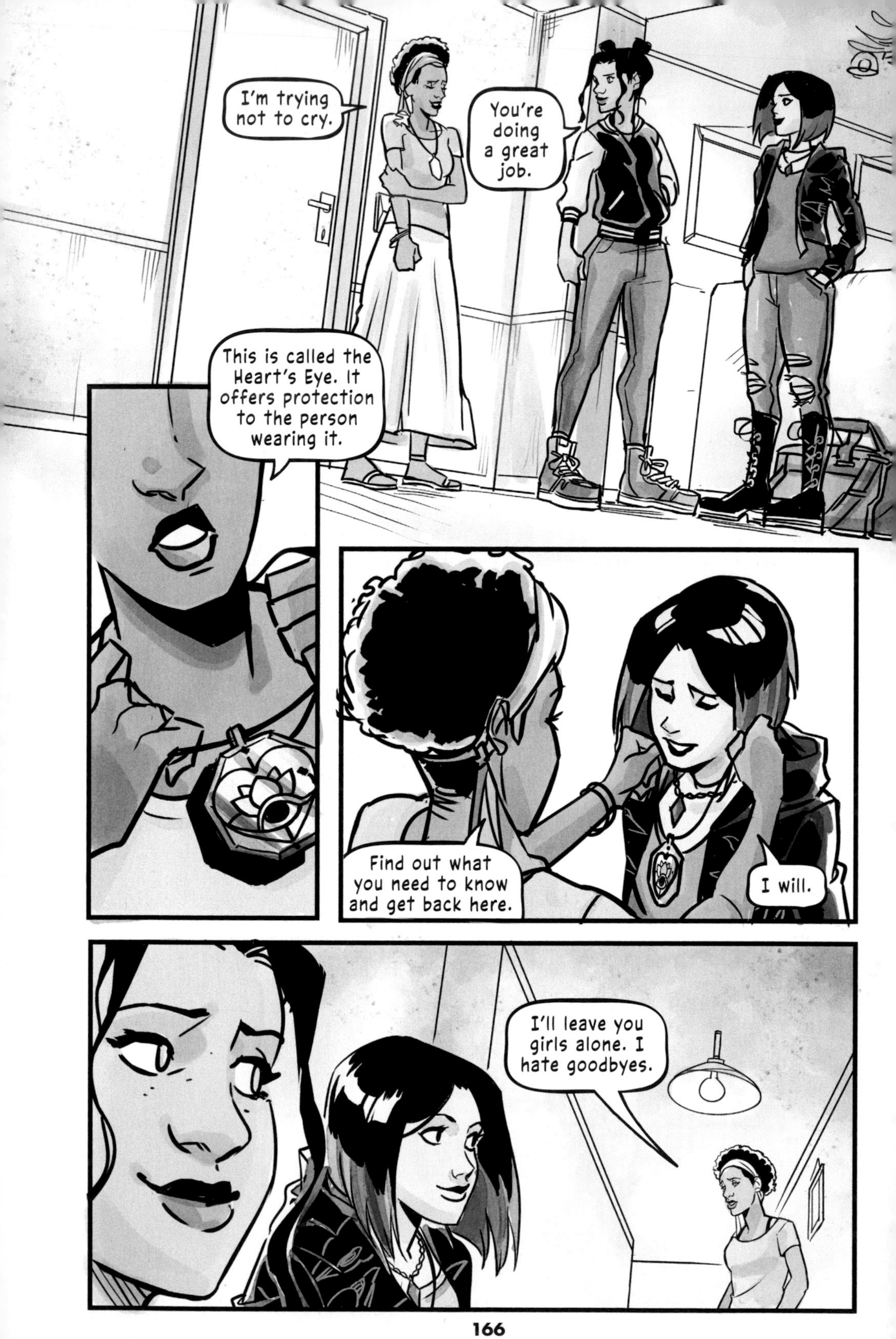
I'm trying not to cry.
You're doing a great job.
This is called the Heart's Eye. It offers protection to the person wearing it.
Find out what you need to know and get back here.
I will.
I'll leave you girls alone. I hate goodbyes.

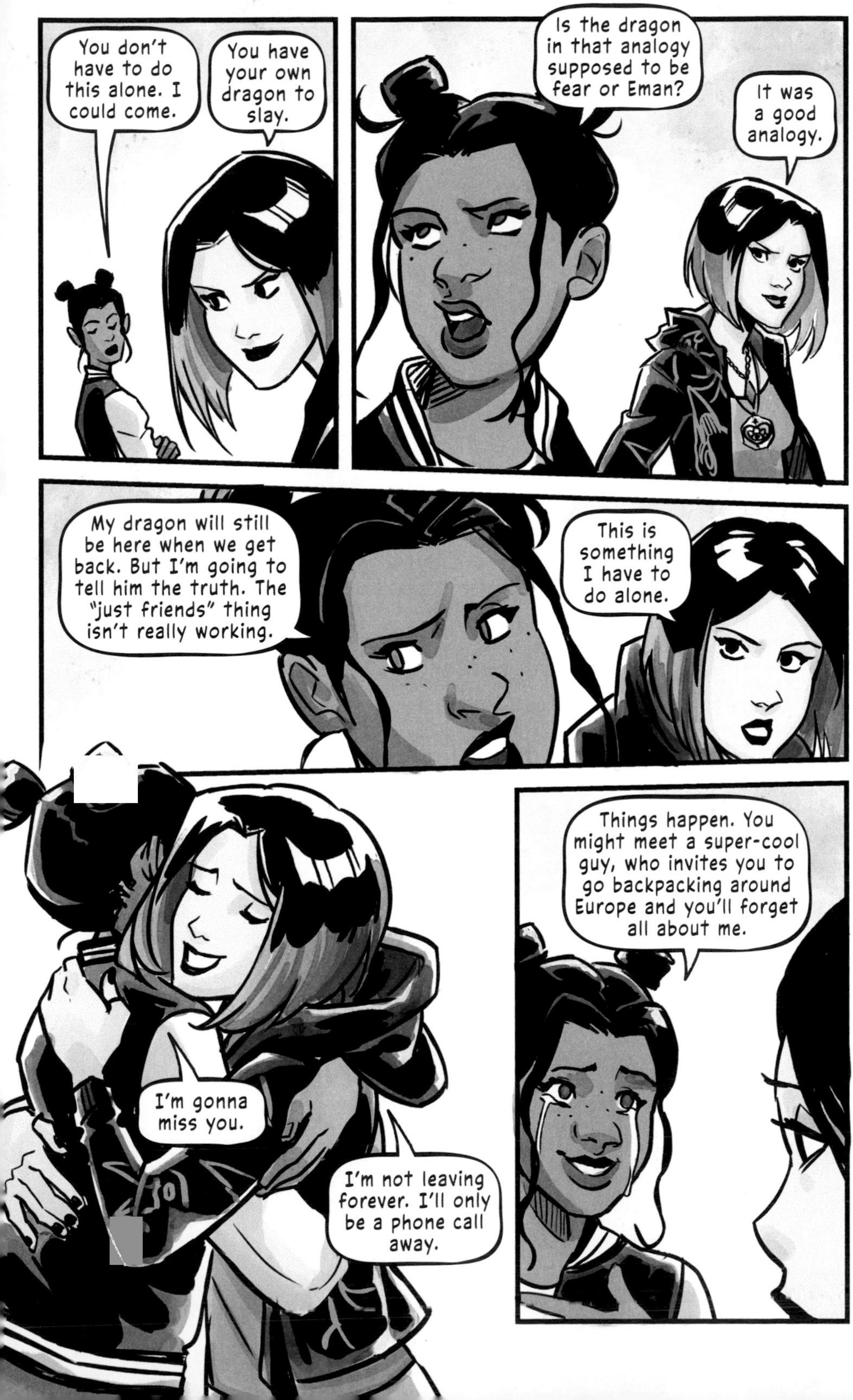
You don't have to do this alone. I could come.
You have your own dragon to slay.
Is the dragon in that analogy supposed to be fear or Eman?
It was a good analogy.
My dragon will still be here when we get back. But I'm going to tell him the truth. The "just friends" thing isn't really working.
This is something I have to do alone.
I'm gonna miss you.
I'm not leaving forever. I'll only be a phone call away.
Things happen. You might meet a super-cool guy, who invites you to go backpacking around Europe and you'll forget all about me.

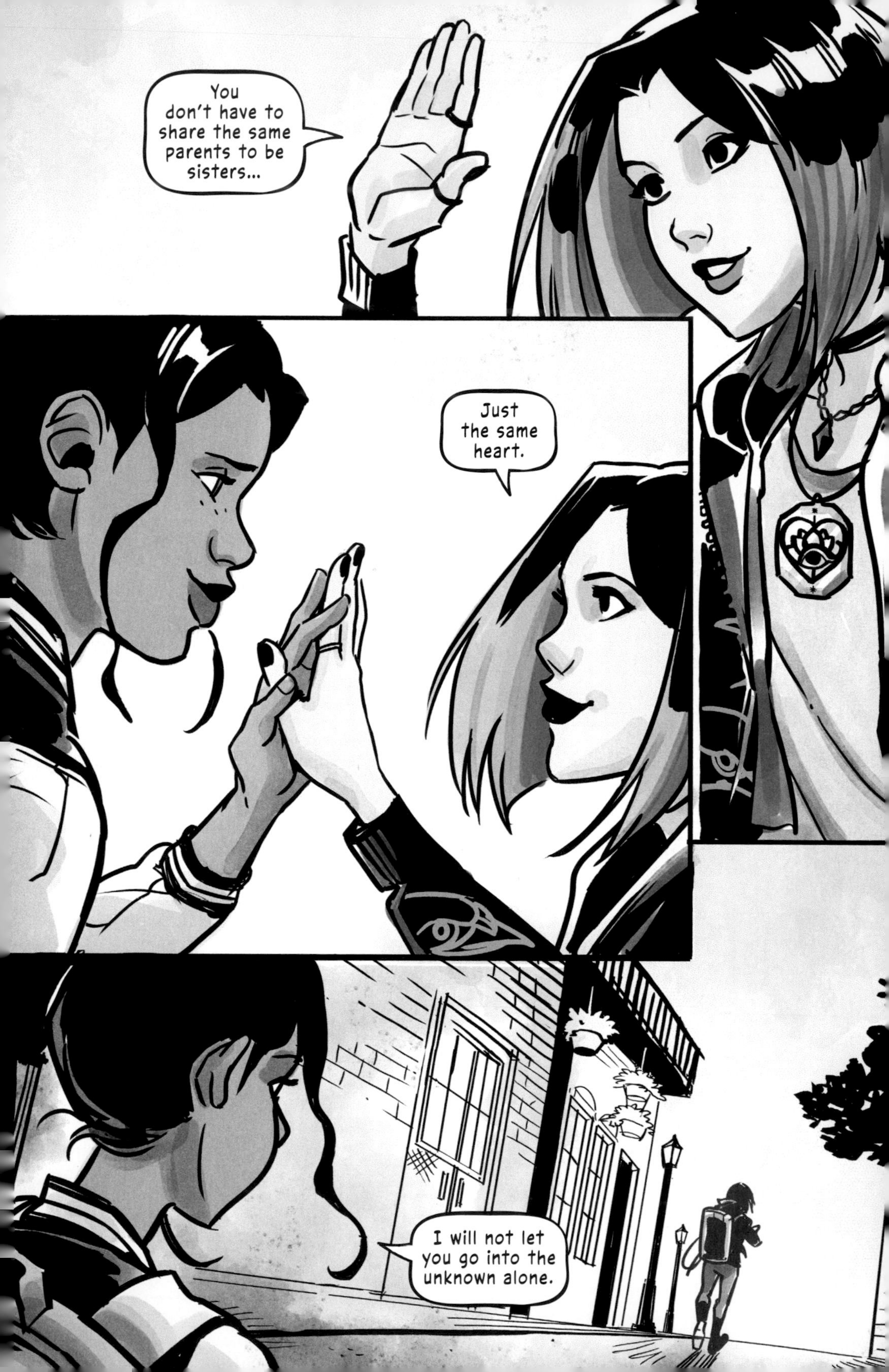
You don't have to share the same parents to be sisters...
Just the same heart.
I will not let you go into the unknown alone.

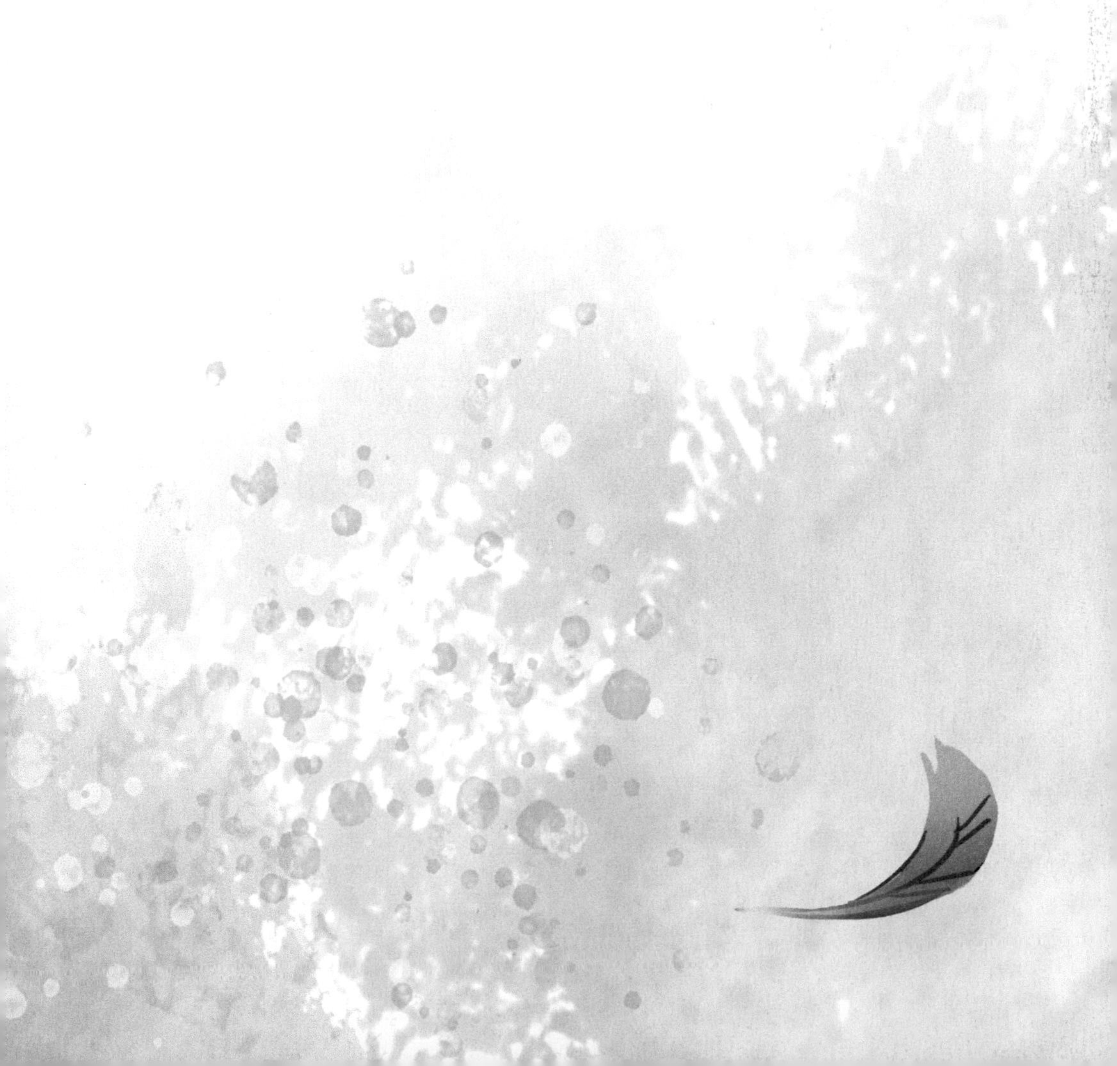

VANIA STOYANVA

kami garcia

is the #1 *New York Times, USA Today,* and international bestselling
co-author of the *Beautiful Creatures* and *Dangerous Creatures* novels.
Beautiful Creatures has been published in 50 countries
and translated into 39 languages.
Kami's solo series, The Legion, includes *Unbreakable,* an instant *New York
Times* bestseller, and its sequel, *Unmarked,* both of which were nominated
for Bram Stoker Awards. Her other works include *The X-Files Origins:
Agent of Chaos* and the YA contemporary novels *The Lovely Reckless*
and *Broken Beautiful Hearts.* Kami was a teacher for 17 years
before co-authoring her first novel on a dare from seven of her students.
She is a cofounder of YALLFest, the biggest teen book festival in the country.
She lives in Maryland with her family.

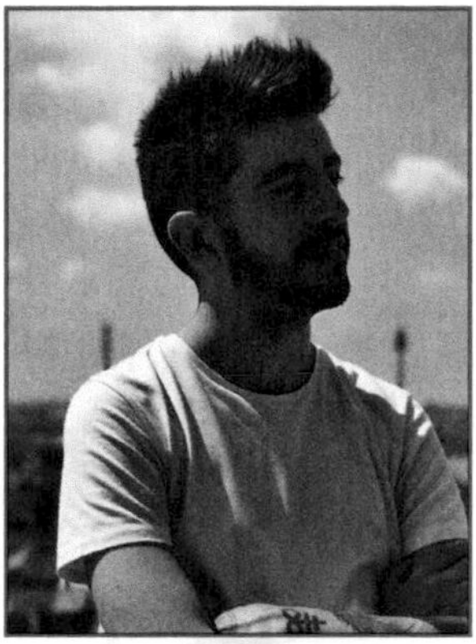

LAURA BROUWERS

gabriel picolo
is a Brazilian comics artist and illustrator based in São Paulo.
His work has become known for its strong storytelling and atmospheric colors.
Picolo has developed projects for clients such as Blizzard,
BOOM! Studios, HarperCollins, and DeviantArt.

special sneak preview

TEEN TITANS

BEAST
BOY

WRITTEN BY
kami garcia

ILLUSTRATED BY
gabriel picolo

COLORIST
david calderon

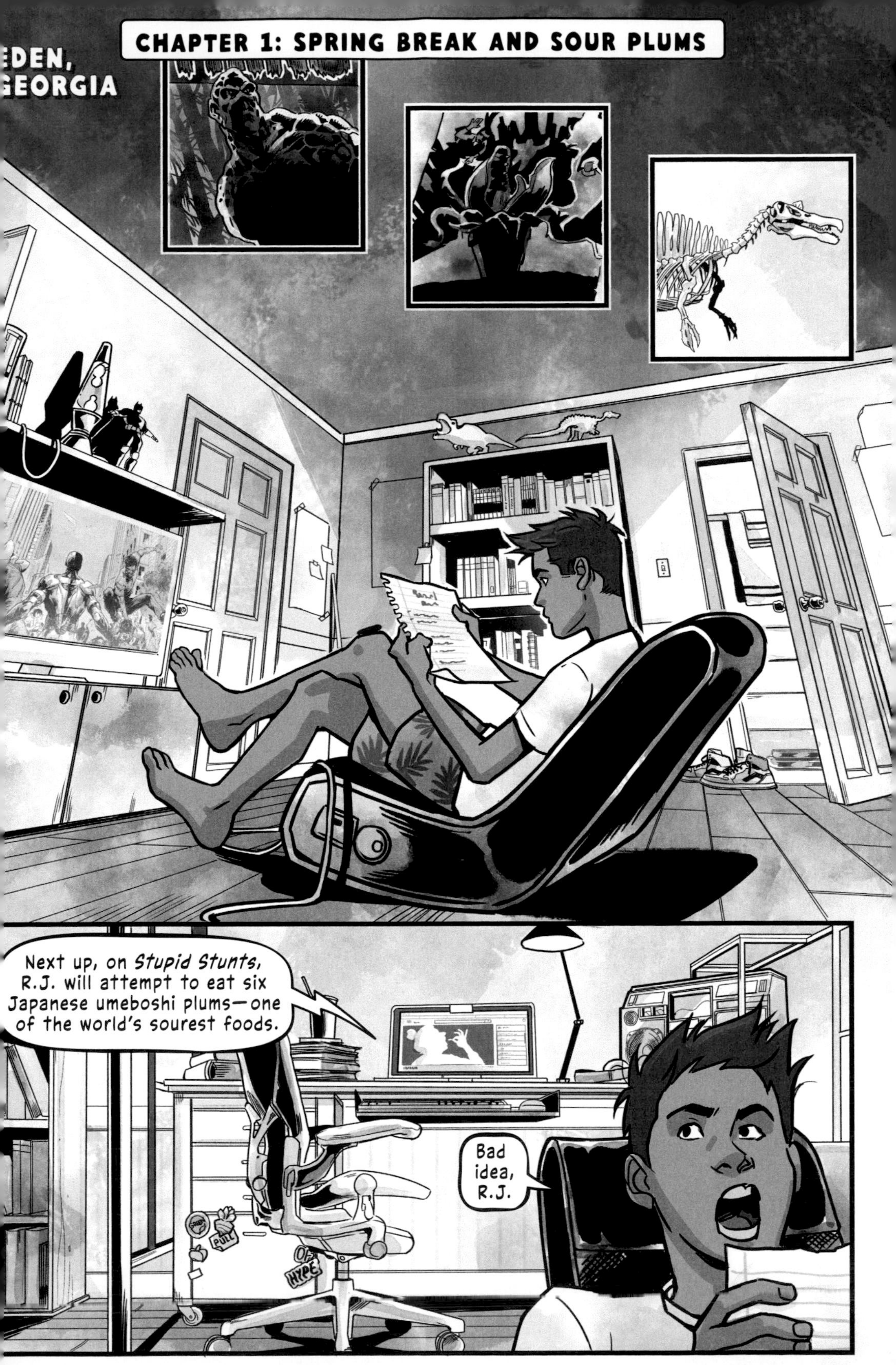
CHAPTER 1: SPRING BREAK AND SOUR PLUMS
EDEN, GEORGIA
Next up, on *Stupid Stunts*, R.J. will attempt to eat six Japanese umeboshi plums—one of the world's sourest foods.
Bad idea, R.J.

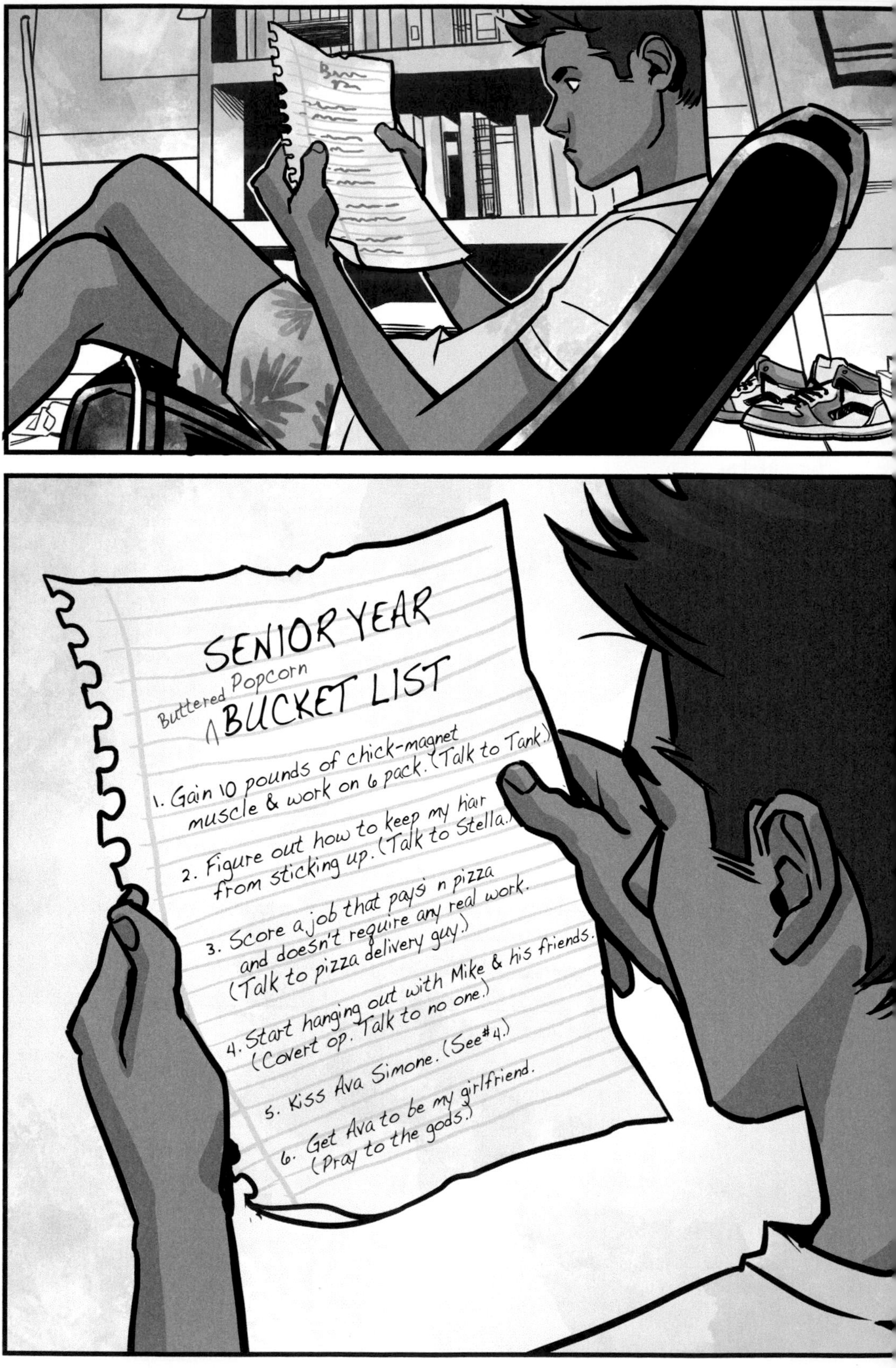
SENIOR YEAR
Buttered Popcorn
BUCKET LIST
1. Gain 10 pounds of chick-magnet muscle & work on 6 pack. (Talk to Tank.)
2. Figure out how to keep my hair from sticking up. (Talk to Stella.)
3. Score a job that pays in pizza and doesn't require any real work. (Talk to pizza delivery guy.)
4. Start hanging out with Mike & his friends. (Covert op. Talk to no one.)
5. Kiss Ava Simone. (See #4.)
6. Get Ava to be my girlfriend. (Pray to the gods.)

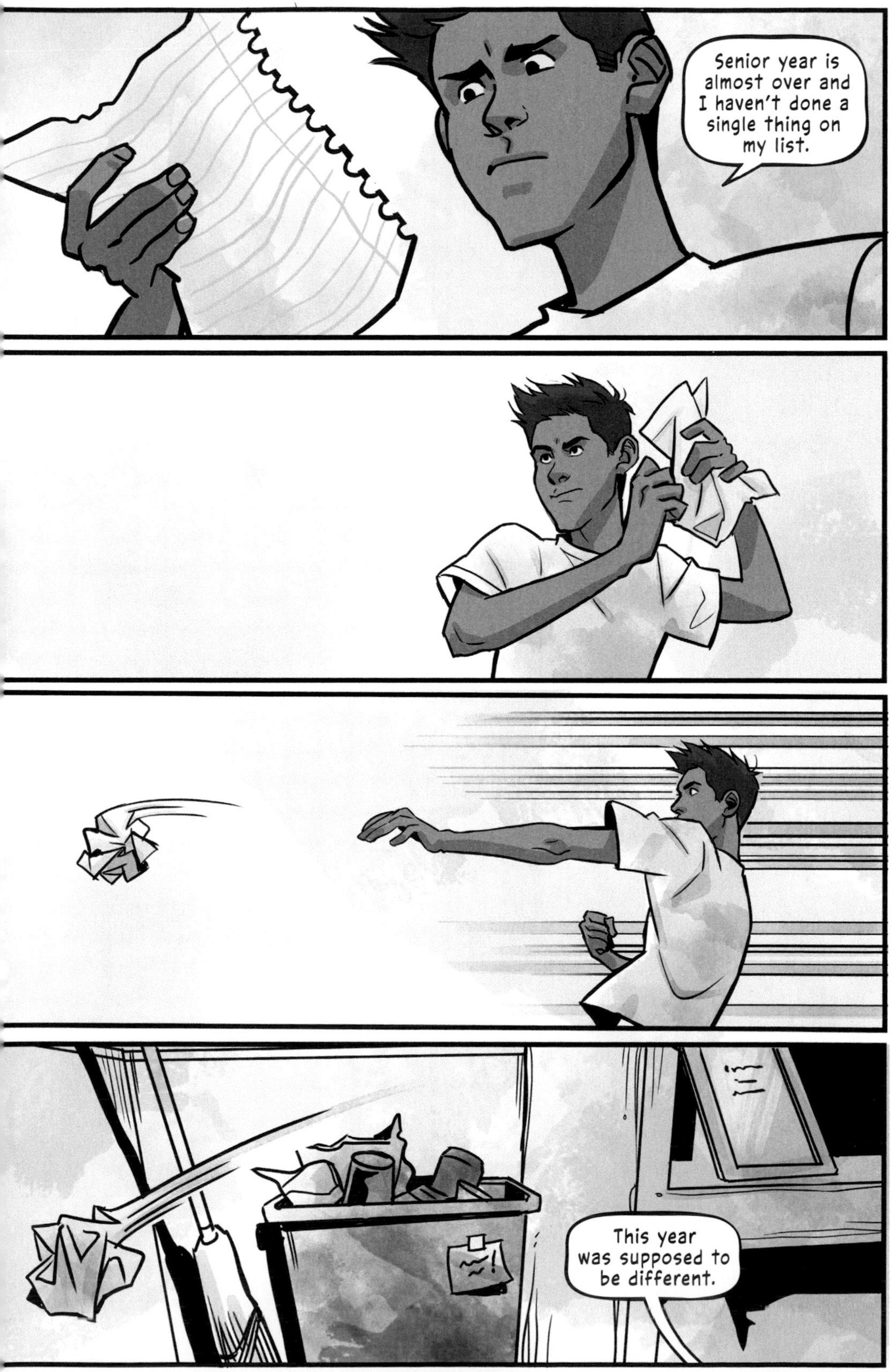
Senior year is almost over and I haven't done a single thing on my list.
This year was supposed to be different.

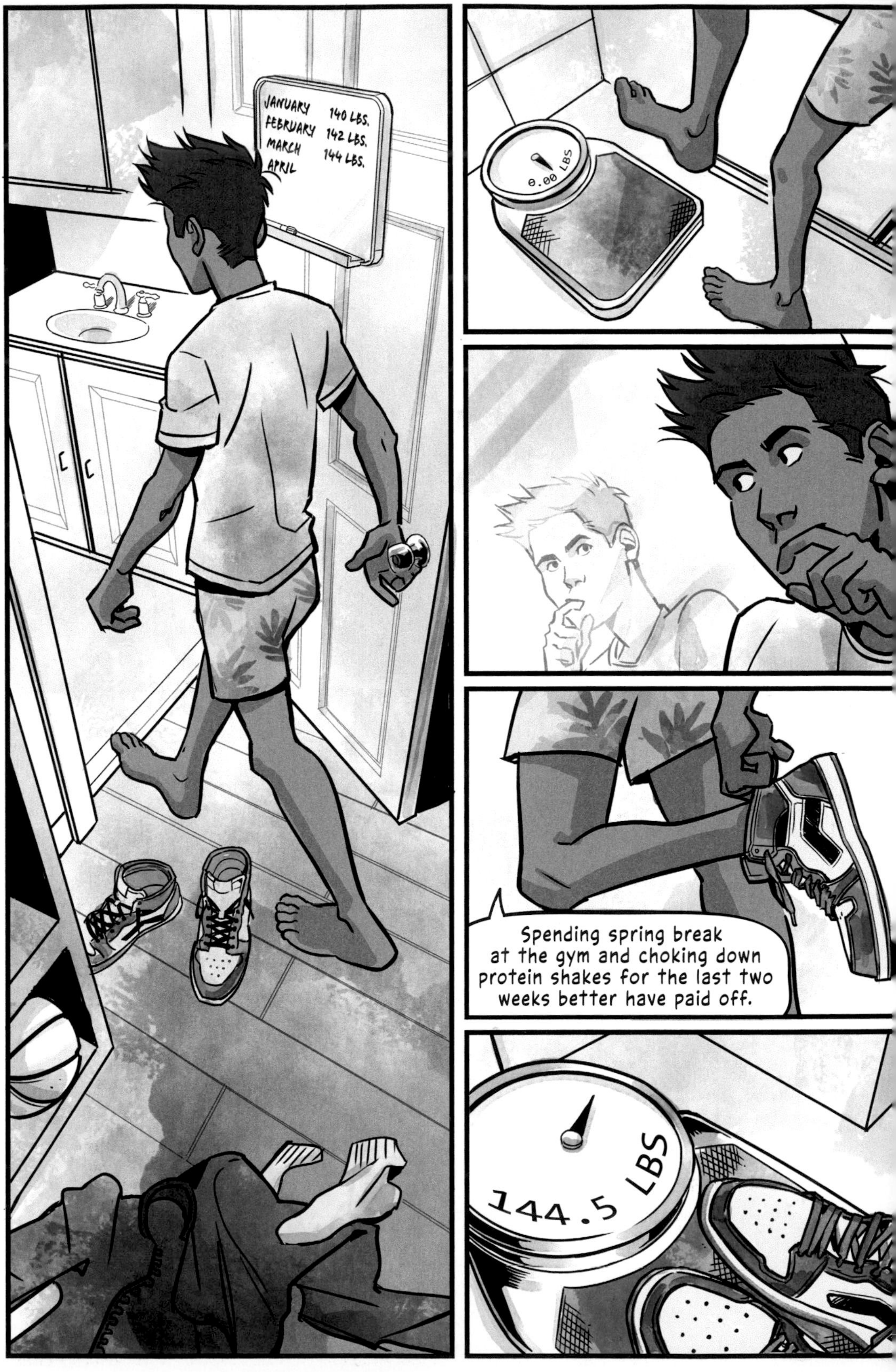
JANUARY 140 LBS.
FEBRUARY 142 LBS.
MARCH 144 LBS.
APRIL
0.00 LBS
Spending spring break at the gym and choking down protein shakes for the last two weeks better have paid off.
144.5 LBS

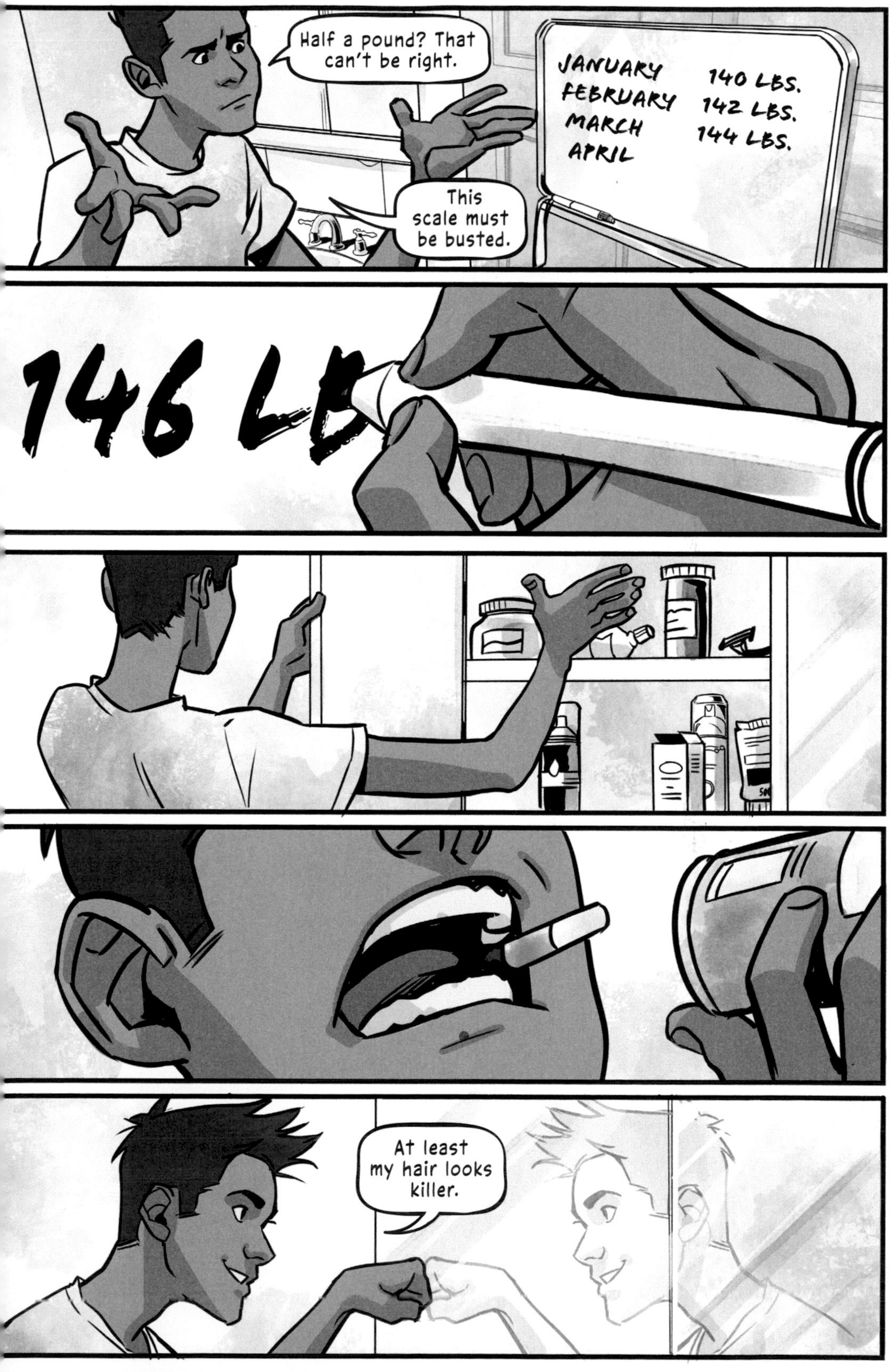
Half a pound? That can't be right.
JANUARY 140 LBS.
FEBRUARY 142 LBS.
MARCH 144 LBS.
APRIL
This scale must be busted.
146 LB
At least my hair looks killer.

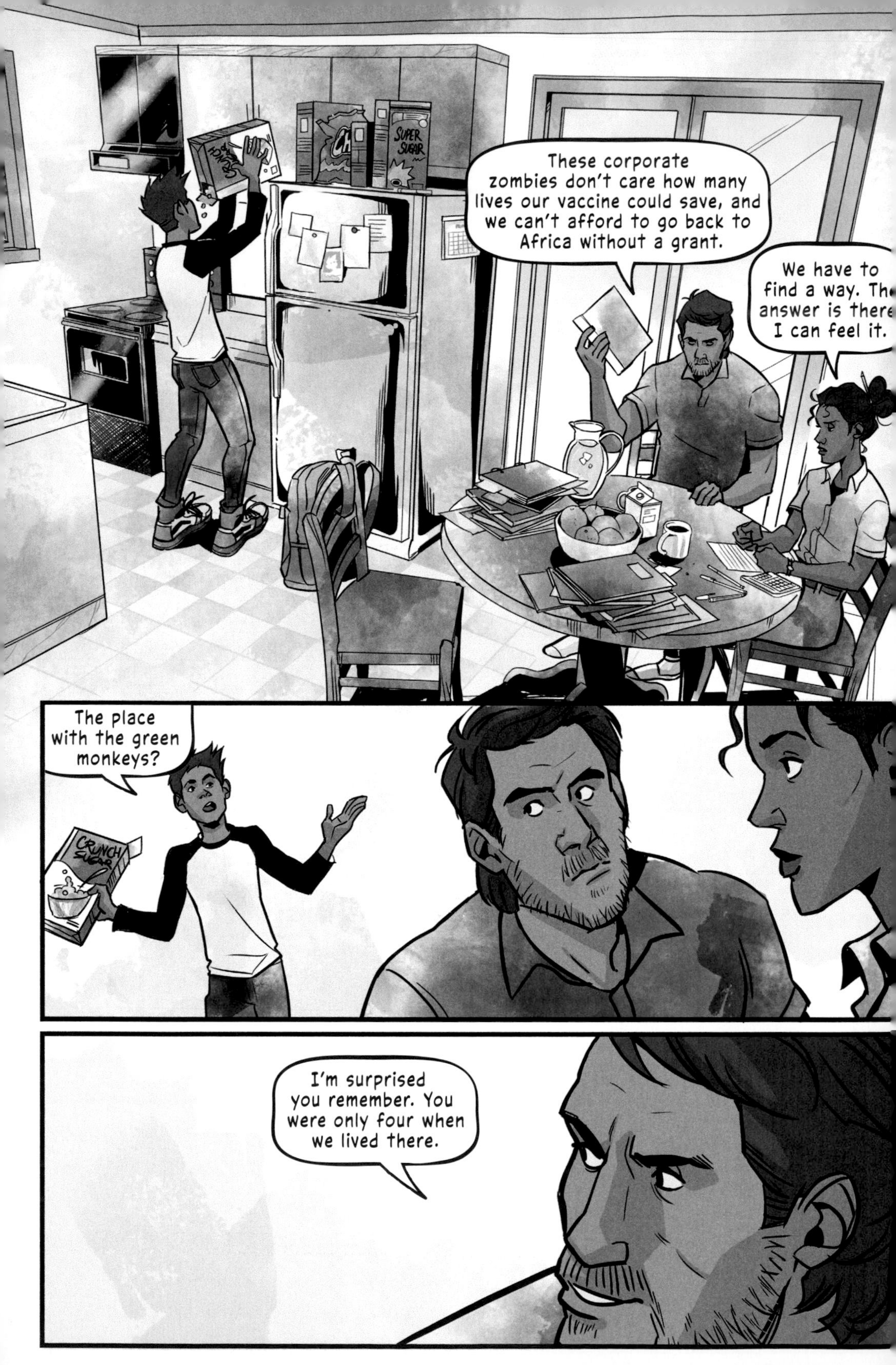
SUPER SUGAR
These corporate zombies don't care how many lives our vaccine could save, and we can't afford to go back to Africa without a grant.
We have to find a way. Th answer is there I can feel it.
The place with the green monkeys?
CRUNCH SUGAR
I'm surprised you remember. You were only four when we lived there.

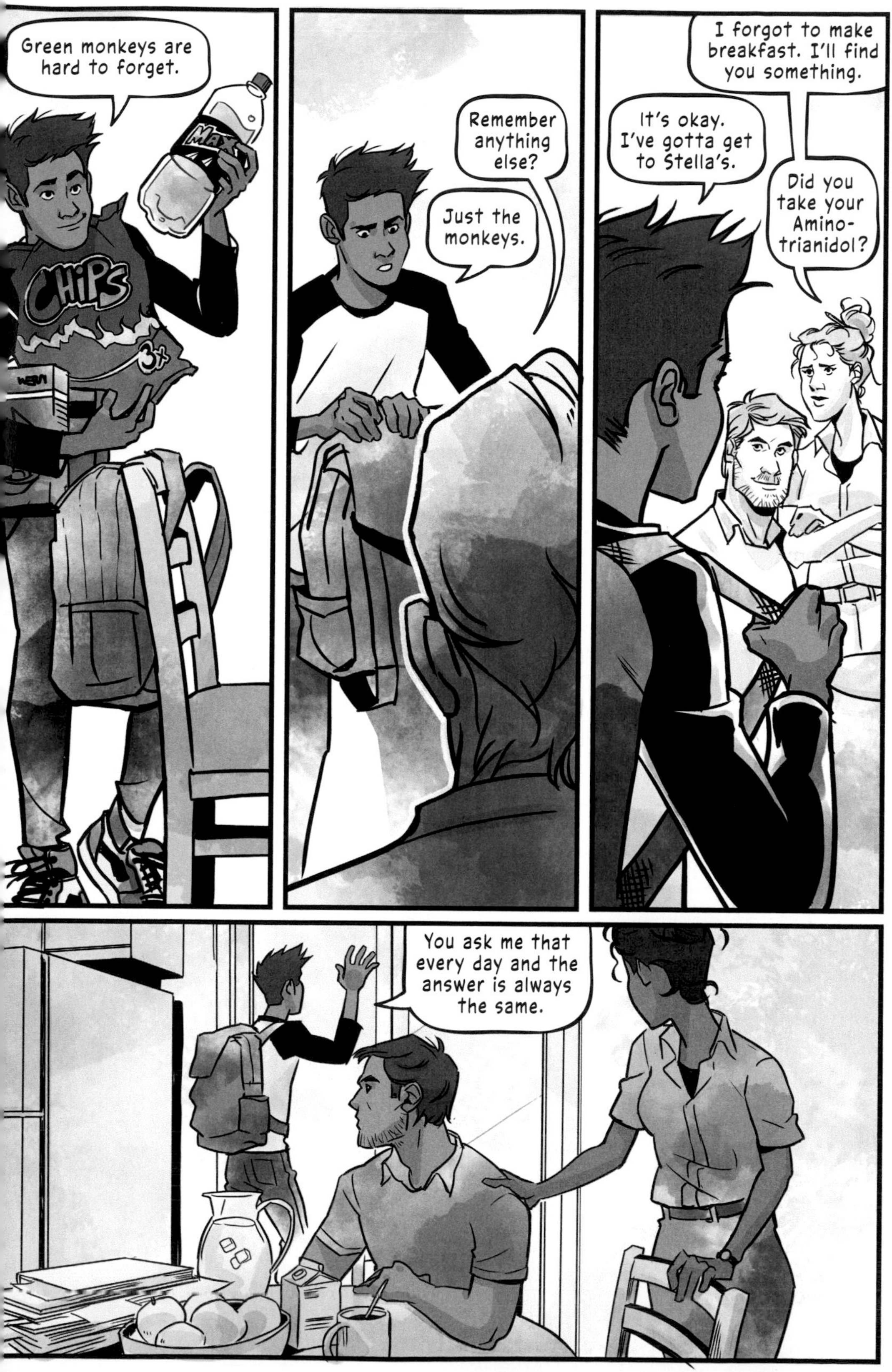
Green monkeys are hard to forget.
MAX
CHiPS
Remember anything else?
Just the monkeys.
I forgot to make breakfast. I'll find you something.
It's okay. I've gotta get to Stella's.
Did you take your Amino-trianidol?
You ask me that every day and the answer is always the same.

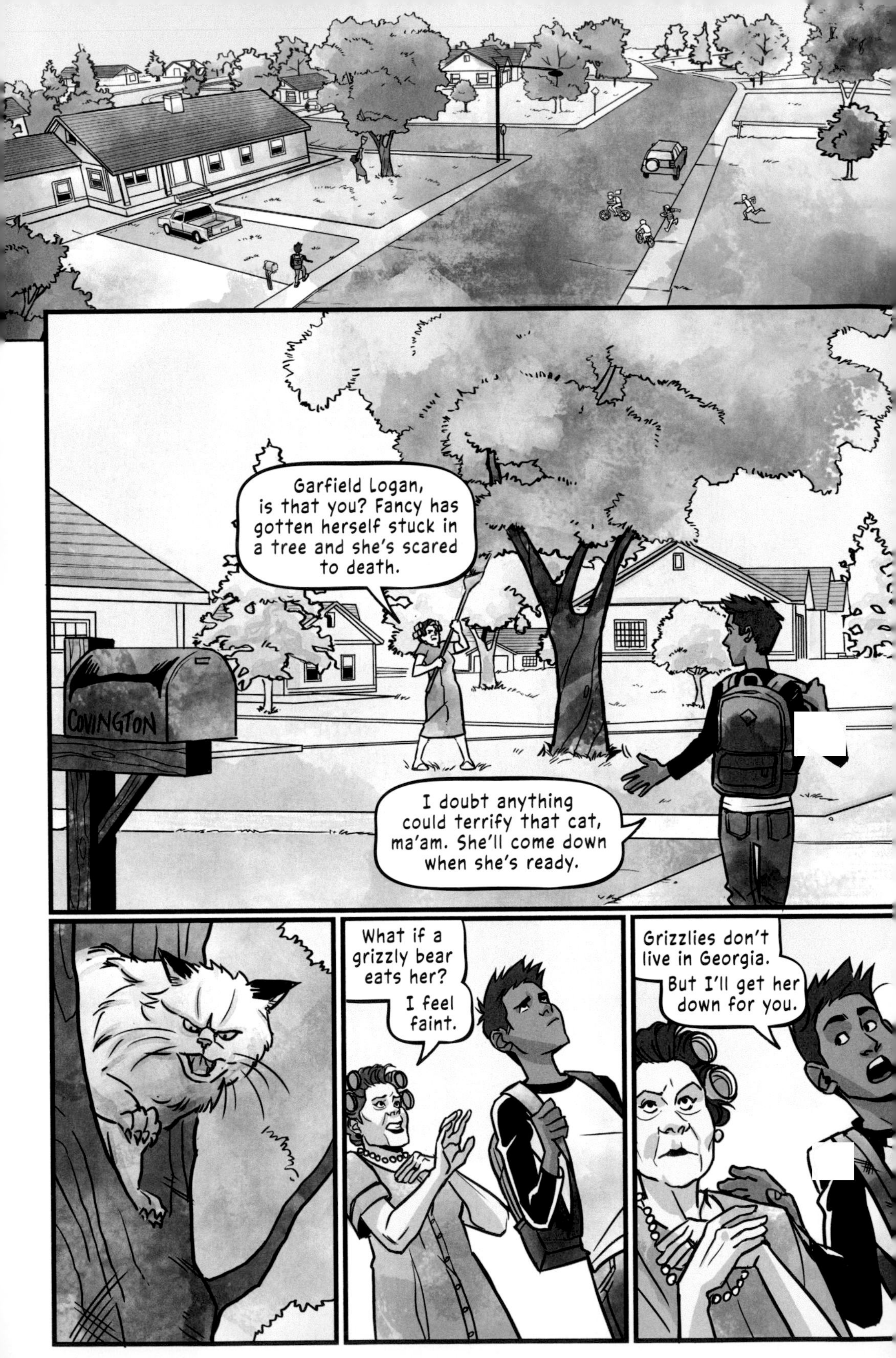
Garfield Logan, is that you? Fancy has gotten herself stuck in a tree and she's scared to death.
COVINGTON
I doubt anything could terrify that cat, ma'am. She'll come down when she's ready.
What if a grizzly bear eats her?
I feel faint.
Grizzlies don't live in Georgia.
But I'll get her down for you.

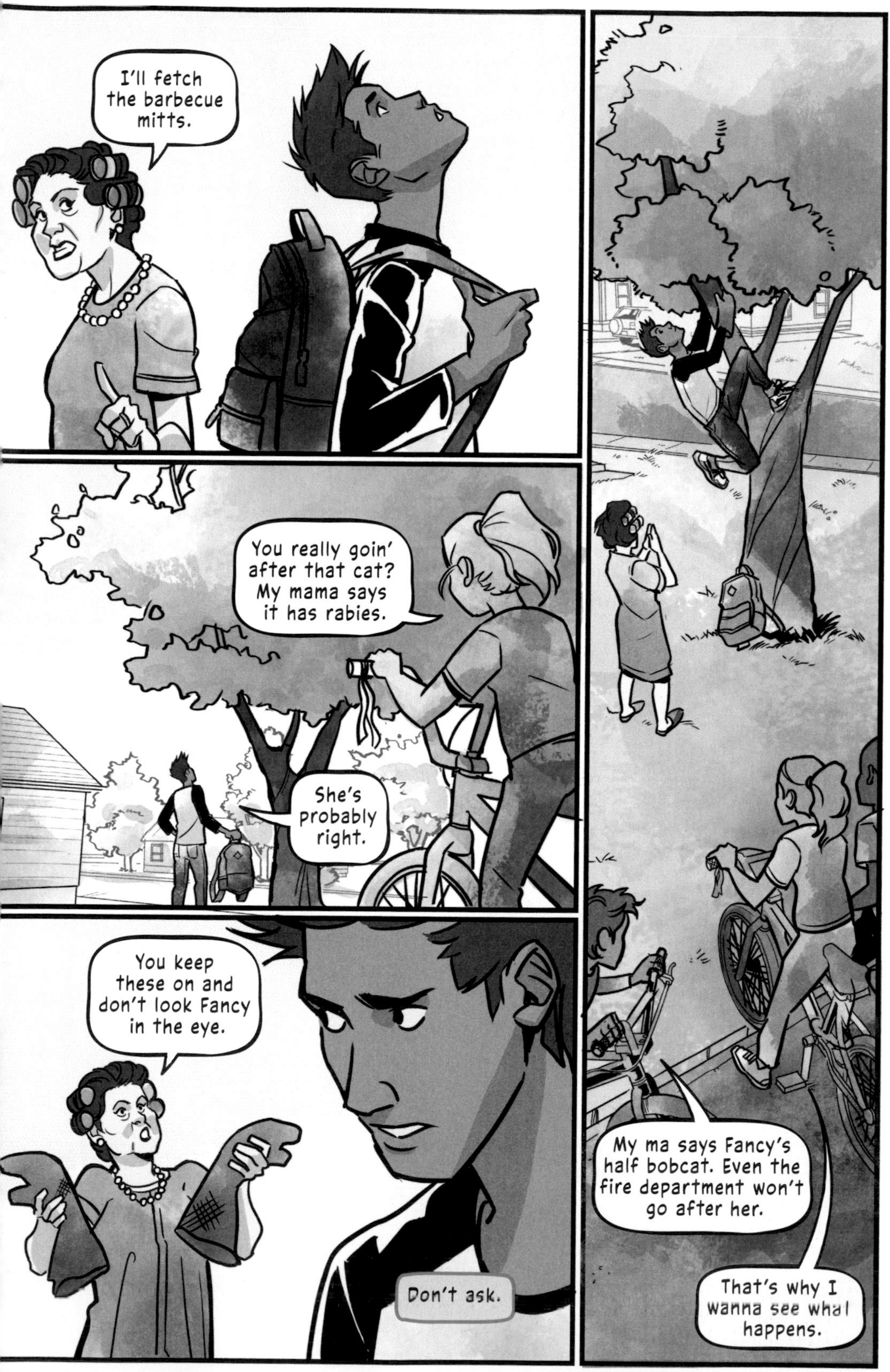
I'll fetch the barbecue mitts.
You really goin' after that cat? My mama says it has rabies.
She's probably right.
You keep these on and don't look Fancy in the eye.
Don't ask.
My ma says Fancy's half bobcat. Even the fire department won't go after her.
That's why I wanna see what happens.

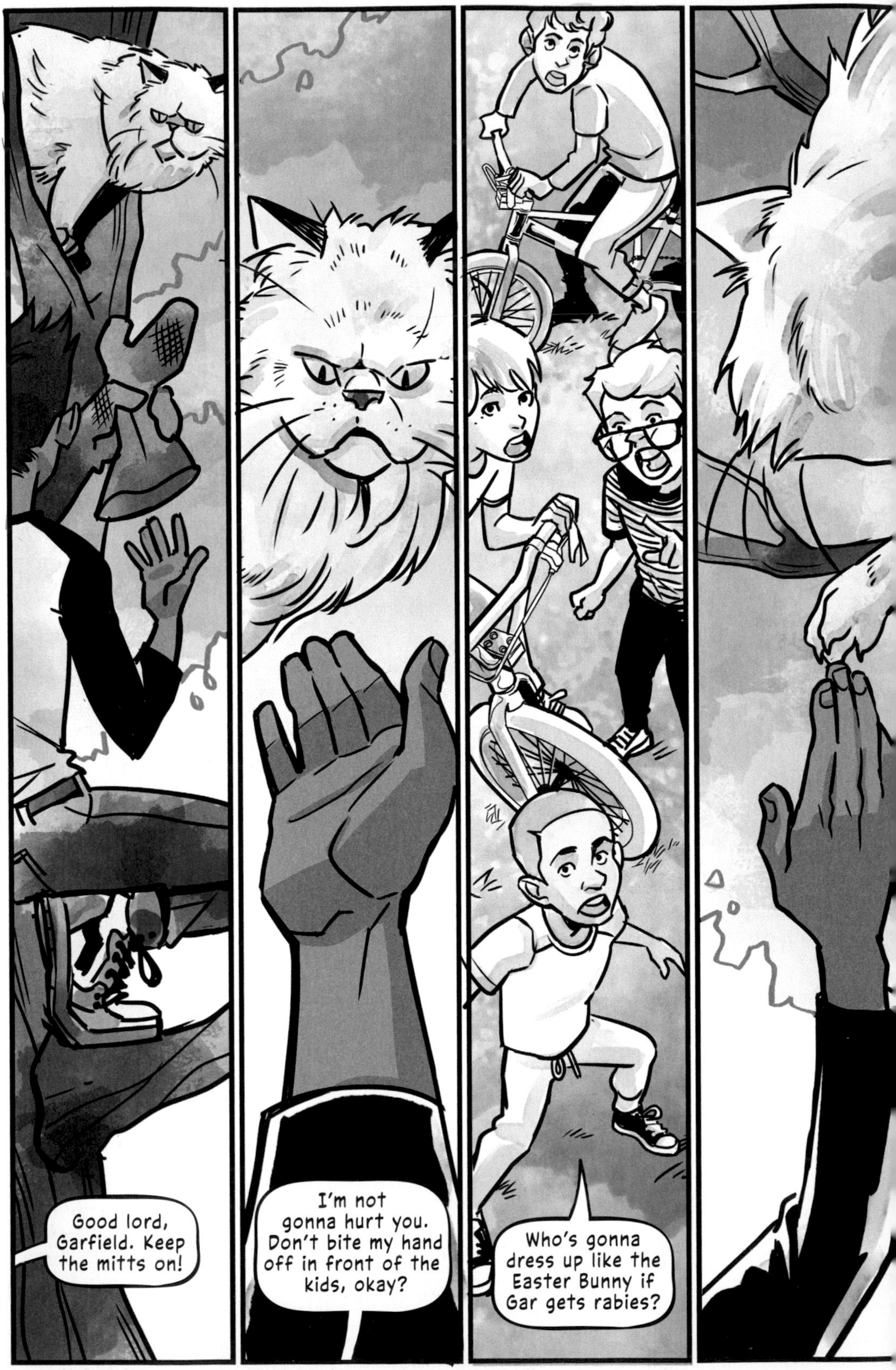
Good lord, Garfield. Keep the mitts on!
I'm not gonna hurt you. Don't bite my hand off in front of the kids, okay?
Who's gonna dress up like the Easter Bunny if Gar gets rabies?

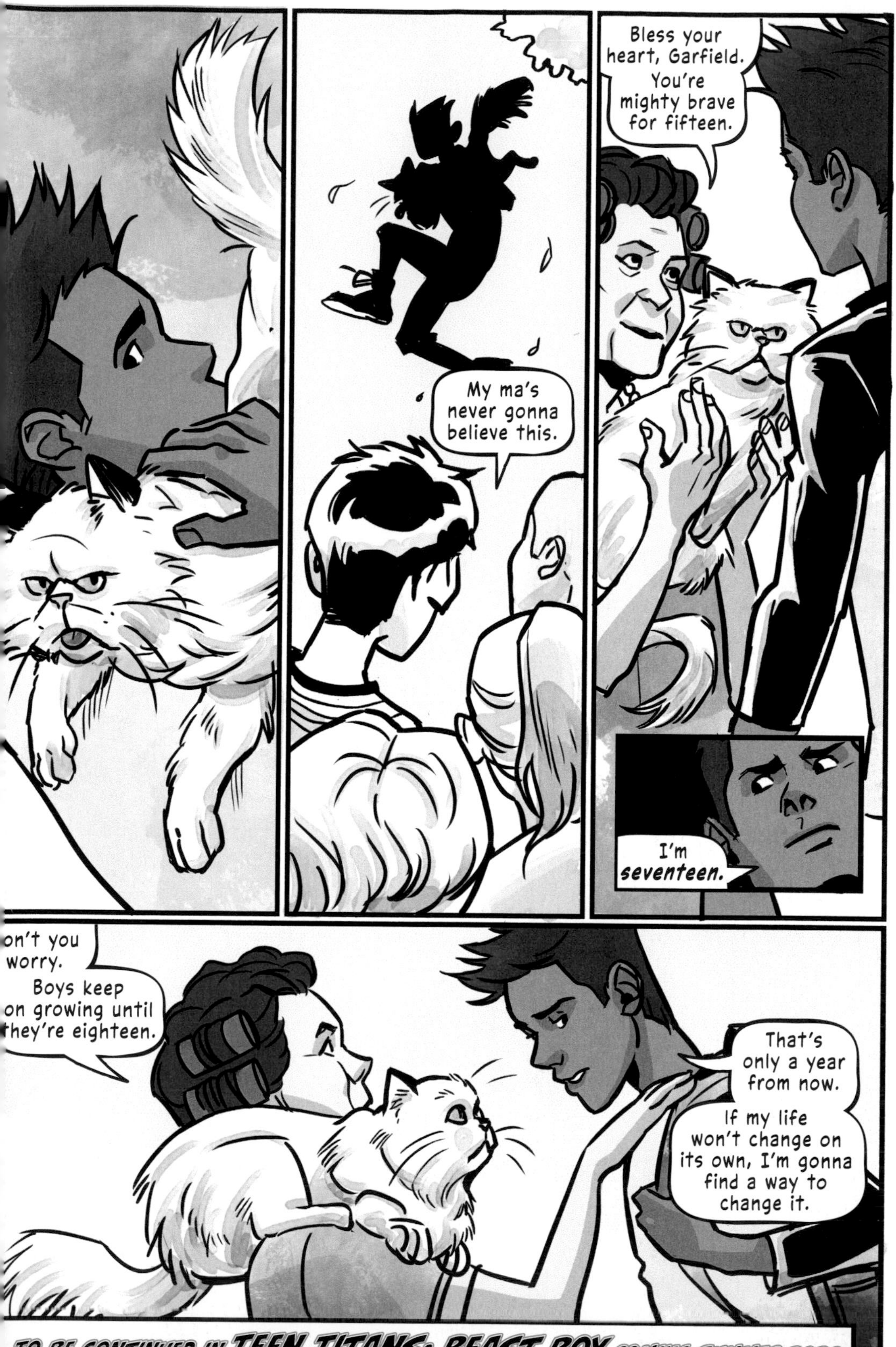
My ma's never gonna believe this.
Bless your heart, Garfield. You're mighty brave for fifteen.
I'm *seventeen.*
on't you worry.
Boys keep on growing until they're eighteen.
That's only a year from now.
If my life won't change on its own, I'm gonna find a way to change it.
TO BE CONTINUED IN TEEN TITANS: BEAST BOY COMING SUMMER 2020

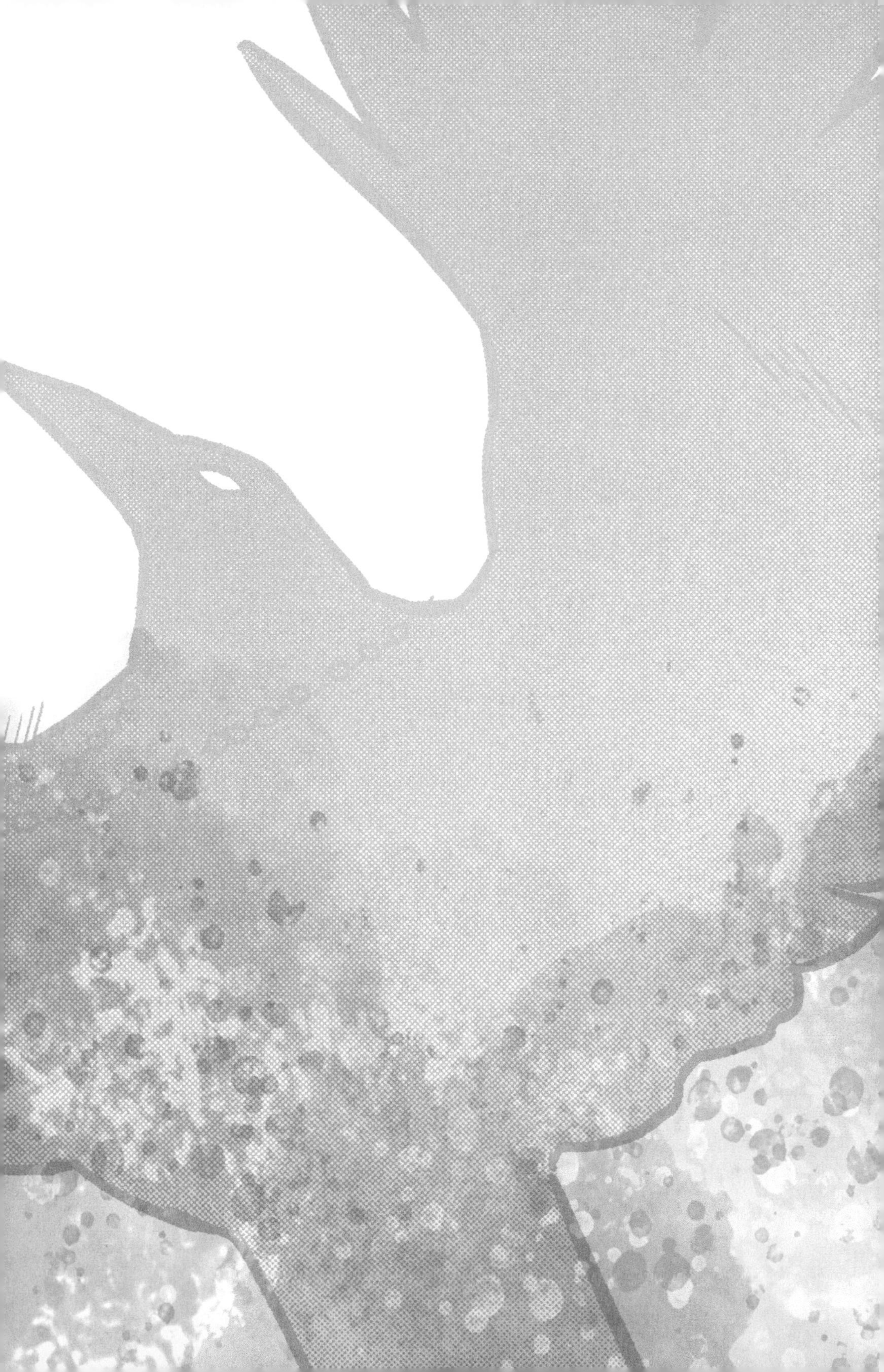